I0819281

# When We Were Brilliant

## Other titles by Lynn Cullen

*The Woman with the Cure*

*The Sisters of Summit Avenue*

*Twain's End*

*Mrs. Poe*

*Reign of Madness*

*The Creation of Eve*

*I Am Rembrandt's Daughter*

# When We Were Brilliant

LYNN CULLEN

BERKLEY
NEW YORK

BERKLEY
An imprint of Penguin Random House LLC
1745 Broadway, New York, NY 10019
penguinrandomhouse.com

Book design by George Towne
Interior art: vector glowing light © Volodymyr Bondar / Shutterstock

Library of Congress Cataloging-in-Publication Data

Names: Cullen, Lynn, author
Title: When we were brilliant / Lynn Cullen.
Description: New York : Berkley, 2026. | Includes biographical information.
Identifiers: LCCN 2025012020 (print) | LCCN 2025012021 (ebook) | ISBN 9780593815854 (hardcover) | ISBN 9780593815861 (ebook)
Subjects: LCSH: Monroe, Marilyn, 1926-1962—Fiction | Arnold, Eve—Fiction | Motion picture actors and actresses—Fiction | Women photographers—Fiction | Photographers—Fiction | LCGFT: Fiction | Biographical fiction | Novels
Classification: LCC PS3553.U2955 W47 2026 (print) | LCC PS3553.U2955 (ebook) | DDC 813/.54—dc23/eng/20250528
LC record available at https://lccn.loc.gov/2025012020
LC ebook record available at https://lccn.loc.gov/2025012021

Printed in the United States of America
1st Printing

The authorized representative in the EU for product safety and compliance is Penguin Random House Ireland, Morrison Chambers, 32 Nassau Street, Dublin D02 YH68, Ireland, https://eu-contact.penguin.ie.

*For Norma Jeane and Little Evie from Philly,*

*and the fierce child within us all*

*There is nothing in this world that*
*does not have a decisive moment.*

—Henri Cartier-Bresson

# When We Were Brilliant

# 1980

**FLASHBULBS POPPED, LEAVING BRIGHT BLUE HOLES IN MY VISION.** The museum hall seethed with elegant women pinching champagne flutes and men biting into savory pastries, crumbs from which were flaking onto their satin tuxedo lapels. The rustling of their finery, the jingling of their bracelets, and the snapping of their lighters made it hard for me to hear the famous television reporter. I leaned closer.

"What is your secret, Ms. Arnold?"

I glanced away as she tipped the mic toward me. *Which one?*

I nudged my coiled braid, stuck with bobby pins like one of the voodoo dolls I'd photographed in Haiti. I'd yearned for my own museum exhibition all these years, and now, finally, that I had one—a grand one, in Brooklyn of all places—I was clamming up. You once told a radio announcer that you wanted to live the rest of your life in Brooklyn, and he'd laughed at you. People rarely took you seriously. Their mistake. You were a master at handling most situations you found yourself in, finessing them so effortlessly that few suspected your terror. What I wouldn't give to have your charm. Looking out over the crowd, primed for something juicy, I wondered, *What would Marilyn do?*

The sequins on my gown winked as I swallowed a laugh.

My interviewer tilted her head, with its famous cascade of honey-brown swoops. "Miss Arnold?" It came out more like *Miss Awnold.* Being from Boston, she dropped her *R*s when she spoke, as had JFK, whom I'd met while photographing Jackie at their house. JFK—now *there* was a secret.

I exhaled. "There's no mystery, really, about how I get people to open up to me. All I do is try to involve them in the photograph, to make them realize, without actually telling them, that it's up to them to give me whatever they want to give me."

"You're saying you empower your subjects to be themselves?"

"That's a way of putting it. If you're careful with people, and if you respect their privacy, they will offer you a part of themselves that you can use. It has more to do with the relationship of the photographer to the subject than it has to do with anything else that might be happening."

She hitched up one side of her mouth. "You get your subjects to offer a part of themselves 'that you can use.' Would you say that you use people, then?"

Is this how it is to be on top? People always trying to trip you up, trying to catch you at your worst, as if one's worst is truly who one is? You would have had a snappy comeback.

"Maybe people are using *me.*"

Oy! What a crab! I didn't even feel that way! I never had the light touch you did.

My interviewer's smile went even more crooked. If she were ever to be my subject, it would be interesting to photograph her with someone she loved, to see if that downward corner could come up. "Your *In China* photos"—she waved her hand toward the exhibition room—"have obviously struck a chord. I understand this is just the first of many shows you're to have across the country. Your fellow photographers have inducted you into the Photography Institute Hall of Fame. You've been nominated for a National Book Award."

It was about goddamn time. I was sixty-eight. I'd been photographing since my twenties, competing with the big boys and learning from the best of them, tramping across the face of the earth and putting myself in harm's way in hopes of capturing the beauty and villainy and wonder of life in this world. My shots were on magazine covers everywhere.

I said into the mic, "I'm humbled by these unlooked-for honors."

"What is your next project?"

"Now that I'm back in the States, I think I'll have a look around. I'd like to have the country of my birth sit for my camera. Do its portrait, so to speak."

My interviewer laughed. "Just a little assignment."

"I enjoy a challenge."

My interviewer paused. "About your Marilyn Monroe photos . . ."

The crowd went silent.

I drew in a breath. Really? Here? Now? Eighteen years since you left us, eighteen years in which I'd scraped my way to the top, and still the conversation always came around to you. Wasn't it enough that I couldn't go anywhere without seeing your face on newsstands or on TV? A poster of you was in the bathroom of the restaurant where I'd had lunch.

My interrogator was watching me. "Other than the photos that your agency, Magnum, published in Marilyn's lifetime, we've seen nothing from you about her since her passing." She tilted the mic back toward me.

"That's right."

"Have you any other photos?"

"Yes."

Seeing that I was being a tough nut, she became chipper in the way one does when coaxing a toddler to wear her mittens. "Tell us about Marilyn. What was she like? Weren't you two friends?"

Friends. I stared at the mic, fear boiling up through the cracks in my armor.

The crowd sensed my panic. They'd pounce if I didn't give them something. *Got to throw the lions red meat,* you used to say.

"I was always the camera, and she was always herself."

My inquisitor narrowed her eyes. Some red meat that was! But what was I supposed to say? How could one forced bleat begin to explain?

She kept up. "About those other photos of her . . . Are there many?"

Only hundreds. Everything about me, everything about you, had led up to and then flowed through them. "Next question," I said flatly.

No one ever said I had your grace.

I DIDN'T LEAVE MY PARTY UNTIL CLOSE TO MIDNIGHT. AS MY taxi crossed the Brooklyn Bridge, I sank into my coat and looked out over the East River, where, in the glow of the skyscrapers of Manhattan, a tugboat pushed a barge heaped with coal. I'd just left the biggest event of my life, and my chest was roiling with loneliness. My family hadn't come, for one, but it was more than that.

Why, after all this time, didn't I talk about you? I'd had good reason not to, once. But who was I keeping quiet for now?

Nearing the bridge, the barge glided with its burden of coal through the sparkling black water. It didn't even have an engine—the tug was doing all the work—but the barge, with its glittering mountain, was what one noticed. Yet only together could the two boats deliver the goods.

Your admirers, whose number only grew by the day—how you must love that!—were desperate for scraps of the girl they thought they knew. But they didn't know anything about you. Not like I did. The proof was in my photos—photos I'd kept buried away for such a long time.

My hair caught on my coat collar when I looked up at the blazing city. It illuminated the river—not with searchlights or floodlights but with the collected light of a million windows. To think that behind each one was someone with their own story of defeat or triumph or, likely, both. Our story began within that city, yours and mine, and there, after a decade, it ended, taking with it all its brilliance. Oh, to feel the warmth of that light again!

What would it hurt, really, to let myself remember?

# 1

## 1952

"CAN YOU IMAGINE?"

A girl's breathy voice sifted through the roar that was nearly levitating the drinks above the bar. Or maybe it was the cigarette smoke that almost held them aloft. The cloud of smoke and testosterone billowing through the 21 Club that night felt dense enough to stir the toy cars and planes that dangled from the ceiling like so many lost boyhoods.

The party was for the director John Huston, still sizzling after his success with *The African Queen* the previous year. It was being thrown by Robert Capa—Bob. My boss. No, my colleague. We were all equals at Magnum. . . . Oh, who was I kidding? I was a five-foot-zero newcomer with a three-year-old at home with an earache, and Bob was the most celebrated war photographer in the world. When he and his famous photographer friends Henri Cartier-Bresson, David "Chim" Seymour, and George Rodger formed a co-op to explore the postwar world, they needed a woman to appeal to "the females." Margaret Bourke-White was busy, Lee Miller had retired to the English countryside, and Dorothea Lange was running an art photography magazine. Hence me, with my single magazine credit, for my coverage of Black fashion shows in Harlem. The Magnum men were that hard up. Experienced photojournalists with two X chromosomes were as scarce as a girdle in a boardroom.

"Oh! It's going to be so *creamy*!"

Crushed together with Robert Capa—Bob—I was unable to turn to see the owner of the baby voice, let alone raise my camera. Bob's gaze wandered over my head, then stalled in the direction of a sweet scent infiltrating the haze: Chanel No. 5.

A hairy hand crowned with a gold signet ring extended past me to Capa. I was able to roll my gaze to its owner, Sam Shaw, as slick in his big-shouldered tweed sports coat with its white pocket square as the playboys in the movies for which he famously shot the stills. Rumpledly handsome Bob, on the other hand, wore a five-o'clock shadow and a borrowed suit coat that strained across his barrel chest. His battered bomber jacket from his war-correspondent years, if not his muddy helmet, hung in the cloakroom, a victim of the 21's dress code.

I looked down at my neat brown wool dress with its nice patent leather belt. What did my much-spot-cleaned, much-brushed, much-loved Saks Fifth Avenue dress—my only Saks Fifth Avenue dress, bought in the spirit of spending money to make money—say about me? I was a field mouse in a room of lions.

That had to change.

Capa—Bob—shook Sam's hand, his gaze still pinned behind me. "Sam." His smile was too wobbly to be meant for Sam—or any man, for that matter. I may have been serious about photographing people only for the past two years, but I could read faces. Maybe I had always been able to. The outsider's door prize.

"Miss Monroe, I presume?" Bob said. I twisted my neck to

confirm: Marilyn Monroe, Hollywood's latest pinup girl, inflating out of her low-cut dress.

You.

"Oh yes!" you breathed. Your Crayola-blue eyes lit and widened, then melted into a smile.

Tough old Bob, he who had photographed the kinetic, watery hell of Omaha Beach on D-Day and the nightmare of the Battle of the Bulge, in which frozen men nestled like hatchlings in snowy foxholes, now squirmed and ducked before kissing your hand, which looked as plump and soft as a girl's. You *were* a girl, just twenty-five.

Sam Shaw's neat mustache skimmed his martini as he winked his hello to me, both acknowledging and dismissing me as a member of the brotherhood of the lens in a single twitch.

"Marilyn was telling me that *Life* plans a cover story," he said to Bob.

"*Life* magazine!" you cooed. "Can you imagine?"

I couldn't. Since when did minor starlets get *Life* covers? No offense, but somebody was sleeping with somebody.

"Congratulations," Bob said.

Sam splashed his drink on a guy's arm. Neither noticed. "She said that a Magnum man was going to shoot it."

"I wouldn't *dream* of anyone else," you cooed.

"Hey!" Sam cried. "I brought you to the party. What about me?"

"Oh, *Samuel.* You know I love you."

"So, who's the lucky guy?" he asked.

"Mr. Halsman," you breathed.

"Lucky dog," said Sam. "Feather in his cap."

A peacock plume on your bonnet, more like. Why *were* the studio stiffs pushing you so hard? As far as I knew, you'd had only minor roles since your big break in Huston's *The Asphalt Jungle* two years earlier. True, you'd burned like a single candle in that dark film noir, your presence jarringly bright in such a small part. It was strange how you alone glowed in the shadowy film. But snagging the cover of the biggest pictorial magazine in the country meant that you were someone. Or, as the studio boys well knew, it would make you someone if you weren't already. Same magic applied to the photographer who shot it, at least among editors. In an age in which magazines dictated what the public saw and believed, still photographers were to movie stars what honeybees were to flowers: symbiotic.

More men pushed into our circle. I found myself crowded to the outside, where I protected my camera from being crushed into my sternum. I gazed at the model train nearly grazing my boss's head. Why had I come to this party? Capa—Bob—knew this wasn't my scene. And though Dora, one of the Beat kids who lived in the apartment below mine, was as devoted a babysitter as she was a fan of jazz and stark poetry, my son had had a fever of 102 when I left. My husband had said he wouldn't be home until late—something about a business opportunity. I'd come only because Cap—Bob—insisted it would be good for me, as had my biggest fan, my husband, and, well, I admit, because I was curious about what made powerful people tick. What'd they have to do on their way up? What was so special about them?

Normally, I was more interested in people who lived outside the gaze of society—maybe because I'd grown up unseen, too. Knowing how being unvalued makes a person wary, I didn't take it for granted when the unseen let me in. I was honored, and grateful, when the designers and models in the Harlem shows allowed me backstage to photograph a realm that was invisible to those outside it. That was why I had become a photographer: to show the world something that it never would have seen had I not shot it.

But the thing about the unseen? No one wants to see them. I'd struggled to place the piece on the Harlem shows until, finally, a magazine in England took it, but its editors redid my captions, rewording my admiration into a racist screed. Thinking about it still makes me see red. I learned the hard way to insist upon approving the text that went with my pictures—not that editors would listen to a novice.

I freed my arm to signal to the bartender, a futile gesture from a minnow in a tank full of sharks. Two movie-studio-executive types elbowed in next to me. One jabbed his cigar toward you, right behind me, and growled to the other, in a smoker's ruined voice, "I want you to talk to this girl."

I heard you coo, "Pleased to meet you."

"We're grooming her." The studio executive smirked. "Or maybe I should say she's grooming herself. This girl will do whatever it takes. She even thinks of it before we do." His chuckle ground into a cough. When he finished hacking, he said, "Whatever—it's working. Kid's going to be the sexiest thing in pictures since Jean Harlow."

You gasped. "Oh, I've given pure sex appeal very little thought. Thinking about it would frighten me!"

If I were drinking the Pepsi I was trying to order, I would have sprayed it. You worked your sex appeal like an organ-grinder worked his monkey.

Capa—Bob, *Bob*—ever down to brass tacks, said, "You must see the effect you have on men."

"Men understand me. I like men."

Sam Shaw laughed. "They like you, too."

"Fox has proclaimed her," the studio exec croaked, "the Woo-Woo Girl."

"All I'm doing," you said, shaking the ribbon of hair that dangled over your brow like a platinum fishhook, "is fighting gravity.

If you don't fight gravity, you sag." You widened your eyes as if surprised when the men laughed; then you threw your head back and laughed with them.

I studied you, wondering how your small, flat face could be both plainer and more beautiful than in the bit parts and magazine fluff pieces I'd seen you in.

You caught me watching. Through your circle of admirers came your hand, fingers pointed down, queen-style. The men allowed us an inch. I thought for an angry moment that you meant for me to kiss your regal paw, until you blurted, "Hi!"

"Marilyn, this is Eve," Bob said as you pumped my hand that wasn't protecting my camera, "Eve Arnold. This tiny terror bakes the best oatmeal scotchies in New York."

"Oh," you said, "I know her."

You did?

"She does more than that."

You met my puzzled look with a blinking one of your own, as if you were afraid to let our gazes fully connect. Before I could draw a bead on you, a baritone voice boomed over the melee.

"How does a man get a decent whiskey around here?"

Our circle opened for a lanky man with little raisin eyes cushioned within great bulging bags set upon a long, narrow face, a sort of Abe Lincoln's hungover brother.

"John Huston, how are you doing?" Sam Shaw slapped him on the back. "Tell us what you're up to."

A glass was passed hand by hand from the bar until it reached the great director's long fingers.

"What I'm up to"—he downed the drink—"is leaving town. There's not enough whiskey in America"—he tapped the last stray drops into his mouth—"to keep me here, not with that jackass McCarthy in Washington."

"Aw," Bob said, "why'd you have to bring him up? We were doing just fine."

"It's my party, and I can do what I want." Huston kissed you on the cheek. "How are you doing, dear?"

"Swell!" You kissed him back. "Are you really moving away, Mr. Huston?"

"I have to."

He wouldn't be the only one. The senator from Wisconsin was putting the heat on artists of all kinds, determined to root out anyone he deemed to be a commie. His drive to get friends to rat out friends to save their own skins was turning America into the Land of the Paranoid.

A pleasant woman shimmied her way between the men—Sam Shaw's wife, Anne, I would find out. She traded his drink for a camera. "You don't mind a photo, do you, Mr. Huston?" Sam asked.

The director put his arm around you as you pushed out your breasts, opened your mouth, and lowered your lashes. The flashbulb lit up the hanging toys. Some magazine would pay big for cheesecake like that.

Whatever good Capa thought I was supposed to get out of being there, I wasn't getting it. I fought my way to the pay phone by the ladies' room to call home. Francis's fever was up. I could hear him crying in the background. That did it. I was leaving.

In the washroom, I'd eyed my braid, coiled at my nape in my dress-up mode, and was rinsing my hands, a towel held out to me by the elderly pinafored woman on duty, when you entered.

Wafting Chanel No. 5, you slipped off your heels, taking you down from your earth-angel pedestal, making you closer to my size. My attention went to your bare legs. A lack of hosiery would be outrageous enough at an event in the summer, but it was downright bizarre in February.

You wiggled your toes like a kid in a sandbox. "Oh, my poor feet!"

Our trio looked at the three-inch heels of the shoes hooked on your fingers. The attendant's eyes rounded behind her glasses.

"Mrs. Arnold." Some of the breathiness had left your voice, replaced by a kind of boldness matched by your careless demeanor. "I saw your pictures of Marlene Dietrich in *Esquire*."

You noticed that those photos were mine?

"I liked the article's title, 'Marlene Dietrich: An Appreciation,'" you said. "'An Appreciation.' It sounds so respectful."

I wiped my hands. Our "appreciation" hadn't been a two-way street. A few months back, when another Magnum photographer had had to cancel a shoot with Dietrich at the last minute due to illness, the editor at *Esquire* had gone down the agency's list until he got to the bottom. Me.

Dietrich and I couldn't have been a worse fit. Besides her being an icon and my being a nothing, my style was all wrong for her. I used a handheld Rolleicord and chased whatever lighting was available while recording action as it happened. I'd never taken a photo in a studio in my life, nor had I ever wanted to. Dietrich, on the other hand, was a studio photographer's dream (or their nightmare, depending on how well they obeyed her), known for controlling every pose, every angle of her shots, even the kind of lighting. She famously offered a lay or a Cadillac, his choice, to any cameraman who could get her right. Worse, I knew she ordered her own retouching. I never retouched. Ever.

Yet, as furious as Marlene was when I showed up with no assistant, no lighting equipment, and no tripod, something miraculous happened when I started shooting her, unposed, as she recorded songs for her new album. When she stopped glaring at me and bent her attention to her singing, I caught Marlene being a real person . . . who turned out to be even more compelling than the coolly glamorous image she'd concocted in photographers' studios.

Fans gobbled up this chance to see the "new" Marlene. The issue of *Esquire* sold out. Magazines in France, England, and other countries snatched up the photos, too. But usually no one other than editors noticed who'd taken them.

"You did well with Marlene Dietrich," you said. "Can you *imagine* what I could do for you?"

"What you could do for me?" *This tough little flash in the pan?* That's what I thought. I'm trying to be as honest as I can be here.

"Yes. You with your new kind of photography—"

"It's not new. It's documentary photography."

"—and me with my Marilyn Monroe."

"Me with my Marilyn Monroe" struck me as odd, like Edgar Bergen talking about his dummy Charlie. I opened my purse to get a tip to put in the attendant's basket. "I don't work in a studio."

"I know."

You did?

"I don't ever retouch."

"I know."

"I mean never."

"I know."

I frowned. How could you know this? You were just a starlet.

You put down your shoes and stepped into them, one at a time. "We could help each other. Do something different. Make a splash." Both shoes on, you exclaimed, "Imagine!"

The attendant offered you a breath mint, a tissue. You declined them and looked at my camera. "Don't you want to take a picture of me?"

"Here? In the bathroom?"

You pushed up the sides of your fluffy hair, tilted your chin down, and then smiled at my reflection in the mirror. "Why not?" You dropped your arms and hair. "Guess I guessed wrong."

You moved to sashay out the door without so much as powdering your nose. Had you made the trip into the washroom just to see me?

Okay, I was curious. And not a little flattered. And you were walking out the door. "Wait."

You turned around.

"What do you mean, 'do something different'?"

You lifted your brows at the attendant, then smiled at me. "I mean show people something they've never seen before."

I stared at you. How'd you know I lived for that?

You put out your hand. "Deal?"

I didn't know exactly what I was agreeing to, but—

The strength in your soft, pearly-nailed hand surprised me when I took it. "Deal."

I'd spend the rest of my days wondering how my life would have turned out had I not stopped you that night.

# 2

UNLIKE YOU AND ME, MY HUSBAND HAD GROWN UP RICH. THE Schmitzes owned a string of luxury department stores in Germany. Under the amused eyes of his mother's Renoir and serenaded by his older sister on their polished black Steinway, Arnold lived a comfortable life in the bosom of his happy family. This came to an end after Chancellor Hitler came into power in 1933. My husband's parents thought to send their son to an English boarding school the following year while they waited for the intellectual leaders in their country to come to their senses and set affairs to rights; things for Jews had become a bit hot. When he graduated from Bedales seven years later, there was no more Renoir, no more house, no more family awaiting him. Everyone but his sister had been shipped to work camps, and she hadn't only because she'd gone to live in the US three years earlier. In late November '41, he fled to her in New York, where he found that the name Schmitz opened neither doors nor hearts in a country on the brink of going to war with his homeland. Combined with his German accent, "Schmitz" slammed them shut. Sick of a name that had brought him devastation as a Jew in Nazi Germany and suspicion as a German in America, he called himself something else.

We met at an Automat at the end of 1941. I was on a lunch break from my job, and in a hurry. I had just been made boss of two hundred employees at a photo-developing plant, a promotion made possible by my boss's running off to enlist after Pearl Harbor, leaving me as the only remaining employee whose first language was English. I found that I liked being the boss. I liked being in a position to improve conditions around the plant—the mostly Chinese employees were being treated abysmally, and I wanted to change that. I just had to figure out how to stay in charge before a male replacement could be found.

I was wolfing down my tuna fish sandwich so I could get back to my twelve-hour day when a man with a German accent said, "Are you all right?"

I stopped munching, then shifted my gaze to the pink-cheeked young man at the neighboring table. Tall and skinny, he looked younger than his voice sounded.

"I don't mean to pry," he said, "but if you're in trouble . . ."

He *was* young—twenty to my twenty-nine, I'd find out later—and so gaunt that his hazel eyes were outsized in his appealingly craggy face. I, a self-proclaimed reader of people, should have known that he was the one in trouble, but he held himself with such confidence, and his smile was so sincere, that I let my guard down.

I swallowed my food. "It shows?"

"Maybe a little." He put out his hand. "Arnold Arnold."

"Arnold . . . Arnold?"

He grinned. "Double trouble."

We spent the rest of my lunch break talking. I confessed that I feared being replaced at work. He scoffed at the thought. The company was lucky to have me—look how conscientious I was!

And obviously so sharp! He told me that he was a graphic artist. He didn't mention an employer.

When I finished work that night, he was standing outside the beat-up metal door of Stanbi Photos, with what turned out to be a homemade greeting card in his hands. *Eve Eve*, it read when I opened its cleverly drawn cover, *will you go to dinner with me? Arnold Arnold.*

Dinner turned out to be hot dogs in the park, but it worked. Now that affable young man, still rangy, still handsome these eleven years later, was peering at the *Life* magazine on the dinette table before me as he looped his tie.

He whistled when I turned the page. "There is your friend Marilyn." He still had his German accent, though his *Deutsch* came out only when he was exhausted, or during lovemaking.

Across the table, our Francis didn't look up from filling in the outlines of a puppy in his coloring book. "Who is Marilyn?"

Arnold bent closer to the headline. "'The Talk of Hollywood,' it says here."

I had to hand it to you. You'd hoisted yourself up a solid rung in the five months since we'd met at John Huston's party. This was your second article in *Life*. In the film columns I'd taken to perusing after your wild claim of being able to help me, you'd popped up an astonishing number of times. Sometimes you were paired with a minor male star. More often you were pictured alone, pushing out your chest in a variety of ways while looking surprised or even amused that you were sexy. Your small parts in Hollywood romps like *Monkey Business*, *We're Not Married!*, and *Let's Make It Legal* had already led to a bigger part, as a crazed babysitter, in a bigger movie, *Don't Bother to Knock*, and this summer you'd be filming an A-list picture called *Niagara* in which you were one of the headliners. Rumor was that you were sleeping with the studio head. Forgive me. I believed it. How else could you have risen so fast?

The thump of bongo drums and the drone of voices rose through the floor, though it was before noon—the Beats in the apartment below us were up early. As I turned the page, my husband leaned over me and rested his chin on my head. "Very clever, *Life* magazine."

I saw exactly what he meant. The eye went instantly to the thumbnail reproduction of the calendar photo for which you'd posed nude three years earlier. One suspected the article was merely an excuse to reprint it. Tiny as it was, it was plenty big enough to titillate.

I picked up Francis's thick green crayon, which had rolled off the table. The public had recently matched the innocently sexy starlet who glowed from photos in *Look* and *Movieland* with the provocative naked calendar girl swimming in red satin. An uproar had arisen. More calendars were bought, so many that the photograph was now being called "The Shot Seen 'Round the World."

I feared you were sunk. Anyone else would be. Two years earlier, Academy Award winner Ingrid Bergman, riding a high since *Casablanca* with hit after hit, had left her husband to live openly with the Italian director with whom she'd fallen in love and become pregnant. Her fall from grace was so fast that her film playing in theaters was yanked out midrun and summarily banned. US senators introduced a resolution naming her a threat to American decency.

I've never heard of a "fallen man." But you were no man, and, like Bergman, you'd broken the rules of propriety. As fast as you'd risen, your plummet could be even swifter. The only thing Americans loved more than deifying a woman was shaming her.

Francis had picked a red crayon from its box and was grinding it into a page of his coloring book as I resumed my reading. You told your interviewer that when you posed for the calendar photo, you'd been between studio contracts and had been desperate for the fifty dollars the photographer paid you, just to buy something to eat. You then clarified that you'd not just grown up in an orphanage, which was already part of the Cinderella tale being spun about you, but been a foster child, too. You wanted to set the record straight: Contrary to the reports that you were an orphan, your mother was still alive, though was not well, and hadn't been able to care for you since you were a baby. You'd not only lived in an orphanage but been taken in and returned by twelve different foster families. When you turned sixteen, you married a neighborhood man just to have a place to go. Now that you were making a little money, you said, all you wanted to do was to make a home for your mother and yourself.

The interviewer observed that you were "naïve and guileless" and implied that you were a sweet kid doing the best that she could in a tough world. An assignment that must have started out as a racy exposé had ended up as a profile in courage, appealing to the reader to protect and coddle you.

How did you do that? I'd never learned the art of begging strangers for mercy. When I was poor and frightened once upon a time, it never occurred to me to ask for help. I'd sucked it up and faked that I was fine, just like my mother taught me.

Francis kept scribbling. Arnold finished reading over my shoulder, then tugged his tie knot to his neck. "Have you made an arrangement with her yet?"

"With whom? Marilyn? No."

I was starting to believe that your talk about what you could do for me was just that—talk. Oh, I knew you were busy, but couldn't you have at least responded to my letter? Well, I wasn't going to beg you. I was doing fine enough. Magnum had thrown me a few bones; I'd just gotten back from documenting the Republican

National Convention in Chicago from "a woman's point of view." I'd done a shoot of Mamie Eisenhower riding a carousel and looking at herself in a fun house mirror at an amusement park—my ideas, but she ran with them. Good training for a president's wife, she'd said. Who says that the women behind the men can't have a sense of humor?

I turned the page of my magazine. The spread was of six shots of you coyly offering either your face, your legs, or your chest to a man at a desk. The headline read, MARILYN DEMONSTRATES HER APPROACH TO A JOB.

I would never pose you like that. I would never pose you at all. Ask Mamie Eisenhower. I only set up the scene, then let my subjects be their own interesting selves. Or, better yet, I caught them when they were busy, like when Marlene was recording her songs, or when the models were scurrying around backstage at the fashion show in Harlem. Finding a person's truth was this documentarian's challenge, but also my joy. Looked like I was never getting a crack at that with you.

Arnold gave his shoes a last-minute shine with one of our dish towels. "Oh, I wanted to say, I booked that rental house again for the summer. Do you want to go to the beach, Francis?"

"Yes!" he piped.

My heart sank. Last summer, at Arnold's insistence, we'd taken a house on the North Shore of Long Island, in the hamlet of Miller Place, a haven for Daughters of the American Revolution types and Manhattan-dwelling "creatives" with new money. I'd felt out of place, the Daughters of Russian Pogrom Survivors type that I was, although Arnold trotted into the village store as if the locals and he were pals.

The rental of the beach place last summer had put us in the negative. There had never been enough money since I'd been forced to leave my decent-paying job at the photo-processing plant when

I got pregnant. Arnold had stepped up, first turning away from the freelancing he loved to go to work in the art department of an advertising agency, then taking a job at Parker Brothers. Their swirl logo? He designed it. Too bad he didn't get a penny extra for it.

He then tried to supplement our income by writing a book, *How to Play with Your Child*, figuring he was an expert on the subject since he worked at a game company and had a child. A year later, it still hadn't found a publisher. He was spiffed-up now because he was going to an interview for a second job, teaching evening art classes at the New School. I just wished he'd waited until he'd gotten the job before booking a summer place.

He picked up his briefcase. "Wish me luck, please!"

"Good luck, Daddy!" Francis said, then hunched back into his crab-fisted coloring.

I turned around in my chair and smiled. "Good luck, darling."

Arnold stopped, came back over, and lifted me in an embrace. "You are my good luck charm."

I looked into those affectionate, more-green-than-brown eyes, and my heart melted the way it had melted on our second date, when I looked into them and burst out: "We should get married." So he wouldn't be deported, I'd quickly added. We wouldn't have to be real married people. It could be just a business deal.

I had not for a moment wanted it to be just that.

The next day he'd bounded up the stairs and into my apartment with a camera, a used Rolleicord. "You develop photos all day at your job. Would you like to take some of your own?" With a grin, he'd added, "Mrs. Arnold?"

Some of the first photos I ever took were of us in the mirror before we left for the justice of the peace's office.

Now I laid my hands on his freshly shaved face. "Don't worry. They're going to hire you. How can they resist you?"

---

SOON ENOUGH, IT WAS SUMMER. I WAS AT THE SINK, UP TO MY elbows in sudsy dishwater, watching Arnold "play" croquet with Francis in the backyard of our rental cottage. Arnold was nudging another of Francis's errant hits through the wickets for him when the phone rang. With one last, loving look out the window at my boys, I went to answer it.

"Mrs. Arnold?"

"Yes?"

"This is Norm Rosten. We haven't met, but I'm a friend of Sam Shaw's."

My blood pressure blipped. Was this *the* Norman Rosten, the famous "Poet of Brooklyn"? Had Magnum sent him? Why would he be calling me directly? "Hello, Mr. Rosten," I answered. "How is Sam?"

"How's Sam? Sam is Sam," he said. "Listen. A mutual friend of his and mine is here, on the North Shore, someone who'd like very much to see you."

"Me?"

"Could you pop down to the beach in maybe twenty minutes, just to say hello?"

"I probably can." Sam Shaw was a big shot, and Mr. Rosten was famous. I was a second-stringer, the girl called to come up with filler material. Who were they trying to palm off on me?

I put away the dishes and went outside, where Arnold was practicing his croquet shots while Francis sat in the grass, singing and picking dandelions. The air was full of the weeds' slick green tang as I dropped onto a metal lawn chair.

"Play you a game?" Arnold looked up. "What's wrong?"

"Nothing."

Francis ran over and climbed into my lap.

"Then play me," Arnold said.

I kissed the top of Francis's head. His hair smelled of sun. "I just got the strangest phone call."

When I'd explained, Arnold dropped his mallet, then took Francis from me. "For what do you wait? This could be good for you. Go! Get ready!"

"It's probably just Sam's cousin, or a buddy from the war."

"What if this cousin is a magazine editor? What if this buddy owns *Life*?"

He was right. I was in no position to say no. And no matter who it was, who was I to shun him? Everyone has something to teach you if you truly listen—which was why I found myself walking down the beach with Arnold a few minutes later, Francis darting ahead of us, turning over interesting stones.

I had to shade my eyes against the setting sun. What photographers called "the magic hour" had arrived, that hour just after dawn or just before sunset, when the light turns everything golden. A tawny glow burnished all: the rocky outcropping jutting onto the nuggety beach; the heaving, molten sea; the slight man trailing behind the plumpish woman with a mop of frizzy hair. She was waving at me with the enthusiasm of a child. With the sun in my eyes, I couldn't make out who she was. Nothing set her apart from the other sunset strollers except her denim jeans, which were unlike the pedal pushers every other woman was wearing, including me. I crooked my fingers in a reluctant greeting.

"Eve! It's me."

Your sweet voice did it.

"Marilyn."

"I'm Arnold." He reached in to shake your hand.

He and Norm Rosten competed for your attention while I walked with Hedda, Norm's wife, Francis skittering like a sandpiper before us, happy to be out past his bedtime. The sky had gone sherbet orange and purple before Hedda rejoined the men and you dropped back to talk to me.

"I haven't forgotten about a shoot. Are you still up for it?" you asked.

Arnold leaned back from beside Norm to interject, "Yes, she is still up for it."

I drew in a breath. I'd run a photo-processing factory, gotten myself into Magnum, and photographed presidential candidates' wives. Arnold meant well, but I could handle my own business. "Sure. Whenever you are."

"Are you busy tomorrow?" You nodded at Francis, squatting to poke at a dead crab. "Is that your little boy?"

Before I could introduce you, you went over and sat on your heels beside him. You looked up at me after he showed you his treasure. "Can he come, too? And your husband? We could go for a swim, have a picnic afterward."

A time was agreed upon for this swim and picnic, and a place, the beach below the cliffs near the Achitoffs' cottage. I knew where it was, a private stretch of the shore. We'd have the beach to ourselves. I figured that by including Arnold and Francis, you meant for me to get to know you at a purely social gathering. We'd do the shoot at another time. I was pleasantly surprised at your professionalism, and, I'll admit, flattered. I'd never had a subject who gave much of a thought about the woman behind the camera.

THE FOLLOWING AFTERNOON, THE AIR WAS THICK WITH THE smell of seaweed, boat exhaust, and the Coppertone suntan lotion baking into my skin as I walked down the beach below the Achitoffs' cliff-top home. Francis skipped along at the end of my hand, his scrawny, tanned legs jutting like clappers from the belled bottoms of his red swim trunks. Arnold, shading his eyes, was sizing up the people out in the water.

There were a lot of them. Too many of them. Men, women, and children were slogging up the shoreline to circumvent the marked boundary of the private land. They joined others up to their knees in the surf at the base of the cliff, box cameras at the ready, or partially submerged like crocodiles ready to splash in for the kill. Boaters puttered up and cut their motors to drift just offshore. Everyone was watching the meadow-topped cliff as if the Messiah should appear.

I didn't understand. Could this crowd be here for you? All you ever played on-screen was some variation of a blond bimbo. Bette Davis you were not. Had someone told these people to come? I thought you and I were to have a swim with my family at a secluded beach, to become acquainted before our shoot. I hadn't even brought a camera. I'd thought it impolite to bring one.

Yet it was becoming clear that you were precisely why these invaders were here. A debate was raging among a nearby group of men in sunglasses and plaid shorts: *Did Marilyn have breast injections or not?* From a circle of women in the water up to the skirted bottoms of their suits, I heard the disgusted words "no underwear" and "affairs." What was it about you that made men want to break you and women want to scorn you, even as they jostled for a view?

The gawkers were all there. I was there—as we had agreed. But you? You were nowhere in sight. I pulled Francis closer to me, to leave.

Just then, against the clear blue sky, you rose from the precipice above us: a Botticelli Venus in a tiny white bikini and open army boots, the overhanging meadow your grassy half shell. The crowd fell silent.

One flapping clunky boot on a shapely leg at a time, you picked your way down the rocky cliffside, setting stones tumbling. You could have used the nearby steps, but no, down the treacherous cliff you descended as intent men, skeptical women, and their puzzled children held their breath. Only when the lug soles of your boots touched the pebbly shingle did the masses surge forward.

The water seethed and frothed as if churned by sharks in a feeding frenzy. The motorboats blurted into action. You widened your eyes at your dripping admirers, then laughed with delight.

Arnold leaped from my side. "Give her room! Give her room!" He made like a traffic cop, hands out, putting his lanky body between the onslaught and you. When space was begrudgingly opened for you, he scrambled for our towel, then flicked it on the sand before you, out-Sir-Walter-Raleighing Sir Walter Raleigh when spreading his cape over a puddle for the English queen.

"Thank you, Eve's Husband," you breathed to him as you folded yourself down onto your knees. "Where's your little boy?"

"Eve," Arnold yelled over his shoulder, "get Francis!"

When I didn't move quickly enough, he plucked Francis from me and offered him to you.

"Hi," you said to Francis.

All ribs and fine, soft skin, my boy curled into himself. You rose on your knees before him, and as the crowd stirred and hobby cameras clicked, you touched a fingertip to his cheek. Your eyes shone under thick, false lashes when you looked up at me. "I think you're just the luckiest girl in the world."

I didn't believe a word of it.

A baseball was produced. You got to your feet and kicked off your boots, and tossed the ball to Francis with much squealing and playacting, until a chunky bigger boy with a pineapple haircut moved in.

The boy held out a stone and made a tough face. "My mother said write your name on this rock."

You beamed. "Sure! You got a pen?"

A pen was found, opening the floodgates for other kids. More stones, bits of driftwood, even someone's white rubber bathing cap, were presented. Emboldened by the children, the men who'd been snapping pictures from a distance now sidled up to put their arms around you and pose for the wives now manning the cameras. You glowed into each cheap Kodak as the crowd oozed closer.

Arnold broke in and put a protective hand on your back. "Come. You need some air."

Elbows out against the invaders, he ran you out into the water, you giggling, he as somber as a boy giving his mommy a rose on Mother's Day until, when up to your bare waist, you splashed forward into a dog paddle. The crowd cheered.

Even when you were in the water, people had to get close. Children bobbed up to you like playful seals, followed by sidestroking men, all eager to get a view. The harbor police showed up in their boat, warning the operators of other craft to stay back from the swimmers. You were being pushed into deeper water. From the shore, I saw your smile collapse into a look of panic.

"Arnold!"

Whether he could hear me or not, he disappeared under the water, then resurfaced, blowing like a whale while struggling to put you on his back. He paddled you toward the harbor police, who lifted you from him and loaded you on board. You waved to the whooping crowd as the police boat roared off.

Cecil B. DeMille would have been jealous.

Arnold panted his way back onshore to drip next to me. "Do you think she'll be okay?"

I'd seen your type. You existed for attention; everything and everyone was in service to it. Shame on me for believing you wanted to get to know me so we could collaborate on a good shoot. There would be no collaborating with someone like you, only using.

"I have a feeling Miss Marilyn Monroe will be just fine"—I picked up Francis, who latched onto my hip, his sandy feet gritty against my thighs—"all by herself."

# 3

YOU CALLED THE NEXT DAY, SAYING YOU WERE SORRY THAT WE hadn't been able to talk. You really wanted to do a shoot with me! Please, please, please, could we get one in before you left for Hollywood the following week? You loved my work.

I nearly sprained my eyes from rolling them. You descended a crumbling cliff wearing nothing but army boots and three little patches of white parachute cloth because you loved my photography. Right.

It turned out that our supposedly private day was such big news that it had reached an editor at *Esquire* overnight, who in turn rang up Capa, who, knowing I was summering nearby, phoned me in turn, not having any idea that your beach production was supposed to be a humble picnic with me. I was still absorbing the improbability of *Esquire* hearing about your dramatic boat rescue less than twenty-four hours after it happened, and of the editor wanting to do a feature on you, when you called. Who was the genius doing your PR?

Well, a feature was a feature. I agreed to a date for a shoot and then went scouting for locations. We might have been near the seashore, but I'd seen André de Dienes's shots of you bursting out of your top as you gamboled on the sand. Everyone had. We weren't doing that.

At the appointed time a few days later, Arnold dropped me and my cameras off at the home of the Rostens, with whom you were still staying, our drivers for the day. I didn't tell you where we were going, just that the shoot would be casual and playful. You interpreted that as a wardrobe call for skimpy swimwear.

I'd tried to keep my cool—literally, sitting in front of the caged blades of a Westinghouse fan—for the four hours you dithered over your makeup, your bikinis, and your hair. I expected nothing less. You didn't respect me or my time.

Finally, I and my gear, you and your bathing suits, Norm and his notebook, and Hedda and her knitting piled into the Rostens' Studebaker and got on the road, heading inland. Several minutes later, when we were in a woebegone area near the town dump, I tapped on my window, kept closed in the stifling heat to spare your hair.

"Stop!"

"Here?" Norm asked.

"Yes, please."

Hedda turned around and frowned, the round, black-framed glasses on her smooth oval face adding to her disapproving-owl look. "Here" was a playground that hadn't been loved much lately. Two of the three swings hung by one chain each. Grass grew up through the middle of the merry-go-round. Rust encrusted the monkey bars.

You gazed out your window. The stripes on the too-tight knit shirt covering your bikini expanded as you sighed. "I see what you meant by 'playful.'"

"We'll wait in the car," Hedda said, not warmly.

We got out. You stroked the galvanized leg of the swing set as I unpacked my cameras.

"You don't have any tripods or lights."

"I don't work that way."

"I guess you don't! You're a documentary photographer."

I draped my neck with my three new Nikons, each with a different lens—a normal, a 35mm, and a portrait—and each a painfully expensive purchase. "What I'd like to do is to photograph you doing what you would do if I weren't here. Be yourself." Whatever that was.

You put your hand to your mouth, then reluctantly stepped from play apparatus to play apparatus as if thinking. Away from your ogling crowd and in this abandoned place, you looked small and plain, unloved, like the abandoned child you had been. I'd thrown you into a weird place and then asked you to act naturally. I felt a tug of guilt. I wasn't in the business of sabotaging my subjects.

I framed you with my camera with the normal lens. "Maybe we should move on to the next place."

"No. I can do this." You raised your chin. "You photographed Mamie Eisenhower at an amusement park. This is sort of like that."

I lowered my camera. "You saw those photos?"

You shrugged a pudgy shoulder. "I do my research."

On me? No one researched me.

Unsettled, I followed you in my viewfinder, then got out my light meter. You'd stopped at the merry-go-round and were scanning the scene. Once I'd adjusted the focus, I could see how your freshly bleached hair sprang from your hairline like flames from a torch, then slumped over your wide forehead in a molten tumble. I switched to my portrait lens and looked. Better. You had an unusual glow—would it show up on color film? I was using color film for the first time, and was nervous about it, but the thinking then was that color photography was for commercial work and black-and-white was for art. I'd pegged you as purely commercial. Who wouldn't after you'd staged yourself as the modern-day Venus?

"The problem is—" You touched a rusted bar on the merry-go-round. "It's just that . . . I guess what I want to say is that I've never been photographed by a woman before."

"Women photographers are just like men photographers."

You crooked the tail end of your brow as if it were jointed. "You think?"

I laughed. "No."

You grinned, pleased to have entertained me. "See? You're not like men!"

"Just don't ever call me a female photographer."

"Okay." You peeled a strip of paint from the merry-go-round bench. "What should I call you, then?"

"A photographer. Period."

"Okay, A Photographer, Period." You gave the merry-go-round a push, then hopped on. "I guess why I'm having trouble is because the men usually tell me what to do. They're like, 'Marilyn, bend over a little more.' 'Marilyn, look over your shoulder.' 'Marilyn, stick out your tush.'"

I waited as the merry-go-round spun. "And do you do what they tell you?"

"No! What's the fun in that?" You smiled. "But what they say does help me to figure out how to flirt with them."

"I'm not going to tell you what to do."

"You're not?"

"No."

You drew your feet up onto the bench of the slowing merry-go-round, then hugged your knees, curling into yourself the way Francis did when he was with strangers. "Sometimes they ask me questions to provoke me. 'Marilyn, how old were you the first time you had anything to do with a man?' 'Marilyn, what do you wear to bed?'"

"I'm not going to do any of that. I just find a location. The rest is up to you."

"I guess so!"

I caught the familiar whiff of glass and metal when I returned my camera to my eye. You were stroking your arms as if to soothe yourself. It occurred to me that you had no idea how to talk without flirting.

I racked my mind for a subject to relax you. "What's your next movie?"

"*Niagara*."

"What's it about?"

You looked up at the sky, then frowned as if aware that the daylight was waning and we were frittering away precious shoot time. "It's about a woman who kills her husband so she can be with her lover." You lay down on the bench, then got up on your elbow, then returned to your back.

"What's your role?"

"I'm the femme fatale."

"Did you enjoy that role?"

You sat up, then crossed your arms, then quickly uncrossed them. You didn't know what to do with yourself. "I'm not really a femme fatale. But that's why they call it acting, right?"

"Do you like acting?"

You squinted at me.

Okay, dumb question. "What have you done while in New York?"

"Ribbon cutting. Radio interviews." You brightened. "I went to Atlantic City, where I was the grand marshal of the Miss America parade. Can you imagine?" You flipped onto your belly and got up on your elbows. "I always wanted to be Miss America. But I would've had to be Mrs. America, because I got married so young."

"How old were you?"

"Sixteen."

You rested your chin on your hand. I squatted directly in front of you to get a head-on shot.

"My aunt Grace, who I was living with then, got married and couldn't keep me. Jim was her neighbor. I'll always be grateful to him for putting a ring on my finger to save me from going back to the orphanage. He was a sailor in the merchant marine—he's a policeman now. But he didn't have a dream, you know? And he didn't want me to have one, either. Everyone should have a dream, don't you think?" You cocked your head, waiting for my answer. America's pinup girl was just an eager kid.

My mentor, Henri Cartier-Bresson, said that when a true expression of life is offered to you, you must be creative enough to recognize it in an instant. *"Oop!"* he'd say. "The moment! Once you miss it, it is gone forever."

*Oop!* I clicked the shutter.

Chin on hands, you seemed to drift away in thought, but even while in this reverie, you moved your head subtly, as if trying to give me angles. Were you acting, or were you being you? I wanted to keep shooting, to see.

"You say your husband didn't have a dream. Did you?"

You started to bite your lip, then stopped, as if realizing you were ruining your lipstick, and licked your teeth. "When I was at the orphanage, they took us to the movies a lot. I guess we must have gotten in for free. I always stayed the whole day and watched the same movie over and over, until they finally had to come looking for me and drag me back to the orphanage. And I didn't even have popcorn to keep me going!" You looked to see if I'd laugh.

I obliged you.

"From my bed in the orphanage I could see out over the Hollywood Hills, to the RKO Radio Pictures lot. The block-long soundstages, the maze of office buildings and bungalows, the water tower with *R-K-O* spelled out in red—why, it was like a magic kingdom, and I was its princess, locked up in the mean woodcutter's cottage. I just knew I belonged *there*, at the studio, not with these girls who teased me by day and cried in their beds by night. I was different, meant for something else." Your chin bobbed against your hands as you spoke. "What an imagination! I talked myself into believing that Clark Gable was my father. I had him coming to the orphanage with coloring books for all the kids, and then taking off with me in his yellow sports car, leaving everyone who made fun of me in our dust."

*Click!*

When I pulled my eye away from the camera, the winsome, dreamy child became a flat-faced twenty-six-year-old in heavy makeup. I put my eye back to the viewfinder.

You sat up. "Wait a minute!" You ran to the car, then nearly skipped back, with a book.

"What's that?"

"James Joyce. *Ulysses.* I just love the sound of it. I read lines out loud just to go where he takes me."

You lay on your belly again and turned the pages. You then sat up and balanced the book on your thighs. Your arm placement, draped across your legs, was too studied to be genuine. You were clearly acting the part of an enthralled child. Even so, when you looked at the pages, you seemed to be retreating into a real part of you, beckoning me, like Joyce with his words, to follow. It was weird and exciting.

*Click, advance. Click, advance.*

I lowered my Nikon. "I'm out of film."

You smiled shyly. "Was I good?"

"Yes. I think so."

You took a breath. "That was me. Norma Jeane. I've never come out at a shoot before."

Before I could ask what you meant, you fled to the car.

"How'd it go?" Hedda Rosten said, doubtfully, when you scooted onto the back seat.

"Fine," you said.

"Do you want to go home, Marilyn?" Norman asked.

You turned to me as I closed my door. Flecks of mascara were gathering under your eyes, somehow making them seem bluer. "Didn't you have another shoot location in mind?"

I thought about denying it. The place wasn't worthy of you. Whoever I thought you were, you weren't.

"We don't have much light left," you said. "Hurry. Where is it?"

Reluctantly, I directed Norm to the spot as you fixed your makeup in a hand mirror. Three minutes later, we stopped at a tangle of bulrushes and bamboo.

You peered out the window. "A jungle?"

"I thought it might lend an air of wildness." My thought had been that you could sex it up all you wanted here, since that seemed to be your goal at our "picnic." "We can forget it."

"No!" You waded into the weeds.

I got out my stuff, then reloaded my camera. When I looked up, you were staring at me, your mouth turned down. You knew I was being a jerk for choosing that place.

"Just a minute," you said, then ran back to the car.

The light had fallen to a rich ochre. At least we'd soon run out of light. You emerged from the Rostens' Studebaker wearing a one-piece imitation leopard skin bathing suit and, before I could react, came over and dropped to your knees in the marsh. Mud oozed up. It was even swampier than I'd thought, yet on you slunk, a tawny, sinuous animal, parting the bulrushes.

I stood there with my camera in my hands.

Your voice was a soft growl: "Aren't you going to shoot?"

A man and a woman on a tandem bicycle happening by on the

empty road swerved, stopped, then took off, the man standing on his pedals to pick up speed.

I brought my camera to my eye. When you lifted your hands and knees, they were covered in mud.

"I'm sorry. I didn't know it was muddy."

"No," you purred, "I love it. I didn't get to play all that much as a kid. I've always wanted to play in the dirt." You dragged yourself through the muddy rushes, a leopardess gone into heat, panting at my lens. I followed you through the mire, sinking in the mud.

*Click, advance. Click, advance. Click, advance.*

You snarled. You slunk. You twisted around to growl at me. When you lunged at me with your claws, I laughed out loud.

"What?" You pushed yourself up onto your knees. Mud slid from your belly.

I lowered my camera. Maybe you didn't mean to be funny. "Is this what you want?"

"This is what *you* want." You dropped down with a swampy squish. "So keep going."

"You think I want this?"

"Yes. You think I'm dirty." You scooped up some mud. *Splat!* A pat of goo landed on my arm. "Now you are, too."

"Hey!" I cried.

You flung another handful. It hit my chest, close to my camera. "Hey! That's my life in a box!" I shoved my cameras over my shoulders. They rolled like rocks across my scapula as I scooped up mud.

"Go ahead." You raised your chin, giving me a target. Without the shield of my camera, I was confronted by a flat-faced bottle blonde, all traces of the sinuous cat in heat, the beautiful actress, the wistful child, gone. "Do it. Get the dirty girl."

My scalp tingled. What were we doing?

I let my handful slide to the ground. "I think we've had enough for the day." I slogged back to the car.

Norm looked up from his writing when we returned. "What happened to you two?"

Hedda clicked her tongue. "Let me get towels." She retrieved some from the trunk, then retreated inside the car while we cleaned ourselves.

"Look," I said as you wiped your legs. "I think we got off on the wrong foot. I'm sorry. I thought yesterday was meant to be just us, discussing a shoot, not a performance. You can see why I might have been offended when it turned out differently."

"Offended?" You palmed back your hair, which the humidity had frizzed into a platinum halo. "Really? I was trying to give you a story. I wanted to show you how it was for me as Marilyn. That 'performance' was all for you. And you didn't even bring a camera!"

My face got hot. "I was being polite. I was trying not to treat you like a commodity."

"But I am a commodity! Why shouldn't you make the best of it?" You snorted. "Oh, don't worry. I'll get something out of it, too, if you get good pictures."

A Cadillac convertible gunned up in the gathering dusk. Five men in straw boaters waved brown bottles as the tires of their car tore into the weeds.

"Hey, Marilyn!"

"Marilyn!"

"Marilyn, show us your tits!"

Norm got out of his car to yell at them, "Hey, what's the big idea?"

You flashed your Crayola blues at me. "We don't have to be friends. You help me, I help you. There's nothing wrong with that."

But there *was* something wrong with that. I could see by the way your mouth turned down that you thought so, too.

"I don't use my subjects to get ahead."

"Don't kid yourself. Isn't your whole goal to get covers on the big magazines?"

The jerks in the convertible were chanting, "Tits! Tits! Tits!"

You kept your gaze on me. "Well, getting big covers is my goal, too. I don't see why we shouldn't team up."

You then turned to the men. Out came your chest; down dropped your eyelids. "Are you boys lost?" Your voice, which I now realized hadn't been breathy all evening, regained its airiness.

"Say, Marilyn," one yelled, "when you gonna do another calendar?"

"Should I?"

"Yeah!" the carload exclaimed.

"Oh, I don't know." You widened your eyes. "When I posed for it, all I had on was the radio."

# 4

TWO DAYS LATER, TOTING A BRIEFCASE FULL OF THE RESULTS OF our shoot, I arrived at the gleaming brass entrance to Oz: the Waldorf Astoria, hotel of the powerful and wealthy. The burly doorman looked down from beneath the patent leather bill of his cap, paused a moment to flick his gaze over my good brown dress (it was Saks, okay?), then ushered me into the revolving brass door.

Across a marble hall fit for a pharaoh, I entered the lobby elevator and was crushed against its mahogany paneling by a pack of elegant men and women whose expensive scents nearly overwhelmed me. After elbowing my way between surprised people upon reaching the twenty-sixth floor—no one realized I was back there—I padded down thick carpet. You answered the door.

I took a step backward. A see-through black robe, tied at the waist, spilled over your body. You hadn't a stitch on underneath.

"I'll come back when you're ready."

"I *am* ready. Come in, silly," you said cheerfully, as if we hadn't last ended on shaky terms. I got a sniff of Chanel No. 5 and hair spray as I passed you. The suite, with its brocade drapes and furniture, smelled of new carpet and of the bushel of yellow roses on the coffee table in front of the sofa.

You exhaled a happy sigh. "I have an interview with a Frenchwoman from *Ciné Revue*. She'll be here any minute."

This was how you dressed for an interview? And I had an appointment to show you your prints. You'd double-booked me.

You saw my expression. "Please don't be mad. Her office phoned to move up our meeting, and I said yes. I called your house, but a girl answered. She kept calling me 'man.'"

"That's my sitter, Dora. She's a Beat."

"You're mad. Don't you see? This will be good for you. I'll introduce you."

"My agency sells my work. I don't need to meet her."

You plucked at the neckline of your translucent robe. "Please understand. It's a Belgian magazine for French speakers. This is my big chance to be seen all over Belgium and France."

I glanced at your getup. "I'll say."

You laughed. "You are so American!" Your voice wasn't breathy in the least. "The French are much more comfortable with their bodies than we are. They don't believe in hiding things."

"Is that true?"

"I think it's so much healthier."

Was it? I'd spent my whole life hiding things about myself. That felt healthy to me.

"Europeans see the body as art. Look at Michelangelo's paintings. Look at Botticelli's. Everyone's naked. It's classical. It's beautiful."

"Europeans wear clothes in real life."

You tipped your forehead at me. "Goddesses don't."

"So we're goddesses now, are we?"

You chuckled from your belly. "I guess so!"

A knock sounded at the door.

I pushed forward. "See you."

"Please don't go! What if she doesn't like me?"

Dressed like that? She wasn't going to love you.

Another knock.

"Did you bring your camera?" you asked.

"Yes, but *Ciné Revue* will have their own—"

As if an inner switch had been thrown, you arched your spine, thrust out your chest, and opened the door.

A thin woman wrapped tightly in a trench coat stood before us. "Miss Monroe—" Her husky French-tinged voice stopped. She slid her gaze down your peignoir.

"Hello." You clutched the front of your robe, and then, catching yourself, let it go, pushed out your chest, and held out your hand. "Pleased to meet you."

The beauty mark above the woman's dark red upper lip bobbed. Was she . . . suppressing a laugh?

You blinked in surprise, then pulled yourself taller, somehow actually increasing your stature.

"Do you know Eve Arnold?" you breathed. "Eve's a photographer for Magnum. I'm sure you've heard of Magnum Photos."

The reporter twitched a glance at me.

"Eve photographed Marlene Dietrich for *Esquire.* The article was called 'Marlene Dietrich: An Appreciation.' Did you see it?"

*"Non."*

"Too bad. It was a work of art."

"Is that what this is?" The reporter nodded at your robe. "I caught you in the middle of photographing"—she cleared her throat—"an *appréciation*?"

You and I glanced at each other.

"Do not let me stop you," the reporter said. "I can send you some written questions."

"No!" You lowered your lids and voice. "No. I have time for some now."

The reporter sighed. "*Très bien.* We will speak quickly about your latest film projects."

"Sure. Sit with me?"

I hovered in the background as the reporter reluctantly followed you to the couch, then unclasped the shiny black purse on her lap and took out her writing things. Your gown, your hair, and your face shimmered under the floor lamp as you arranged the flimsy material of your negligee over your knees. A close look revealed that a fine golden down covered your skin, trapping and reflecting light. You literally glowed. I couldn't resist—I raised my camera.

The reporter shook her finger at me. "*Non! Ciné Revue* has their own photographer."

"Oh, Eve has my permission."

"She does not have mine."

You bit your lip, getting your lipstick on your teeth, then pulled yourself straighter and lifted your chin. "Eve," you breathed, "won't you come sit with us?"

With a longing look at the door, I perched on a chair. *Just get this thing over with.*

The woman uncapped her fountain pen with a hollow click. "Tell me about *Niagara.* I understand you will be getting the top billing in it—your first top billing, the studio publicist advised me. How does that feel?"

"Wonderful!" You whispered, as if the reporter were your equal and you were letting her in on a secret: "I'm to be the villainess."

*"Oui?"*

"I was set to play the heroine of the picture, the smart wife, but they switched me to being the villainess. They thought that it suited me better to play 'a raging torrent of emotion that even nature can't control.' That's what the promotional posters are going to call me. Can you imagine?"

The woman snorted. "Did you enjoy playing this 'raging torrent of emotion'?"

"I did. I try to make the most of every role I get."

Above her ruby lips, the woman's beauty mark bobbed in disdain.

"Tell me about your co-stars."

You began to talk about Joseph Cotten, and what a gentleman he was.

The woman interrupted. "I understand that you went to his cast party dressed only in a terry cloth hotel robe."

"Who told you that?"

"Your studio publicist."

"He did? Hmm. Mr. Cotten's party was just down the hall of the hotel we stayed in. And I was comfortable in that robe."

"The publicist also said that, during the shooting, you crossed the studio lot wearing only a nightgown." The reporter idled her pen to glance at your robe. "You seem to want to be . . . 'comfortable' . . . often."

"That was my costume—" You stopped. "Well, yes, I guess I do want to be comfortable. I believe in being natural. As I was just saying to Eve, I don't believe in hiding things. Do you?"

The woman pushed back her peekaboo hair with a red fingernail. "All of us must hold back something, *non*? It is how we get along."

"Well, what if someone didn't hold something back?"

"Then I would say he or she was extraordinary."

You smiled.

"Extraordinarily stupid," she said.

You sniffed as if poked in the chest.

The reporter's gaze went to the magazines stacked on the coffee table, your image beckoning from the cover of the uppermost one. The headline proclaimed, WHO NEEDS TALENT? MARILYN MONROE HAS OTHER ASSETS. The reporter half smiled, then consulted her notes.

"Tell me about your background. You are completely untrained, *oui*?"

I could feel you coiling into yourself as you stared at her. She smiled back, proud to have dinged you.

At last, you said, "Do you mind if I brush my hair?"

The woman raised penciled brows, then recovered. "*Bien sûr.* Please do."

You glanced at me with a strange look, then disappeared into the bathroom. The woman flipped a page of her notebook, scratched the nib of her pen on the paper, then dug into her bag for another pen. I might as well have been the vase of roses.

I nudged through the stack of magazines. All featured you on the front, next to titillating cover lines: THE M BOMB . . . MARILYN MONROE: SHE BREATHES SEX APPEAL . . . HAS HOLLYWOOD GONE TOO FAR WITH SEX?

On the bottom of the pile was the current issue of *Focus.* The cover line, next to you in a skimpy gold two-piece swimsuit, read, A PSYCHIATRIST LOOKS AT MARILYN MONROE.

I sat back. Would a psychiatrist be called in to evaluate any other movie star? I tried to imagine the headlines. A PSYCHIATRIST LOOKS AT JERRY LEWIS . . . FRED ASTAIRE ACCORDING TO FREUD . . . JOHN WAYNE ON THE ANALYST'S COUCH.

I reached through the roses for the card. *I love you I love you I love you. —Joe*

How strange it must be to be so adored and so reviled at once.

You came out, swinging your hips, with an embossed silver

hairbrush in your hand. I shoved the magazines into rough order. Your tight smile, lost upon the reporter, who was scanning her notes, alarmed me. I could feel tension thrumming within you as you settled onto the sofa.

"So, tell me about your co-star Jean Peters," the reporter said, "the woman who got the role of the heroine. How did you two . . . get along? Was there friction after she took the role you were supposed to have?"

"Oh, I like Jean. We did fine."

"You did? Miss Peters said—" The beauty mark froze. You had parted your gown, and were brushing the tuft just visible above the V of your crossed legs.

The reporter sputtered a question about your next film, then stood while you were still answering.

"I'm going to star in *Gentlemen Prefer Blondes* with Jane Russell," you said as she raked her things into her purse, "and in *How to Marry a Millionaire* with Betty Grable and Lauren Bacall. I'm getting top billing." You followed her across the room. "Can you imagine?"

*"Non,"* the woman said, and was gone.

You leaned against the door, then raised those heavy lids. "Maybe I shouldn't have done that."

I didn't have to verify that.

You saw the brush in your hand and dropped it as if it were hot. It hit the carpet with a muffled thud. "What was I going to do? She wasn't paying attention."

AFTER THE REPORTER LEFT, YOU SLUNK TO THE BEDROOM, THEN returned dressed in a Harvard sweatshirt and loose blue jeans. You glanced at me, at the door, ready to leave, then went over and dropped onto the sofa.

"I raised myself, you know. I had to, passed around all those homes the way I was before I landed in the orphanage. I guess that makes me feral." You plucked at your sweatshirt. "You know that story about the boys who were raised by a wolf, Romulus and Remus? I used to be jealous of them. At least they had the wolf."

I thought you were kidding.

You weren't.

"Problem is, I don't know how normal people are supposed to behave." You threw your head against the cushions. "I keep getting myself in trouble because I just don't know." You looked up at me. "I had to dress myself and wash my own clothes for as long as I can remember. Ha! They didn't get washed much. I was on my own, you know? I had no idea that panties were not optional until I went to kindergarten. I only figured it out when I got stuck on the slide and lifted my dress to see why I wasn't moving and kids yelled, 'Norma Jeane's got no underpants!' Can you imagine?"

What would it be like to navigate this world with no compass other than your own desperation? My family had been outcasts, poorer than most and the only Jews in an Irish neighborhood, but at least we'd had one another. Dressed in hand-me-downs that had been handed down too many times, too poor for shoes, and unable to bathe but once a week in our cold-water apartment, I'd been called dirty by kids at school. But I'd had a father who taught me history and literature and to love life, and a mother who worried about me, so I'd been able to stand it. I even considered my childhood to be happy. But no one had loved you. Not even a wolf.

I sat down beside you and popped open the latches of my briefcase. "I brought you something." I offered you a stack of prints.

You took it and, scowling, slowly looked through the shots of yourself slinking and growling through the reeds.

"I think they're good," I said.

Your eyes begged me to be telling the truth. You sucked in a breath, then went on to the playground prints.

With color film being a first for me, I hadn't exactly brimmed with confidence when I'd lined up the additional trays in our apartment's bathroom/darkroom. My experience from the photofinishing plant, which had given me an edge when it came to coaxing the most from black-and-white film, couldn't help me with color. But as each image in the developing tray came swimming into view like the answers in a Magic 8 Ball, I forgot to be afraid.

Moment after captured moment, the frames of you reading on the merry-go-round were of a brave, sweet, determined child reading a book as if it might save her. The fierceness of this young girl's hope made the hair on my arms stand up. She—you—were the most enigmatic, compelling, and frighteningly . . . I don't know the best word—vulnerable?—subject I'd ever photographed. You'd given me something I hadn't seen before when shooting. Was it real? It was so heartbreaking, I almost hoped it wasn't.

You stopped at a photo of yourself with your chin on your hands. "I've always been sure that I could be someone special someday, if only I dreamed hard enough and worked hard enough and believed hard enough. Isn't that dumb?"

"It's not dumb at all." I hadn't fully seen how vulnerable you were when we were shooting. Only my camera had caught it—something, some essence of you, communicated only through my lens. I'd never had this happen with a subject before. It spooked me.

You unbuttoned the top button of your jeans and rubbed your belly as if it hurt. You saw me looking. "Cramps. I get them bad, all the time. I have a condition."

"I'm sorry. Can I get you some aspirin?"

"No, thanks. I already took a couple."

Were you an otherworldly being in a human's body, or a human in an otherworldly body? Neither seemed an easy fit.

I must have been staring at you. "You don't have to feel sorry for me," you protested. "I don't! I think I'm the luckiest girl in the world."

"You're lucky?"

"Sure!" You smiled shyly. "And I guess I try to give my luck a little poke. The gods help those who help themselves, right?"

The phone rang. Joe DiMaggio was calling from San Francisco. I'd heard—everyone had heard—that you and he were dating. You pointed to the prints you liked best, then settled down into the cushions with the receiver nestled under your chin.

The gods also help her who dates the most popular man in the world.

I let myself out.

AFTERWARD, AT THE *ESQUIRE* OFFICE, THE EDITOR, A BRAWNY brown-haired man with an orange mustache, was shuffling through the prints at his massive battered desk when I mentioned that I'd just shown them to you.

He stopped midshuffle. His chair creaked as he leaned forward to ash the cigarette that was smoldering in my face. "Kid, what were you thinking? You never show proofs to your subject. What if they don't approve, or they like something you don't? You never put them in the driver's seat. Biggest amateur move you could make." He sat back with a squeal of his chair. "You bring the contact sheets for these?"

I reached into my briefcase.

"Don't bother," he said before I got them out. "I can't use these. Well, maybe these ones of Marilyn slinking around in the weeds, playing leopard, I can. Looks like she's horsing around, kind of pulling our leg. I don't know if readers will like that, but you did get some good body shots. But these others . . . Who's interested in seeing Marilyn Monroe on a playground, reading a book, with most of her clothes on?"

"I think it will appeal to people. They'll see she's a real person. She's—" I spread my hands. "There's a lot more to her than we think."

He rocked in his squeaky chair. "Who cares?"

"I do."

"Evie, sweetheart, come on. *Esquire*'s for men. We're making guys' dreams here, not psychoanalyzing bimbos. Besides, this photo with the book right here? Not fresh. Halsman just published some shots of her reading. At least she was wearing a little nightie in those." He rapped the prints on his desktop to straighten them.

I stood, which put the desk at waist height. Reaching over it caused me to beach myself across the middle like driftwood at low tide, but so be it. I snatched the photos from his hand.

"Hey!"

"I want them all back." I beckoned with my fingers. "Give me the rest."

"But I kind of like some. I want this leopardess-in-the-reeds one for sure."

"You publish them as a set." I remembered the way the story for my article about the Harlem fashion show had been perverted by the editors of the magazine that published it. "And I write the copy, or I take them all back." Seeing that my point would be better made with my belly off the top of his desk, I unbeached myself. "All of them."

He raised his orange mustache in a smile of disbelief. "Are you crazy?"

"Yes. I am."

That was how I published my first feature article that came complete with my photos *and* my text. I would publish my work no other way from then on. As I walked out the office door, leaving the editor and his 'stache to cure in the smoke from his own Pall Malls, it occurred to me that it was your photos that had given me power. He wanted your prints badly enough that he'd met my "crazy" demands. Could I have succeeded had they have been of any other subject?

I'm still trying to square myself with that.

# 5

THE SALE OF YOUR PHOTOS TO *ESQUIRE* WAS GOOD, BUT I couldn't exactly sit back and riffle my stack of dollar bills. I lived in fear of being penniless, a bad fit for a freelance artist, who, by definition, never knows from where the next penny will come. I came by my phobia of going broke honestly. I can pinpoint the day; I was eight years old.

That morning, my mother had put on a huge pot of soup. My father had been gone for several nights. His rag-and-bone collection route, for which he drove a horse-drawn cart, often took him far afield—the twenties did not roar for Jewish refugees from the Ukraine—but something had detained him for longer than usual. My mother had manned the stove all day, stirring and tasting her concoction in its pitted cast aluminum pot as she waved out the window at the Lynches across the courtyard, at the Connellys, the Boyds, the O'Sheas. Though the soup didn't smell like much, I couldn't wait to eat it. My sisters and brothers and I'd had only a see-through slice of bread for breakfast.

When dinnertime neared, I couldn't stand it any longer. Stomach growling, I put a step stool to the stove, climbed up, and slid back the heavy lid. All that was in the pot was water.

You can see why, then, a couple weeks after I'd last seen you, I was biting my thumbnail as I sat on the other side of the mayhem of magazines, letters, and tear sheets that was Robert Capa's desk, watching him squint through his jeweler's loupe at the contact sheets for a feature I was proposing. I never trusted that all was well. I feared the water soup.

To the right of Capa (face it, he would never be Bob to me), Inge Bondi, broad-cheeked, sloe-eyed, and whip-smart, tapped at her typewriter. Inge, from Austria (was anyone at Magnum—make that in New York—back then *not* an immigrant or first-generation?), had been a photographer but had left her camera days behind to run the office. A recent women's college graduate clacked away at an ancient Remington with sticky keys in a corner behind her. On the other side of our basement window, flocks of wing tips and high heels flashed past the pink brownstone town house that contained our subterranean office. Inside, our pit reeked of cigarette smoke, mildewing magazines, and photography chemicals, through all of which threaded the almond scent of Inge's Jergens hand lotion.

Capa, the greatest living war photojournalist, had waded—no, run headlong—into unspeakable horrors. His exterior, from his coarse nest of hair and his black bottlebrush brows, to the thick lips upon which a cigarette was generally cushioned, matched the toughness that had required. He spoke with a Hungarian accent, his vocal cords wet only by coffee and his preferred drink, champagne. Empty champagne magnums—the agency had been named after them—lined the mantel of the boarded-up fireplace at my back.

Tough old Bob was given away by his hands, with their slender, tapered fingers, as sensitive as a poet's. How had this empathetic creature ever endured the atrocities he'd seen? I was staring at those beautiful fingers supporting the edges of my contact sheet when he sat back.

"Holy shit," he rasped. "Is this how it is at birth?"

Inge stopped typing.

"In hospitals in American cities," I said, "I think usually, yes."

His snort rerouted the smoke curling from his cigarette. "Damn."

Inge and I followed his magnifier's path as he went back over the frames:

—A DOCTOR SUSPENDS A NEWBORN BABY BY HER FEET.

—ON THE OPERATING TABLE, HER LEGS BOUND INTO STIRRUPS AND DRAPED IN WHITE, THE MOTHER SLEEPS.

—NOW THE DOCTOR WORKS BEHIND THE MOTHER'S DRAPE WHILE, BLURRED IN THE BACKGROUND, THE BABY LIES SLACK ON A STEEL TABLE.

—CLOSE-UP OF THE LISTLESS BABY.

—THE NURSE RUSHES TO THE INFANT.

—THE NURSE HOOKS A GLOVED FINGER INTO THE CHILD'S MOUTH.

—THE NURSE PUTS AN OXYGEN MASK OVER THE BABY'S FACE.

—THE BABY IS BAWLING.

Capa looked up at me from under those half-inch-thick brows. Another thing that gave away his sensitivity was his eyes, when he'd let you meet them. "Was the baby all right?"

"I know for a fact that she is. She's a month old now, and perfect." My heart swelled. "She's my niece."

"Your niece?" Inge blurted in her Viennese accent. "*Das* is your sister?"

I nodded.

"Poor you!" she cried. "How could you watch?"

Capa tapped a cigarette on his palm before lighting it. "Damn."

My sister had invited me to photograph the birth, and her doctor, a friend, finally agreed. I was not prepared for the violence of it. Like most women having babies, I'd been knocked out for Francis's delivery. I'd been shocked, therefore, to see the doctor delve into my sister with forceps and pull out the infant by her head, like a turnip from stubborn soil. I was startled by the speed with which he hung the baby from her feet to force that single sharp, blessed *waa.* But my heart banged to a stop when, satisfied by the baby's yelp, he left her on a table to attend to my sister, and the newborn turned a dusky cobalt.

I shouted for the nurse, then quaked so hard as she battled to save my tiny blue niece that I had to bury my elbows in my ribs to keep my camera still. Tears seared my eyes as I clicked and wound, clicked and wound. *Don't look away. See it. Record it. Bear witness.*

Capa blew out smoke. "Well, I can't use these."

"Really? I have a scoop here. Some doctors and nurses are starting to wonder about the safety of the anesthesia used for births. Don't you want to know what goes on in the delivery room?"

Inge's stare commanded him to say yes.

He grimaced. "Okay, okay. It's good work. But can you imagine these in *Life,* spread out on the coffee table in someone's living room? Americans don't want to know how babies get here, let alone imagine the mother birthing."

Inge snatched up her bottle of Jergens and tapped out lotion, releasing a fresh gust of almond fragrance. "*Ja*, better to drug the mother and baby senseless and send congratulations with greeting cards with storks on them." She offered the lotion to me.

I shook some into my hand. "I was thinking of *Ladies' Home Journal* for these. Well, maybe not the photos of my niece when she was in trouble, but enough of them to show that deliveries aren't as simple as people think."

Capa's guffaw rang out. Then he saw that I wasn't laughing with him. "Eve, come on. *Ladies' Home Journal*? That's the last magazine for this kind of realism."

I rubbed the lotion in. I'd been gunning for *LHJ* because they paid better than anyone else, for their new How America Lives series in particular. The series was supposed to be about families finding togetherness as they sought the American Dream, but we all knew it wasn't serious journalism. Features about families cooking together were thinly disguised excuses to print recipes using ingredients from the magazine's advertisers, just as articles about the family relaxing at home were jumping-off points to sell home goods and back-to-school features were sales pitches for children's clothing manufacturers. What was I thinking? I'd gotten so deep in my project that I'd lost sense of its salability. And no one would ever see this story if it wasn't salable, no matter how important or true it was.

On the wall behind Capa's tornado of hair were some of the world's most iconic photos by Magnum photographers. There were Capa's own photos of Omaha Beach and the falling loyalist soldier; Chim's *Pablo Picasso in Front of* Guernica; Henri Cartier-Bresson's *Seville, Spain*, of children playing in the ruins of a bombed-out building in 1933. Each of these photographers crystallized their world, their time, into images unbearable in their clarity. Why was my story less important than the ones they told?

Capa took a folder from the stack on his desk. "Take cheer, my tiny terror. I have a little assignment. *Coronet* wants a photo-essay on immigrant families trying to find the American Dream. They mentioned you."

"Me?" My heart blipped.

"You. Inge told them this kind of stuff was right up your alley."

I raised worshipful hands to Inge.

She shrugged, grinning. "I reminded the editor about your Marilyn Monroe shots in *Esquire.* He thought they were inventive."

Capa poked his cigarette into a Pepsi bottle with a hollow hiss. "Nice. You're getting a reputation."

I was fired up during the whole train ride back to the Village. Editors thought I was inventive! How could I prove them right? What unexpected angle could I take on a story about newcomers to America chasing the Dream? As I cast my mind through the war brides, refugees, and dream seekers who had tumbled into the US in the fallout of World War II, a little thought tickled the back of my mind.

Who had been the inventive one on our shoot, me or you?

THAT EVENING, ARNOLD BURST THROUGH THE DOOR OF OUR apartment pumping a bottle of champagne like a dumbbell, his suit flapping around his lanky frame. Francis and I looked up from the dinette table, where we were eating lo mein from paper containers in celebration of my *Coronet* assignment. I hadn't expected Arnold this early. He taught a Wednesday-night class at the New School.

"Good news!" He winged his hat to the sofa and unbuttoned his coat, the bottle under his arm.

I lowered my chopsticks. "I've got some, too."

"Evie, I got a book contract. Ballantine is publishing my book."

I pulled back my chin. "*How to Play with Your Child*?"

"That is the one." He scooped me up in a bear hug, his arms strong and warm, and the champagne bottle cool against my back. "I am going to be the Benjamin Spock of playtime. How do you like that?"

I laughed with delight. "I do like that!"

He held me out, his bony, winsome face beatific. "Our lives are going to change. Oh, the advance is not as big as I'd hoped, but it will be bigger the next time, and the time after that."

Now was not the moment to ask about the size of the advance. "Congratulations, Arnold. This really is wonderful."

"I have more good news. You know our rental on Long Island that you love so much?"

Arnold was the one who loved it so much. I was a city girl. I thrived on traffic noise, crowded sidewalks, and all kinds of people. Give me Beats drumming below my living room floor, and steamy delis that smell of spices and toasting bagels. "Yes?"

"It is ours now."

"Ours?"

"I called Mr. Jones from the phone booth in Ballantine's lobby. It seems he was ready to unload the place. I will go to the bank tomorrow." He went over and picked up Francis, who clung to him like a koala. "Frankie, how would you like to go to the beach every day?"

"Arnold! You're buying it? We can't afford—"

"We can! A few more contracts, and I will pay it off."

I felt sick. I knew too well the life of the freelancer. There was no depending on anything.

He must have seen my hesitation. "I have ideas for other books. Ballantine's interested!" He put Francis down. "It is finally working for me. You must not worry about money anymore. Think of it—you could have a real darkroom. You would not have to use our bathtub to make your prints."

Several years after the water soup incident (after which my mother had banded together with the neighbors to turn our courtyard into a garden, to avoid another such calamity; I can still taste the sweetness of those carrots!), I'd seen my strong, wise father sag behind the front door when the creditors came knocking. With horror, I watched him throw it open to their torrent of threats. Not until I was older did I understand that we were forever short on cash because he'd paid those needier than us for their rags and bones on his collection route, even though those scraps should have been free. The damage had been done. If my respected abba could get into trouble over money, no one was safe.

"I cannot believe I did it," Arnold said. "Do you realize how hard it is to get a book contract?"

I imagined it was as hard as landing a feature article in a major magazine. Before I could tell him about my *Coronet* assignment, he drew me to him again. "Finally—*finally*—I can take care of you in the way you deserve"—he glanced upward and laughed—"just by using this poor noodle. It will be better for us from now on. Trust me." He tucked a stray wisp of hair behind my ear. "You do trust me, don't you?"

It was the impermanence of things that I didn't trust, the unpredictability, the injustice, not this beautiful man so devoted to me and his son. My heart hurt with love for him. "Of course I do."

# 6

AFTER THE *LEOPARDESS IN THE REEDS* SHOOT, I DIDN'T THINK our lives would cross again anytime soon. That fall your career was making strides on the West Coast—in Hollywood, where you were creating a stir in the run-up to making *Gentlemen Prefer Blondes.* Mine was baby-stepping forward in the East—in Hoboken, New Jersey, to be exact. Maybe my life wasn't as glamorous as yours, but I was in heaven.

For my *Coronet* assignment, I'd gotten to know a starry-eyed teenaged mother and her young husband, both from Sicily and now proud residents of Jersey. After photographing them in their apartment, I took them to a nearby park on the Hudson, where they posed with their six-month-old son, the beaming mama in bobby socks and with her scarf tied into a headband, and the duck-tailed papa, his fingernails black from his welding job at the shipyard, eyeing my camera. The session had stopped when the baby got fussy and the mother, excusing herself, had sat down on a bench, nursed him, and then put him in his buggy and rocked it with her foot. As I aimed my camera elsewhere, looking for other shots, she nudged the pram and chewed on a pencil while poring over a list of things she hoped to buy. When her husband, weary from working the night shift, slumped down next to her and stared off into space as she dreamed of how to spend their money, I saw it, the decisive moment. *Oop!*

*Coronet* liked that photo. The feature I built around it and other shots of the young family prompted the editor to ask me to follow up with a second story on the American Dream, this one maybe with the dreamers up a rung or two on the ladder, maybe more American—code for "more bourgeois white."

I went to Newport News, Virginia, to photograph a navy family my brother knew. Blondes they were (white enough?), from Dad, a sailor, and Mom, a housewife, down to the two little daughters, squabbling in crinolines. I was invited into their home on the base, a tidy little house among thousands of identical tidy little houses. My plan was to accompany them, in their new Chevrolet, to the man's parents' home.

As Mom fixed the two-year-old's hair for a quick family portrait, Dad showed me the features of their prize possession, the large Zenith TV lording it over the living room sofa and chairs. Dad's duty to entertain me fulfilled, he sank into his armchair and took up his newspaper as I got out my cameras. Meanwhile, Mom was putting white gloves on her five-year-old, who was allowing her hands' imprisonment with the resignation of a just-broken mustang. Gone were the girl's years of running free. Already, she was being hobbled by femininity.

I couldn't focus quickly enough.

I got a call from *Fortune* the week *Coronet* ran that feature. The editor loved the article. He thought it clever the way I captured the father reigning over his little kingdom, newspaper in hand. I didn't set the editor straight. My job was to lay out the moment. The viewer took what she or he wanted from it.

The editor said I got the hopefuls right. Now how about finding him a family who'd actually *achieved* the American Dream?

Not sure what that would look like, I took myself to the Advertising Association's awards banquet being held in Manhattan. Where better to search for the winners of the Dream than among the people who'd made up the fantasy in the first place?

Outside, on the streets, a cold November rain plastered hosiery to skin, filled shoes, and flipped umbrellas. But in the fake Polynesia of the Hawaiian Room in the Lexington Hotel, palm fronds wafted in the wake of barefoot, grass-skirted women bearing trays of food and drink to rowdy admen. Already, during the cocktail hour, I'd zeroed in on the most compelling young man in the room—judging by the crowd gathered around him. As I photographed him amusing his colleagues, his wedding ring flashing as he gestured, it became clear to me that this debonair gentleman was not the marrying type, regardless of the ring, unless his wife was a front. The madly-in-love guy and gal and the little fruits of their passion, all living the high life that *Fortune* was desirous that I should document, were unlikely to be modeled in his home. Don't ask me how I knew. An outsider knows an outsider.

Back on the hunt for Dream Dad, I cruised between tables, my cameras around my neck like a blocky lei. The admen had just been served dinner when the hula dancers onstage swished off and the master of ceremonies took to the podium to begin presenting the awards. I receded to a bamboo-paneled wall.

An older gent with a naked dome save for a few beige strands came up and leaned against the bamboo next to me. "She sent you, didn't she?" He raised the straw in his coconut-shell drink to his mouth.

I couldn't think who he meant. "Inge?"

"Who's Inge?"

"At Magnum."

"She tell you to say that?" He sucked at his straw. "Very clever, sending a girl photographer, trying to rub it in our faces. That Kay!"

"Kay?"

"Quit playing around. Kay. Kay Daly." His gaze traveled to a table on the other side of the room, where a petite strawberry blond woman was writing something on a napkin as her colleagues caroused around her. She was the only woman in the room besides the Hawaiian girls and me.

He saw me looking. "Pretending you don't know her—that's cute." He shook his coconut and then Hoovered in more drink. "Her and her *Fire and Ice* campaign. Who's she think she is? My *Nothing Draws a Man to a Woman Like Crushed Rose* for Max Factor won awards! Now here's her harebrained campaign suggesting that women buy lipstick *just to please themselves*! She even talked the magazines into printing a second page of the ad, with that dumb questionnaire to see if gals were daring enough to wear Fire and Ice." He rattled the cubes within the hairy shell. "Do *you* buy lipstick just for yourself?"

"I don't buy lipstick."

He raised his brows as his gaze fell to my ring finger, as if to verify that I was a real woman, properly claimed by a man.

The band struck a sultry tune. The spotlight wavered, then hit upon a blond woman oozing over to the podium in a tight white dress.

You! Here? You certainly got around. I found that I was glad to see you.

The admen were whistling and shouting like GIs at a wartime show. The MC gathered you in and then spooled you out to display you to the crowd. "I give you—Marilyn Monroe!"

You lowered your lashes and loosened your jaw into that

open-mouthed smile. It occurred to me that no human emotion corresponded to that expression in nature.

The MC hushed the crowd. "Did you know that Miss Monroe has been nominated by our colleagues in California for a new category, the Most Advertised Girl in the World?" You chopped on high heels as he reeled you in to him again. "The Most Advertised Girl in the World—sweetheart, does that mean we're advertising you a lot, or that you are advertising our products?"

You leaned to the microphone. "Well, both."

Everyone laughed.

"Marilyn, how do you like New York?" He tipped the microphone to you.

"I love it."

He took the microphone back. "What are you doing while you're here, besides stopping traffic?"

You waited until the men stopped chuckling. "Well," you breathed, "I'm here to promote my new movie, *Niagara*."

"Hmm. How about that? Sounds like a case of you advertising yourself!"

You bunched your shoulders as if naughty. "Oops!"

The audience laughed.

"What else are you doing?"

"I recorded a radio show."

"Oh? Edward R. Murrow?"

You cooed, "No, Edgar Bergen and Charlie McCarthy."

"You mean the ventriloquist and his wooden dummy?"

"Yes."

"What'd you do?"

"Well, we did a sketch together. I got married in it."

"Got married? Isn't Edgar Bergen a little old for you?"

"No." You smiled shyly. "I married Charlie."

The men roared.

My new pal shook his empty coconut. "The broad has good timing—you got to give her that. Who knew?"

"Boys," the MC said, "how would you like to have Marilyn give out the awards tonight?"

They pounded their tables in response.

"There you have it." He handed you an envelope. You hesitated.

"What's the problem, honey?"

"Do you mind if I borrow your glasses? I'm going to wear glasses in the next picture I'll be filming, and I guess I should get used to them."

"All right," he said as if appeasing a child.

His horn-rims perched endearingly on your soft toddler's nose, you opened the envelope, lisped the winner's name, and gave out the trophy, surprising the winner with a kiss. By the next category, the winner had his cheek ready.

The men were sauced on you and rum drinks by the time the Advertiser of the Year was to be named. To a drumroll, you took the envelope from the MC and held it to your chest.

The MC growled into the microphone, "I'd like to be that envelope."

"Hey," someone yelled, "does the grand winner get a date with Marilyn?"

"What do you think, Marilyn?" the MC asked. "Is that all right with you?"

There was a blink of discomfort. And then it vanished. "Gee. I can't. I don't think Charlie McCarthy would like that."

The admen roared.

My companion shook his head in admiration. "She's funny. Bet she can sell all sorts of shit."

You waited for the men to quiet, then nodded to the drummer.

To the trilling of snares, you opened the envelope, then announced the winner, who trotted up and demanded kisses on both cheeks before prancing back to his table, trophy held high.

"Thank you, Marilyn!" the MC exclaimed. "And this concludes our evening of bliss, tropical and otherwise."

"Wait a minute." You laid a white-gloved hand on his arm.

He looked down at it, then up into your eyes. "Yes, sweetheart?"

"I just want to say that, as a woman"—you paused for whistles—"I think the new campaign for Fire and Ice lipstick is brilliant. 'For you who love to flirt with fire, and dare to skate on thin ice'—that's me!"

The room fell quiet. Frowns flashed toward Kay Daly, who stopped writing on her napkin.

The MC took the microphone from you. "Thank you, sweetheart," he said, his tone suddenly flat. "So, tell me: Who do you wear lipstick for when you're on a date? The man? Or for you?"

You looked out over the audience. The men, arms crossed, looked back. The air in the room seemed to have contracted. How quickly the mood had turned. I lifted my camera.

You lowered your lashes and opened your mouth in that one-of-a-kind smile. "Well, I don't know, but I should wear *something*, shouldn't I?"

Laughter burst forth. You did a little shimmy.

*Oop!*

AFTER THE AWARDS, I FOUND MY SUBJECT FOR THE *FORTUNE* feature: a tall twenty-something blond man whose hair was as perfectly clipped as his mid-Atlantic accent. In Cary Grant tones, he let it drop that he loved to row, went to Harvard, and had a wife, a little daughter, and a baby son waiting for him in an apartment in fashionable Stuyvesant Town. *Bingo.* Once I'd gotten him to agree to a shoot and had taken his phone number, I looked for you, but you were so mobbed that I gave up. I was packing my cameras when you came up to me on the arm of your escort, a suave black-haired gentleman.

You extracted yourself from him and hugged me. "This is the photographer who took those pictures of me looking like a leopard for *Esquire*," you told him.

The guy aimed his slick black Tony Curtis sidewalls at me. *Wait*—it was Tony Curtis.

"I saw them. You photographed her in a swamp." He'd stuck a cigarette between the pillows of his lips. "Why'd you photograph her in a swamp? She deserves better than that."

"I liked it!" you said. "I've never had so much fun on a shoot."

Was that true?

"Huh," he said, cigarette bouncing. "Don't you know she was making fun of you?"

You shook the curl over your forehead. "No. I was making fun of myself."

You apologized for him when we met up in the bathroom later. "We dated once, a couple years ago, and now he thinks he owns me—and he's married now!" You frowned at my reflection in the bamboo-framed mirror. "Why do they always want to own us?"

You reapplied your lipstick—Fire and Ice, was it?—then rubbed your lips together. I noticed that you had emphasized the small beauty mark above your lip, placed exactly where the reporter from *Ciné Revue* had hers. Jean Harlow's hair, the reporter's beauty mark—it was as if you were watching everyone, picking up bits from whomever, to build your Frankenstein's bombshell upon the body of the feral Norma Jeane.

"That was a close call back there," I said, unfolding my plastic rain bonnet for the trip home.

"You mean when I said I liked that lipstick?"

"I'd never seen a room turn so fast."

You inhaled, then let your breath out loudly. "They don't scare me," you said, your voice gone breathy. "I like to imagine that the boys are like a great big lion, ready to turn on me at the slightest provocation. I'm locked in a cage with it. There's no escaping. I've got to throw it red meat before it kills me." You pantomimed flinging a steak. "But when I've got it purring and eating out of my hand, there's no better feeling in the world. It loves me and I love it, my nice big kitty." You saw my expression. "I'm not worried!"

I laughed as I tied on my plastic bonnet. "You're crazy."

Your friendliness drained from your face. "Crazy," it appeared, was not a word to be used lightly around you.

I warmed my voice. "Congratulations, by the way."

You clicked your lipstick into its case. "For what?" you said coolly.

"For getting Miss Most Advertised."

"Thanks." You dropped the lipstick into your purse. "I worked hard for that. Nobody's ever given me anything."

"Then you must be extra proud of your achievements."

You stared at me in the mirror. With your sexiness turned off, you looked like a tired tough girl.

I shouldered my packed cameras. "I know what it's like to have to be more on your toes, more persistent, more creative than your peers. Do you think I've had anything handed to me? I'm the only woman in a man's world. It's hard."

You snorted. "Men think they are in charge. Well, let them think that! Let them think of you *solely* as a woman, as *nothing more than a woman.* No, more basic than that—as the woman they want you to be. A fun-loving piece of ass! A little girl to be spoiled by her daddy! A bad girl to be punished!"

"A lightweight who can't get a scoop?"

You shrugged. "Yeah. Let them think that's who you are while you keep doing what you need to do, and, in the end, who has gotten what they wanted? You. It's a woman's world, and men are just living in it."

"I wish that were true."

"It *is* true. Try it."

I laughed.

You frowned as you hooked your purse on your arm. "When are you going to call me about another shoot? Or are you afraid to be with me now, since"—you exhaled—"*Ciné Revue*?"

I'd thought our business was finished after the last shoot. You wanted to do more?

"You wouldn't be the first girl to drop me. I'm like poison to respectable women. Tell me now, and I'll leave you alone."

"No! I'll call you."

"Oh, thank you!" you said in a rush. "You won't be sorry! You did all right with the *Esquire* shoot, didn't you?"

I'd only gotten my name out there with editors and won the authority to write my own captions—that's all. "I promise I'll call you."

"I just want to see what I look like through the eyes of someone who's not trying to get into my pants. Can you maybe show me who I am?" Your sigh was long and sorrowful. "Because I really don't know." You shot me a wistful glance. "Okay, Miss Documentary Photographer?"

You meant that. You really didn't know. My voice was as tender as it was teasing. "Okay, Miss Most Advertised."

You laughed.

Outside, taxi drivers honked and vied for lanes, the bright shafts of their headlights painting the wet street. Being around you made me feel off-balance. The crazy—sorry, unusual—things you said about men and women were either completely untrue or completely genius; I didn't know which.

I had to figure it out.

---

THE FOLLOWING WEEK, I WENT TO THE ADMAN'S LUXURY APARTment in Stuyvesant Town and waited with his wife and kids for him to come home from work. I photographed the young woman soothing her screaming baby boy, and then I stopped to take the child when she had to comfort her sobbing four-year-old daughter, who'd just wet her dress. I put the baby in his playpen and then, in silent sympathy, recorded the mother changing her distraught little girl out of three wet, scratchy layers of crinoline. The woman's dogged strength, even when she was exhausted by her children, shone through my lens—I took frame after frame. Women would understand her.

*Fortune* didn't want those shots.

I receded to the coatrack when the head of the household finally made his hero's entrance. I snapped him as the mother, pearls intact, and with only a few damp wisps escaping her perfect French twist, presented their baby boy like an offering to a king. The infant laid plump starfish hands on his father's face while the little girl reached up, unseen, for her daddy's arms.

*Fortune* used it for their cover, without the slightest sense of irony.

I had my doubts. Was it really a woman's world?

# 7

## 1953

**THREE MONTHS LATER, LONG AFTER YOU'D GONE BACK TO CAL**ifornia, I was out on the North Shore, chasing my own American Dream—tricky, because this dream required me to be in the city. That day, I had five hours to zip Francis into his snowsuit, drive him to school, aim our secondhand DeSoto between banks of snow toward the train station, grab the express to Grand Central, hoof down slushy streets to the *Look* office, watch Mr. Gordon pick apart my contact sheets, pray that I got the feature, and then reverse course at insane speed to end up waiting in line with the other mothers picking up their children at school. Arnold had two jobs in the city of his own to worry about, and he was working on a new book. He couldn't see how he could possibly help me, although he declared that if his book took off, we would both quit our jobs. That was hardly a solution to my time shortage. I *wanted* to work. I wanted to be a great mother and mate, too, but this madness was not sustainable.

I was not admitting that.

At the midpoint of my five-hour window that day, I calmed myself by scanning the framed photos on the grass-cloth walls above me while Mr. Gordon perused my shots, his cigarette smoke charring my lungs. Unlike the iconic stills on the scuffed walls of Magnum, these photos were pure kitsch. Here were Bob Hope and Bing Crosby dancing the Highland fling in kilts and Scottish bonnets. There was Jane Russell curled upon a bale of hay. Behold Stan Gordon himself, receiving smooches from Elizabeth Taylor, caresses from Joan Crawford, and tickles from Martin and Lewis. The photos were as devoid of real emotion as a circus clown's smile, but what did one expect? Stanley Gordon was the editor of the Hollywood section of *Look* magazine. I was in the land of make-believe.

Jeweler's loupe to his eye, he shuffled through my contact sheets. "You got a shot of Richard Burton in attendance."

I pulled my gaze from his wall of fantasy.

"Very good. And Cagney, too." He sucked on his cigarette with a crinkle of burning tobacco. I'd recently given up my own habit, cured of it by being hermetically sealed into too many magazine offices with chain-smokers. "These are decent shots of the performance"—he deposited an inch of ash in a green cut glass ashtray— "though the play looks like a snooze. Was it?"

"I thought it was riveting."

His grin added to his boyish good looks. He could have given Frank Sinatra a run for his money with the bobby-soxers. "A play about Puritans?"

"About Puritans betraying each other," I clarified.

He laughed. "And that makes it better?"

Joke as he might, in these times *The Crucible* was a brave play. Senator McCarthy, flexing his strengthening muscles, had doubled down on going after Hollywood—the bigger the player, the better—dragging actors, directors, and writers suspected of having the slightest ties to Communism before the House Committee on Un-American Activities. McCarthy had struck pay dirt when he'd gotten Elia Kazan, the country's top director of screen and stage, to name names.

To keep himself and the hundreds of people who worked on his productions on the job, Kazan had made the calculation that anyone he named could prove that they were loyal Americans and be okay. They weren't okay. They were blackballed out of work. Enraged, his best friend, playwright Arthur Miller, wrote *The Crucible* to shame him publicly, though Kazan had made Arthur Miller "the Great American Playwright" with his staging of *Death of a Salesman.* Miller's rebuke of his mentor seemed to go beyond moral indignation and into something sharply personal. One wondered what that was.

Now frowning, Mr. Gordon sluiced through the contact sheets. "Did you get any starlets?"

Neighbors were turning in neighbors, children were starving in migrant camps, Black men were being lynched for "looking funny" at white women, babies were being born blue to mothers being knocked out in delivery rooms, and shots of starlets were all he cared about?

He paused to peer at a frame. "Can you believe Marilyn Monroe once had an affair with this stick?"

I leaned in to see the image under his loupe, of a man talking to reporters. He was built like an actual stick, a sapling with black glasses, although a handsome one. You had an affair *with him*?

I pulled back. "With Arthur Miller?"

"They met in Hollywood when he and Elia Kazan were trying to cut a deal with the studios on a picture. The affair made him run back to his wife like a scalded cat, and then Kazan took up with her. At least, that's what I've heard. Can you verify?"

"No!"

"Aren't you Marilyn's friend?"

Was I? My letters had gone unanswered since you'd returned to Hollywood, but I tried not to be disappointed. You were busy and we didn't live close to each other. There was no prayer for us to have another shoot. You'd already kept your promise of doing something for me. I guessed I should be happy.

"I hear she got kinky with the *Ciné Revue* reporter when you were there." He flashed his appealing smile. "Don't look so surprised. I have contacts everywhere. We're all connected in this business." He drew on his cigarette. "You know that Loretta Young had Clark Gable's baby, right?"

"What?"

"It's old news, common knowledge to anyone in the biz. Kind of separates insiders from the outsiders." He sat back. "Maybe Hollywood isn't your beat."

I could have lived with that. Too bad I needed the money.

"But"—he sat forward—"your photos have something about them, like they're pulling back the curtain. You got a side of Marilyn Monroe that made me wonder, who the hell is she? I liked what you did with Marlene, too, and with all those others you've been photographing during their recording sessions at Columbia: Tony Bennett, Kate Smith, Sammy Davis Jr.—who else?"

Editors were forever trying to pigeonhole photographers. Once pegged as a recording session photographer, always a recording session photographer.

"What's your trick?" he said. "You make the viewer feel like he knows these people, maybe knows something secret about them. I'm not sure how you get in people's business and do that, little bitty girl that you are, but keep it up."

There was no "trick," no trying to "get in people's business." I wasn't trying to expose my subjects; I was just showing them how they were. But he didn't want to hear that.

He ashed his cigarette. "I need someone to cover the *Photoplay* magazine awards dinner next week, out in LA. You'd be an interesting fit. You ever think of traveling?"

Oh, I'd thought of traveling. I'd dreamed of it since going to Chicago to photograph the candidates' wives. But recently I was stretched so thin. It felt like a bad time to leave my family for days on end.

He saw my hesitation. "Never mind. I got a guy out there who I can use. Thanks for these shots. I'll let Inge know which ones I'll take." He ground out his cigarette. "Goddamn television. I can't compete with it. People are getting addicted to their boob tubes. But can TV viewers study their favorite stars at their leisure, not just when the show airs? No. Can they get the inside scoop on their idols? No. And for that reason, they're always going to come running back to the magazines." He opened his arms and grinned. "And when they do, Papa will be here, waiting for them."

No one was putting my delivery room shots on their covers. But maybe they would if my work got famous, and to get famous I'd have to do what it took.

He got up to usher me out.

"I could go to California—"

"Don't worry about it. My guy there can handle it. Milton Greene—you know him?"

He had me out the door before I could answer.

When I rolled up to the school two-plus hours later, Francis was sitting cross-legged under the flagpole in his snowsuit and rubber boots. Not a soul was in sight, save for the janitor, Mr. Jenkins, who was scraping the already-shoveled walkway.

I threw the car into park and jumped out. "Francis! Oh, my baby! I'm so sorry!" I hugged him, then led him off by his mittened hand, his head bowed with the grief of the abandoned. It was the second time I'd been late that week.

"Thank you," I called to Mr. Jenkins, leaning on his shovel.

He saluted from the bill of his red plaid wool cap.

We climbed into the DeSoto, its exhaust blackening the snow. I tugged myself around in my bulky coat to look at Francis in the back seat.

"When I'm late, it doesn't mean that I don't love you. You understand that? You deserve a mommy who is never late. But you have me. And I love you. Do you understand? I love you more than anything."

He fed his snowsuit zipper into his mouth, then let it fall to his chest. "You were supposed to send cookies today. It was my turn."

I gasped. "Oh no. That's right."

I faced the windshield, with its half-moons carved from snow. He really did deserve better. My gut burning with anxiety, I put the car in gear.

# 8

THERE WERE NO MENTORS TO HELP ME FIGURE OUT HOW TO juggle having a vocation and a family. Had it been up to my mother, I would have dumped my photography at the altar and thrown myself into being a stellar wife and future mom of many wunderkinder. Oh, Mother. Was there a more prideful woman alive than Bessie Cohen? Pride was what drove her to boil water for show when we had no food. The only thing worse than starving was having your neighbors know that you were starving. And it was pride that turned her into Lady Bountiful when we did have food. Just give her a bumper crop of beets and potatoes, and a five-pound bag of flour, and soon she'd be doling out soup, challah, and latkes to our neighbors, Irish and otherwise. *I hope it is good*, she'd say as she distributed her manna, even though everyone knew she was an excellent cook.

When a group of aunts, uncles, and cousins escaping the Russian pogroms landed at our door, her charity kicked into gear. Flour powdered her face and the floor. The reek of onions made eyes water all over the house. Beets left her and our kitchen looking like she'd slaughtered an ox with her bare hands. Leaving an aftermath of blackened pans and pots on every surface, she'd made enough knishes and bowls of borscht to feed an entire village.

*How generous is Bessie!* the relatives exclaimed. *Such a fine cook! Such a fine house! All these fine children—count them: five, six, seven, eight, nine! And her husband a rabbi, too!*

Mother glowed. For three days, Papa's loss of a congregation when they'd fled to America, his horse-drawn scrap wagon in an era of trucks, and her children's bare feet were forgotten. No one would ever know how many extra loads of wash she had to take in to afford her largesse. For weeks after the relatives left, clothes boiled on the stove instead of soup. To her, it was worth it.

Papa's illness and death when I was seventeen gutted my family. Even after the month of *shloshim*, I didn't feel like leaving the house, gloomy place that it was. Though I was of an age at which finding a husband was supposed to be my reason for being, I had no interest in the few suitors who stepped forward. They weren't half the man my abba was. Mother saw my unmarried state as a *shande*, an embarrassment. *A scandal!* I was too proud!—a prime case of the pot calling the kettle black.

When I finally pulled myself out of my darkness and announced that I would be a doctor and applied for college, she nearly rent her clothes in grief. What medical school would take a woman? What patient would go to me if I graduated? And what man would choose a doctor for a wife? A life of disappointment, I was asking myself for! And for her, a loss of potential grandchildren.

I got into college. Only when it dawned on Mother that she might spin my strange choice into something bragworthy did she ease up on the garments. *My youngest girl, the smart one, is not going to* marry *a doctor*, she told the neighbors. *Evie is too smart for that. Evie is going to* be *the doctor.*

But soon I burst her bubble again. "Evie the Doctor" tired of starving while competing with men who discounted her every word. I left school after a year and took a job at Stanbi. Renewed maternal lamenting ensued . . . until I'd worked up the ladder to management and, again, Mother could hold up her head. *My Evie, the boss of a whole factory!* She was prouder yet when I left the job to have a son.

Oh, bitter were her protests when I took up the camera for a career! "Photography?" Mother cried. "*Pictures*? You throw everything away to take *pictures*? It is a *shande*! A scandal! You have a husband from a good family, and a healthy baby—a son! There are your riches! There is your happiness!" She tore at her hair. *"Koptsen vu krichts du?"* "Pauper, where are you crawling?"

When my first *Life* article came out, I went to where she lived with my brother in Philly, to show her my photographs of Mamie Eisenhower. I'd just met the wife of the president of the United States, and here were my photos of her, in the biggest magazine in the country. Mother and I sat on the sofa, turning the pages of the magazine in her lap. I readied myself for her praise.

She'd shoved the issue from her knees. As it splatted on our shoes, she exclaimed, *"Koptsen vu krichts du?"*

IT WAS THE WEDNESDAY BEFORE HALLOWEEN. I'D WALKED FRANcis to school in a rain that stripped the remaining leaves from the sugar maples, and now I was back home, in the basement, developing prints from some film I'd shot on spec. The bad news was that, during the months after I'd passed on Stanley Gordon's offer to shoot the *Photoplay* banquet for *Look*, demand for me had, let's just say, quieted. Everyone in journalism knew everyone else's business—who was getting the stories, who was not; who would travel to shoots, who would not. We were like Hollywood, with its secret love children, in that way.

The good news was that I had the time to chase the local stories that called out to me. I'd long been interested in the migrant families that were living in grinding poverty just beyond our barbecue grills in town. During the last potato harvest, in September, I started visiting them with Francis, taking muffins I'd made and gallons of apple cider, which they were too hungry and thirsty to refuse. Finally, after Francis got over his fear of going to what he called "that awful place" and started playing with the toddlers—the bigger kids had to work—the parents got used to our hanging around and let me shoot. I stuffed down my emotions and documented a baby, a diaper pinned around his belly, staring at the sun from his cardboard box while his mother dug potatoes with a hoe. I recorded a little girl blowing bubble gum as she hauled bags that weighed more than she did. I snapped a weary young mother applying lipstick in front of a mirror in her shack when the working day was done. I noticed that the woman used Rose Morgan cosmetics. When invited into the quarters of the other ladies in the camp, I saw that they used that brand, too. At the library, I traced the products to an actual Rose Morgan, in Harlem, who agreed to meet with me in her beauty salon.

The Sugar Hill mansion in which she'd opened her place was once a haunted house. Now it bustled with workers, including twenty hairdressers, three licensed masseurs, skin care specialists, and a registered nurse, making it what *Ebony* magazine named "the biggest Negro beauty parlor in the world."

"Everyone has beauty inside them," Mrs. Morgan explained as she showed me around. She stopped often to encourage her hairdressers and admire their work or ask clients about their families. Touched to hear about her products' use among the migrants I'd photographed—she was the daughter of a sharecropper herself—she invited me to cover a Black debutante ball at the Waldorf Astoria.

"There isn't just one Negro experience in America," she'd told me, lifting the bonnet of a hair dryer to check on a woman's coloring process.

Now I was washing one of the results of her invitation, a print of dozens of gowned young Black women promenading with dozens of young Black men, elegant in their tuxes, when I heard the phone ring through the ceiling of my darkroom. After a minute, Arnold called down through the kitchen floor, "It's for you," his voice exceptionally light.

"Tell them I'll call back!" I yelled up through the unfinished rafters.

"*E-eve,* you had better come *he-ere.*" He was almost singing.

I hung the print next to one of a debutante in a deep curtsy, her dark shoulders sleek against the white lace skirt of her gown. Upstairs, in the kitchen, Arnold, with a silly grin, held out the receiver. My hands smelled vinegary from the stop bath as I took it.

"Hello?"

Arnold crowded me to listen at the phone.

"Hi, Eve!"

"Marilyn?" I gave Arnold a nudge and a playful glare, belying my happiness. I'd given up on you—nearly a year had passed since we'd been at the advertising banquet.

"I'm in town. Can you come see me? Tomorrow night. And your nice husband can come, too."

Arnold gave me an eager thumbs-up.

"I'm going to be at the Waldorf," you said. "I'll be getting ready for the advance screening of *How to Marry a Millionaire.* There's going to be a big party afterward. A lot of important people will be there—can you imagine?"

"Yes. I can."

You chuckled. "Can you come? I've got tickets for the show. That is, unless you're busy . . ."

Arnold turned up both thumbs now.

I rolled my eyes. I didn't need his prompting. "We can come."

"Good! And bring your camera. You can shoot me getting ready, like you did Marlene Dietrich at her recording session. You could call it *An Appreciation*"—you cleared your throat—"if you wanted."

I laughed.

You didn't immediately laugh back. Oh, you were serious. You hadn't gotten over this "appreciation" idea. Was that what this was about?

"I'm kidding!" you said, lightly. "I just want to see you. Just come, okay?"

THE FOLLOWING NIGHT, ARNOLD AND I WERE PADDING DOWN a hall on the forty-fifth floor of the Waldorf with our dripping umbrellas, looking for the room number you had given me, when a door opened.

A male voice barked, "Going to Toots's." The speaker jerked down the brim of his hat, then strode by, all shoulders, in a flashy suit with a crisp white pocket square.

Arnold winged me. "Joe DiMaggio!" he said from between clenched teeth. "That is Joe DiMaggio!"

We went to the same door as it closed. It was reopened by a man holding what looked like a short black centipede in a pair of tweezers. He had one of those voices that often cracked. "It's a lady with a CAMera!" he announced over his shoulder.

You cried heartily, "Well, bring her in, Whitey! Hello, Miss Documentary Photographer!"

"Miss Most Advertised."

You were perched on a stool, in a white bathrobe, while a shiny-faced young man unfurled your hair from curlers, letting the end-papers flutter to the carpet. A sturdy woman in rolled-down hose sat on a burgundy sofa, holding up the formal gown draped over her arms as if it were a sacrifice for the gods.

You introduced your makeup man, Whitey Snyder, your hairdresser, Leonardi, and your seamstress, Olga, to Arnold and me before exclaiming, "You brought your camera! Thank you!"

Arnold retreated to a sofa perpendicular to Olga's. "I made her."

He didn't. (A) You had requested it, and (B) I had at least one camera on me at all times these days. I was in danger of viewing the world through my camera lens first and my own eyes second.

"We saw you in *Gentlemen Prefer Blondes*," Arnold said, his accent at its most charming. "You were great."

You obediently closed your eyes as Whitey closed in with the clump of false lashes. "Gee, thanks."

Arnold watched, squinting in sympathy. "We took our son—"

"Francis!" you exclaimed from under Whitey's hands.

"He did not recognize you," Arnold said. "When I told him that you played ball with him last summer, he could not believe it."

Arnold had thought it would be fun for Francis to see someone he knew up on the big screen. On the way to the theater, Francis had bounced in the back seat, excited about seeing the lady who played catch with him at the beach. Yes, he remembered her. The harbor patrol boat had to take her away! And she had stinky hair that "smelled funny when it got wet." But at the show, he'd sat in his scratchy velveteen seat with his legs straight out and a disappointed look on his soft face. That wasn't her up there. The stinky-haired girl was "regular."

The hairdresser, Leonardi, jumped in while Whitey delved into the cloth belt tied around his waist for mascara. Leonardi fastened a curl next to your cheek with bobby pins, then stood back to let Whitey lean in.

From her sofa, Olga said, "How much longer?" She spoke just like my mother. "To sew you in takes time."

You sat docilely amid your handlers, a golem, still in its lump-of-mud stage, with rabbis laboring over it to bring it to life.

"The golem," I murmured.

My mentor, Henri, had been assigned to photograph the coronation of the English king, George. To his editor's initial chagrin, Henri had gotten so caught up in recording the behavior of the crowd lining the streets to see their new monarch that he hadn't shot a single frame of the king. I could imagine Henri, in his ever-present cardigan, mentally *oop*ing as he snapped children waving Union Jacks and kerchiefed matrons wiping away tears and old soldiers holding their salutes as the new king passed by. Ultimately, his photos became famous (and his editor, thrilled). The jubilant subjects said more about the majesty of the king than any portrait of him ever could. What did the people creating Marilyn say about you? My fingers went for my light meter.

You opened an eye.

"Don't look at me," I said. "Forget I've got a camera. This is just for fun."

"For an appreciation?" you said hopefully.

When I paused, you said, "You know I'm just kidding around."

Were you?

Whitey guided your face back to him with his thumb to your chin.

You swallowed, as if resetting. "Well, what's your story's angle? What should I be doing?"

Could I ever get a shot of you that you didn't try to control? "My angle is that there isn't an angle. You're just getting ready for an event. Do what you normally do."

"Oh, like Marlene did for her appreciation?"

I lowered my light meter.

You chuckled. "Got you!"

"Got me." I uncapped my camera. "Don't even think about me. I'm just here as a friend."

You caught my gaze. We looked at each other as if testing out the idea. *Friends.*

Even under the hands of your stylists, the sun came out on your face.

Arnold asked, "Miss Monroe—"

You broke from our gaze. "Marilyn!" you exclaimed. "Or Norma Jeane, if you want," you said as Whitey repositioned you under his mascara brush.

"Marilyn," Arnold asked, "what was it like working with Lauren Bacall?"

"Oh, she's all right."

I set the aperture, then focused.

"No, she's NOT," Whitey honked, touching up a final lash. "She was cranky."

"Whitey did my makeup for the picture," you said. "Look for his name in the credits tonight. Whitey's been doing my makeup since—"

"Stay still! Since her first screen test. Back when she was Norma Jeane Dougherty. And a bruNETTE."

"Whitey and I created Marilyn."

"Oh, I can't take credit for that." He stood back to study his work. "You created MARilyn. That walk, that talk, that hair . . ."

"But you made her face look just the way I hoped it would."

"I made her look the way you TOLD me she should look." His sharp young face softened with affection. "Now I'm just here for old times' sake."

You returned his warmth. "That's not true."

I shifted the two of you into focus as he leaned forward with a pointed pencil. "Bacall was cranky," he said. "That's all I'm going to say."

He retouched the eyeliner extending downward from your lower lid, echoing the thicker, longer upward swoop he'd drawn above it, and then whipped a white pencil from his makeup bandolier to sketch a tiny, pale V between the diverging wings of dark liner. I thought of the lesson on chiaroscuro Henri had taught me: The viewer's gaze goes first to the darkest dark next to the whitest white in a composition, be it a photo or a painting. The juxtaposition of dark and light demands attention.

Having applied a dot of red pencil to the innermost corner of each of your eyes to make the sclera seem whiter, he stood back. Now that I'd witnessed your makeup application, I could see the optical illusions he'd created. Yet, with a blink of your freshly crafted cat eyes, the tricks fell away. All that could be seen were beautiful eyes. Commanding eyes. Marilyn eyes. Whitey held up your chin and beamed as you gazed at us.

*Oop!*

Leonardi moved in. "Lauren—I should say Betty—" you said, your head bobbing with the tug of his wide-tooth comb, "her name is really Betty—that's what Bogey and everybody calls her. Betty wasn't cranky. She just didn't like me being late. That's all. I shouldn't have been so late."

"It's not YOUR fault," Whitey honked. "You don't want to be late! She just needs someone to tell her that her makeup's done," he told me. "It's never GOOD enough."

"Your makeup job is always good, Whitey." You sighed. "It's me. I just need to be better."

Everyone in the room protested.

Except me. *Oop!*

Leonardi formed peaks in your platinum meringue. "I just need a friend like Jane Russell," you said from under his comb. "I was never going to be done, and Jane knew it, so she just came down to my room, took me by the arm, and said, 'C'mon, kid.'"

"Jane was nice," Whitey agreed, going in for a microscopic fix when Leonardi pulled back.

*Oop!*

"So was the other Betty," you said.

"Who?" Arnold asked, clearly enjoying the show.

"Betty Grable. She was nice to me. This person I grew up idolizing! Nice to *me*! I used to pose like her in the bathroom mirror at the orphanage when no one was looking. Peeked over my shoulder and lifted my knee as if I had on a bathing suit and heels, not my ratty old jumper and clodhoppers." You sighed. "I've always had a good imagination."

"Don't move!" Leonardi unpinned the curl at your cheek.

"The studio wanted to give me her dressing trailer."

Whitey scowled. "That was TERrible of them."

"I didn't have one, you see," you told Arnold. "They never gave me a dressing trailer for any of my pictures. But I told them, if I was going to be the first person listed on the marquee, but they weren't going to pay me as much as everyone else, at least I should have a trailer."

"They're always treating Marilyn crappy." Whitey took a makeup brush from his belt as Leonardi gingerly pulled at a curl. "It's because she wouldn't sleep with Zanuck."

"I didn't. I won't. I don't give myself to anyone I don't want to. There are a lot of someones I do want to give myself to, but that's my choice."

Arnold looked away, pulling on his upper lip, too respectful to say that he was uncomfortable with a woman making whatever choices she wanted, for her own reasons—though, like most men and even women, deeply uncomfortable he was.

"Zanuck wanted to give her Betty Grable's dressing room," Whitey explained. "BAStard."

"I wouldn't take it," you declared. "Not for all the tea in China!

Betty made more money for the studio than anyone during the war, but as soon as she turned thirty-six, they canceled her contract and gave away her trailer. This is her last picture with Warner."

Leonardi shook a can of hair spray as if to kill it. "Betty Grable! Without a trailer! Bums."

"They'll do it to me someday," you said, "when I'm thirty-six."

"No, they WON'T!" Whitey squeaked.

"They won't," Leonardi said as he gave his heavy glasses a staunch push. "You're Marilyn Monroe, Fastest-Rising Star."

"Most ADvertised," Whitey added.

"Grand marshal of the Miss America parade," Olga said from over on the sofa.

"The Woo-Woo Girl," Arnold said.

Everyone turned to frown at him.

"Thanks, guys," you said. "We're all working hard at this. Can you believe how far we have come?"

"How far YOU have come, Norma Jeane," Whitey squeaked affectionately.

*Oop!*

Leonardi started spraying.

Your smile faded. "You know how me and Jane Russell got our stars in front of Grauman's Chinese Theatre this summer?" you said from within the mist.

"Sure!" said Whitey. "On the Walk of Fame! It was a dream come true."

"Well, there I was, on the biggest night of my life, trying not to sweat. I didn't want to ruin your makeup, Whitey." You swiveled your sad gaze to me while holding still for additional blasts of Aqua Net. I think you really had forgotten my camera. "The crowd was going nuts. The police had to form a human chain in front of the barricades to keep people away, just so I could put my hands in the cement. The cops were taking all kinds of shoves and blows. It was crazy!"

Leonardi stopped spraying. We were all listening.

"There I was, down on my knees, with my hands in the wet cement, when I thought I saw one of the cops on the other side of a barricade looking at me funny. I was squinting through the flashing cameras, trying to see who it was, and all of a sudden I knew.

"'Jim!' I cried. My hands were still in the cement soup. 'Jim, is that you?' He got pushed, regained his footing. 'Jim! Jim! It's me.'

"He broke into a huge smile. Then he said, 'How are you, Marilyn?'"

Your smile faded; you shrank back into your robe. In the awkward silence, a heat register rattled under a window. Finally, Leonardi shook his can of spray. "Who's Jim?"

Whitey looked away.

You closed your freshly done Marilyn eyes, then opened them. "Someone gave me a towel. Walter Winchell came up and started interviewing me. I got my smile back—your good makeup gave me strength, Whitey. When I turned around to see if he was there, he was gone."

"But who was he?" Leonardi asked.

"Jim Dougherty. The guy I married when I was sixteen. He's an LA cop."

Arnold laughed. "He must have felt like a dope."

Sadness pulled at the corners of your mouth. "Why'd he have to call me Marilyn? He knows who I am."

We were quiet after that. Whitey applied the deep scarlet lipstick he'd loaded from a tube onto a pointed brush. He then pulled another tube, a lighter scarlet, from his belt, loaded the brush again, and applied the orange-red within the darker color outlining your lips. With a lighter coral, he proceeded to paint the center of your lips, effectively shading them as one would draw an apple in art class, then dabbed a pale gloss over the very center.

At last you'd been properly powdered, fluffed, and sprayed. When you unselfconsciously dropped your robe, Arnold hurried off to the lobby, and you were then stitched into your gown. Your pickup time for the premiere had long since come and gone, and still you studied yourself in the mirror and asked for touch-ups.

"You're LATE," Whitey said. "Zanuck is going to go bananas."

You turned your face in the mirror. "There's not enough sheen on this cheekbone, Whitey. Can't you fix it? Maybe hit it with a little Vaseline?"

This was nuts. You were getting yourself into trouble with the studio for nothing. I let my camera hang from its strap, offered you my arm, and, in my best tough-girl Jane Russell imitation, growled, "C'mon, kid."

You looked at my forearm, then into my eyes, and, biting your lip, laid your hand, encased in a glove past your elbow, on my arm. You peered down from your height, augmented by your heels. "Jane, what happened? You shrank."

"Better to nip at your ankles, my dear."

Your gown rippled with a chuckle.

"Do not laugh!" Olga exclaimed. "You pop the seams!" She bustled over and laid a gold brocade stole over your shoulders.

Thusly enrobed, you proceeded with me and the Merry Marilyn Makers to the service elevator.

Whitey pressed a button on the control panel as we got in. "Are you SURE you want us in your limo, Norma Jeane?"

"Yes! I need you to knock me into the car and then pull me back onto my feet," you said, pantomiming the action with the hand not holding on to me. "Olga sewed me in good!"

Olga looked stricken. "I am sorry, Miss Norma!"

"Don't be sorry. I wanted you to sew me in tight."

So tight that it was clear that you had no undergarments on? Joan Crawford was leading a highly publicized charge against you in the press, claiming that the American public wanted their female stars to be ladies, and show restraint with their clothing and sexuality. People, she sniffed, would soon sicken of your freedom. I glanced at you, trembling next to me. If freedom was what this was.

When we got to the garage under the hotel, the car wasn't there. We trooped up the ramp to the street, your high heels clicking on the rain-slicked concrete. Almost at the sidewalk, you stopped.

"Wait. Marilyn walks like a queen."

You recommenced slowly, majestically, batting your hips from side to side as you turned your head, a monarch acknowledging her subjects. We followed as if carrying your train. I could almost hear the bombastic music playing for the just-crowned lion in *The Wizard of Oz*.

At the sidewalk, no limo was in sight, just lines of stalled traffic strung together by their headlights. The gutter ran with the recent rain.

"You should have had Joe take you," Leonardi said.

Whitey harrumphed. "He wants no PART of this. He'd rather be with his PALS at Toots Shor's."

"Aw, don't be mad at Joe," you said. "He's shy. Just like me."

Whitey and Leonardi glanced at each other.

A limousine driver trying to make the turn onto Forty-Ninth trumpeted at a traffic policeman, who coaxed delivery trucks and cabs out of the way with his whistle and rotating hands.

Next to me, something was happening to you. A light seemed to have sparked within you, activating your very molecules, expanding them, illuminating them, so that by the time the limo splashed up to the curb, the soft, sweet girl who'd pretended to be a queen was somehow taller and brighter and crackling with life.

You had *willed* your body into magnificence, as bizarre and impossible as that seemed.

I found you in my viewfinder. There was no time to check the lighting, but I made just a few quick adjustments as this divine new being put out her hand to the man emerging from the vehicle. "Hello, Mr. Zanuck," you breathed.

He gave you a curt peck on the cheek. "You're a half hour late. This fine gent made us go around the block. Twice." He nodded toward the policeman. "Idiot."

"Hey!" You hiked your brocade wrap around your shining shoulders. Your voice was as airy as cotton candy. "That's not nice! He's someone's daddy, or son, or husband."

Mr. Zanuck just grunted, then led you, clip, clip, clipping, to the door behind the waiting chauffeur.

"Wait!" you cooed, fully Marilyn now. "My friends!"

"No room," he snapped.

"But I promised!"

"Go!" we all said.

You blew us kisses as he ladled you into the car.

"Watch your LIPstick!" Whitey called.

The taillights flashed as the limo took away from us the fantastical creature you'd created.

Why did I fear for it?

# 9

FLOODLIGHTS, SPOTLIGHTS, HEADLIGHTS, SIZZLED MY RETINAS. Lit-up two-story ads hawked booze, TVs, men's suits, their glare illuminating the people on the crowded sidewalk, some of them dressed for Halloween, which was in two days. A message spelled out in light bulbs chased itself around the Times Tower: QUEEN ELIZABETH OF ENGLAND TO TAKE FIRST WORLDWIDE TOUR.

Arnold put his arm around my shoulders as I caught my breath at the stoplight on Broadway. We'd been running since we'd left the Waldorf. "Are you okay?"

I glanced at the man in the devil costume next to me, and at his date in a Catwoman outfit. I nodded, panting.

"Two more blocks. We can do it." He hiked his closed umbrella under one arm and put my hand on his other. Together we strode across the street and to the next block, where we turned the corner and stopped.

We tipped back our heads.

Atop the theater marquee, a four-story wooden cutout of you

in a red bathing suit looked over its shoulder as it aimed its ten-foot-tall backside at us.

Arnold whistled. "That is a lot of Marilyn."

"I'll say." You were the size of an actual golem now, ready to pull free of your braces to tramp through the city and wreak revenge for the underdogs. I half expected the creature to move as Arnold piloted me by the elbow, between its giant legs, to the theater door.

Closed.

"Do you kid me?" he exclaimed.

He banged on the glass of the entry booth, where a young woman took her time getting off the phone.

"We are friends of Marilyn's! Check your list."

The woman consulted a clipboard, fluffing her blond pageboy.

He craned his neck to see. "Eve and Arnold Arnold."

"Arnold Arnold?" She smirked.

He was past caring about slights. "Please. We are Marilyn's friends." He saw the woman look at my camera. "My wife is a Magnum photographer."

The woman shrugged. "Every Tom, Dick, and Harry in there has a camera. I was told Miss Monroe wants people to take all the pictures they want." She found our names, then signaled for a doorman to let us in. "Wish I'd brought my Brownie!"

Inside the packed lobby, Arnold and I wove our way past women in heavy perfume and men in elegant suits. Flashbulbs strobed red satin walls hung with gilt-framed posters of you preening in a swimsuit, your fully dressed co-stars looking on like Cinderella's dowdy stepsisters. A crowd was swarming the grand staircase, angling for position like bees on a honeycomb.

You began to rise from them. One step at a time, you mounted the stairs sideways, alone save for the photographers who flanked you like cupids bearing Venus to Olympus. When you had gained the top, you closed your eyes, shivered, opened them again, and, with a squeak, threw your head back and laughed. My vision went blue with a barrage of flashes.

You knew exactly what you were doing.

The crowd pushed forward to follow you. "God," the man next to me said, "I could just eat her up!"

"Stop." The woman next to him winged him with her glove-encased elbow. "Can't you see that she's shy? I feel sorry for her."

"Shy, my ass," said the man at the woman's other side. "She just wants to have fun."

By your design, you were whoever your beholder wanted you to be—a fun-loving piece, a little girl needing a daddy, a shy bird. Everyone staunchly believed he or she knew you. And maybe everyone was right, at least in the way that the blind men who touched parts of an elephant in Kipling's tale were, confidently describing the entire animal after feeling only its trunk or its tail. Or maybe you were like a Rorschach inkblot—people's perceptions of you said much more about themselves. How did you do that?

Arnold, overhearing the others, shook his head. "They do not know what a nice person she is."

Oh, Arnold. I nearly laughed with affection, thankful for his sweet interpretation of you.

At the top of the stairs, you waved, blew a kiss, and then disappeared into the auditorium. The rest of us herded up behind you.

After speeches by studio people, and much fanfare, and the parading of personages, the lights went down. The curtains opened . . . and opened and opened. The crowd gasped.

On the movie screen that spanned the vast stage, a larger-than-life orchestra swung into motion. The violinists' sleeves waggled with their bowing; the cellists sawed lustily; trombonists jabbed their slides at the backs of puffing clarinetists. Unused to so many choices, on such a wide field, the eye darted from musician to musician like a kid in FAO Schwarz.

I'd heard that the movie was to be in CinemaScope. Who hadn't? For months, Twentieth Century-Fox had trumpeted in every newspaper in America about the superiority of their new wide format. CinemaScope's supersized screen was meant to lure back the millions who'd abandoned the movies for their puny little televisions. That the studio chose you to star in the first movie shot in CinemaScope and the second movie shown in it said something about their regard for your star power. They must have calculated that only Jesus could outdraw you—the first film shown in CinemaScope had been *The Robe*.

And yet, I thought, watching the flutists raise their slender instruments, the studio wouldn't give you a dressing trailer. They singled you out for their contempt, paying you far less than everyone else, although you were their biggest draw. They played to your popularity by erecting a four-story version of you above the theater, yet they loved to fan the rumors that you were difficult and unprofessional, a dumb blond diva who screwed anything that moved. What was it that they had against you?

The film credits dissolved into dizzying aerial shots of New York. Like Tinker Bell in the latest Disney movie, the camera hovered over the busy harbor to gaze lovingly at the ocean liners sailing in the shadows of the world's tallest buildings, before it whisked off to the top of Rockefeller Center, where it floated down, down, down, to admire the stylish humans swarming at the base. One quick visit to an idyllic cove in Central Park, and then off it shot, across Gotham, to a complex of high-rise apartments known to anyone familiar with the city: Sutton Place, the chicest address in town.

As stirring as the panoramas on the huge screen were, the interiors, strangely, weren't. Lauren Bacall, dressed like the *Vogue* model that she played, flitted around her cavernous apartment interior like a stage princess in an empty castle. In all that space, the stylish furnishings lost their visual impact, as did Bacall herself. As a photographer, I sympathized with the cinematographer. That was a lot of volume to fill in every frame.

And then you minced into the scene. Like when Technicolor was switched on when Dorothy arrived at Oz, the screen bloomed with life. It wasn't just your beauty that lit the screen. Lauren Bacall was beautiful. Into a role that was supposed to depend on the silly schtick of your myopic character running into walls and mistaking identities because she was too embarrassed to wear her thick glasses, you infused charm, sympathy, and genuine vulnerability. Somehow, you'd dug into yourself and brought out a character who endeared with her sweet humanity, dimming everything and everyone else on the screen. When you said you didn't believe in hiding yourself, you meant it, because that girl up there, though written to be a joke, was genuine.

I looked around at the crowd with delight on their uplifted faces. People couldn't get enough of you. We humans crave to see, to feel, real emotion, but how often do we actually do so, on the screen or anywhere else? It took a feral child, unaware of what was acceptable, to deliver it.

In the lobby after the show, you moved through the lines of your well-wishers, cooing and laughing with men as they whispered into your ear, smiling earnestly and shaking hands with women. Trailing outstretched hands and faces, you inched on through the crowd. No one seemed to be able to let go of you.

Waiting for my turn to congratulate you, I was on my tiptoes to see which other stars in the show were at the reception, and how well, or not, they were handling your popularity, when Arnold lunged at you. I dived after him to save him from embarrassment. Too late.

"Marilyn!" he cried. "You were superb!"

You started, then patted your throat. "Oh, Mr. Eve!" You pecked his cheek, then saw me. "Miss Documentary Photographer! How'd you like Marilyn?"

"Wonderful." Even though I understood why you did it, would I ever get comfortable with you referring to yourself in the third person?

"That was me up there on that great big screen—can you imagine?"

"Yes. I can."

You laughed. "You always say that."

"Well, it's true. You work hard."

You clasped my hand with your gloved one. "Thank you, friend."

Even in that hubbub, warmth streamed between us.

An elegant man with meaty features inserted himself next to you. He wafted expensive aftershave when he extended thick fingers to you. "Allow me to introduce myself. I'm—"

You became serious. "You're Bosley Crowther. I love your reviews in the *New York Times.*"

He receded into his dimpled slab of a chin as if surprised that you knew him.

"I have admired your work since I read your review of the film adaptation of *A Streetcar Named Desire.*" You closed your eyes as if to quote: "'It throbs with passion and poignancy. Indeed, through Vivien Leigh's haunting performance . . . this picture becomes as fine as, if not finer than, the play.'" You opened your eyes. "I think films need more Vivien Leighs, not wider screens, don't you, Mr. Crowther?"

His fleshy brow shot upward as if he was surprised by your

opinion, or that you could even read. "I guess you wore your glasses when you read that."

You cocked your head. "You're confusing me for my character, Pola. I have twenty-twenty vision."

"Well, you play a very convincing man hunter. Just like you played a very convincing gold digger in *Gentlemen Prefer Blondes,* and a very convincing femme fatale in *Niagara.* They're all the same role—aren't they?—and you play it very well: the sexy blonde with more ulterior motives than brains."

You blinked as if slapped. "You think I play the same role?"

"You don't think so?" Mr. Crowther lifted that chin. "Tell me, then: How do you prepare for your part?"

"Well, it's hard, isn't it?" you said warily. "I mean, it's not easy. I have to pull from way deep inside myself. It hurts—well, it doesn't feel good."

He pursed his lips. "Uh, to play Pola Debevoise?"

You saw that he hadn't been on the level with his question about your acting. You went pink. I wanted to pop him.

"Whatever you're doing," he said, patting your arm, "keep doing it. Your dumb-blond-girl act will keep you busy in Hollywood."

You lowered your lashes. When you raised them, your voice was breathier than ever. "Thank you for your interest in my acting, Mr. Crowther. I'm so glad that you don't think I'm just another sweater girl. I don't know why people are so interested in sweater girls." You touched your décolleté in innocence. "Take away their sweaters and what do you got?"

He threw back his head and laughed, as did the well-wishers who'd been eavesdropping. "You're a stitch." Then he wrote something on his pad and moved off.

I was so furious at that jerk I was afraid to let my eyes meet yours. When I did, you sighed. "Give them what they want, right?"

"No! Do you let a child fill up on candy just because he wants it?"

Your face fell.

"Sorry. I'm not trying to attack you. But who's going to believe you have something important to say when you let Marilyn play dumb?"

You blinked at me. Arnold wedged between us, only to be bumped aside by a slight young man whose tanned good looks were set off by the whiteness of his collar. "Marilyn?"

You turned from me. "Milton!" you cried, then kissed him on the lips. You took his hands to turn him to me. "Milton Greene, meet another great photographer, Eve Arnold."

So, this was the guy *Look* had sent to the *Photoplay* banquet instead of me. He blinked, grinning good-naturedly, as if trying to place me.

"She works for Magnum."

"Oh, that's right," he said cheerfully, clearly unfamiliar with me.

"Milton just did a photo shoot with me for *Look*."

I told myself not to be jealous. I didn't do staged studio shoots. We weren't in competition. "I took a job with *Look* once."

"They're great, aren't they?"

"It was just the one assignment."

"Eve is a documentary photographer," you said. "Like a war correspondent, but for people."

He gave his head a sympathetic shake. "Kind of out of work without war, aren't you guys?"

"There are plenty of interesting people in the world to keep me busy."

"She doesn't use a studio, a flash, or even a tripod," you said. "And she never ever retouches, not even if you ask her to."

He winced as if sorry for me. "So, how is that going for you?"

Arnold firmly inserted himself. "She just had a spread in *Fortune.* She has been in *Esquire* and *Coronet* and what else, darling? I am her husband, Arnold."

"Mr. Eve," you added as the men shook hands.

Milton laughed. "I want to be that lucky dog called Mr. Marilyn."

"You're already married, Milton," you said, "with the cutest little son."

You gazed at each other a moment too long.

Later, waiting in Grand Central Terminal to catch the last train home, Arnold and I were scouting a bookstore window for possible competition for Arnold's book, due out the next year. *Sexual Behavior in the Human Female* by Alfred C. Kinsey took pride of place, in the center of the display. Below it, as if for the fallout of the subject of Kinsey's book, were paperbacks of Benjamin Spock's *The Common Sense Book of Baby and Child Care.*

"What are the odds that those two are lovers?" I asked.

Arnold peered at the display. "Kinsey and Spock?"

"I'm serious. Marilyn and that photographer, Greene."

"I do not see any books on children's play." Arnold addressed the photo of Dr. Spock behind the window: "Too bad you did not think of it, old friend. I guess you have not cornered the entire childcare market." He noticed that I was waiting for a response. "The odds that Marilyn is sleeping with that photographer? Yes. Sure, she is."

"I've heard talk of her sleeping with her photographers. I chalked it up to my esteemed colleagues' wishful thinking until I saw those two tonight."

"You are in doubt? She *told* us she sleeps with whoever she likes." He shifted his arms over his closed umbrella. "It is just another example of male photographers having an advantage over you. You cannot get her in the bed."

"That's insulting."

"I am sorry. I should not have said that. But maybe you should rent some studio space—if you are serious about making it big."

"You," I said, my anger rising, "of all people, know how deadly serious I am about my work."

"I do know, and that is why I suggest a studio."

Would Capa ever be told to try studio work? I wheeled away from the display window.

"Evie, come on."

"I don't need a studio," I said when he caught up. "Guys with studios have to scramble even harder than I do, because they're a dime a dozen. At least I'm doing something different."

"When you are able to do it." He saw my face. "I am just being honest. And you would not have to travel so much if you had a little studio. You could stay home more with Francis. Be a mom. Join the PTA."

I couldn't believe my ears. "I am a mom! I am in the PTA!" I stormed toward the train platform.

"You are going to the wrong track. Ours is number twenty."

I turned around, nearly bumping into the briefcase of a man with lipstick on his cheek. At this hour, the only people out were partyers and cheats.

Arnold tipped his hat at him as if to excuse me. "If you insist upon being a photographer," he said, following me, "maybe you should take advantage of your friendship with Marilyn a little more. She seems to be the ticket to go places. Her makeup man—"

"Who is named Whitey."

"—appears to have figured out how to use her."

I stopped to stare at my husband. "Whitey hardly seems like he's using her. And if he is, it isn't working out for him. Didn't you notice he wasn't listed in the film credits? Some other guy was. Poor Whitey."

Arnold shrugged. "All I know is that Marilyn gets people to work for her and it comes out to her advantage. I do not say she is not a sweet girl. She is. I like her. But she is a user. She knows that is how it is done."

Our train came screeching in. I bounded down the steps to our platform.

"Why are you so angry?" he called, tramping after me.

"I'm not angry!"

We entered the train and headed down an aisle. I dropped onto a seat behind a grown-up pair of Halloween hoboes going home from a night on the town. I wasn't mad, not at him. I'd wasted my time with you at our one-on-one shoot, sticking you in dumb settings such as a swamp and the playground, making it hard for you to deliver. Before the premiere tonight, I'd thrown away the chance to let you show me who you were, focusing instead on the Merry Marilyn Makers and their creation, and refusing your participation. You, Norma Jeane—bravely revealing a slice of your feral, unfettered, hopeful soul—were what was compelling, and from now on I'd do whatever I could to work with you to bring you out.

Arnold was wrong. You weren't a user, not when it came to me. When it came to getting covers, you didn't need me. The newsstands were already loaded with them. No, you were giving me every chance to use *you*, anything to help in your desperate search to find the girl in the mirror.

THREE DAYS LATER, THE MAILMAN WAS HEADING UP OUR SIDEwalk with his pouch when I got home from walking Francis to school. "Thanks. I'll take that," I called.

A copy of *Look* was in the pile. Inside the house, I dropped the letters next to Francis's grocery bag of trick-or-treat candy on the kitchen counter and flipped to Milton Greene's photos of you.

They were all the things my pictures were not—posed, retouched, and artificially lit.

But unlike in your other studio portraits, you didn't look like you were *trying* to be sexy in these—you *were* sexy, though fully clothed. Dressed in a heavy sweater, you leaned on a mandolin in one. You seemed relaxed and artsy, wise for your twenty-seven years.

In the serial images of you kneeling in an unrevealing black lace and white satin nightgown, you looked more confident and less vampy than I'd seen you elsewhere. This wasn't pinup silliness, but two intelligent artists communicating through the camera.

I was jealous.

The phone rang.

*"E-eve!"* Inge Bondi's Austrian-tinged voice sang into my ear. "What is wrong?" she asked after I said hello.

"I've lost my touch."

"What?" She laughed on the other end of the line. "Well, get it back. I just got a telegram about you."

"Me?" I raked through the candies in Francis's bag for a Baby Ruth.

"Yes, *meine liebe*, I have a job for you. A big one. *Picture Post* requested you."

"*Picture Post*?"

"I know, I know, you are angry at them for changing your captions about the Harlem models. But—Eve! They want you to go to Jamaica to photograph the new, young English queen, Elizabeth."

"The queen?"

"It is her first foreign trip since her coronation—a big deal, as Americans say." She laughed. "I can hear you frowning over the phone. Do not worry. I told them that you insist upon having full control over the words that go along with your article."

"You did?"

"Of course. And they agreed."

My chest ached as if it had been pumped full of air. I'd never had a foreign assignment. My mind went into instant overdrive, thinking about the research I'd have to do on the queen, and the travel preparations I'd have to make. To photograph a monarch! Step aside, Capa. I was moving up.

"They think you will have an advantage as a woman when photographing a queen."

I wished they thought I had an edge because I was good, not because I was a woman. "Did they see my American Dream stories?"

"They didn't mention them. They liked your Marilyn Monroe photos."

Why couldn't my photos of the Black debutante ball at the Waldorf, or of the potato pickers, or even of the president's wife in the amusement park be what they remembered, instead of photos from a shoot I wasn't particularly proud of? "Oy vey."

"'Oy vey'? The queen is calling! Pack your bags, *meine liebe.* Her Majesty arrives in Kingston on November twenty-fifth."

"How long will I be gone?"

"For as long as you need to set up there, and then to follow her once she has arrived."

My very molecules seemed to contract. My family. I didn't have just the particulars of Jamaica, the queen, and the travel to worry about; I had to find care for Francis. *Help!* Old Mrs. McArdle down the street, Francis's usual sitter, wouldn't cut it! Besides plotting out, shopping for, and preparing meals for a week—no, more like two—and ironing enough shirts for Arnold, I had to find a better sitter. My brain jammed with everything I had to do.

"Is there a problem?"

"No. No. Thank you, Inge."

When she hung up, I put the receiver to my aching head. Capa never had these worries when he went on assignment.

I set my jaw. But he had never got the terrific shots I was going to get for this story.

# 10

## 1954

THAT SHOT OF THE QUEEN STILL GAVE ME GOOSE BUMPS WHENever I looked at it. And it didn't make it only into *Picture Post,* but had been picked up around the world. I supposed I was now an official photographer of Her Majesty the Queen. But at the door of Toots Shor's lounge, four months after I'd returned from Jamaica, none of that meant zip. Unless a woman was a famous man's doll, and then only if she kept her mouth shut, she wasn't welcome no matter what she'd achieved. In fact, achievements were strikes against her. Toots's lair was a place where the legends of sports, film, and literature (that is, men's literature—read: Hemingway) could get sauced and pound their chests with other powerful gents, or keel over and peacefully sleep off a drunk, as Jackie Gleason was rumored to do—often. A he-man could brag about his home run, his bestseller, or his new gold record over a dinner of shrimp cocktail and steak or, better yet, get thumped on the back and insulted by Toots. Being called a "crum-bum" by Toots was as potent a mark of masculinity as the gun belt riding John Wayne's saggy rear.

As I stood with Toots blocking my way in on that blustery March night, I was mentally murdering Capa for choosing a place so hostile to women. The joint was bad enough for men. Even they had to pass a vetting process that only Toots understood—Toots, the guy who, not liking the cut of Charlie Chaplin's jib, had told the comedian to go outside and entertain the crowd waiting to get in, and then *maybe* he could enter. When studio head Jack Warner had complained to Toots about being kept waiting for twenty minutes to enter, Toots had snapped that it served the movie mogul right; *he'd* been kept waiting in line for longer than that for one of Warner's lousy films. Then there was the time Toots had sent the young, rising Frank Sinatra across the street with a dime, telling him to buy him a pack of gum while Toots decided whether he was man enough to come in. The list of humiliations went on. A lone woman didn't have a prayer.

Toots, a bull in a pinstripe suit, said, "Where's your date, little girl?" His eyes had a sweet downward slant to them when he arranged his big face into a smile. It was the smile of a boy . . . who pulled the wings off butterflies. "Kinda little for a hooker, ain't you?"

"I'm here to meet Robert Capa."

Pinstripes swished against pinstripes as he crossed his thick arms.

"The Magnum photographer," I added.

"I know who he is." He looked me up and down. "What are you to him, babe?"

"A colleague."

"You're a photographer?"

"Yes!" I was making progress.

"Huh. Nice little girls like you shouldn't be sticking their cameras in people's business."

I could see Capa in a distant booth, craning his neck to see the drama at the door. I shot daggers across the smoky room. *Could you help me, please?*

Capa turned back around.

*You little twerp!*

Toots was waiting. There had to be a key to his meaty heart. "I heard you're from Philly. Me, too."

"Which part?"

I told him.

"Don't know it."

He peered over my head at an approaching group of freshly showered athletes—baseball players, I guessed by their average builds—their hair still wet above their spread-collar shirts.

And then it occurred to me: "I've photographed Marilyn Monroe for *Esquire*."

He squinted. "You know her?"

"We're friends." Since the premiere of *How to Marry a Millionaire*, those words meant even more to me. I feared that wasn't true for you.

"Marilyn, huh? My pal Joe married her."

And there was the rub. In January, two months after I'd last seen you, you'd wed the baseball great in the San Francisco courthouse, with the press as your only guests. I'd read about it in the papers, along with everyone else in the world. You retreated from public life, claiming that you wanted nothing more than to be a good wife to Joe and a good mother to his son. Your acting days, you said, were over. And also, now that you'd jettisoned everything to be Mrs. DiMaggio, maybe our friendship.

"Joe's got his hands full," Toots said. "I wouldn't be him for all the tea in China." He rolled his head to one side of his beefy neck. "Take some pictures of Joe and her. Be kind."

I opened my mouth to reply. He waved me in. "Get in there

before I regret it." He reached behind me. "Mickey! Yogi! What are you crum-bums doing here?"

At our red leather booth during dinner, A.1. Sauce and meat juice sizzled as Capa put out his cigarette next to the remains of his T-bone. "You are probably wondering why I called you here," he said in his Chesterfield-baked Hungarian accent.

My other Magnum colleagues at the table paused in various stages of eating: Capa's thirty-five-year-old "kid" brother Cornell, scraping the bottom of his shrimp cocktail cup with a tiny fork; fluffy-haired Elliott Erwitt, his eyes nearly closed behind his big glasses as he gnawed on a hard piece of bread; and Ernst Haas, elegantly handsome in his reserved Austrian way, even when chewing on some gristle. Indeed, I *had* been wondering why Capa had rounded us up, and I wondered anew when he'd stopped me from ordering a grilled cheese sandwich—the cheapest item on the menu—and told the waiter, "She will have the steak."

He'd seen my grimace. "It's on Magnum."

I'd thought times were tight for Magnum. The last time I was at the office, trying, and failing, to get Capa's blessing to pursue a story about Senator McCarthy, he'd muttered about how demand for photojournalists was down. Goddamn magazines were using their own staff photographers. When I suggested that television news might in part account for the dip, he'd curled a corner of his mouth in scorn.

"Are you kidding me?" he'd said. "Who in their right mind would want to watch Edward R. Murrow on the tube with their baby crying in the background, or their neighbors playing Sinatra too loud, when, whenever they want, they can study our photos and get all the information they need?"—an argument that would have carried more weight if more people weren't buying television sets every day. I'd read that nearly half of the households in the US currently had them.

Now Cornell laid down his tiny fork. "Is Magnum closing?"

Capa made his living by recording the very worst of mankind. Exposing his soul to the brutal hideousness of war and escaping death so frequently and narrowly should have made him a grim and humorless zombie. Yet the man had a glorious, toothy smile that he flashed often. His entire coarse face would shine, as it did now, as he grinned at his brother.

"Quite the opposite, Corn."

Toots ambled up, king of his domain. "Any you crum-bums need another drink?"

*Crum-bums?* Honored, the guys raised their glasses.

"Hey, how about me?" At the table next to us a man lowered his newspaper, revealing jellied waves, squinty eyes, and a triple chin. Jackie Gleason pointed at his empty schooner.

"You live here," Toots said. "Get your own."

Gleason folded the paper back to the entertainment page and flopped it on the table. The picture up top was big enough for me to see from where I sat: you, bare and glowing above the tips of your white fur stole.

Toots bent to look. "Joe's going to shit his pants. That girl cannot keep herself covered."

"Says here she won Most Popular at the *Photoplay* banquet last night," said Gleason. "I thought she quit Hollywood."

"That's what she wore to it?"

"You shoulda seen what she wore to it last year," Gleason said. "It was an anatomy lesson."

Toots picked up Gleason's glass. "If she were my missus, I wouldn't let her out of bed. But that one does what she wants. She *had* to go with Joe to baseball training camp in Japan. She *had* to entertain the troops in Korea, and then—surprise, surprise—she got pneumonia running around almost naked there in February. Hear she just got over it. Some honeymoon they had."

Truthfully? I was surprised you'd married Joe. You'd hardly talked about him when I'd seen you last—and if Arnold was right, you'd been sleeping with Milton Greene—yet now you'd given up acting for him. I just couldn't get used to seeing photos of you two, you wearing a modest suit, him wearing that gap-toothed grin, both of you as tickled with each other as a couple in an ad for Swift hams. The new Marilyn, Mrs. DiMaggio, wore buttoned-up silk blouses or fur collars that closed at her throat—except, apparently, at the *Photoplay* banquet, or when wowing soldiers in Korea. Had you retired into a life of spaghetti making and connubial bliss, or hadn't you?

I don't mean to insult, but had you wed him because you were in trouble with your studio bosses for refusing the flimsy script they'd sent you? Because that's how it looked. I'd heard—anyone with a heartbeat had heard—that you were on a personal strike against them, declining their calls, but not because of the money, though they still weren't paying you half as much as your fellow headliners. All you'd ever wanted, you said, was the right to choose your projects and directors. So you got yourself a sugar daddy and quit?

The studio had fought back by promoting your look-alike, a buxom young blonde named Sheree North, as if to say that Marilyn Monroe was just a replaceable set of knockers. I'd seen Miss North on the cover of *Life* just this week. The lead photo in the issue was a close-up of her rear in tight white pants as she jumped a hurdle. A hurdle! Who jumps hurdles? Could there be a more contrived excuse for a cheesecake shot? Oy vey, I wished you'd battle back against those jokers! I thought you'd do anything to keep creating. Didn't you care about your art? You'd left me holding out against the lions, tossing steaks they gulped down in a moment.

Gleason shambled to the bar with Toots. "Listen up," Capa said when they were gone. "I do not have much time. I am shipping out to Paris tomorrow."

"You got your passport!" I exclaimed. "Great! Can I do my McCarthy story now?"

The others glanced at the boss. We weren't supposed to acknowledge that he was under investigation by McCarthy's subcommittee, and that his passport—a globe-trotting photojournalist's lifeline—had been held up for months. No one was supposed to acknowledge anything about McCarthy, Communism, the hearings, or one's private thoughts about any of it. Better to know nothing if dragged before the Senate to name names.

Capa, a Jew like me, gestured as if he were the pope giving a blessing. "You may do your McCarthy story now."

My colleagues held up their glasses.

I bowed. "Thanks, guys. I'm going to nail that bastard."

After we took a drink, Cornell said, "Tell them where you're going after Paris."

Elliott, a cuddly teddy bear whose short black brows perpetually shot above his specs, popped them farther scalp-ward. "Another war, Bob? Where?"

"Not this time."

"Where are you going?"

"Japan."

"What he won't tell you," Cornell said, "is that they're having a major exhibition—"

Capa tamped him down. "Not a major exhibition."

"—a major exhibition of his work," said Cornell. "It was arranged through the Paris office."

Capa shrugged. "It is all of us old characters' work—mine, Henri's, and Rodger's. What I was saying was that I called you all here for some big news."

Cornell, as handsome as his brother in their beetle-browed

way, leaned forward on his elbows. "But Magnum isn't closing, right?"

Though, at forty and thirty-five, the Capas were grown men, they retained their childhood roles, Little Brother following in Big Brother's footsteps. I didn't envy Cornell, living in the shadow of a giant.

"Right, Corn," Capa said. "Magnum's not closing. Here's the deal: I was at a card game last night with the editor of *Holiday.* And let's just say I won."

"Bob's great at poker," Cornell said.

"We know," Elliott grumbled, his brows diving beneath the tops of his glasses. We all knew. You couldn't work at Magnum if you didn't play some kind of cards with Capa. When Capa came out to a Fourth of July cookout at my house last summer, he'd even played Francis at Go Fish. And won.

He spread his hands. I noted, once again, how sensitive they were. "What can I say? I've got a poker mug. You'd have one, too, if you'd knocked on the Pearly Gates as often as I have. Anyhow, I took all his money, but he wanted to win it back. So we kept playing." Capa shrugged. "And I kept winning. I ended up with a promise from him to run a weekly series in *Holiday* using only Magnum photographers. And *still* he insisted on playing. When he lost again, I got him to promise to run *another* series." He shook his head. "The man could not play poker."

"What are the series?" asked Haas, ever serious and to the point.

"Why'd you stop playing?" asked Cornell.

Capa laughed. "I had to think of a subject on the spot, one that would keep us busy and on nice, fat expense accounts, courtesy of *Holiday,* for a long, long time. Our friend Cartier-Bresson popped into my mind, and his photos of kids after the war."

We nodded. Anyone who knew Henri knew of his sympathy for children and women, and of his concern about what the war had done to them. He felt that men had mucked it all up with their stupid aggression, and now women and children had to live with the mess they'd made—something women have always known about the way the world works. At least Henri acknowledged the situation. Right after the war, he'd photographed kids all over Europe and published a book of them, *The Children's World.* The loss and grief that he captured on his subjects' soft faces, but also the toughness and hope, had fired my early desire to be a photographer.

"As you guys know," Capa said, "Henri and I formed Magnum on the strength of those pictures. We wanted to record what the war had done to the world and what it was like to live in it, what it was like to be a kid in the postwar era—"

"What's Henri call those kids?" said Cornell. "The X Generation?"

"Before my poker victim could change his mind, I blurted out the titles of Magnum's new series: Children of the World and Women of the World." Capa grinned. "Get ready to travel, pals. Lots."

I pressed my lips together. I'd long been forced to make women and children my turf, and now my colleagues wanted it. Of course they did, because, as men, they felt they had a natural right to everything. They'd believe they could get better shots of my own specialty, too, flitting off around the globe without a worry about who was going to make their children happy or starch their wives' dresses.

Cornell lifted his glass. "To the kids—may they rule the world."

Capa lifted his to me. "To women—who are ruling it now."

"It's a woman's world, and men are just living in it." I held up my glass, daring them to refute me.

They paused, then, with big belly laughs, toasted me, which was worse than if they'd argued.

I seethed.

It took two rounds of booze on *Holiday*'s tab to chip the edge off my irritation. Erwitt, Cornell, and Haas ended up at the bar, arguing with a couple of mobsters. Jackie Gleason dozed at his table. Only Capa and I were left at ours. We scooted closer together to talk over the shouts of the baseball players in a neighboring booth.

"Listen, *Arnoldné*," Capa said in his Hungarian accent. "I know we are encroaching on you. Women and children have always been your beat."

"That's okay," I said. "I'm going to get better shots than the rest of you guys, or die trying."

He laughed. "I do not know why I laugh. I know you are not kidding. I see the tiger lying just beneath that pussycat exterior. Which is good. I will only have tigers at Magnum."

I wasn't ready to be pandered to. "I prefer to be a lioness."

He rumpled his already-messy hair. "Yeah? Why is that?"

"While the lions do all the roaring, the lionesses are out making the kill."

He studied me. "Okay, Lioness."

We sat in silence, letting the possibility of a comradery sink in.

"Why are you a photographer?" I asked him.

He pulled back. "Huh? No one asks me that." He dragged his glass toward him. "They assume that I was born with a camera in my hand and was shooting pictures before I could toddle."

I waited.

"If you must know, it is because of my mother. She decided I was destined for greatness from the moment of my birth. She based this on the very sure sign of me being born with the beginnings of an eleventh finger." He pointed to a white scar next to his left pinky finger. "The midwife bound it with a string until it fell off. It is not such a rare abnormality, but that extra finger was all my mother needed to determine my specialness. Poor Corn—he only had ten fingers. She had no expectations for him, not like the ones she piled on me." He took a sip, then laughed. "With that kind of pressure, I had to find something to prove her right. Perhaps it is correct to say that this long-lost finger made me." He turned his hand from side to side for us to marvel. "And what about you?"

Should I admit that it was my own photo—of myself—that sent me down my path? Early on, while I was still figuring out the settings on the Rolleicord that Arnold had given me, and I was hoping to be able to record us before we went to the justice of the peace, I'd taken a photo of myself while looking in the mirror. I was stunned when I'd developed it. The camera had caught a different me than the one I confronted in the mirror each day. I saw a determination that I did not know I had, and also a surprising calmness. That was me? I was excited to think that the camera could reveal the person waiting inside each of us. I wanted to run out and photograph everyone I knew, to see what I might learn about them. I hadn't thought about that picture for a while. Maybe that was a mistake.

"I saw an interesting photograph," I said.

"Oh, something of Cartier-Bresson's? Chim's?" He signaled to Toots for another round. "I have not told you enough—your photo of the English queen was spectacular. The old governor of Jamaica bows to the young woman—" He shook his head in appreciation. "In one shot, you caught the passing of the old world to the new. This is why we will always need still photography. Nothing tells the story like a singular moment caught on film." He turned to face me. "Cheers to Cartier-Bresson and his decisive moment."

"To the decisive moment." We tapped empty glasses. I glanced across the restaurant at Toots, badgering a group of his cronies, but Shor wasn't really registering in my thoughts. I was thinking about the English queen.

---

MY HEAD WAS SWEATING FROM THE HUMIDITY—JAMAICA IS still steamy in November. I was leaning through the window of a pink stucco building, my eye to my viewfinder. A hush had fallen over the women and girls in cotton dresses, and the men and boys in shorts, lining the streets as far as the eye could see. The wizened governor of Jamaica, neat in morning dress tails, was shuffling his spats across the blazing pavement in front of his palace, his goal the young English queen. Flanked by her tall husband, uniformed in white, and a dignitary wearing a helmet stuck with fluttering flamingo feathers, she waited, the skirt of her filmy organdy dress rippling in the breeze.

At last, the old gentleman's labors took him close to the waiting queen, where, like an automaton winding down, he stopped. The crowd grew so quiet that you could hear the rattling of the palm trees along the street as, sweeping his top hat from his bald head, he pivoted from his waist and bowed.

The queen—it was her first stop on her first foreign trip as monarch—hesitated. I felt her uncertainty. She'd left two children at home, a boy near Francis's age and a baby girl. She was on her first foreign trip without her young, as was I. I ached for her, and for myself.

The breeze caught the veil on her hat and lifted it. She caught it and laughed as a girl would laugh—she was just twenty-seven, like you.

Still bent over, the governor rolled his gaze up to her.

As if remembering who she was, she straightened. Tentatively, she lifted a hand, then, fully blooming into the queen she was, resolutely extended it. The smile that grew on her face was pleasant but firm. She was every young woman just realizing her power.

I swallowed the lump in my throat. *Don't move. Get your shot.*

The governor put withered lips to her strong, young hand.

I released the shutter. *Oop.*

CAPA WAS WATCHING MY FACE. "WHAT ARE YOU THINKING?"

"Just"—I spread my hands, then sighed—"that I love being a photographer."

Holding my gaze, he held up his drink, his face tightening, his eyes intensifying, until the man before me became the Robert Capa who inserted his camera between himself and death. "To getting our shot."

Slowly at first, then resolutely, like a woman coming into her own, I put my glass out. "To getting our shot."

# 11

WHO'D EVER BELIEVE THERE'D BE A MEMORIAL SERVICE TWO months later? It was enough to make me wonder, when I'd just returned from it and was in the red-lit cocoon of my darkroom—was Arnold right? Should I throw in the towel and open a studio and photograph brides and graduates and naked babies on a fluffy rug? Or toss away the camera altogether and take up chairing the PTA bake sale committee, with a side job burping Tupperware in neighbors' homes? Because this photojournalism gig was breaking too many hearts. Including mine.

Maybe I was just exhausted from attending the service, hard on the heels of a two-week work trip to Cuba. I hadn't even had time to change out of my mourning clothes before heading to the basement. I became aware of the thumping of a barroom brawl filtering through the rafters overhead; Francis and his friend were playing in the kitchen. I paused to assess the horseplay. Glass was not breaking. Smoke was not seeping in. Screams were not curdling my blood. I returned my weary attention to my film. The service had put me behind on my deadlines, and I needed some prints to show Inge for my first—and possibly my last—entry in the Children of the World series.

Through the rippling fluid of the developing tray shone eight-year-old Juana, up a palm tree on her island off the shore of Cuba. She was heaving down a coconut, her feet clinging to the trunk like a tree frog's, the breeze exposing the ragged underwear beneath her too-small dress. My two-seater plane had just landed on the beach, and she had raced the kids of the island's eleven families for the honor of being first up a tree to pelt me with coconuts in welcome. In the print hanging behind me, Juana was hunched over her desk in the one-room school hut that her parents had built. A shiny black hank of hair was licking her nose as she bore her pencil down on her paper in concentration. The child did nothing by halves.

Even as I smiled, my mind slipped to the memorial service—it was a Quaker meeting—from which I'd just returned. I could still see my dear Henri Cartier-Bresson, who'd come all the way from Paris, sitting next to me in the circle of friends participating in the meeting. He must have heard me sniffing back tears, because he patted my hand before he stood. His voice, thick with emotion, had echoed in the room, which was bare save for our folding chairs and us.

"The goal of the photographer—" He stopped to gaze around our group. "The goal of the photographer is to find the inner silence of the subject. Find the inner silence, and you have found the truth. He knew that."

Shoes scraped on the linoleum floor. The *cheer-cheer-cheer* of cardinals floated through the open windows of the simple church.

"But—it is an illusion that photos are made with the camera. They are made with the eye, the heart, and the head," he said, pointing to each. "He knew that, too. He wasn't afraid of opening his heart to his subject, any more than he was afraid of being killed."

I returned my consciousness to my darkroom. In the tray, red light was dappling the fluid that covered Juana's young face. Her zest for life shone through in the print. She radiated the wonder common to every young girl, but in her that wonder was tripled in strength. She had allowed me to see the inner silence at her core. No—she'd made a present of it for me.

I looked away quickly and saw a third print, floating in the holding bath by the sink. Beaming, Juana's father was lifting Juana above his head as her mother reached up to her. It was the opposite of my American Dream photo in *Fortune*. Here, the father worshipped his daughter instead of being the worshipped one receiving his child in tribute. And the mother—oh, I couldn't bear it—Juana's mother caressed her daughter like the precious jewel that she was.

I squeezed my eyes shut. "Francis!" I yelled up through the ceiling.

The thumping stopped. "What?" sifted down through the rafters.

"What are you doing?"

"Playing!"

All was still overhead, as if he was waiting for my response.

I held my breath. The bumping on the ceiling resumed.

I nudged the print with my tongs and remembered.

THE LOWERING SUN WAS GILDING THE WAVES AS JUANA WADED along the foamy edge of the sea. At the little table set up under a double palm tree, her mother urged me to take the last piece of *doncella de pluma* caught by Juana's father and roasted under the sand. I'd never tasted such delicious fish.

"Juana is such a happy child," I told her mother as she slid the fillet onto my plate, even after I suggested that she give the piece to my translator, a woman from mainland Cuba. "I commend you."

The translator relayed my words.

Juana's mother sat down, looked at her husband, and then drew a breath. *"Llévatela."*

The translator seemed not to understand. Juana's mother repeated: *"Llévatela."*

Uncertainly, the translator told me, "'Take her.'"

I laughed.

Her mother waited, her expression solemn. The translator shifted in discomfort.

"Take . . . Juana?" I was confused.

Juana's mother said, *"Te quiere."* She looked between the translator and me, waiting for the translation.

"'She loves you,'" said the translator.

The week I'd spent with Juana and her family for my Children of the World piece for *Holiday* had been pure joy. I'd gone fishing with her jovial father, sewn nets with her bright and serious mother, and been dragged down the shore in search of conch shells by Juana, her affection sizzling from her hot little palm straight into my heart.

When I'd first photographed her, the translator at the ready, Juana had hammed it up for my camera, making it impossible to get a good shot of her. She clambered up trees and grinned down at me like the Cheshire cat; draped herself over the middle of a double palm and rested her chin on her hands like Shirley Temple; ran into the surf and splashed it over her head like a pirate luxuriating in his doubloons. She could have given Gloria Swanson a run for her money in the silent movies. The shots were trash.

I thought to let her look through the viewfinder and focus in on a subject: her mother grating coconut at a table.

"That's what I see," I said as she peered through the viewfinder, the translator conveying my words. "The rest depends on the person I'm taking a picture of. Do they like me enough to talk to my camera?"

Juana's mother, hearing me, looked up and, though not understanding what I said, smiled at Juana through the camera, her love shining in her eyes. Had I had the camera in my hands, I would have clicked it.

Juana handed my Nikon back and gruffly announced, "I want to talk to your camera." She wedged herself into the base of the double palm as the translator interpreted, her eyes telling me what the interpreter could not: She meant it. She was determined to talk to me through my lens. I pressed the camera against my nose.

Now she didn't smile. She didn't have to. Her eyes were lit with pure Juana-ness.

*Oop!*

I told her mother, now waiting for me to respond to her request, "I love her, too. Very much."

Her mother said something, firmly, then nodded for the translator to repeat it. The translator drew a breath. "'Then you will take her.'"

My throat tightened. She couldn't possibly be serious. "But she loves you!"

"Yes," she said through the interpreter. She drew in a breath. "She does."

"And you love her."

Her mother spoke, then swallowed as the interpreter translated, scowling.

"'That is why you must take her.'"

"I can't—"

Her mother spoke in a rush.

"'There is nothing for her here. You saw how it was in Havana.'"

The translator and I exchanged glances. We'd spent a week the previous month scouring Havana for an assignment *Esquire* wanted to call "The Sexiest City in the World." I found sex, all right.

In a city sagging under the oppression of the Batista regime, despite the snappy Latin music lilting from the cafés, I recorded dozens of listless prostitutes and the aggressive American sailors who hired them. My photos were not what *Esquire* had in mind, but they accepted my pictures of the prostitutes, and, finally, those of the sailors, too—after I'd airbrushed out the bulges in their white trousers. My first and only retouching.

"You live in paradise here," I'd told the mother, "away from the ugliness of the mainland."

The translator looked worried at her response.

"'I am not well.'"

I tamped down my dismay. "Then you will need her. Your husband will need her."

Juana's father spoke through the interpreter. "'I'm a fisherman. How many old fishermen do you see here?'" He went on before I could answer. "'Being a fisherman is a dangerous life. If I go, then what? Juana will go to Havana. You know what happens to girls there. We want better for her. You can see that she must have better.'"

I'd tossed and turned in my hammock that night, thinking about how it might work to take her home.

—Francis might like having a big sister.

—No. He'd resent getting a smaller piece of my attention. He already got too little of it—now even less than ever, since I'd begun traveling so much. In the past few months, his sitter, a young woman from Port Jefferson, saw more of him than I did.

—But you love her.

I'd pressed the heel of my hand against my breastbone. I did love her, to the point of pain. Thinking of her actually hurt my heart.

—And that's why you would divide your attention. Francis would get less of an already meager pie.

Neither move would be right. Who should I hurt less?

---

DOWN IN MY DARKROOM, THE NEED TO SEE MY SON SUDDENLY overwhelmed me. I washed the prints, hung them up hurriedly, and ran upstairs, still in my rubber apron. "Francis!" He wasn't in the kitchen. The house was quiet. I called up the stairway: "Francis, where are you?"

No answer.

Were he and his friend playing with matches? Drinking Drano? Cutting themselves on Arnold's razor? I stormed upstairs, the hair on the back of my neck rising. He wasn't in his bedroom, the bathroom. I stood, panting, in my bedroom. My gaze went to the conch shell on my bedside table. I was reckless with my son. I'd been reckless with Juana. I was reckless, and selfish, always going after my shot, and for what? For what? Pride? Fame? *Koptsen vu krichts du?* I deserved to be sentenced to a life locked in a studio with brides demanding retakes.

MY DEAR HENRI'S WORDS HAD ECHOED IN THE EMPTY QUAKER meeting room.

John Morris, formerly of *Life*, now our director at Magnum New York, stood when Henri had sat back down. "Our friend left behind a thermos of cognac, a few good suits, a bereaved world, and his pictures, among them some of the greatest recorded moments of modern history." He ran his hand over his narrow face. "For *Life*, I'd sent him to Omaha Beach. I'd sent him to the Battle of the Bulge. Okinawa. He survived those. He got his shots." He sighed. "After the war, I thought we were done with all that, so I sent him to photograph uplifting stuff: the immigrants arriving to live in Israel, Picasso romping on the beach, Hitchcock filming *Notorious*. Why didn't I stick with sending him to Hollywood?

Why'd I have to send him to war again? I should have told *Life* no. Everyone knew that the conflict in Vietnam wasn't even a real war, just a quagmire of guerrillas and booby traps." He turned to our boss's mother, sitting next to him. "I am sorry, Júlia."

She regarded him for a moment, then rose, slowly, unbending, as if stiff with age. Her voice was thick with the Hungarian of her youth.

"I would beg my son to not go to such dangerous places. 'Why do you insist on going to war?' I asked him. 'You hate war. You have never taken up arms in your life, not even when men are shooting at you. You hate man's inhumanity. You fled Berlin when Hitler came to power, because you hated his cruelty. Why do you keep putting yourself at risk going where you hate it so?'"

Birdsong trilled into our silence. He'd gone to Vietnam to report on the northern part of the country's war with France. Leaving his jeep to get to a skirmish on foot, to record the killing that he abhorred, Robert Capa had stepped on a land mine.

Júlia looked at each one of us. "His students would ask him, 'What is wrong with my work? Why are my shots no good?' My son told them the same thing he told me: 'If your shots are no good, you're not getting close enough.'" She smiled fiercely. "His shots were good."

After the meeting, I held her hands and gazed into her face. She smelled of baby powder and metal. "I am so sorry for your loss."

Within their delicate webbing, her eyes were a stronger, wiser version of Capa's. "He was not mine to lose. He was never mine. He was never his own. He was always the world's. Just as you are the world's. You must accept that, and act."

"FRANCIS!" I CALLED, SCARED NOW. "FRANCIS!"

I heard noises outside. I ran to the bedroom window and looked through the branches of our tree. Francis was running with his friend in the yard. I drooped with relief.

I went downstairs and mixed a pitcher of cherry Kool-Aid, then took it, condensation rolling down its aluminum sides, to the picnic table outside. "Who's thirsty?"

Francis hurtled himself at his friend. Mikey raised a stick to his eye as if sighting with a rifle. "Bang!"

Francis threw his arms out and arched his back like the shot soldier in Capa's photo, then scrambled up from the ground with his own stick and fired back.

"Stop it!" I clanged the pitcher down and snatched the sticks from their hands.

Francis gaped as if I'd slapped him in the face.

"You know how I feel about guns, and you make one out of a stick? What's wrong with you?"

Mikey slunk out the gate.

Francis went red. "We weren't hurting anything."

"Do you think that playing at killing is fun?"

"It's just a stick."

"You were pretending to kill."

"We were playing!"

I stopped him from walking away. "Don't you *ever* play at killing someone. It's not a game."

"All the other kids have toy guns."

"I don't care. You don't have one."

He hung his head. When he raised it, his eyes were bright with a child's raw fury. "Why can't you be like the other moms?"

I looked with pity at his twisted face.

*You are the world's*, Capa's mother had said, her eyes as fierce as they were wise from decades of enduring. *You must accept that, and act.*

And then I understood: when a person was the world's, her

family was the world's, too. Was it right of me to make that choice for Francis?

I knelt before my son and took his arms. He turned his face away.

"What if I can't be like other moms?" I waited until he glanced at me, almost frightened. I was frightened, too. I had no choice in this. I was born seeing with my eyes, my heart, and my head, and I could no more stop showing the world what it might have missed than Capa could have helped being born with an extra finger.

It hurt to exhale. "Because I don't think I can be like them, Francis." He glanced at me again. "And you're not going to be like other kids."

His arms hung at his sides when I hugged him and told him I was sorry. When I pulled back, disappointment was written all over his soft features. I could see it dawning on him that it was true, he was not going to have a normal family. We were not to be like the families on *Ozzie and Harriet* or *Father Knows Best.*

"There will be good parts to our being different." I pushed the curls from his sweat-damp forehead. "Let's try to make it worth it, okay?"

"I don't want to."

"I know." I stroked his hair. "I know."

Slowly, he tipped forward until, as I held my breath, his head rested against my chin.

He put his arms around my neck.

Fighting off the burning in my eyes and throat, I held him tight.

My work had to be worth a six-year-old's trust. I could not take unimportant assignments. I had to get as close to the truth as Capa ever dared, and not flinch. Because I was not only the world's, but Francis's and Juana's. To them I owed my very best.

I put my nose to my son's hair and inhaled, memorizing his scent for the times ahead.

# 12

AFTER THE DAY OF THE MEMORIAL SERVICE, I PURSUED THE McCarthy story with a ferocity Capa's mother would be proud of. I was exposing that jerk terrorizing our country, no matter the personal cost, though it took me a good month of knocking on closed doors and getting hung up on to find someone willing to talk to me about how it felt to be targeted by McCarthy. His victims weren't keen on criticizing him and running the risk that he would destroy their lives all over again, preferring to cling quietly to whatever miserable existence they could cobble together since being blacklisted. The former NYU mathematics professor I'd managed to interview had been stripped of his job, his friends, and his house after he lost his head and talked back to McCarthy at a hearing. He'd agreed to meet me at night, in a dark alley off the waterfront in Hoboken, and even there he'd kept looking over his shoulder. He was trying to support his family by hanging on to the only job he could find, as a traveling salesman selling toilet seats, based in West Virginia.

His face hadn't been visible in the shade of the warehouse, tugboats moaning out on the foggy river.

"You want to know how low McCarthy brought me?" He snorted bitterly. "Right after my hearing, I saw a driver hit a child playing in the street, then keep driving. A driver! Hit a child! Did I help? No. I watched as others came to help the boy. Best I could do was to go to a phone booth and report the license plate number, then fade away like a shadow." He'd drawn a breath. "That's what I am now, just a shadow."

Months later, that exchange leaped to mind as I crouched under the recorder's table in the Senate chamber in which McCarthy was bullying a defendant. There were more reporters than senators in the packed chamber, but only two of us were allowed up front, beneath the table; I'd been in Washington for weeks beforehand to make sure I was one of those two. I'd trained for the assignment with the determination of a boxer preparing for a match, hanging out at the back of the hearing room to figure out my shots, hardening myself to Senator McCarthy and his henchman Roy Cohn's bullying their marks, and slurping down the Senate dining room's famous bean soup in order to fraternize with the reporters on the DC beat. If I had to be away from my family, I was going to do this right. But despite my training, I was getting upset about McCarthy's treatment of his current victim, a decorated lieutenant colonel, when old Satan himself turned away from his harassing and spied me under the recorder's table.

McCarthy's face, as red and shiny as a skinned rabbit, stretched in a wet-lipped grin. "Well, well, well. What do we have here?"

He stopped the hearing and indicated that he and I should meet outside the hearing room. I could feel everyone's gaze upon me as I followed him out.

"I usually approve the two reporters who are up front," he said when we got out into the hall. "I don't recall OK'ing a lady."

Through the hallway door, I could see his prey at the witness table, head in hands. I swallowed back my fear. "I'm a stringer for the press. You authorized me. E. Arnold." I hadn't mentioned Magnum on the clearance list. Photojournalists were especially reviled at the hearings.

"What's the *E* stand for, honey?" He raised his black hockey-stick brows.

My god, he was trying to be darling! I'd expected him to bully me. I'd prepared for him to throw me out. What I hadn't foreseen was that he would flirt with me.

My stomach lurched. "*E* is for Eve."

Reporters were pushing out of the rear door of the hearing room now and hustling our way, flash apparatuses raised.

His voice was smarmily kind. "Why, you're just an itty-bitty thing."

I burned at the thought of the professor selling toilet seats, of the lieutenant colonel just stripped of his rank, of all the people this man had ruined. I scraped my brain for words to skewer him properly.

A *New York Times* photographer dropped into a crouch before us. McCarthy ignored him. "Well, congratulations, sweetheart."

*Flash!*

"Covering this important work is a real big accomplishment. You're playing in a man's world now."

*Flash!*

A McCarthy aide rushed up and kneed the *Times* photographer, who fell onto McCarthy, who then stumbled against me, reeking of whiskey and peppermints.

He clung to my arm. "What's the big idea?" he said to the photographer. "Sorry, sweetheart. These press guys are vermin." He rubbed my forearm. "Are you okay?"

I raised my free hand to knock him off. He would destroy my photos. I dropped it. When my hand brushed his hairy knuckles on the way down, he trapped it under his paw. "There, there."

Every pore of my body screamed.

He turned his peeled-rabbit face to the closest reporter. "Smile for the camera, honey."

*Flash!*

He let me go. I lurched my way to the ladies' room, where I scrubbed my hands until they hurt. Many deep breaths later, I went to the Senate cafeteria, where the photographer from the *Washington Post* was in line, putting a goblet of Jell-O on his lunch tray.

I spoke over the rumble of male voices and the clanking of glasses and plates. "Did you see McCarthy paw me?"

The *Post* guy frowned, then slid his tray toward the cashier.

I waited for him to pay. "You saw him, right, Jim?"

"Saw what?" He waded into the crowded dining area.

The AP stringer was sitting with some guys I didn't know at a nearby table. I pulled up a chair and sat at his elbow. "Did you see McCarthy get fresh with me?"

"Is that what you call that?" He turned away.

I approached other colleagues with whom I'd roamed the marble halls, gulped down shitty food, and swapped work jokes. No one would talk with me.

I stalked from the room, my cameras bouncing on my chest, and didn't stop until I'd made it back to the ladies' restroom, where a splotchy-faced young woman was at the sink, trying to staunch her tears with a paper towel. I locked myself in a stall. My colleagues hadn't seen a powerful man pushing himself onto a disgusted woman who was half his size. What they'd seen was a dame fraternizing with the enemy. They thought I was using my sex to get an inside scoop. Regardless of the experiences I'd shared with these men, when push came to shove they'd not seen me as a colleague. They'd seen me as someone whose greatest potential was to be screwed.

A COUPLE WEEKS LATER, RAIN BOUNCED ON THE SIDEWALK outside Magnum's basement window as I drank a bitter cup of Maxwell House from the percolator set up next to Inge Bondi's desk. The place was neater now that John Morris had taken charge. While Capa's champagne-magnum dead soldiers still lined the mantel—no one could bear to move them—magazines were no longer splayed around the office like a flock of dead birds. Instead, a neat pile of upcoming issues for mid-September rested by Morris's brass lamp. On the other side of wire baskets holding letters and tear sheets, John himself, plain as a plowed field like the Midwesterner he was, glided his loupe over my contact sheet.

"These are good," he pronounced. "I'm impressed." He sat back. "How'd you manage to get so close to McCarthy? I thought he ran his hearings like a general on a battlefield—closest the coward ever got to real action."

Sensations zipped through my mind: the hot glare of the light banks; the rasp of coughs and shuffled papers; the man smell of Vitalis, cigarettes, and dirty suits; the hard marble floor hurting my knees as I knelt between McCarthy and his sweating target, my camera pressed to my face.

Morris squinted at an image. "I can see the hairs in McCarthy's nose. What lens did you use?"

"Just a normal. I had the disgusting pleasure of being six feet away from him." No sense in telling Morris that I'd gotten even closer. I shuddered, remembering McCarthy's thick fingers on my skin.

"Ugh. Well, I hope I can use these. Who'd have ever thought the tables would turn on the old bastard?"

Not me. When I shot the images, I hadn't dreamed that the Army-McCarthy hearings would screech to a stop the very next day. It had come to light that he'd driven a fellow senator to suicide—the last straw, finally, for the legislators. Now he himself was being brought up for censure, but would that stop him, or undo the hatred he'd whipped up in Americans for other Americans?

Beyond the office window, two pairs of wing tips dashed by; the outer door on the other side of the office wall opened. I could hear my big teddy bear of a colleague, Erwitt. "Who knew that lying on the floor," he bellowed, "trying to get a nickel off your nose without moving your head or body, would be the party rage of 1954?"

"Exciting times, Elliott. Exciting times." I recognized the other voice—the features editor from *Life*. "Be glad I'm not asking you to report on our fashion item for that issue: covering ladies' buns with a little hat."

"What?"

"Hair buns, Erwitt. Get your mind out of the gutter. Chignons. Evidently ladies are putting little hats on them."

"I'll pass."

They must have had at least a two-martini lunch.

Erwitt and the *Life* editor ambled into our inner chamber. "Get you coffee?" Inge said.

Morris had stood up to shake hands with the editor, when the front door opened again and the new guy at Magnum, Bob Henriques, trotted in. Bob waved off Inge's offer of coffee and nodded to me before telling the men, "You have to see these photos." He slid some eight-by-tens from an envelope.

Morris took a look. "Wow."

The *Life* editor agreed. "Stunning. Where'd you get them?"

"Here in town." Henriques, Hollywood suave and handsome, with slicked-back hair, whistled through his teeth. "It's all Marilyn. I just pointed my camera." His modesty was precious. "The eye loves looking at her like it loves looking at any extraordinarily beautiful thing, like a Monet, a diamond"—he swirled his hand as if to conjure up his dream—"a Ferrari."

Were they shots of you? I didn't know you and Joe were in New York. It had been how many months since I'd seen you at your *How to Marry a Millionaire* premiere, ten? I didn't hold it against you. We'd both been busy fighting our own battles.

*"Pffft."* Inge poured coffee for the *Life* editor. "I hope someday a man appreciates me as much as a car."

The editor kept his sights on Henriques's prints. "So, where'd you get these, again?"

"Sixty-First Street, yesterday. I heard they were shooting an exterior for her new movie."

Now I wanted to see the photos. "She's back to making movies?"

"With a vengeance. By the time I got there, a thousand people were milling around outside, waiting for her to show. Sam Shaw was there and waved for me to come on up. Say, weren't you there, too?" he asked Erwitt.

"Yeah. But I got there late. Was Joe DiMaggio there?"

"No. I hear he hates her doing this kind of stuff."

"Poor slob," Erwitt said. He tipped Henriques's prints toward me so I could see. "I didn't get any shots like these."

There was one of you wearing a white terry cloth robe and leaning out a third-story window. Another was a close-up of you in the robe, resting your chin on your hands as you gazed up into the camera.

"Looks like she liked you, Bob," Erwitt said. "A lot."

The *Life* editor chuckled. "You know what they say about Marilyn and her photographers."

Henriques grinned. "I did feel like there was something between us."

I examined the print. Did you come on to Henriques? I didn't think so. What I saw was a plea in your eyes, kind of like that of a puppy hoping not to be hit. I looked up at the men. No one else saw this?

The *Life* editor tapped the prints. "I want these for my next issue."

"Evie's just brought me some great shots of McCarthy and his goon Cohn at one of the hearings." Morris picked them up to show him. "Really close-up, really chilling."

The editor glanced at my images. "Full of themselves, aren't they?"

He didn't know the half of it.

"These shots should make the issue, too," Morris said, "especially now, with him being investigated."

A crooked grin grew on Henriques's face. "*Ohhhh*, so you're the one who McCarthy . . . liked."

I didn't care for his tone. "What do you mean?"

"Just that pals of mine at the AP were talking about some Mata Hari with a camera who wiggled her way up close to him. I should have known it was you. How many girl photographers are there?" He smiled as if I'd find that cute.

The *Life* editor looked amused.

"I didn't 'wiggle my way up close.'"

"Of course you didn't," Inge said, her Austrian accent tinged with annoyance. She sat back down at her desk, her coffee duties over. The *Life* editor was busy trying to bum a smoke from Erwitt and no longer paying attention.

"What was McCarthy like, Eve?" Inge asked.

I let my impressions congeal. "Needy."

"Hitler was needy," she said. "Needy men are the most dangerous."

Bob Henriques took his photos from the *Life* editor, who was now drawing on a Pall Mall. "If you want me to do a spread on Marilyn Monroe," he said, putting them back into their envelope, "you should give me another couple days. She's going to do a big shoot on location tomorrow night, outside the theater at Lexington and Fifty-Second."

"What's the name of the film?" the editor asked.

"The press is supposed to be there at midnight," Henriques said. "There're rumors she's going to strip."

"What'd you say the name of the movie was?"

"*The Seven Year Itch.*" Henriques nodded at me. "Aren't you and Marilyn friends?"

The *Life* editor turned to me, then heaved a torrent of smoke. "You're friends? Why didn't you say so?"

WHEN I GOT HOME, ARNOLD WAS AT THE TABLE, GRADING PApers for his teaching gig, unbothered by the dirty bowls, the Shredded Wheat box, the broken head of lettuce, the open package of Wonder Bread, the unboxed roll of wax paper, the empty ice cube tray, the bottle of Pine-Sol, the rocket-ship thermos, the scattered *New York Times*, and the dress shoe—his dress shoe?—cluttering the counter behind him.

"Marilyn just called." He pushed his papers around and came up with an envelope with a number penned on it. "She said she was in town and wants to see you."

My mood muted my pleased surprise. I shoved the envelope into my pocket, ignoring everything else but the shoe, which I knocked to the floor. I poured myself a glass of water, drank it, and then leaned against the counter. "*Life*'s not running my McCarthy photos."

He stopped reading to swipe his shoe up from the floor. "I stepped in gum. How do I get it off? How do you know they are not using your photos?"

"Because a *Life* editor was there when I was at Magnum, and he passed, at least for now. He wants me to cover Marilyn at a shoot in town"—I tossed my hand—"from a lady's point of view."

"Good!" he said. "You should call her back, then."

"Good?" I pressed the glass to my forehead. "I take impossible shots, shots no one else can get—I mean, Capa couldn't have gotten any closer—and still my colleagues think of me as a woman first and a serious photographer a distant second. I am never going to get past that."

"You will," Arnold said. "What do you use to get gum off shoes?"

"What? Soak it in vinegar for ten minutes and then scrape it off."

Once upon a time, you ran into the fire by flaunting your sexiness. Guys saw you only as a woman? Fine! You promised them their dreams until you had them under your control. But then you abandoned that strategy to become the wife of the most beloved man in America, as if his popularity could boost yours. What hope did I have of fighting off the lions when the chief tamer had turned in her whip and her stool?

Arnold looked in a cupboard. "Where is the vinegar?"

I pointed to a shelf.

"What do I use to scrape it?"

"A knife."

But now you were back to making pictures. Was being Mrs. Joe not getting you where you wanted to be? What new twist did you have up your sleeve? Because the feral kid with no rules to constrain her was nothing if not a scrapper. And I could use some inspiration. If I couldn't place my McCarthy photos, I couldn't place anything of value, because my work didn't get any better than them.

Arthur held out his shoe. "Can you do it?"

I absentmindedly took the shoe and dropped it on the floor, then dug in my pocket for your number.

# 13

THREE THOUSAND–SOME MEN WERE ALREADY THERE WHEN I ARrived at the address you gave me, or so a cop told me, and now, in the wee hours of the morning, we were all waiting behind police barricades at the Trans-Lux Theatre at Fifty-Second and Lex. Some of the men stood rigidly, tobacco-smoke wraiths escaping them to swirl in the klieg lights trained on the movie set. Others shuffled on their patches of concrete, as uneasy as stud stallions when a mare is nearby. Magazine photographers jostled for position, while TV newsmen idled behind cameras that were bigger than they were, watching like Cro-Magnons leaning on their spears as Neanderthals chased a mammoth with their clubs.

You were late. You needed your Jane Russell.

I looked around for something to photograph. None of my lenses were right for the skyscrapers down Lexington, backlit by a full moon. I pivoted my camera to the twenty-foot-tall lizard man atop the theater marquee—a promo for the B movie *Creature from the Black Lagoon*, and part of the set for this shoot. With thousands of randy men now stirring beneath him, the monster seemed to be carrying the damsel in his arms away from danger, not into it.

A vehicle approached. It crunched over empty cigarette packs and beer-bottle caps, nudging the crowd with its enormous, cowcatcher-like chrome fenders, until at last, churning exhaust into the crisp September night, it stopped. A car door swung open. A tousled blond head emerged. A stockyard bellowing went up.

The plunging halter top of your white dress buckled as you lifted your bare arm high above your head to turn your hand languorously in greeting. You processed through the booms and rigging, a goddess gliding between the columns of her temple. When you stepped under the kliegs, your hair, your button earrings, your skin, your dress, your high-heeled sandals—all of you white—glowed. The men nearly beat their chests. I think some of them actually did.

The pockmarked Everyman actor Tom Ewell and the director Billy Wilder trotted next to you into the illumination of the klieg lights, Wilder smiling so hugely that the corners of his down-curved eyes and his upcurved mouth nearly met. Extras were positioned. Whitey dipped in to powder your face. Mr. Wilder stepped back for you and Ewell to find your marks.

"Quiet on the set!"

Three thousand leering men held their breath. Mr. Wilder barked, "Action!"

You and Ewell strolled from beneath the marquee, with its damsel-toting beast. A police siren wailed in the distance. Somehow, I managed to hear you speak over my neighbors' ragged breathing.

"Didn't you just love the picture?" you gushed in your Marilynest voice. "I did! But I just felt so sorry for the creature at the end."

"Sorry for the creature!" Ewell exclaimed. My neighbors' shuffling blotted out his next line.

I glimpsed the swish of your skirt as you sashayed on. "He was kind of scary looking. But he really wasn't all bad. I think he just craved a little affection. You know"—your words came out in little puffs—"the sense of being loved and needed and wanted."

I came down from my tiptoes. What kind of bull was this? Maybe the screenwriter thought your ditzy character had the simple needs of a swamp creature, but real women's needs were a whole lot more complicated. *Look at you, with your need to beat men at their own game, and me with my drive to illuminate the unseen.* What about the desires of any housewife at home? None of us was just hanging around, waiting for a man's touch. But real women never made it into the movies. Real women were more frightening to many men than seaweed-strewn beasts.

Wilder cued the special effects man waiting under a subway grate with a fan, there to simulate the displacement of air by a train roaring under the street.

The fan kicked on. Your pleated skirt wafted up around your knees.

"Ooh!" your character said. "Do you feel the breeze from the subway? Isn't it delicious?"

Thousands of men whistled their response.

"Cut!" Wilder shouted.

You rubbed your arms.

Wilder asked for another take. The man with the fan made your skirt blow higher. Then another take was ordered, and another, with your skirt shooting ever upward, first to your thighs, then to your waist, and then to your shoulders. Each time the crowd yelled, "Higher! Higher!"

If you were surprised by the increasing length and intensity of the fan blasts, you didn't show it. With every strafing of the fan, you pushed down the front pleats of your skirt with your hands and poked down the side sections with your elbows, making a dance of it while smiling, as if essentially being publicly stripped was the very thing you wanted. The crowd went berserk as the fan man jetted your skirt higher and higher, until you were nothing but panties and dancing legs.

I lowered my Nikon. Who'd told the special effects man to keep turning up the fan? Had Wilder planned this outdoor strip show? It couldn't possibly be part of the movie. The Legion of Decency would flunk it. And with all the noise, the sound quality would be terrible; I couldn't imagine how Wilder could use a single take. This world's largest girlie show was just a cheap trick to whip up publicity for the film.

I turned around to escape. I hadn't gotten far through the ranks of howling men when I saw Sam Shaw with your husband. Arms over his broad chest, Joe was watching you with a glare that could torch wood.

Steadying the cameras that were strapped around his neck, Sam waved me over as if he were a passenger on a burning ship. "Evie, hi!" he exclaimed when I got to him. "How are you? How are things at Magnum? Say, have you met Joe?"

"Yes. Hello, Mr. Di—"

"What the hell is going on?" he growled, eyes on you. "My wife is inviting all these sons of bitches to tear her clothes off. Hell, they're almost off her already." He lowered his burning gaze onto me. "Why can't she be a regular wife?"

THE NEXT MORNING, I WAS LEAVING THE FANCY DIGS YOU'D RESERVED for me at the St. Regis. Four hours of sleep had done nothing to soothe the sick feeling that had come with seeing you used like a piece of chuck. Billy Wilder was now on my shit list. I had just finished checking out when you came from the elevator wearing a black short-sleeved turtleneck, white slacks, and clear Lucite mules.

"Miss Documentary Photographer!" You clipped over on your Cinderella slippers.

"Miss Most Advertised."

We pecked each other's cheeks.

When you glanced around the lobby, I noticed bruises on your bicep. "Have you seen Joe?" you asked. "He took off while I was getting ready. I'm meeting Milton Greene. He has a business plan he wants to go over with me."

"Are you all right?"

You rubbed your arm when you saw me frowning at your bruises. "I am now." You lifted your chin. "Were you there last night? I didn't see you."

"Oh, I was there."

You opened the purse on your arm and pulled out a folded section of newspaper. A photo of you holding your flaring skirt down commanded the top quarter of the page. By the height of your hem—below your waist—I guessed the shot must have been taken in the earlier part of the evening.

"Isn't it terrific? Sam Shaw took it. Front page—can you imagine?"

"I guess."

Your smile dimmed. "Did you not get any photos? If I'd seen you during the press shoot, I would have had you come up front."

"I wasn't at the press shoot."

"Why not?"

You didn't get it. Or maybe I didn't get it. "Mr. Wilder couldn't have gotten any usable footage from all that . . . whatever that was. There's no way the soundmen could have dealt with all that racket. Weren't you furious?"

"Furious?"

I swallowed. "I saw Joe there. He seemed pretty . . . upset . . . by how they used you."

"*They* used *me*! You think they used me?" The silvery curl over your eye bounced as you laughed. "Eve, I used them! I made front-page news, and it didn't cost me a dime. The fan under the grate was my idea."

You subjected yourself to that on purpose?

"I was going to call the *New York Times* myself, but after Billy saw how these things could help the picture, he got Publicity to do it." You held up your picture in the paper. "Isn't it just grand?"

"But"—I glanced at your arm—"didn't Joe hurt you?"

You were opening your mouth to speak when the revolving door whooshed around to produce a gangly teenaged boy holding a home movie camera. "Marilyn!"

The concierge, who'd been pretending to work behind his elegant desk, stepped out to confront him. "Have you business here, young man?" he demanded in a tony British accent.

The boy, all plaid shirt and pimples, went pink to the base of his brush cut. He charged toward you, but he was no match for the reflexes of the older man. Collared, the boy yelped, "Marilyn!"

The concierge gave him a shake. "Now, look here—"

"Marilyn, I'm your biggest fan!"

"I've seen you. You were there last night. You were right behind all the professional guys, with your little movie camera."

The boy's face shone. "You were beautiful."

"Oh, let him go, Godfrey."

The concierge released him. Now tomato red, the boy gasped, "I love you, Marilyn."

You glowed. "What's your name?"

"James."

After you signed the newspaper he'd produced, he stumbled away as if drunk.

You were smiling when you turned back to me. "What were you saying?"

Getting a teenaged boy to worship you was worth exposing yourself to thousands of jackasses and your husband's abuse? "I'm trying to understand. I really want to."

You shrugged. "I got tired of waiting, stuck out there in San Francisco with Joe. The way I get to the top might not be pretty, but in the end, I'm going to get there. We underdogs have to be creative, you know?"

"Yes, I know, but Joe hurt—"

"But Joe proved who he is, and the sooner I found that out, the better. I don't have time to waste on a dead end. This"—you playfully circled your face with your finger—"doesn't last." Your glow dimmed when you saw that I wasn't buying your frivolousness. "Nothing lasts, does it? Just ask someone who's gone through twelve foster families. I'm never surprised when things don't work out."

A handsome young man in a Hawaiian sport shirt strolled in through the revolving door. I was thinking that he looked familiar when you clasped your hands together. "Milton!" You clopped over on your clear plastic mules to hug him.

Joe would have strangled him if he saw how long you embraced.

You looped your arm through his. "Milton, you know Eve. Eve, you've met Milton Greene."

"The documentary photographer," he said. "Sure."

You beamed as he pecked my cheek. "We're working on a secret new business plan."

"Does Joe know of this secret plan?"

"Of course," Milton said.

You snorted. "Though he doesn't believe we can pull it off. For all his success, Joe's not much of a dreamer. But we're dreamers, aren't we, Milton?"

You grinned at each other. I wondered if Joe knew what was coming. If he hurt her, he deserved it, but, regardless, it was coming.

"I'll let you two go, then."

You didn't argue with me. You left, arm in arm with your next new thing.

# 14

## 1955

"GREAT PORTRAIT, PHILIPPE," JOHN MORRIS WAS SAYING. WE were crowded around his desk, talking about a photo of you that Philippe Halsman had just shot for *Life*. Like many New Yorkers on this freakishly warm day at the beginning of February, we had the window cranked open as far as its aged sash would go. We knew the weather wouldn't last. Tomorrow, snow might pile against the window of our belowground bunker. Best to seize the day, never mind the mushy cardboard boxes and browning Christmas trees lying at eye level.

Halsman dipped his head in response to the compliment, accentuating the high forehead from which his fine, dark hair was ebbing. "Thank you."

After decades outside of his native Russia, one of them spent partially in an Austrian prison on a false charge of murdering his own father while on a hiking trip—anti-Semitism had been on the rise in the Tyrol, and Halsman was a Jew—Halsman still spoke with a heavy accent. I was one of the few at Magnum who didn't, unless you counted Philadelphian as an accent. Most of us sounded foreign and, save for Morris, we were Jews, our families having been run out of their countries by pogroms, recent or ancient.

Bob Henriques (family expelled from Spain, 1492) sniffed. "Interesting shot, Philippe. Looks like she forgot you were there, pal. The opposite"—he coughed—"of my experience."

"Not all of us try to seduce the girl," said Halsman (escaped Russia, 1933).

Henriques shook his head. "What a waste." Inge Bondi (Austrian refugee, 1939) and I (family fled the Ukraine, 1918), the only women present, caught each other's glances and rolled our eyes.

"Seducing her is a cheap trick." Elliott Erwitt (American via Russia, France, then Italy) pushed up his glasses. "I treat Marilyn Monroe the same as I do any other subject."

"Well, that's dumb," Henriques muttered.

Erwitt pursed his long upper lip, a grumpy teddy bear. "It's not my way to smarm up to celebrities. I just walk around and look at things and try to put them in the frame—and then hope that I've got something interesting."

Henriques cocked his head. "No 'smarming' for you, huh?" He knew—we all knew—that taking a great shot was never that easy. "And what if you don't get something interesting?"

Erwitt grinned, his cuddly self again. "Would I be at Magnum if I didn't?"

I studied the print as Henriques and Erwitt traded boasts. Halsman's subtle use of side lighting made me jealous. You couldn't get dreamy results like that outside of a studio. (I would never admit that to Arnold—not that I'd have much of a chance to in those days, busy as we both were.)

But the atmospheric lighting didn't fully explain the pensive look Halsman had caught on your face. The photo was remarkable for the fact that, in it, you weren't trying to project something.

Even in the newspaper photos of you and your lawyer outside the San Francisco courthouse in which you'd just divorced Joe after nine months of marriage (you'd filed mere days after I last saw you, leaving the St. Regis with Milton Greene), I thought your distress looked ginned up, as if you were the heroine threatened by the villain in a silent film. I was embarrassed for you, if you want to know the truth. Here, though, you weren't vamping. You weren't flirting, sobbing, or exuding charm or glamour or sex; you were just floating in the camera's eye and letting it love you. Was this—drumroll, please—the New Marilyn?

In a better-kept secret than the invasion of Normandy, in the dead of night on New Year's Eve, three months after your divorce, you flew from Hollywood to New York. There, you announced to a startled press that you'd broken your contract with Fox and were teaming up with Milton Greene to form your own film company, Marilyn Monroe Productions. All you wanted, you said, was to choose your scripts and pick your directors—and have your own damn trailer, I presumed.

This "New Marilyn," as you called yourself, said she was a serious actress who wanted to act on Broadway. She'd like to have the lead in a Chekhov play someday. She'd come to New York to study with the greats to do so.

My first response? Brilliant. Who in America, the Land of the New and Improved, could resist a jazzy new model of Marilyn Monroe? On the stage, no less. But if the theater was your aim, you'd need a Jane to peel you out of your dressing room, because there was no such thing as being late on Broadway. And I was just a phone call away.

I was still waiting for you.

Erwitt passed your photo to Henriques. "Have you put the moves on"—he coughed—"I mean photographed—Marilyn lately?"

"Not since her last presser." Henriques rubbed his jaw, already purple with emergent stubble before noon. "I'm not sure how well this New Marilyn's going to go over with reporters. She wouldn't bend over like she used to when they asked her to show her tits. Made guys mad." He grinned. "She remembered me, though."

"Of course she did, Pretty Boy Floyd," Erwitt said.

Morris displayed another of Halsman's eight-by-tens. We gathered in again.

At first glance, the print looked to be of an unexploded missile, small, centered, and in sharp focus against a soft gradient background. A closer look proved it to be of you, shot straight on in midair in a jump, with your legs tucked under, your arms pinned to your sides, and your chin tilted down.

"Christ, she's cute," Erwitt said. "Look at that little smile."

Henriques grinned. "Looks like you got her to love you after all, Halsman. Did you have to 'smarm'?"

Halsman's bulbous Eastern European face grew serious. "She rattled me. When I said, 'Marilyn, loosen up when you jump,' she asked me what I meant. I told her that the real character of a person appears when they are up in the air—they can't help it. It was a little trick I had." He shook his head. "As soon as I said it, she froze. She said, 'You mean my real self will show when I jump?' After I told her yes, she would not move, though I tried to encourage her. Only when I put my camera on a timer and jumped with her would she do it." He studied his photo. "I am just out of the frame. But it came out nice. She is like a little girl jumping rope."

Were you? Did little girls jump with their fists clenched at their sides? The anxiety in those hands said everything. You—New Marilyn, Old Marilyn, Norma Jeane—were under a great deal of stress.

I looked up in alarm. How could my colleagues not see this?

As hard as you were working to conceal your stress, I wasn't going to be the one to blow your cover. "How clever, Philippe. You got the blond bombshell to look like an actual bombshell."

When I showed the guys how your silhouette resembled a falling missile, they laughed.

"You should have no problem selling this," Morris said. "*Vogue*, *Life*—they'll all want it."

"Not *Look*," Henriques said. "Her boyfriend has that sewn up."

"Milton Greene, boy wonder," Erwitt said.

Henriques huffed. "At the press conference, Marilyn hardly said a sentence without checking with him first."

"He's married," said Morris, recently wed himself.

"And? So?" Henriques said. "The New Marilyn seems a whole lot like the Old Marilyn, if you know what I mean."

They all laughed. Apparently, a woman aspiring to better herself was funny.

THE FOLLOWING SUNDAY, FRANCIS AND I WERE ON THE LIVING room floor, playing Television Star, a board game that Arnold was developing to pitch at his work. The smell of chicken soup simmering on the stove drifted in from the kitchen—at least my son would never know what it was like to wait for water soup. But my McCarthy photos still hadn't sold in the US. I'd put myself and my family through the grinder, for what? Because of photos that should have established me as a journalist to watch, my reputation had taken a leap backward. My only recent assignments had been maddeningly condescending, like shooting the first televised Miss America pageant. I had to come up with a story to redeem myself.

Maybe Arnold was onto something by focusing on kids. While so far sales for *How to Play with Your Child* were far short of the copies Ballantine had printed, thus killing his chances of publishing subsequent books with them, try as he might to come up with irresistible ideas, he still swore he was on the right track. He could see it at his work. Parker Brothers was selling kids' games faster than they could make them. In the 1930s, Charles Darrow had made a million on Monopoly. Think what a breakthrough board game could do in this era of Silly Putty, Slinky, and Mr. Potato Head!

*Goodbye, loser book proposals. Hello, successful kids' game!*

Arnold did have a point. From teenagers grabbing the popular imagination with their rock and roll, soda fountains, and cars, to the newborns flooding the hospitals, the young were driving the economy. All the kids born since the war were being catered to with circuses, Westerns, and roller-skating rinks. In America, Cartier-Bresson's X Generation kids knew little of their fathers' war but a lot about Tiny Tears dolls and Tonka trucks, thanks to what they were being told by their TV sets. And which parents among us who'd survived the deprivations of the Great Depression and the slaughter of world war could deny their children whatever they dreamed of?

Along these lines, I'd been circling around shooting a story on a man out in California whose whimsical children's books—including his most recent one, about an elephant named Horton—were selling in numbers that Steinbeck, and poor Arnold, could only wish for. I was also following the teenaged kids in my area, shadowing them when they were at dances, in their cars as they "buzzed" the Port Jefferson village square, or at the malt shop. Even as Francis and I pushed our tokens around the board of Arnold's silly game ("It's *supposed* to be funny!"), my wheels kept turning. I would zero in on the Great Idea yet.

I had taken a "Star Turns" card from its pile when the phone rang.

You exclaimed into the receiver, "Miss Documentary Photographer? It's me! You called?"

It was your real voice, from the belly, and a bit on the brassy side, a rough little kid's kittenish growl—nothing like the Old Marilyn's breathy puffs, or the studied and hesitant remarks stammered on the radio by the New. I wondered how many people had ever heard your real voice.

"How are you doing?" I cradled the receiver under my chin and, stretching the phone cord to its limit, went over to stir the soup. I'd called right after I'd seen Halsman's photo of you jumping. I was concerned.

"Eve, I got invited to go to the Actors Studio."

"Wonderful! Congrats." Well, that was a coup. Only actors serious about performing on the stage or in important films need apply to the most prestigious acting school in the country. Few were accepted, and the ones who had been were changing the film industry with their "Method" approach to acting. Emoting was out; showing raw, personally experienced feelings was in—terrible news for the likes of Joan Crawford and Katharine Hepburn.

"Gadg Kazan invited me."

Nicknames now? I tested a carrot with my spoon. Still not tender. "That's some invitation."

Elia Kazan had served his time in Hollywood purgatory after his McCarthy testimony and was back to directing pictures. His last one, *On the Waterfront*, had won Oscars for him and his two leads, all of them alumni—in Kazan's case, a founder—of the Actors Studio.

"I'm scared! Everyone there is so good. They're going to look down on me."

"They only wish they were you, Miss Most Advertised and Most Everything Else." I dunked a chicken back into the broth.

"I don't think so. The greats that I grew up worshipping hate me, and the new stars who I want to be like hate me even more."

"That's not true." Was it?

"Will you come with me? Please?"

"Me? To the Actors Studio?"

"You're my only real friend."

I was? I secreted this nugget to my heart even as I told myself you must not mean it.

"What about Amy Greene?" I heard you were living with her and Milton, which sounded like a very bad idea.

"Milton keeps running her around, buying clothes for me and getting props for our photo shoots. He had her comb Manhattan to buy up every square yard of black velvet for one. She had to find a ballerina tutu for another. And she has a one-year-old baby to take care of!"

A very bad idea indeed. I pushed the chicken back down. It would not stay submerged.

Your sigh flooded the receiver. "She cooks for me. We eat breakfast, lunch, and dinner at their *table*, like you see on *Ozzie and Harriet*. Did you know families really did that?"

"Well—yes."

"Oh, you're so lucky! She taught me how to do my laundry, too. And got me a dog! She does all this for me, and there I am, taking up all her husband's time. She must be sick to death of me."

"No," I murmured.

"Hey! I have an idea. You can take your camera! To the Actors Studio. Do a story on it."

The hair on my arms tingled. A story about the Actors Studio was a great idea. It would be culturally significant—I could examine who these people our society worshipped really were—with the added benefit that I would be able to sell it all over the place. I could really use a notch in my belt just now. "Kid, you are a marketing genius."

You chuckled from the belly.

"Just don't take pictures of me there."

"What? Really? Why?"

"Take pictures of everyone else. They'll love it. But promise you won't take any of me."

"No pictures of you. I promise, I guess. But why?"

"Because I can only stand to be hated so much."

"You aren't hated." I clanged the lid onto the pot. "When are we going?"

# 15

AS PREDICTED, THE BALMY FEBRUARY WEATHER LASTED EXACTLY one day. It had been snowing ever since, the thick, wet kind of snow that was murder to shovel. My camera cases thumped on my coat as I powered down Fifth Avenue, crushing slush under my translucent booties. I was late, but I knew you'd be even later. I arrived at one of the lions in front of the main branch of the library, our agreed-upon meeting place, and prepared to freeze.

I heard my name. A woman swaddled in a camel coat and a white silk headscarf was navigating the slush in my direction. I saw the chafed stretch of bare ankle between her slacks and soaked black flats. Not a New Yorker.

"Miss Documentary Photographer!"

"Miss Most Advertised?"

In the shadow of your scarf, your makeup-free face was plump and sweet; you looked like a mild version of the Miss America contestants who'd lined up before my camera for the story in *Life* last fall. The pointy, downward-turned tip of your nose—how had I not noticed this minor defect before?—was red.

I glanced around. The people hurrying by paid us no attention.

"They won't look, you know," you said. "No one looks at Norma Jeane."

You pulled your collar closer to your throat as we negotiated the slippery sidewalk. At a corner, we waited for a bus to maneuver around a pothole at which a worker was lighting a flare. The worker stepped back, the oil in the smudge pot having caught fire, and did a double take at you. *Here we go—cue the catcalls.*

He looked at you again, then, frowning, went over to his truck to lug out another smudge pot. The intersection cleared, and we went on.

"I thought he was going to ask you for your autograph."

"I told you, no one ever asks for Norma Jeane's."

Ten slushy minutes later, we stopped in front of a church.

"This is it. Wish me luck."

A plain sign above the door of the dour New England–style façade read ACTORS STUDIO. How fitting that the new gods, those deified in movies, on television, and on the stage, were taught in a former church.

Behind the door that had once admitted a starched and pressed congregation, we hung our coats on a rack. I unhooked and kicked off my plastic booties while you rubbed the wet toes of your flats against your ankles. Closed doors to the former sanctuary funneled us to a stairway where an arrow on a sign pointed upward as if to heaven: TO THE ACTORS STUDIO.

You turned away from the railing. "I can't do it."

"Yes, you can."

Several attractive young men and women entered and shed clothing down to their suit coats or cardigans, hailing one another as they unwrapped, before one of the girls saw us by the stairs. The others followed her gaze. The air seemed to contract.

"Hi." The walls swallowed your soft voice.

They glanced at one another, then filed by as if we didn't exist.

You turned to leave.

I grabbed your arm. "Oh, no, you don't."

"They hate me."

"Don't take it personally."

"Don't take it personally!"

"It's not you. They're jealous."

You moaned.

"Hey, where's that girl who throws the lions red meat until she gets them eating out of her hand?"

"Gone. These people are worse than lions. These are the kids in seventh grade, and I'm the new girl wearing a crummy jumper and blouse that look exactly like what they are, a uniform from an orphanage." Your blue eyes were filled with misery. "My new foster mother didn't get me any other clothes. Kids called me dirty. Everyone thought I was dirty. And there was nothing I could do about it but be dirty."

My stomach pitched. I'd been called dirty a few times, too. Poverty looks dirty to some kids—to some adults as well. But remembering childhood slights wasn't helping either of us. I grabbed your arm and put on my best Jane Russell swagger. "C'mon, kid. We're going up."

IT WAS AS BAD AS YOU FEARED. ONCE WE'D MET THE DIRECTOR, Lee Strasberg, and you'd taken a seat on a back riser in the black-walled room, the actors around you leaned away, their hostility rising from them like stink from a cartoon skunk. I was free to roam around the edges with my camera.

A pair of students acted out a scene after which Mr. Strasberg, an elfin, balding man with big black glasses, solicited critiques from the students. My first and only photography teacher, Alexey

Brodovitch, had used the same technique with his class. The results had been brutal. My fellow students had ripped my green efforts to shreds. I swore I'd never return to the class, and Arnold only too happily supported me. "Stay home," he'd said. "Let's have another baby."

I'd gone back the next week, with better and stronger photos.

Now I lifted my camera to the pair being torn into. The boy was cocking his head and looking skeptical of the criticism, but the girl drooped, forlorn. Why were women so quick to believe negative comments while men explained how their critics were wrong?

I got shots, too, of the students doing the grilling. One cool customer in a white T-shirt leaned forward as if watching a boxing match, one of his feet, in a bobby sock and a loafer, resting on the chair in front of him. Paul Newman, he later told me his name was.

Pretending to be a nobody, you hunched into yourself like an overgrown kindergartner trying to make herself small. But even with flat hair and no makeup, and though no longer dewy at twenty-eight, five to ten years older than most of the other students, you drew one's eye. Normalcy was unavailable to you no matter what you did, which was both your strength and your curse.

But I didn't take a single shot of you. A promise is a promise.

Mr. Strasberg came over to you and me when class was over. "What did you think of our little session, Miss Monroe?" For a man who stood a scant few inches taller than someone who'd been called a tiny terror, he had the big presence of a person who thought well of himself.

"Call me Marilyn," you told him, with no breathiness whatsoever. "I thought it was magnificent."

His nod was meant to be humble. "We try."

"I could learn so much from you."

"Would you like to be a member of our group?"

"Yes!"

"Then you shall be." The Lord at creation spoke with no more authority.

"I can come to your classes?"

"My sessions, we call them. Yes, dear."

You scream-sighed. "Oh! Thank you!"

He glanced at me and my camera, assessed that I was good for him, nodded, and then went back to you. "But there's one thing I ask of all my members."

"Yes? How much does it cost?"

"Oh, we can talk about that later. No, what I ask is that everyone get psychoanalyzed."

Your face fell.

"Have you been analyzed?"

You shook your head.

"It's imperative that actors examine their past and lay themselves bare, because we draw on our experiences to propel us through a scene. We do not so much act as use our past to animate our characters." He flashed a smile. "Is this something you're willing to do?"

Terror flashed over your face, then was gone.

"Why not?" You lifted your chin. "The whole world's already seen me with all my clothes off."

# 16

YOU WERE STILL CAUSING STAMPEDES, LIKE THE ONE AT THE PREmiere of *East of Eden* in March, when your fans had heard that you would be one of the celebrity usherettes. (Gee, I wonder who told them.) I was getting a little recognition, too. The Tiny Terror had a photo hanging in the Museum of Modern Art.

Okay, it was one of eight hundred photos, part of an exhibition called *The Family of Man*, but MoMA was MoMA. Not too shabby for a first show. I was inordinately proud of my inclusion, so I wasn't going to turn you down when you called and said you wanted to go see it with me. Sure, I might have been there with Arnold three or four times already, but I hadn't gone with you.

You'd come to the museum that day as Zelda Zonk, an identity that you said you used for traveling. Zelda favored a black wig with bangs, and a beat-up black trench coat, a thin disguise that worked as long as you didn't put on your Old Marilyn act. I came as me. Well, not the usual me. I didn't have my cameras.

We stopped at Wayne Miller's photo of a baby being delivered.

You pushed back your fake black fringe and exclaimed, "Isn't birth wonderful?"

I glanced at you. "I don't know about the delivery part, but I like the net result."

The photo centered on the attending doctor. The baby, pale and suspended by his ankles, was the only hint that the print wasn't of a surgeon performing an appendectomy. The mother was shrouded and out of sight, the unseen terminus of the umbilical cord. My photos of my niece's nativity told a fuller story, yet a man had been the one allowed to tell the story of childbirth here. I still thought babies and mothers deserved better.

"I want a baby," you said, "but I'm scared I'll be terrible at being a mother."

The seriousness in your voice made me look twice. You were truly disturbed.

"Stop. That you're worried about it is a sign you'll be a good mother, when you're ready." I had another thought. "Are you—?"

"No, I'm not pregnant, though Joe and I really tried. You'd have thought, as much as . . ." You looked troubled. "Well, good thing it didn't work out with him as the dad."

"Good thing." I took your arm.

We strolled into a room hung with photos of mothers cradling their infants. Few of the shots had been made by women; many felt staged and emotionless. Only my friend Elliott Erwitt's photo of his wife and baby raptly studying each other, with their cat perched Buddha-like between them, came close to catching a mother's experience. I reminded myself to commend him for that—even as I swore to outdo him.

The next room contained images of children with their mothers. I held my breath as you got close to it—

"Oh, Miss Documentary! Your photo!"

You lowered your face when several patrons looked our way.

"Oh, Eve," you whispered, "it's so real. They look so happy. Look how much her parents love her. What a lucky, lucky little girl."

Juana. The funny, bold child I'd left behind. Of all my photos, the curators chose hers, and rightly so. Her vivaciousness, and her parents' love for her, radiated from the photo. I'd captured love so pure that it was almost hard to look at.

Was this photo proof of my creativity, or was I just in the right place at the right time, and my camera had simply recorded it? My friend Henri would have me believe that my connection with and my love for the subjects was coming through, and as I gazed at their beaming faces, I knew that much was true. But I also realized that Juana and her parents wanted me to see and record their true selves. The photo was a collaboration; they'd given me the gift of themselves.

"I've been going to Lee's psychoanalyst," you said, startling me.

I swallowed the lump in my throat. You were on a first-name basis with Strasberg now. Of course you were. You had a knack for getting onto a first-name basis with everyone within two minutes of meeting them—though, come to think of it, precious few would ever come to call you Norma Jeane.

"My headshrinker is making me go back to the beginning."

I trod lightly. "The beginning of . . ."

"My life. My first memory." You looked at me. "What was yours?"

"Hm. I do remember. I was two years old. I was reaching up to the kitchen table, where my grandmother was ironing, and she swatted me, hard. I was crushed. I steered clear of the mean old lady after that. She died not long afterward. I held that swat against her for years, until I was grown enough to understand that she'd been trying to save me from getting burned."

You smiled crookedly. "Mine is of my grandmother, too."

I waited.

"She was trying to suffocate me with a pillow."

You had to be pulling my leg.

"I still can't bear the smell of old feathers. Now that I have a little pull, I ask for foam rubber pillows wherever I go."

What could I say to that?

You wrinkled that funny little nose with its downward tip. "It's good for me to remember. I can use it for my acting."

What kind of role called for having been smothered by one's grandmother?

"I mean, I can use my anger," you said, watching my face. "I thought what I felt was fear when I remembered it, but Margaret, my headshrinker, says what I was feeling was anger. We're all angry about something." You laughed. "I guess I might be more angry than most."

"You have a right to be."

A few minutes later, you excused yourself to go to the restroom, your second time since we'd gotten to the museum. I wondered if you had an infection. I'd gone back to look at Juana's family when a man said, "I like your work."

I turned around.

A smile lit the man's scarred, narrow face. "Gordon Parks."

"Thanks," I said, blushing. What kind of narcissist stares at her own photo in a collection of hundreds? "I know who you are. I like your work, too."

"I've been following you ever since your Harlem runway-show feature."

"You saw that in *Picture Post*?" He must have thought I was racist. "I promise you, I had nothing to do with the copy. I felt so betrayed."

"I suppose the ladies in the photo did, too."

I covered my face. "I'm appalled. I meant to do those women justice."

"You'd have to ask them, but I thought you did, though I dare you to photograph a famous white woman's ass."

My face was on fire. He was referring to my photo of the model Fabulous, whose backside I'd shot while she was putting on clothes in a wardrobe change. "She was just so impossibly beautiful, a work of art."

He frowned. "Hey, you letting me ruffle your feathers? Come on, now. You've got to be tougher than that."

"Believe me, I know." Gordon Parks must have seen plenty to toughen him. How had he felt when he shot his photos of Black boys and girls repeatedly choosing pale-skinned dolls over dark ones when they were offered by a psychologist, or when he photographed Black children gazing longingly through a fence at a playground at which they weren't allowed? How infuriated he must be to see kids still going through the pain he must have grown up with.

"Did you see this?" He led me to a photo of a Cuban woman propped on her elbows at a bar. I sucked in my breath and looked at the image info: the photo was his. "I know," he said. "You did a photo of a woman in a bar in Cuba just like this. I saw it in *Esquire*."

I laughed. "You and I took the same shot."

We'd taken similar photos before. In addition to his fashion photography, Gordon Parks had done shoots of many of the same subjects as me, from sharecroppers to old women on the street. "I admire your work."

"Of course you do. We're flip sides of the same record. Nice to meet you, Flip."

We shook hands. "A pleasure, Flip."

Is it possible to feel a person's kindness through his palms? It seemed I could feel his. He was one of those rare people with whom I instantly and inexplicably connected. How could I adore someone I'd just met? But I did.

We grinned at each other. "Well, you stay out there, Eve Arnold. And stay mad."

"Who said I was mad?"

"Your photography wouldn't be any good if you weren't."

It was crazy—had we known each other in another, richer life? I didn't want him to walk away, but I didn't know how to keep him.

Zelda Zonk returned from the ladies' room, still in the worn trench coat but sans the black mop. You'd slicked your hair behind your ears, which stuck out a little. Without any makeup, and with those ears, that flat face, and that funny little nose, it was hard to imagine that millions thought you were the most beautiful woman in the world.

"Where's the wig?" I asked.

You opened your purse to reveal what looked like a curled-up Scottie pup. "Itchy." You snapped the clasp closed. You saw my grin. "What is it?"

"I just met a guy who told me I was angry."

"And you're smiling?"

"He told me nicely."

You laughed. "Why are people always telling us we're mad?"

I spread my hands. "Because we're not as serene as we think?"

"I guess not!"

We walked through the room filled with images of children with their parents, you studying the photos while I threw you glances. How were these shots of "the family of man" sitting with someone who never had a family? Oy vey, I wanted to hug you.

**I SAW YOU NEXT A COUPLE WEEKS LATER . . . ON TELEVISION.** Arnold and I were watching Edward R. Murrow's show *Person to*

*Person*, broadcast live from the Greenes' country home in rural Connecticut. You were still living with them—this couple and their son, possibly the first family you ever had.

"He is still schtupping her," Arnold said.

My hand froze knuckle-deep in warm popcorn.

"That Milton Greene is schtupping Marilyn. Look at them. She will not look at him; he will not look at her. Guilty."

"Oh, so you're an expert on who's schtupping whom now?"

But it was horrifying. Amy Greene was doing all the talking—plucky of her, considering that Murrow, live from his studio in New York, hadn't addressed her.

"See how Mr. Greene puts his hand over his wife's? He is saying, 'I am her husband. No fling is going on here.'"

"Shh! I can't hear!"

Mr. Murrow had cut off Amy and asked you a question.

You answered so quietly that I had to strain to hear, and your voice was so meek that I could hardly recognize it. This bland creature, with the droopy hairdo and the plain white open-collar knit shirt, first smiled wanly into one television camera, then into the other, as if never quite figuring out which to use. This was not the spirited person I'd seen at MoMA a couple weeks ago. Were you trying to make yourself look small and dumb to show Amy how harmless you were? Were you sabotaging yourself as a way of atoning before the woman who shared her house, her life, even her baby son, with you, while you slept with her husband?

Amy interrupted Mr. Murrow and jumped up to lead everyone from the kitchen to the den, where she and you curled up with your knees tucked under yourselves, the two of you beautiful bookends, one dark, one light. Greene, for his part, affected a casual slouch on the arm of the sofa behind his wife, occasionally massaging her shoulders.

Amy tried to talk, but Murrow wasn't having it. He asked you about your smallest roles, of all odd questions. You couldn't decide which TV camera to look at when you gave your hesitant answer, and even after settling on a camera, you turned your face this way and that as if giving a still photographer angles. It was clear to me that, accustomed to having the safety net of cuts and retakes when filming a movie, and control over your position in a photographer's studio, you had no idea what to do with yourself on live TV. This did not bode well for someone looking to play Lady Macbeth—or anyone—before unforgiving audiences on Broadway.

Arnold and I watched to the end of the interview. "Wow." He turned off the TV. "They were so guilty."

"Why do you care so much?"

He shrugged. "I am going to bed."

I watched him climb the stairs, the sight of his lanky figure still stirring my heart. Not long ago, he would have asked if I wanted to go to bed then, too, or he would have waited for me to go up with him. We used to be lovers, not old fogies wondering about other people's love lives. Did time, or raising children, or chasing dreams, loosen every couple's bond like this?

*Oh, we're just "old marrieds,"* I told myself. *Embrace this comfortable stage of marriage. It's just a sign of stability.*

# 17

AUGUST CAME TO THE MAGNUM OFFICE, AND WITH IT THE sharp stink of elephant pee oozing through our open window, courtesy of the Central Park Zoo, just around the corner. John Morris had insisted that I go to the annual meeting, and I'd resisted, knowing it would be the usual kvetching about magazines using their own staff photographers and about the poor visual quality of televised news compared with the beauty and art of photojournalism. But there I was, crowded into the space between Morris's desk and the empty fireplace, with its dusty row of Capa's magnums, passing a bottle of Chivas Regal to the guys and ruing not being at the beach with Francis. His nanny spent more time with him than I did.

"Next order of business." John Morris loosened his tie, then raised his voice over the clicking of lighters and the scuffing of wing tips on the gritty linoleum. "This needs no explanation. We're going straight to the vote. All those in favor of admitting Eve Arnold as a full member of Magnum Photos, say 'aye.'"

*Me? Full member? What?*

My dear Henri, in from Paris, reached over and patted my arm. "Aye."

"Aye!" Ernst Haas, Cornell Capa, and Edward Steichen raised hands or drinks.

Over in the corner, the watercooler glugged as Elliott Erwitt filled his pointed paper cup. "Aye!"

Inge Bondi took her hand from her typewriter and waved it over her head. "Aye. And it's about time!"

"The ayes have it." Morris plucked up the empty champagne bottle on his desk and held it aloft like Zeus with a lightning bolt. "The Magnum has spoken. Welcome, Eve."

"I've been waiting for this." Inge rolled back in her chair to take a bottle from the drawer of her desk. After a pop and a hurried wipe at the froth fizzing onto a letter, she distributed warm champagne in paper cups Erwitt brought over. The title was largely ceremonial—pretty much all it meant was that I could now vote for other members—but that my colleagues thought I was their equal meant something to me. I was the first female photographer to be a full member at Magnum.

I was tipsy at midday when I started the trek along the park to the station. Sparrows hopped, cheeping, from their pickings of cigarette butts and peanut shells on the lumpy sidewalk buckled by the roots of venerable elm trees. A mother, young, glowing, and oblivious to the zoo smells, wheeled her baby buggy over the bumpy pavement. We exchanged smiles. At forty-three, I was past the age of having babies . . . likely halfway through my life, I thought idly, with fewer days ahead of me than behind me.

*Wait.*

*Halfway through.*

This life, this waking up each day, this looking out from these eyes, was going to end. This heart, this steadfast tin soldier in my chest, was going to stop marching. This human being, Evie Cohen,

Eve Arnold, Mom, was going to be no more. How had I never fully felt this before?

A small green sports car zipped up to the curb. Gordon Parks leaned toward the passenger window. "Need a ride?"

My surprise turned into a rush of gratitude. "Yes. Please!" I jumped in with the haste of someone grabbing a lifeline.

Still dizzy with drink and my reckoning with mortality, I looked over my shoulder. Light reflectors and camera bags packed the rear seat. He was smiling at me when I glanced back at him. My giddy heart "swarmed up" to him. (Halsman, you dear phony.) "Heading to a shoot?"

"Finished one yesterday. Followed the Italian premier around New York for *Life*." He checked for traffic, then gunned into the stream of vehicles. "You know what he wanted to do most? Go to the top of the Empire State Building! What a crazy shoot." He grinned at me. "How about you, Flip? Staying mad?"

What was it about this man? His voice flowed through me like warm syrup.

"At this particular moment, I guess I shouldn't be too furious. I just got voted in as a full member of Magnum."

"You did?" He took his palm from the stick shift to squeeze my hand. "Congratulations! First woman, right?"

"First woman photographer," I said, my hand glowing. "Inge Bondi insisted on being a full member if they were going to make her give up her photography to run the office." I was about to gripe about how long it had taken me to become a full member when I realized—there were no Black Magnum photographers, full or associate.

He could see my cogs turning. "That's all right, Flip. *Life*'s been good to me."

"The magazine or the thing we live?"

He smiled at me, then changed lanes. "Both."

A taxi driver laid on his horn. Gordon waved in the mirror. "What are you working on?"

I found myself admitting that I was still shooting at the Actors Studio and that I'd had a run on celebrity subjects the last couple of months. I liked to capture them in their element, like James Cagney doing a soft-shoe routine in the barn outside the country home that the former street urchin had always dreamed of owning, or Danny Kaye, a conductor at heart, although he couldn't read music, at the Met, pretending to conduct, using a flyswatter as a baton.

"Not exactly exposé work," I said, suddenly ashamed. The photos weren't exactly *The Falling Soldier* or Gordon's own shot of the little boy choosing the doll that didn't look like him.

"Don't apologize. There's something unseen that needs to be seen in every situation, in every person."

I almost laughed—those could have been my own words. Of course my flip side shared my search for the unseen. But he shouldn't let me off the hook. "Even hammy actors trying to hog the camera?"

"Maybe them most of all. What are they hiding behind their theatrics?" He glanced at me. "Right?"

I nodded, grateful. "Right."

Too soon, we came to Grand Central, where he swerved the car to the curb. "Here we are. Go get 'em, Flip. For us."

My hand on the door handle, I let my eyes meet his. A connection burned between us like fire down a clothesline. I knew he could feel it, too.

I forced myself to open the door. "Stay mad, okay?"

"You, too."

Though it was hard to be mad when my flip side was smiling at me. God, I adored that man.

---

THAT NIGHT, I MANAGED TO FIND SOME SPARKLERS TO CELEbrate my partnership. Francis and I pranced around our backyard, waving the sizzling sticks like drum majors and humming "The Stars and Stripes Forever" while Arnold sat in a lawn chair, sipping a Scotch. Francis was still giddy when I put him to bed; he settled down only when I read a chapter of a Hardy Boys book with him. I went downstairs to Arnold, slumped on the couch with a fresh drink.

I sat next to him. "You okay?"

"Yes. Congrats." Ice clinked in his glass as he took a gulp. He wiped his mouth and glanced at me.

"What's wrong?"

He shook his head.

"No, what?"

His rough, handsome face was a picture of misery. "They turned down my Race to the Moon game."

"Oh no. I'm sorry, Arnold." This was the third game Parker Brothers had rejected since Television Star, nixed soon after Francis and I gave it a run.

He took another drink. "Careers, meanwhile, is selling like gangbusters."

*Selling like hotcakes. Going like gangbusters.* But now was not the time to correct his English. "I'm really sorry, Arnold. Why didn't you tell me earlier?"

"At least one of us is doing well."

"I love you," I said, more as an offering than as a declaration. When he kept staring at the television, I leaned in and gently kissed his neck.

In one swift move, he cupped my head and brought his mouth

to mine, his probing kiss muffling my bleat of surprise. With the TV gabbling in the background, he pushed himself onto me, and after fumbling briefly as I protested, he pulled back.

"You're never in the mood." He stalked upstairs.

I sat up on the couch, unnerved by his clumsy attempt to demand what he wanted from me. While I hadn't for one moment feared for my safety—he'd never hurt me, and he hadn't been rough now, just rude—his pitiful show of dominance saddened me. Didn't he know he'd just made himself look weaker?

I listened until he was done getting ready for bed and had had time to fall asleep before I followed him upstairs. When I finally lay beside him, I was too disturbed to sleep.

I had just drifted off when the phone rang. Next to me, Arnold rolled over. It rang again.

"What time is it?" he groaned.

I got up on an elbow. The Baby Ben read five until four. Only bad calls came at four in the morning.

Last time I talked to my mother, she'd had a deep cough. . . .

My unease burst into fright. I threw on my robe and sailed down the stairs to the dark kitchen, where I snatched up the receiver, my heart thumping. "Hello?"

"Miss Documentary Photographer?"

"Marilyn?"

"Sorry to wake you up."

"It's not even four!"

"I know! I'm sorry. It's awful. But when my alarm went off just now for me to get up and get ready for my flight at ten, I thought, *I need Eve. Get me Eve! Call Eve! Only Eve understands how important this is to me.*"

I sighed loudly. "Oh, Marilyn."

"I wouldn't ask you to go if it was just some dumb movie promo. But it's art! Carleton Smith, the head of the National Council for the Arts—*the National Council for the Arts, Eve!*—wants me, Norma Jeane, to open a museum."

In the dark beyond the screened window, crickets chirped. "What museum?"

"It's in Bement, Illinois. In the Land of Lincoln! It's some kind of celebration of art and Lincoln. And you know how much I love Lincoln."

"I do?"

"Yes! Haven't you noticed all my Lincoln books? I used to dream he was my daddy."

I wasn't sorting this out at four in the morning. "Marilyn, I—"

"And bring your cameras. If you're not ever going to do an appreciation of me, at least you could document me bringing art to the masses. Who knows if I'll ever get a chance to do *that* again?" You laughed.

That you thought you could call me in the middle of the night to come work for you bothered me most. I hadn't thought you could be so selfish. "I'm trying to travel as little as possible these days, for my family's sake."

"Don't worry. I'll have you back by midnight tonight. We're just popping there and back."

"I really shouldn't."

The clock ticked in the still kitchen. A cat screamed in a nearby yard; I flinched.

"Eve, all I am—" You started over. "All I am is just a dirty girl. I need you, someone who's so wise and smart and cool, to help me not to be so darn feral. Please—" Your voice was shy now. "As my only female friend, won't you please go with me?"

"Damn it, Marilyn."

I was making toast when Arnold came thumping down the stairs in his robe. "What is going on?"

We stared at each other. I wanted to talk. I wanted to assure him, without hurting his pride, that I still desired him but that forcing the issue had repelled me. I wanted to ask him what had made him so desperate and angry that he thought he should treat me so crudely, and I wanted to tell him that it made me feel desperate and angry, too. I wanted to ask what was happening to us. I could feel him slipping away from me, and I could feel myself slipping away from him, and I wanted it to stop. But as he stood there in his brown robe, just six feet away, he might as well have been on Jupiter. I didn't know how to start.

My toast popped out of the toaster.

Silently, he handed me the butter dish from the counter.

I should have sat him down and hashed it out, or at least begun the process, in the little time I had. Instead, I took the butter from him and scraped some onto the toast.

"I'm going with Marilyn this morning. In fifteen minutes."

When he said nothing, I added, "We're flying to Illinois, but just for the day. It's some big art show."

He went over to the sink for a glass of water and stood with his back to me.

My voice strained with civility. "I'll try to be back to make dinner. Will you be able to call Elaine to come sit? I would, but it's too early."

"Whatever you say." He drank his water, then went back upstairs.

I finished my quick breakfast and went up to the bedroom, where Arnold lay on his side, under the covers, as I packed. I would not admit what my heart suspected: marriages die one silence at a time.

# 18

OUR PLANE WAS EMPTY SAVE FOR A HANDFUL OF BUSINESSMEN who had unusually tiny bladders, at least judging by the number of trips they made to the bathroom to pass your seat. LaGuardia Airport had been the opposite. The tarmac had teemed with grinning airport workers in coveralls, teenaged boys zooming up on their bicycles, and reporters shouting to get your attention. You'd performed for them all at the base of the stairs to the plane, striking poses in a white cinch-waisted, sleeveless eyelet dress, your personal copy of Carl Sandburg's dictionary-sized biography of Lincoln under your arm.

Now you were sucking your thumbnail as you gazed through the double glass of your airplane window. Your Sandburg tome on Lincoln was opened across your lap, and atop it lay a blank sheet of paper and a pen; you'd yet to write the speech you were to give in a couple hours. Behind us slept Leonardi, commissioned by you to do your hair for the ceremony.

"Can you believe there are so many trees?"

I looked up from the list of ideas for future stories I was making.

My mother had too often decried the crime of putzing away time for me to enjoy sitting idly. I leaned to look past you and out over what must have been Pennsylvania.

"I never saw a forest when I was growing up—not a real one, just the ones in schoolbooks or in the movies. I was never in the woods until I started living with Milton and Amy in Connecticut." You chuckled. "Can you believe it? When I got there in January, I thought all the trees on their property were dead, just a bunch of sticks. Boy, was I surprised when green shoots came out on the branches in the spring!"

"They're good to you, aren't they?"

"Milton and Amy? Yes. Very good."

"And here Arnold thought you were having an affair with Milton. Please, tell me differently."

You switched those blue eyes at me. "He wanted me, really badly, and I wanted to give him something, because he is so good to me." You saw my face. "I told you I was feral! I told you I don't know how to be!"

I sighed. "I don't think that applies here, Marilyn. Knowing not to sleep with someone's husband is just plain human decency. I hope Arnold's secretary doesn't want to hop in bed with him just because he is nice to her." I paused. Where did that come from?

You hunched down into yourself. "You can't imagine all the offers Milton and I are getting. I'm going to make him and Amy rich. Their little Joshie, too. Scripts are pouring in. Good ones—not like the trash Fox was sending me. Tennessee Williams wanted me to be in his new play! He actually wrote it for me."

"Oh, Marilyn."

"Don't you see? I'm going to make it up to Amy and Joshie."

"And what about you? You hurt yourself by doing things that you know are wrong."

"Am I wrong? By trying to be good to someone who's good to me?"

"Isn't Amy good to you?"

You crossed your arms and legs. "I told you how I'm being good to her."

Your pen rolled from the book on your lap and onto the floor. I reached down to get it. "Money isn't everything." I gave you the pen. "What if she'd rather have her husband?"

"I'm not taking him from her! I don't want him! She's got him! I was just trying to do something nice for him."

The stewardess came and offered us coffee. We both turned her down. I tried to get back to my list of feature ideas, the airplane rumbling under my feet.

You said, quietly, "No wonder my father doesn't want anything to do with me. I'm a bad person."

"What?"

"I had a detective find my real father. He lives in Iowa. He wrote back after I sent him a letter. He wants me to leave him alone." You put the collar of your dress in your mouth, then spat it out. "What kind of father would write to his daughter, *No, thank you, I don't want to meet you. I know who you are—you're Marilyn Monroe.* That was all he needed to know. *Good luck and goodbye.*"

You toyed with the little curtains at your window as if ashamed to look at me.

"You're not a bad person, Marilyn."

"You don't have to say that. I know I am."

"You're a good person. You might have made some bad decisions, but we all do."

"You don't."

"The hell I don't."

You didn't push me to explain. You weren't holding me to any standard or making any judgment. You saved that for yourself.

The front of your eyelet dress expanded with your sigh. "Will you forgive me the next time I make a bad decision?"

"What am I, some kind of rabbi?"

"I mean it. Will you?"

"Of course I will."

I didn't know that I would be the one who would need forgiveness.

WE EMERGED FROM THE PLANE TO A ROARING CROWD THAT was bigger and wilder than the one in the morning. This time not just reporters, workers, and teens on bikes showed up, but businessmen, housewives, and the local chapters of fan clubs were on hand. They cheered as television cameras recorded your antics on the plane steps.

"Marilyn, what brings you to Chicago?" a television man called up to you as you posed on the metal stairs.

You raised a red United Airlines umbrella against the sun, then rested it on your shoulder like a geisha. "I'm bringing art to the masses!"

"Like paintings and sculptures?" he said.

"Yes!"

"Miss Monroe, aren't *you* a kind of living sculpture? Like the *Venus de Milo*?"

The old Marilyn would have widened her eyes, then lowered her lashes with a pout, but the new you just laughed. "I prefer to keep my arms, thank you."

The crowd, pressing closer, laughed with you.

"Marilyn," a news photographer called, "what's the craziest thing you've ever done?"

"Well, I rode a pink elephant once. It was for a benefit for the Actors Studio."

"How was that?"

"Oh, the elephant and I got along. We had a lot in common. We were both painted up to look pretty."

So often your jokes were at your expense. The crowd loved it.

"Hey, Marilyn," a reporter shouted, "look over here and lean over." He raised his camera.

Your disgust was quickly replaced by sweetness. "Sir, would you ask your sister to lean over for a picture?"

"My sister don't look like *that.*"

Some people chuckled.

You gave him a friendly smile. "Here's a little advice for the future: Treat all women like they are your sister. If you do, you'll be surprised how many will want you for more than a brother."

A plane roaring down a nearby runway drowned the crowd's happy laughter.

They pressed even closer. I could feel their whipped-up energy as the police escorted us into the airport terminal, where you and I headed for the shelter of the ladies' room. The crowd pushed to follow you in. I turned, all five foot zero of me, against a revved-up horde.

With you gone, they seemed to be surprised to find themselves clamoring at the ladies' room door. They seemed as amazed at their altered selves as Odysseus's men were when Circe broke her spell and they were transformed from pigs back into men. They receded, subdued. I swung into the lavatory to check on you.

You were at the mirror, with your back to me, your hands up, ratting your heat-tattered hair, your dress hiked up to your thighs. Under the bunched white eyelet, the gams of the world's most famous sex siren were endearingly short and chubby. And this small, plain woman thought she could take on lions.

I swung my camera up.

Under your raised arms, you watched me in the mirror. I

tensed, my finger on the shutter button, ready for you to pull your clothes down and transform yourself from a guttersnipe into a princess in your uncanny way.

But you didn't. Your gaze trailed back to the reflection of the plain, pudgy girl, the gritty orphan fixing her hair. There was no pretense here, no game; there was just trust. This was you, Norma Jeane, making a present of your inner self for my camera.

I found that my heart was pounding.

*Oop!*

I lowered my camera, and you switched your gaze to me.

I felt the absence of my camera between us. I never realized how much I'd grown used to letting it put me at a remove from my subjects. You—your real you—kept watching me until I got the nerve to meet your eyes fully, human to human.

Your gaze was at once tremulous and defiant. I knew how you felt. It is a frightening thing to let your true self out.

A toilet flushed. A woman came out of a stall and, ducking her head with a giddy smile, sidled up to the sink next to you. You smiled at her, then, with a glance at me, busied yourself with your hair.

I raised my camera, focused, and, wishing you back again, shot.

YOUR DRESS WAS FIRMLY BACK IN PLACE AND YOU WERE MARILYN again, and fully in charge as you strutted from the airport to the waiting plane in which we made the short hop to Champaign. There you were handed over to the local mayor, who perched you upon the back of a Cadillac convertible the glistening red of a candy apple. I plunked myself and my camera bags on the white leather seat below you, and with the governor's own motorcycle escort revving their engines on either side, our car rumbled onto the road and through a sea of green, green fields.

"Come here, you." You pulled me up next to you, on the seat-back, where the wind from the car's motion pummeled us. The air smelled sugary with ripening corn, and of warm dirt and Chanel No. 5.

"Wave."

You meant for me to wave to the men, women, and jumping-up-and-down children lining the fields along the road, but all I could do was marvel at you. With your white mop ruffling as you leaned back on your hands, you made being a goddess look so easy, so fun, so cool—literally, on that hot and sticky afternoon.

A half hour passed in this way, with waving people standing shoulder to shoulder along the highway, before we came to a cross-road studded with three white houses and a church, and a row of brick storefronts just beyond. When we stopped, the mob surged forward. Half the state must have been there.

A portly man dressed in a top hat strutted through the crowd. "Welcome to Lincoln Days!" He stroked the black beard spilling onto his shirtfront. "Dick Meyer, mayor. Thank you for joining us in the great town of Bement!"

"Thank you." You looked around as if for the museum. The storefronts, the single gas station with its two glass-topped pumps, and the clapboard houses with T-shirts and bloomers hanging from clotheslines held no clue as to where this art trove might be. Many of the men wore black beards and top hats. I'd heard of the Amish—were these them?

"Would you like to go to my house to gussy up?" Mayor Meyer asked. "It's two o'clock. The wife's made you some refreshments to tide you over until the ceremony, at five."

You perked up at the word "ceremony." "That sounds lovely."

"Potluck's at six. Do you like cherry pie?"

"I do."

"Then you're in luck. Bement women make the best cherry pie in the country."

"How long would you like me to speak?" You and I had finished writing your speech on the plane.

He seemed surprised. "Oh, for as long as you like."

We returned to the car. Mayor Meyer marched down the street, with our Cadi lumbering after him. He led us to his home, a white-columned clapboard affair, where his wife, a thin woman with much hair heaped high upon her head, ushered us inside and to a downstairs bedroom from which she seemed reluctant to leave. After comments about your hair and clothes and movies, she finally backed her way out, gripping her string of pearls.

You dropped onto a flowered armchair. "Whew!"

I went to a window and pulled down a V in the closed aluminum blinds. Women in cotton print dresses, little boys in striped shirts and shorts, and little girls in Sunday crinolines milled among the menfolk in the yard. All the men were in top hats and black beards, some real, most false—their nod to Lincoln, I realized. I let the blinds ping closed.

You slumped back, knock-kneed, on the chair. "This is nuts!"

"Understatement." When I brought my camera to my eye, you threw your arms out as if shot, then chortled like a girl as I photographed your amusement. You were playing with me and I was in on the game—we were two kids who'd gotten a new camera. I felt young and goofy and clever.

We romped until I ran out of film. "Shit! Let me reload."

But by the time the camera was ready, you were flat on your back on the bed, with your hand to your belly.

"Are you okay?"

You rubbed your stomach through your eyelet dress. "It's just my condition. I have endometriosis."

"You do? I'm sorry. What is that?"

"You don't want it! All this crazy tissue grows between your organs." You winced. "It gives me terrible cramps."

"What can I get you?"

"Nothing. I forgot my pills." You lolled your head to look around the room, then pitched yourself up, snatched a bunch of grapes from a fruit bowl left by the bed, and fell back down. You started eating them.

I sat next to you. "Here." I took the bunch from your hand. "Goddesses don't feed themselves their own grapes."

I put one to your lips. You put out your tongue, then rolled the grape into your mouth.

I gave you another.

"This is dumb," you protested.

"Yeah, it is. Shut up and eat."

You obeyed, then closed your eyes and laid your arm over your head. "Keep shooting," you murmured. "This is me, too."

Suffering had stripped your face of any pretense. You were allowing me to see you completely vulnerable.

Now I knew why Henri said *oop*. When someone chooses to share their innermost self with you, it knocks the wind right out of you.

I fitted my camera to my face.

"Eve," you whispered as I shot.

"What?"

"Thank you."

It felt awkward, and yet right: "Norma Jeane?"

But you didn't answer. You had drifted off before I could return the thanks.

---

WHEN YOU WOKE, I WENT DOWN TO FIND LEONARDI, THEN photographed you coming to life under his hands, becoming more firmly Marilyn Monroe with every brushstroke . . . until you winked at me and laughed for my camera. I was now an official Merry Marilyn Maker, too.

When you went outside, bearded men solemnly led you down the street like a virgin to sacrifice. Inside the sweltering little courthouse, more bearded men parted for you to process until you came to a bronze bust of Lincoln on a pedestal. Near it, on another pedestal, was a squat, gritty sculpture of a human hacked out of rough rock—some kind of ancient fertility god? A cornstalk had been stuck between its thick stone hands as if to give it an agrarian theme. It dawned on me: This weird little display was the exhibit. The complete exhibit. This was the art you were to bless for the masses.

Mayor Meyer took off his hat, his hair stuck to his head with sweat. His droning rose to the plain wooden rafters: "Thank you for honoring us—and Abraham Lincoln—today, Miss Monroe. Would you like to say a few words?"

Your understanding that this was not a museum, this was not an exhibition, this was not even art, flashed through those cornflower blues. For one microsecond the corners of your mouth lowered. You'd been duped.

The beards, the art, the audacity—I couldn't help it: a laugh popped out. I hurriedly stuffed it back, but when you glanced at me, I heaved with stifled laughter.

You bit your lip, looked away, and then, your white eyelet bosom shaking, you burst out laughing.

The town fathers exchanged frowns.

You smiled fondly at those men in spite of their rotten little con, then gave your speech graciously, sincerely. Such hearty applause went up in that small, hot space that it hurt my ears.

Afterward, you were delivered to the grounds of a church where tables laden with cheese-topped casseroles, Jell-O salads, and pies awaited under banners for Lincoln Days. Without even a plate in your hands to shield you, you allowed grandmas, pigtailed girls, and mothers toting babies wearing only diapers to crowd around. I snapped away on my Nikon as you shook each of their hands and genuinely listened to them, even the babies.

As gathering clouds blocked out the sun, the Bementers grew more demanding, shoving and grabbing at you like starving people breaking a breadline. You were holding a toddler away from a surge of hairy men demanding autographs when we were separated. A stooped older gentleman in a top hat and faded overalls receded from the fray with me. He spied my camera.

"You know Marilyn?"

"I came with her from New York."

He chuckled as he drew an envelope and pencil stub from his bib pocket. "Bet you're glad to get out of there! Could you sign this?"

"Sign it?" Me?

"Just say 'Marilyn Monroe's friend.'" He pulled down his false beard to mop the sweat underneath as he watched me write.

THE CLOUDS THAT HAD BEEN GATHERING BECAME A DARK greenish purple. A sudden gust lifted top hats from the heads of farmers, and a long, lazy crackle of thunder sent women whisking their gouged-out casseroles and Jell-O creations from the tables and to the shelter of the church porch. An elderly woman, her apron and flowered dress hem wild in the growing wind, led you into the church as quickly as her black brogans would allow her.

As I gazed at the weekly attendance and offering totals reported in movable numerals on the wall, Mayor Meyer announced that the plane at the Champaign airport was too small to fly over the storm. You, he said, his glee hardly suppressed, would have to spend the night. His house was ready and available.

After you'd given these people your all, even as they trampled you, fear blazed through your eyes for the first time that day. You'd played your part. You'd given them what they'd come for, and you'd keep giving it as long as they were in front of you, though you were desperately weary and ill. You didn't know how to disconnect any more than you knew how to be on time.

I knew what I had to do.

I took your arm and, in my toughest Jane voice, growled, "Come on, kid."

I asked the sheriff, who'd been looking on, twiddling his brown tie, if he could take us to his office. There, I got on the horn and called the Chicago airport. As I worked my way through different airlines, you slumped on a bench and clutched your hair in a topknot, the sheriff and his deputy smirking down at you, waiting for you to perform. You looked up at me from under your arms as if to say, *See what it's like?*

Oh, I did.

I chinned the phone and whipped my camera to my eye. *Oop.*

I found a plane from Los Angeles that was stopping to refuel in Chicago before going on to New York, leaving in two hours. One more call, to strong-arm the governor into letting his motorcycle escort clear our way to Chicago—I wasn't taking no for an answer because you were so ill—and we were huddled in the buttoned-down red Cadillac, the rain drumming on the canvas stretched over our heads, the windshield wipers slapping. The temperature had fallen a good thirty-five degrees. The heat blasting from up front was no match for it. I wondered how Leonardi was doing in the car that followed us.

Your reserves gone, you withdrew into yourself, a sick young woman with tangled bleached hair. I took off my cardigan and swaddled you.

You scooted into me, then settled your head upon my shoulder. "Thank you, Mother."

Anger flared up in me. How could your real mother never have cared for you? She'd almost destroyed you. No one deserved that.

At the airport, we ran through the rain to our plane, then bounded up the steps, entered, and dropped, soaked, onto our seats.

I looked around in the dark. The craft was full of Angelenos sleeping as if a spell had been put over them. Even before the plane bucked and shuddered its way above the rain and lightning, you were sleeping, too, your head leaning against mine. I felt its weight, and the weight of your neediness, and my responsibility to you. I thought I could protect you. But I hadn't counted on your worst enemy.

# 19

TWO WEEKS HAD PASSED SINCE WE COMMUNED WITH THE LINcoln lovers of Bement, an eternity when *Life* was signaling that they were interested in the photos. I needed the career boost, and my family needed the moola—Arnold had not yet struck the mother lode (he'd actually called one of his board game ideas Gold Rush)—but I'd promised you that you could okay the shots before I submitted them. They were pure Norma Jeane, not a hint of Marilyn in sight, and I wanted to make sure you could handle being seen like that.

Just . . . I didn't realize that you were going to leave the Greenes' as soon as we got back. I didn't know you'd then spend the next couple weeks shopping for and furnishing a new apartment. You claiming your independence was great, but couldn't you have at least taken the time to tell me yourself that you'd decided to strike out on your own? You had your new secretary, May Reis, take my calls. I don't mean to be a baby, but my feelings were hurt. I would have liked to have cheered you on.

Now this Miss Reis—a cheery middle-aged woman about my

size, with short, flat hair, and chipmunk cheeks—let me into your apartment in the Waldorf Towers. She went to fetch you, leaving me to sink into your plush white sofa and gaze at the books that crowded the shelves by the fireplace, and at the pale green orchids gracing the coffee table. You'd moved up in the world since I'd first visited you at the Waldorf for the *Ciné Revue* interview.

"Miss Documentary Photographer!" You came out in Keds and black Jax slacks, glowing as if lit from within.

You were awfully happy. It was infectious. "Hello, Miss Most Advertised!" I opened my briefcase to show you the prints.

"Can that wait?"

My hands froze on the latches. If there was one thing you loved, it was your photos, and you knew *Life* was interested in them. At least, I'd told Miss Reis that they were.

You saw my face, then lowered yourself to the couch.

I watched as you went through the prints. These were good, maybe my best work of showing someone heretofore unseen. Here you were, knock-kneed and laughing after you'd thrown yourself into the chair. There you were, holding your hair up in a topknot and looking bug-eyed at me to save you as the sheriff and his deputy hovered over you. Look at you touching a grape to your mouth, or contemplating the lone bust of Lincoln, or holding hands with an elderly woman at the potluck. All were imperfect compositions, many off-center or dully lit, but when I'd worried about the composition of my photos early on at Magnum, my dear Henri told me, "Do not look for the perfect composition, *chérie.* Nature is not perfectly composed; truth is not perfectly composed. Composition is not what makes them beautiful."

You stopped at the photo of yourself in the restroom at the airport, where you were peeking past your raised arm at me in the mirror, your dress hiked up on your thighs. Your face was in the far upper-left corner of the print. Yes, it was a wretched composition, but your face, in that little corner of the photograph, was riveting in its honesty. You'd found me behind the lens and given me you.

Softly, you said, "Is this how I look?"

I could not help but be moved. I nodded.

Almost shyly, you said, "Am I—am I even pretty?"

You . . . weren't. "You're so much more than that."

You looked at me as if wondering what I might mean.

"I think it's time we shoot that 'appreciation' you wanted me to do. It's time we show people Norma Jeane."

You bit your lip. "Really?"

The phone rang. We both jumped.

You were on alert as May Reis answered, then called you to the phone. You ran back to the bedroom to answer. When you came dancing out a few minutes later, you were all charged up.

"Come with me to Brooklyn!"

"Brooklyn!" I knew you'd told Dave Garroway, on his radio show, that you wanted to retire to Brooklyn, a pronouncement that made him and everyone else laugh. Brooklyn was a lot of things, but Palm Beach it wasn't.

"Why are we going to Brooklyn?" I asked as you threw on a wrinkled white polo coat.

"Because you're my best friend."

Those words took me by surprise.

"Your shoes don't look comfy." You frowned at my business heels. Before I could respond, you went back to your bedroom and returned with a pair of white Keds like the pair you wore.

"There. That's better," you said when I put them on. You stood back and clapped your hands. "We're twins!"

I was going to scoff at that—no two people looked less like twins—when I saw the affection in your grin. Maybe running cold and hot, freezing me out on one day and dressing me like yourself on another, was your feral girl's idea of friendship. It was going to take some getting used to.

"I guess we are."

"So, you'll go with me to Brooklyn?"

"Now that I'm properly shod, I suppose I have to."

Thus, it was decided: like the red and green subway lines, I was Brooklyn bound.

My too-large tennis shoes caught on the doorframe as I climbed into the cab that your doorman had hailed. Soon we were looking out over the East River through the cables of the Brooklyn Bridge. "Did you know that there's an air-raid shelter under the bridge?" you said. "One of the hollow support caissons is stocked with emergency items in case of nuclear war."

"Really?"

"That's what I've been told."

"By whom?"

You asked the driver to take us to a neighborhood not far off the ramp from the bridge. We got out on a street of brownstones, many of them made cheery with window boxes of red geraniums. We strolled down a tree-shaded sidewalk.

"This is a ginkgo." You smiled to yourself as you touched a fan-shaped leaf, then tapped the peeling bark of the next tree as women wearing white gloves and men sporting summer panamas passed. "This is a sycamore. Some people call them plane trees."

"Thanks, Teacher."

You chuckled. "Did you know that Brooklyn Heights was the first official neighborhood in America?"

"All these facts already! Why the tour?" I read the sign when we came to a corner: WILLOW STREET. "Am I supposed to be looking for something?"

Just then, down the grand stone steps of one of the largest

homes, tripped a waiflike boy whose glasses looked heavier than he was.

"Marilyn!" he cried in his whiny drawl. "Marilyn! Marilyn!"

No one gave us a second look. Apparently, people in the first neighborhood in America cared more for their geraniums than for movie stars.

"Walk fast," you whispered. "We'll never get rid of him."

We rushed down two blocks—a person can really move in Keds, even big ones—before he caught up and started walking backward in front of us. "Marilyn, didn't you hear me?"

He saw my camera, then wiped his hand on his striped short-sleeved button-down before holding it out to me. "Truman Capote. You've probably heard of me." He dropped my hand before I could tell him my name. "Marilyn, what are you doing here?"

"What are *you* doing here?" you asked back.

"I live here!" He swiveled his thumb in the direction of the mansion from which he'd sailed. "That's my place—didn't you see it? Let's go back. I'll get you something to drink."

You glanced at the house in front of which he'd caught us.

He followed your sights. "Arthur Miller lives there. You know him?"

"No." You were a terrible liar.

Something was going on with you.

He took you by the hand and, with you glancing over your shoulder, led you back to his manse. Inside, he showed us the many rooms while telling us long-winded stories about his antiques and the guests he'd had there. He eventually took us to the open-air veranda out back, where a massive wisteria vine was shedding papery pods onto the planks of the floor. He took a wicker peacock chair and, jiggling his foot in its black-and-white saddle shoe, began to expound about the challenges of being a writer.

"Each story presents its own technical problems," he said in his strangled voice. "Obviously, one can't generalize about them on a 'two times two equals four' basis. Finding the right form for your story is simply to realize the most *natural* way of telling the story. The test of whether or not a writer has divined the natural shape of his story is just this: After reading it, can you imagine it differently, or does it silence your imagination and seem to you absolute and final?"

You stared through the wisteria vine like a prisoner planning an escape. He saw that you weren't paying attention.

"What did you think of the *Times* review of *The Seven Year Itch*?"

You blinked to attention.

"That stuck-up Bosley Crowther," he whined. "What a little bitch!" He quoted the review from that July. "'Thus it is that the undisguised performance of Miss Monroe, while it may lack depth, gives the show a caloric content that will not lose her any faithful fans. We merely commend her diligence when we say it leaves much—very much—to be desired.'" He shrugged. "I have a photographic memory."

"I don't want to talk about it," you said.

"He is wrong, wrong, wrong. You created that role for laughs. There's an art to being funny! One has to play the joke through. One can't pause for the laugh, or act like one knows one's being funny. That takes work!" He wagged his large head on its tulip-stem neck. "I know you, Marilyn. You're a serious girl. You make people believe that you're someone you're not, and that takes lots and lots of work. Do you think Jayne Mansfield knows how to do that?"

I knew the actress Truman meant; Hollywood had made damn well sure everyone knew her. Sheree North was not exactly catching fire, so Fox had come out with another replacement for you since you'd left the studio: Jayne Mansfield, who Fox was billing as the "King-sized Marilyn," based on her 44-18-36-inch statistics. Mansfield, for her part, was running with it, gleefully amplifying Old Marilyn's white hair, breathy speech, and Jell-O-y tush.

"You are the most famous woman in the world," he said, "and no one—not Jayne Mansfield, not Bosley Crowther, not your studio—can take that from you. Everyone, everywhere, knows you. I bet that even in the jungles of New Guinea—"

Leaving me jangling, you jumped up from the porch swing upon which we were sitting. "I have an urge for ice cream."

Truman hopped to his feet. "Let me look. I might have some."

You pulled me out of my seat when he'd scampered out. "Let's go. Truman's bluffing. This isn't even his house. He rents the basement apartment."

I wondered how you knew that.

He came trotting back. "No ice cream. Sorry."

"That's all right." We started for the back stairs.

"Where are you going?" he cried.

You seemed to consider lying but knew it was no use. "Schrafft's."

That was news to me.

"Oh! I'm coming with you. I know just where it is. Only two blocks away."

You were down the back steps, out the iron gate, and back on the sidewalk of Willow Street. And so were Truman and I.

He tugged me along to keep abreast of you. "Did *you* bring money? Marilyn never has any. She's like the queen of England. Someone follows her with a purse full of farthings. I know this," he said, letting go of me to wag his finger at you, "from when she took me out for champagne at the Stork Club and then made me pay."

"*You* took *me*!" you said, gazing up at Arthur Miller's house as we passed it.

Truman was nearly skipping alongside you. "I'm writing the

most perfect story. It's going to be a huge hit." His last book, published years before, was more famous for the controversial photo of him coiling suggestively on the back cover than for his writing. "You're in it."

"Me?" You didn't slow down.

"It's about a call girl who window-shops at Tiffany's when she goes home in the morning after her dates. She lives by socializing with wealthy men, who take her to clubs and restaurants and give her money and expensive presents. She's what you might call an American geisha."

You stopped. "That's not funny, Truman."

White lashes fluttered behind thick lenses. "But—she's adorable! I want you to play her when it goes onstage—or to film."

"I'm not a geisha! Your story is not about me."

"Okay! Okay! It's not."

"Everything I have, I've gotten myself."

"Okay!" he cried again.

We entered the lunchtime bustle of Schrafft's, with its whiff of spoiled milk, sugar, and egg salad on toast. At our booth, you were distant, unaware of the waitress who was cocking her head as if to decide whether this nervous woman in tennis shoes and a rumpled polo coat really was Marilyn Monroe. Truman was asking me if I knew the *marvelous* photographer Richard Avedon—I really *ought* to study him if I wanted to become famous—when you stiffened.

I followed your gaze to the entrance, to a lanky man whose denim work shirt hung from his broad shoulders.

"Look who's here! Arthur Miller!" Truman jumped up to go over to talk to him.

"Please get Truman out of here," you whispered across the table. "He's got the biggest mouth in New York."

"Why? What are you worried he'll say?"

You shook your head.

"Where do I take him, if I've got to take him? Though I don't know why I'm doing this." I could be home with Francis. This was ridiculous.

"Anywhere. Back to his house. I'll come meet you. Just give me a few minutes. I'll be there, I promise." You made prayer hands at me, as wistfully as a little girl hopeful of getting a pony. "Please?"

As one little girl who never got a pony to another, I softened. "Just hurry, okay?"

You hopped up and kissed my cheek. "Thank you."

When Truman came back to the table, I asked him if he wanted me to take photos of him at home.

"She's had photographs in *Life*," you said.

"You didn't tell me that!" The big, nodding bloom of his head bobbed on his tulip-stalk neck. "Say, what's your name again?"

I told him. You added, "She's with Magnum."

His eyes enlarged behind his glasses. "The agency? You should have told me. Are you coming, Marilyn?"

"I'll catch up."

We left. Over my shoulder, I saw you go to where Arthur Miller was seated, then sink down across from him. Your coat, your sunglasses, could not contain your glow.

I didn't know it then, but you were already morphing into your next identity.

This one would cost you.

# 20

YOU HAD TO BE QUIET ABOUT YOUR AMOUR AT FIRST. ARTHUR'S wife didn't know about your affair when you met him in Brooklyn that time with me, though he was adamant that his marriage was over and she *should have* known. Eventually, she found out. Wives always do, sooner or later. She threw him out; she was better off now, Arthur said. You needed to believe him. You loved him.

I'd never seen you as happy as you were during those dog days of '55. From the pebbly beaches of the North Shore to where the earth petered into the sea at Montauk, you and Arthur joyrode around Long Island in your black Thunderbird. I, half pal, half documentarian, followed with Hedda and Norm Rosten in their car. Francis was at summer camp; Arnold was staying at a friend's place in the city, "doodling on a book idea" (his words) when he wasn't working. I was surprised that Arnold chose to miss this chance to rub elbows with the famous—our jolly circle did picnic with Elia Kazan and drink with Jackson Pollock—but I was too involved with you to question him. I was on the watch for an angle to shoot your "appreciation," though, shockingly, you constantly put me off. *We'll do it soon*, you promised, but you were so busy with Arthur now. Meanwhile, though Milton Greene still owned 49 percent of Marilyn Monroe Productions, he and Amy had fallen away entirely. Arthur, you said, didn't like them.

"Arthur understands me," you explained to me on one of those heady evenings. He and the Rostens were back at Norm and Hedda's house, cooking lobster with "Gadg" Kazan, who was restored to Arthur's good graces now that Arthur had won you. You and I were walking the pebbly seashore not far from my home, you in a tiny black-and-white checkerboard halter top and no makeup, and me cradling my Nikon to my chest. I snapped the occasional shot of you, although you rarely acknowledged my camera. Neither your heart nor your head was in our collaboration, nor had they been since your affair had flamed into seriousness. The resulting shots were unsurprisingly soulless. A fan with a Polaroid Land camera could have made them.

"He's so tender and kind," you were saying, "and oh, how I love his mind. He's a genius, you know." Your eyes, sans makeup, were bright blue beneath your windblown hair. "He loves me. He really, really loves me."

How could I begrudge a friend so sorely in need of love? Although I felt sorry for Arthur's wife and kids.

You picked up a flat stone, then flung it with a flop of your hair. It skipped across the quiet water three times before it sank. "Don't you think he looks like Abe Lincoln?"

"Arthur?"

You nodded, hair bouncing.

"Looks like Lincoln?" I chuckled. "I guess so."

"When I was a girl, I used to pretend that Lincoln was my father."

Yes, you'd said. "Did he and Gable drive around together?"

But you weren't laughing. "When I'd lie alone in my little bed after the dad or a friend of my foster family had come in and made me do things, and then I couldn't go back to sleep, I pictured dear Mr. Lincoln telling me a story."

I stared at you. Were you saying what I thought you were saying?

You found another flat pebble. "Mr. Lincoln was so kind." You sent it hopping. "Don't you think he looks kind in his photos?"

I forced myself to think of Lincoln's portraits and not your mistreatment. "Lincoln always looked sad to me. He suffered. Greatly. Not only did he take the deaths of the fallen personally, but he lost his favorite son— Norma Jeane, did somebody molest you?"

You picked up another stone, then turned your face to me. Your tough-girl façade had dropped away. You looked young and defensive. "Yes."

My rage flared. What kind of abominable person would take advantage of an abandoned child? I would kill him. "Who was this monster?"

"It's been twenty years."

"I don't care. You need to report him."

"*Them.* Report *them.*"

"There's more than one?"

You nodded.

"Oh my god. Then report *them*! Report every despicable one!"

"Why? So that they can deny it and I'll look like a nut who makes things up? Why do you think I was in so many foster homes?"

It hurt to breathe. I grasped for your hand. "Oh, Norma Jeane."

You slid from my reach. "It's okay. Just—" You took a ragged breath. "Just ... thank you for believing me. No one ever does."

"What about Arthur? What's he say?"

"I don't want him to think less of me."

"You haven't told him?"

"And I never will." You tugged at the bottom of your checkered knit halter and frowned. "Anyway, it wasn't all bad."

"'Wasn't all bad'!"

You curled into yourself as if to ward off my ill judgment. "It seemed to make the men so happy. Oh, my body didn't feel good. My body hurt. But it felt good to be special to somebody." Your eyes beseeched me to understand. "I had a power. My only power."

A shout made us turn. Arthur was stalking around the base of a cliff. "Girls!" he yelled, waving his arms. "Cocktails are ready. Come back!"

"Don't tell him, Eve. Promise! You cannot tell him. He'll think I'm a slut, and I cannot lose him."

He didn't deserve you. Oh, my poor child. I blew out a breath. "Okay."

"And, Eve, please don't call me Norma Jeane around him. He doesn't like it."

You ran for him. He caught you, swept you from your feet, and swung you around. "How's my little baby?"

A MONTH LATER, WE WERE AT THE PREMIERE OF *WILL SUCCESS Spoil Rock Hunter?* You'd been invited by the playwright, your *dear* friend George Axelrod, who'd written your career rocket *The Seven Year Itch* . . . the guy who thought all women ever yearned for was to be "loved and needed and wanted," with no complex thoughts in their pretty little heads. It was a rare night out in the public eye during those halcyon days of your affair, and you'd posed happily on the red carpet with Arthur as he stared threateningly at the photographers. You knew the play was to star your "king-sized" imitator, Jayne Mansfield. You'd told me so when you called to see if I was going—and I was, with the Rostens, since Arnold had said he didn't feel well and told me to go on without him. If you had any misgivings, you wouldn't say so. You were going to go to support your friend Georgie. I was learning that you'd walk across the bed of coals in the Hawaiian Room for someone you thought was good to you.

The play started. I watched in horror as Jayne Mansfield wiggled across the stage, her voice, her hair, her mannerisms, obviously lampooning yours, her speeches blatant spoofs of your real-life comments. I blushed when Mansfield repeatedly cooed her motto, "You do something for me, I'll do something for you." Had you told Axelrod the same line you'd once used with me—a line I now realized you must use with everyone, to get them on your side—and was he now publicly mocking you with it?

From my seat two rows behind and to the left of you, I could see people leaning to look at you. You hid your face in Arthur's shoulder.

We went to Sardi's afterward, escaping the main dining hall, with its famous caricatures of the stars covering the walls, for a private room upstairs. You and Arthur included me, the Rostens, Milton Berle, and Berle's vivacious wife at your table, all of us merry and bright to make up for your silence.

Suddenly, Hedda, her owl's face fierce, said, "Imitation is the sincerest form of flattery."

You smiled stiffly.

Arthur shook you by your shoulders, like a dad cajoling a son who'd just caused the loss of a Little League game. "Don't worry, Hedda," he growled in his Brooklyn accent, tilting his head down to look you in the eye. "Marilyn can handle it. She's got other fish to fry. Did she tell you that we're in talks with Laurence Olivier?"

"No!" Hedda cried. "Fantastic! Marilyn, you must be so proud."

Arthur let go of you to address the rest of us. "Olivier's full of himself, but we'll bring him around to our terms. Marilyn's a good little businesswoman. Who needs Milton Greene? She's reeling Larry in all on her own."

"Milton helped me," you protested.

"No. It was all you, kid."

"But Milton really was good to me. He believed that I could beat the studio, and he put all his money behind me. He mortgaged his house for me."

Arthur blew a raspberry. "Riding your coattails."

"Laurence Olivier!" Milton Berle's wife exclaimed. "Why, he's the most respected actor in the world! What's it like wheeling and dealing with God, Marilyn?"

"Aw, she's a master at it." Arthur knocked against you. "Aren't you, kid? She hardly needs me at all."

"I'm trying," you said quietly. "I really am."

"My girl's going to run circles around Olivier," he said. "Wait and see. She's my champ."

The next day, you resumed your sessions at the Actors Studio as if your life depended on them. Maybe you thought it did.

# 21

SEVERAL WEEKS LATER, YOU INVITED ME TO A SESSION AT THE Actors Studio, where you were scheduled to perform a scene. I was busy arranging a shoot of the faith healer Oral Roberts in Oklahoma, and I had lots of details to tie up—though at least Arnold had volunteered to make the arrangements with our nanny. But you sounded so nervous that I went.

Hunched and miserable at the front of the little auditorium, you were a mess. Marie Antoinette could not have looked more terrified while being carted to the guillotine. With the appearance of Maureen Stapleton, with whom you'd been practicing daily, you unfroze enough to run and hug her so long that she had to unpeel you. The other students, already dug in on the risers, watched the pair of you with unsympathetic eyes.

The bespectacled elf himself, Lee Strasberg, appeared next to you. "Ready to do your scene?" he said solicitously.

"I can't," you whispered.

When I'd arrived to pick you up at your new Sutton Place apartment, Arthur pulled me aside while you were getting ready.

"She couldn't sleep all night, yet she wouldn't take the Seconal her psychiatrist prescribed her." His Brooklynese was always heavier when he was agitated. "She said it would make her dull. Some headshrinker Dr. Hohenberg is. She makes Marilyn dredge up her childhood five days a week, thinking it'll fix her, and Marilyn goes for it because *Lee*"—he snarled the name—"says it will make her a great actress. Well, all it's doing is making me and her miserable."

And now miserable you were indeed, even when Miss Stapleton stroked your hand and talked to you as if you were a child about to enter the classroom of a new school. "Sweetie, we've got to go on now," she crooned, leading you to your place offstage. She continued to pet your hand as Lee Strasberg announced the scene you'd be playing, from *Anna Christie.*

I wasn't the only one holding their breath. Even though the actors surrounding me grimly readied themselves to find proof of your incompetence, they were holding theirs, too. It's hard to see someone readying to self-immolate.

You slouched onstage as Anna Christie. You dropped at a table, and then Maureen Stapleton, playing aging barfly Marthy Owen, guzzled a pretend beer, swiped her mouth, and sidled over to you.

Before our eyes, you became the brittle and broken Anna. Fury progressively corroded your Anna's steely demeanor as she lashed out at her father for abandoning her when she was two, then at her male relatives who abused her after her mother died, and at the men who rode her body in the only work she could find. With each admission, your Anna retreated into her wrecked shell, but within that tattered ruin, a fragile hope flickered. She wanted to believe that her father might still love her.

I felt ill. Why did you do this to yourself? Why did you take a role that cut so close to your bones?

"If my old man doesn't help me"—your Anna swayed her head, a chained elephant prodded by captors—"it's back to men. It's all men. Men all the time." Your Anna stopped, as if remembering the horrors she'd come from and knowing what going back would do to her. But her father's rejection would give her no choice. "I'll clear out and go back to the old job in St. Paul."

Your Anna stared into her unbearable future.

An awed silence rang out, and then—your fellow actors leaped to their feet. Against the express house rule never to applaud for a class performance, they banged their hands together, then banged them together some more. *What a performance!* they cried.

But it wasn't a performance, was it? It was you ripping open your deepest wounds, wounds you'd spent a lifetime stitching up. You were ripping them open and letting them gape for your peers' approval.

You didn't speak during your classmates' critiques, all of them glowing. Afterward, as the others shuffled out, Lee Strasberg hugged you. "You're a great new talent, Marilyn."

You burst into tears.

He must have thought they were tears of joy. "You're going to be the biggest actress of our times. Lady Macbeth, Cleopatra . . . You name your role, you name the stage—you can do it." He beamed at you, his prize student.

You didn't speak until we were in a cab, heading home. We were sitting in our capsule of exhaust fumes as it passed St. Patrick's Cathedral when you said, "I spilled my guts in front of people who wanted me to fail. With no retakes! With not even a *chance* of a retake."

"I know. You were astonishing."

You flashed me a glare.

"Don't worry, Norma Jeane. I hear all the greats have stage fright. They get over it."

"There was no do-over, no revising, nothing to do but bleed while they just sat and judged me." You hit the seat with your fist. "I am *never ever* doing that again."

Offers for roles on the stage and on television were still pouring in for you. Magazines and newspapers were full of your plans to do a TV production of *Rain* and an Elia Kazan play on Broadway—once you'd finished filming *Bus Stop* out West and your proposed movie with Olivier in England. Your New Marilyn was getting you everything you'd ever wanted.

"Sure you will."

Your glance had the disdainful fury of a starlet who'd just been let out of the office of a producer who had just defiled her. "Like hell."

AFTER I RETURNED FROM PHOTOGRAPHING THE FAITH HEALER in Oklahoma several weeks later, you called asking me to go with you and Arthur—it was always you and Arthur then—to James Beard's new ice-cream parlor. Mid-November seemed an odd time to open an ice-cream shop in Manhattan, but that didn't stop the cookbook author from opening Maxfield's; and you, his loyal friend, from visiting it; and me, whose husband was behaving aloofly since I got home, from tagging along. Going would be an antidote to my trip to Oklahoma; I'd pick up the pieces with Arnold later. Photographing thousands of people who unquestioningly—no, gleefully—put their trust in a man who promised the unpromisable had baffled me. What need in them made them so blind? When their mass hysteria subsided—when they saw that they needed their crutches, their glasses, their medicines after all—what would they tell themselves?

You, Arthur, and I started at the Thanksgiving muscular dystrophy drive at the Waldorf, where you kissed all the children, continuing long after the cameras had stopped flashing. Still high from the energy you always seemed to take from being around the young, you swept into Beard's ice-cream place. On Arthur's arm, you were resplendent in head-to-toe mink as you received cheers from the opening-day crowd.

You'd signed snatches of paper for every last fan—or at least every fan who could get past a glowering Arthur—and were hugging that big bear Beard, who was patting you clumsily with those huge paws capable of making the most delicate soufflé, when a disturbance arose just outside. Someone was shouting, "Marilyn! Marilyn!"

You lifted your head from Beard's solid chest, ready to humor yet another fan.

A woman approached, a sparkly top strategically draped over her considerable bosom. The gazes of onlookers traveled to those fleshy hills and mostly stayed there, with an occasional glance at the proud curl of the woman's nostrils or her drastically arched brows, or at the little girl she led by the hand.

The man who was shouting your name while trailing her froze when she stopped in front of you. "Two Marilyns?"

You stared at her as if looking into a fun house mirror in which all your features were exaggerated to the point of absurdity. She wasn't your spitting image; she was your grotesque.

She held out the hand not connected to her little girl. "Hello, Marilyn. I'm Jayne Mansfield."

You took it. "I know who you are."

Miss Mansfield's ivory face lit. "You do? Well, I so admire you and what you're doing. You're a genius."

When I raised my camera, you waved me off. You squinted as you looked her over, then asked, "Why are you trying to be me?"—not unkindly, but as if you really wanted to know.

If the question surprised Miss Mansfield, she didn't show it.

"I'm not being you. I'm being me. You say you don't believe in hiding yourself." She patted her breasts. "Me, neither."

Arthur tried to pull you away, but you wouldn't go. "That's wonderful, but don't you see? Fame built on a curvy body only lasts so long. I saw it happen to Betty Grable. It'll happen to us, too."

Miss Mansfield laughed. "Well, it hasn't happened yet."

"You aren't listening. Once you get boxed in, it's hard to get out. If you're a blond bombshell, that's all they'll ever think you are. I heard you're very smart. Why don't you go for something that lasts? Something real. Something that matters."

Miss Mansfield's nostrils flared. "You're twenty-nine years old, you have your own company, and you choose your own scripts, directors, and co-stars. I don't see any other women in Hollywood calling their own shots like that. And you say this doesn't matter?"

"Yes. Of course it matters. But it's not what's most important."

"Are you kidding?" Miss Mansfield scoffed. "What's better than being in charge?"

Arthur butted in, anger sharpening his Brooklynese. "Why don't you leave her alone?"

"Why don't *you* let the lady speak for herself?" With a dip of her overdone hair, she turned the floor over to you.

Her little girl tugged at her mother's hand. "Mommy?"

"What, honey?"

"Can we get ice cream?" Her plaintive smile revealed two missing front teeth.

You crouched, your mink brushing the tile floor, and reached out to the child. "What flavor do you like?"

Revealing tiny fangs bared by the absence of her front teeth, she said, in her little voice, "Cherry."

"Me, too."

You looked up at Arthur with hopeful eyes.

He pulled you up to standing. "What kind of ice cream do you want? He's asking." Arthur hooked his thumb at James Beard, who was greeting well-wishers. "He says to try the cognac-coffee flavor."

You trailed wistful looks at the child as Arthur led you away.

We got our dishes of ice cream and sat in a booth, where Arthur immediately dug into his cognac-coffee scoops and you laid your temple on his bony shoulder, your own dish untouched before you.

"Eat," Arthur said—to which of us, I don't know.

My spoon paused over my ice cream when I understood—Miss Mansfield had the one thing you didn't have, the one thing you thought might fix you: a child.

# 22

## 1956

AH, FEBRUARY, WITH ITS DAYS OF GROUNDHOGS AND CUPIDS. And for me, that ninth of February in '56, a day to survive the guys shouting and shoving and using their Graflexes as battering rams to get to your press conference. Capa had his Omaha Beach; I had my Waldorf Hotel when you were in the building.

The previous week, *Time* had granted your frame an extra inch and a half and declared that you, "a five-foot-five-and-a-half blonde weighing 118 alluringly distributed pounds," had brought the mighty Twentieth Century-Fox to its knees. Your production company, it said, had just signed Laurence Olivier, reigning king of the theater and the movie house, to star with you in a film with a script that you'd chosen—and that you would get top billing. A press conference had been called to mark the momentous meeting.

"You'll be my date, like when we went to see the beards" was how you'd put it when you phoned to ask me to photograph you at the presser.

"Your date with a camera."

"Best kind!"

"Arthur's not going?"

"Oh, you know how he hates these things." With that belly chuckle of yours, you exclaimed, "I'll be bringing Art to Olivier!"

And so it was that, hunched over my Nikon like a soldier keeping his powder dry, I made a break for your dressing room in the Waldorf. The faces of New York cops, a pained Milton Greene, and a big-eyed May Reis flashed by as I stormed the hall and barged into the ladies' lounge, where you looked up from a vanity. A sweet-faced young man was spraying your hair.

"Miss Documentary Photographer! Thank you for coming. That crowd is nuts. Isn't it exciting?"

"If you enjoy D-Day." I waved away the hair spray fumes to air-peck your cheek. "Miss Most Advertised. You nervous?"

You shrugged, your shoulders completely bare save for the thinnest of spaghetti straps holding up your velvet gown—a cold look for February. "I'm always nervous. What was I thinking, signing Laurence Olivier? How is Norma Jeane going to look next to him?"

"Gorgeous," said the hairdresser, whom you then introduced to me as Kenneth Battelle.

May Reis, who'd rode my wake in, said, "She's legally changing her name to Marilyn Monroe. You are Marilyn," she said to you. "There is no Norma Jeane."

You winced. "Go see what Olivier's doing, could you please?" you asked May. When she was gone, you said, "I'm in a fix this time. Eve, I'm going to look so dumb! Larry's so much smarter than I am."

I took a camera from its case. "Is he? Or is he just a regular guy who plays smart people in the movies?"

You pressed your lips together, then laughed.

Your wardrobe woman brought in accessory choices: a mink, a filmy white scarf, a velvet jacket. Seeing me take position as you tried on the mink, you slid it down your shoulders and pouted into my lens. I took the shot. With each new item, you played a vixen or little girl or tramp, spoofing yourself, spoofing the absurdity of the circus outside the door, spoofing the ease with which you controlled men through their fantasies. You played to my camera, and when I lowered it, you kept going. Only my expression of pure affection stopped you.

*Thanks,* you mouthed.

*Thank you,* I mouthed back.

Watch out, world. The lionesses were back.

I lifted my camera again.

I don't know how much time had passed—five, ten minutes—when May Reis popped back into the room. She frowned as if surprised to see us laughing, and then she exclaimed, "Mr. Olivier is waiting! And he doesn't look very happy about it."

I supposed Mr. Olivier was not used to being kept waiting for anything.

"What's he doing?" you asked.

"Chain-smoking," she said. "Barking at people."

Your sigh ran down the scale. "Okay. I'm coming." You rose. Then you sat back down and pushed at your hair. "This side isn't right."

Kenneth stepped in to rat a curl and comb it back into place.

You flapped your hands as if they were wet. "How am I going to stand out next to him? I shouldn't have agreed to do this. What was I thinking? What was I *thinking*?"

Kenneth rounded his eyes at me in the mirror. *Save her.*

Your plummet from joy to despair shocked me. But that wasn't helping you. I racked my brain.

"Did I tell you about the feature I did a while back on Rocky Marciano?"

"That big brute," Kenneth said. "Ugh."

"Actually, he wasn't what you'd expect at all. He was gentle and kind—a bit like your Lincoln, Norma Jeane."

You glanced at my reflection, still ready to jump from your ledge.

"He's not even that big in person," I told Kenneth, "not as big as you'd expect for the heavyweight champ of the world. He's your height, just broader."

You were listening.

"His trainer told me Marciano had the shortest reach of anyone in his weight class. He said Marciano shouldn't have been a champion. Oh, Rocky works harder than everyone—I saw it with my own eyes in a training session—but what makes him a champ is that he works *smarter* than everyone else, too." I shifted the camera strap on my neck. "He said a fighter should go with whatever's different about him. If he's tall, he should make himself taller. If he's short, he should make himself shorter. And that's what Marciano did: learned to fight 'short,' down in a crouch, tightening his punches and narrowing his stance, forcing his opponent to come down and look for him. And when the opponent did—pow!"

"Ouch!" Kenneth exclaimed.

"The point is," I said, watching you in the mirror, "champs work with what they've got. They make whatever's exceptional about them even more exceptional."

May dipped into the room. "Olivier says he's going to leave."

Time for the patron saint of tough girls. I put my arm up for you to take. "C'mon, kid."

You stood slowly.

"You got this?" I asked you at the door.

You switched your gaze to me. "I might have an idea."

I pushed the door open to a roar of reporters.

Milton took you from me, then paraded you down an elegant

stairway in a hail of bursting camera flashes. How were you not blinded? I hopped up on a balustrade, balanced myself against the wall. In my viewfinder, your hair and bared shoulders glowed pearlescent against the black suits and drab hair of the horde pushing against you. You stood out among them, a fragile sprite from another world. How did you bear your apartness?

But as I brought you into focus, I saw you jut out your neck and jaw. You battled through the mob, your arms crooked behind you as if you were a racer throwing herself over the finish line. That sprite was as fierce as she was fragile. She'd win, with no care that she'd break.

Tears blurred my vision.

*Oop!*

You were seated at a table with Olivier; then you laughed for the reporters' cameras as you received dry pecks from your visibly irritated co-star, all the while turning your head to give the photographers good angles. When the questioning began, you put on your velvet jacket and let Olivier speak for both of you, his British accent tighter and his chin dimple seemingly deeper with each answer.

"—Yes, we expect the film to be *veddy, veddy* successful."

"—Yes, I *veddy* much look forward to working with Miss Monroe."

"—Yes, the shooting begins when we have finished our current engagements. I expect that to be *veddy* soon."

Someone asked, "Is this the beginning of a long collaboration?"

He took a cigarette from a gold case and tapped it on the lid. He held his dimple aloft. "I *veddy* much doubt so."

The reporter asked, "Marilyn, is that true?"

You looked at Olivier as if deciding something, then, smiling sweetly, wriggled out of your velvet jacket. Your sheer scarf fluttered to your lap as you thrust yourself forward to speak into the microphone Olivier held for you.

A spaghetti strap snapped.

"Oh!" Your bodice dropped with a flash of nipple. Your hand flew to your shoulder.

All hell broke loose. Flashbulbs erupted as if in a grand finale. Cries lifted for a safety pin. Pockets, purses, were searched.

A reporter pushed forward, holding a magic pin aloft. He beamed as you let him reconnect your strap to the back of your gown. The room zinged with electricity as, pressing your finger above your bosom to the strap as if it might—it just *might*—snap loose again, you leaned into the microphone. "I do look forward to working with Mr. Olivier."

*Champs work with what they've got. They make whatever's exceptional about them even more exceptional.*

Oh, Norma Jeane. After all you'd achieved, you thought your body was the most exceptional part of you?

After a few more photos of you and Olivier, I withdrew to the back to stand next to Milton Greene.

"I can't control her!" he exclaimed.

"Are you supposed to? Does she need controlling?"

"Beats me! Frankly, I have no idea what the vice president of Marilyn Monroe Productions is supposed to be doing."

Bitterness pinched his boyish face—the look, I realized, of a cast-off lover. Arthur had won, and Greene was taking it hard.

"Where'd she get this crazy idea, popping her dress strap? How's this going to help the New Marilyn? Does this say 'serious actress' to you?"

Not to me, it didn't. But maybe that was not what you wanted to be.

When I photographed Josephine Baker at a club in Harlem a few years ago, she told the audience things about herself that made me run to the library to verify them. Few matched the facts on file. When I was showing her the prints, I asked her which were right, the accounts in the archives or the tales she told at the nightclub. She shifted within the stiff bodice of her strapless gown, looked down her nose at me, and smiled. "I don't lie, honey. I improve on life."

Was there such a thing as improving truth? Wasn't the truth the truth? Old Marilyn, New Marilyn, any Marilyn in between—they were all Norma Jeane. Would you ever believe the plain truth that you were extraordinary just the way you were?

# 23

I LEFT FOR CALIFORNIA ON A CLOUDY DAY IN MAY, BUT GRAY skies weren't all I left behind. I'd pulled out to leave for LaGuardia with Francis hunched on the driveway and my mother on the porch step behind him, her arms crossed over her apron front. His usual nanny, Elaine, had been called out of town on an emergency; I wondered, with a pang, if he was crying for her or for me. Arnold was in the city, spending the night there as he often did that semester. It just made sense, he'd said, since he'd increased his teaching load at the New School. He enjoyed the kids, he'd said.

The children's book author had finally agreed to let me do a feature on him—a relief. I'd been stewing in my juices, taking a few unsatisfactory local assignments here and there, since you'd left, soon after the publicity shoot with Olivier, to film *Bus Stop*, the first of your Marilyn Monroe Productions films. After throwing months away tagging after you and Arthur, and with little to show for my time besides the story on the faith healer, I had gotten out of step at Magnum. I needed this fresh start.

Now, still a little fuzzy from my cross-country journey, I gazed through the open window of the author's La Jolla studio. Outside, in the bright sunshine, butterflies danced above his bristly green hillside property. Beyond that, a wash of deep azure lolled clear to the pastel blue horizon. With a view like this, how'd the man get any work done?

I tightened my grip on my camera. *Get your act together. Make this trip out here worth it. Make leaving Francis, and Arnold, worth it.* I had to face it—I'd left things a mess back home.

"I used to wander around Pop's brewery." Ted Geisel, the fifty-two-year-old former adman with the funny pen name, a genial air, and eyes like chocolate drops, kept sketching at his desk. "It stank like hops. Ever smell them?"

"Hops? No."

"Well, they stink like puke. I loved that smell! Those were wonderful days." His drawing pencil stilled. "When Prohibition came, the neighbors were only too happy to smash our boilers and close the brewery. They'd been spoiling to do it since the anti-German ugliness of the First World War. We went from riches to rags overnight—the American way in reverse." He saw me looking outside. "You see whales?"

"Whales!"

"It's May—maybe a little late for them, but possible. Where was I? Oh yes—riches to rags. Believe me, I had plenty of ragged years, and I suppose I'd still be broke if it weren't for Flit."

"The bug spray."

He nodded. "My illustrations for government publications during the war, and my book of children's sayings, kept me afloat, but it was Flit that bought me this house and made me enough for us to travel. My wife and I love to travel. Do you?"

I nodded.

"When you get out there, you realize there are a thousand ways to eat dinner."

I laughed. "I get what you mean."

He leaned forward to fetch a back copy of *Redbook*—May 1955—then opened it to a poem illustrated with his strange drawings. "'The Hoobub and the Grinch.'" He tapped the page. "These guys got me a contract at Random House. Did you read *Horton Hears a Who!*? Came out the year before last. Kids' books are the way to make money now."

I thought of Arnold and his sole book, and his flight into the arms of the world of board games, which had only wounded his pride more when it spurned him. I was glad that he was increasing his teaching load if it made him happier. Thank goodness we had a good nanny.

Mr. Geisel pulled some drawings over to show me. "This one comes out next. It's called *The Cat in the Hat*." He grinned, a papa proud of his whimsical child.

I snapped their photo.

"I had to find some other way of making a living," he said as I wound my film. "Illustrating for advertising is going the way of the dodo bird. You, of all people, should know that. The magazines only want photographs for their illustrations now. I bet you've done work for advertisers."

"Some." I was shooting more ads than ever. I wasn't proud of it.

"Well, thank your lucky stars that you have a skill that'll always be bankable. The big magazines will always need photos."

After lunch, I packed up my cameras and left with one of his fanciful drawings for Francis and some brownies that Geisel's wife had baked for me. I drove up the coast in a rented car, chocolate crumbs trailing down my shirt as I marveled at the palm-tree-studded landscape with an East Coaster's sense of awe. I was headed to Los Angeles, where I thought I'd surprise you. Okay, okay, Dr. Seuss wasn't the only force pulling me across the continent. Plain truth? Life wasn't as exciting without you.

In Bel Air, I followed my map past green lawns cushioned by flowering shrubs, which in turn cushioned sprawling Cape Cods and mock Italian villas and French palaces, all of them with pools, and houses for their pools, homes that epitomized the American Dream, though it was hard to imagine people living in them.

At 595 North Beverly Glen Boulevard, I stopped the car. Within this five-dormer Cape Cod, you lived with Milton and his family while Arthur remained in New York, working on a screenplay. How quickly Milton had let you back under his roof! I wondered if Amy was as enthusiastic about your return.

Milton greeted me at the door. "Eve?"

"Hello, Milton."

Confusion was all over his boyish face. "Was . . . Marilyn . . . expecting you?"

"No. I was taking my chances. I had a job in San Diego, so I thought I'd drive up and surprise her."

"That's some drive."

"Is she here?"

"She's here." He remained in the doorway.

I peered behind him.

"She's doing a photo shoot. For *Life*. PR stills for *Bus Stop*."

"Can I watch? Out of view, of course. I won't bother them. I'd just like to see how he works with her." Because I knew it would be a "he." I was the only "she" ever to have done a shoot with you.

"It's a Black guy. He usually does poor people. I'm surprised *Life* sent him. Guy named Gordon Parks."

"Gordon? Gordon is great! I'd love to watch them."

"I don't know how much longer it'll take. They've been at it over an hour."

Amy came to the door, bright and pretty and sleek like the fashion model she once was. "I thought a particularly persuasive encyclopedia salesman was making a score, as long as Milton has been out here. What are you keeping her outside for? Come in, Eve."

She led us into the kitchen. There was a bounce to her step—the strut of a woman who'd gone up against the world's sexiest woman and won.

She held up a percolator. "Coffee? I can make some in a jiff."

I had a car to return in a few hours and a plane to catch. "Yes, please."

As Amy shoveled coffee into the percolator basket, and Milton extolled the beauty of Sun Valley, Idaho, where you had finished filming for *Bus Stop*, I peered through the red-checkered kitchen curtains. Outside, beyond the concrete patio, against a steep, vine-covered hill next to the pool house, you were posing for Gordon.

With your tiny black camisole stretched low across your breasts, you pivoted on spike heels, stuck out a hip so that the black stripes of your stretchy slacks slithered down your curves, and threw a slit-eyed sneer over your shoulder like a smutty Betty Grable.

"Have you been there?" Milton asked.

"Where?"

He followed my troubled gaze out the window. "Sun Valley."

"What is she doing?"

Milton closed his eyes and shook his head.

Outside, Gordon, his legs braced as if he were in combat and his face serious, shot as you turned around and bent from the waist until your breasts fell almost completely from your top. You'd refused to pose like this for reporters now that you were the New Marilyn, and here you were giving blatant sexuality to Gordon, your expression coolly aggressive.

"What is going on?"

Milton hung his head like a kid who'd been caught breaking a window with a baseball—that is, like a manager whose client was misbehaving. "They just started doing this. I guess I can tell the editor not to use these shots."

"Don't worry. They won't." Not even *Playboy* would. They wanted their girls soft and easy, not confrontational like this woman posing outside the window.

The phone rang. Amy strutted over and answered. She held her hand over the receiver. "It's Arthur."

Milton rolled his eyes upward and pressed his palms together in gratitude for an answered prayer. "Thank you." He went outside and called you.

You skipped into the kitchen, and stopped when you saw me. "Miss Documentary Photographer! What are you doing here?" All traces of the bad girl by the pool house had melted away. "Don't leave. I've got to go talk with Arthur. He went to Reno! Eve, he's getting a divorce!"

You ran off to another part of the house to take the call. Gordon entered the kitchen.

"Flip!" He did a backstep, then chuckled with delight. "Well, well, well. My day just got even better."

Oy vey, I loved his smile. "Mine, too."

Milton demanded, "You aren't using those shots, are you?"

"Hell yes, I am."

Milton's voice cracked. "You can't!"

Gordon's eyes cooled. "I can. If Marilyn wants me to."

"But she looked—slutty. This is not the New Marilyn that we've worked to project. She looked so"—he searched for a word—"hard."

"She is hard, Milton. She's doing this for all the hard girls out there."

"Did she tell you that?"

Gordon smiled sadly, as if sorry that Marilyn had a manager who would have to ask him that. "She didn't have to."

Two cups of coffee and some good conversation with Gordon later, you were still on the phone with Arthur. I couldn't wait for you. Gordon walked me to my car, both of us carrying my cameras in their cases. I never leave them in a car, not even in Bel Air.

"How'd you like shooting Marilyn?" I asked him.

"I can see why she's your friend."

I wondered what that meant. "What was going on at the end of your shoot? I was watching you guys."

"That? That was her trusting me."

I unlocked the trunk and we put the cameras in it. I knew what he meant. You had opened yourself to him out there. You'd let Norma Jeane out, the hard and ugly girl, the Weird Dirty Girl in junior high. You had never completely opened your ugliest side to me on camera, never completely told me that truth. I was . . . hurt.

He shook his head. "She's the most fearless chick I know." He chuckled. "Save for my mother. And my wife. And every Black chick in America." He saw my look. "And save for you, Flip, competing with me and all the cats."

He didn't have to soften his compliment to you to spare my feelings. What he thought about me wasn't my concern, at least not in this case. But he'd gotten something wrong.

"Marilyn isn't fearless. She's the most scared person I know."

"Oh, I saw her fear. Don't think I didn't. I shouldn't have said 'most fearless.' I should have said 'bravest.'"

"Bravest?"

"Bravest. Because the bravest person is the most terrified person, who goes on and gets it done."

He was right. Of course he was.

"Words to live by." I opened my door, dropped onto the driver's seat, and squinted up at him. Being with such a kindred spirit was both the rose and the thorn. It hurt to like someone so much.

He leaned down and kissed me on top of my head. "See you, Flip. Soon, I hope. Keep being scared."

"You, too, Chicken."

He blinked, then guffawed. He was still laughing as I drove off.

How proud I was of entertaining him.

My heart too big for its cage, I wound through the streets of Bel Air, between the swards of green that buffered mansions in which martinis were being sipped to dull the pain of success.

# 24

SEEING GORDON IN CALIFORNIA DROVE HOME THE FACT THAT while I was playing your personal photographer over the summer, I'd strayed from my mission to hold up a mirror to the world. Even if my photos of Dr. Seuss got some attention when published, and they did have some cultural significance, I yearned to take on meatier subjects. Therefore, when I returned to an empty house—Francis was at school, my mother had left a note that she was at the store, and Arnold was God knew where—and got a call from Inge about a shoot for *Ladies' Home Journal*, I didn't bite.

"What?" Inge said when I demurred. "You must be mixed up after that long flight."

I laughed. *LHJ*, the Moby Dick of photography, at least when it came to pay, wanted me to do a feature on Joan Crawford. Crawford, the queen of Old Hollywood, had asked for me specifically. "You will get top dollar photographing her and her daughter together," Inge said. "All you must do is to show them a few sights in New York and record it. You won't have to leave Francis and

Arnold." Inge knew how much doing so bothered me. "You could sleep in your own bed at night."

There's something unseen in everyone, Gordon had once said. Maybe finding it in one of the most seen women in the world would be a worthy challenge. And Arnold would kill me if I turned down the money.

A few weeks later, Miss Crawford arrived at the Murray Hill showroom of clothes designer Tina Leser with her hands stuffed in a gray Persian lamb muff—although it was a warm morning in June—and precisely on time. I would find that, unlike you, she made a point of being punctual—one of the many things that put her a cut above, she would later inform me. Her clear plastic heels snapping against the marble floor, she and her broad shoulders blew by Miss Leser and barreled straight for me as I was taking my cameras from their cases by a sofa.

"Eve!" she cried in her stagy voice, though we'd never met in person. She pulled her hands apart, stirring awake what was not a muff but two tiny poodles. They bowed in a stretch on her gloved palms, their piss tinkling musically on the floor. She kissed them both on their mouths, shoved them into her secretary's arms, and then kissed me deeply on the lips. I tasted vodka.

She patted her black dormant volcano of hair. "Tina, what *togs* have you for me today?"

Swiping my mouth with the back of my hand, I followed her and Miss Leser into the dressing room, where an array of clothing in tropical colors awaited her and her teenaged daughter, Christina, for a mother-daughter spread.

"How is the lighting?" Miss Crawford asked me, turning her cheekbones for me to test her angles.

"Oh—we're starting now, Miss Crawford? Is Christina coming soon?"

"It's Joan, darling, and yes, we're starting now. Time. Is. Money."

She toed off her shoes, taking herself down from a queenly height to a commoner's five foot four. Your height. She was swaying as she peeled her gloves down. "Aren't you going to shoot?"

"I thought Christina—"

"Where's your light meter? Where's your camera?" Seesawing her hips as if to the beat of burlesque music only she could hear, she unzipped her sheath.

"Shouldn't we wait?"

"For what?"

"Christina."

"No!"

I reluctantly took light readings as she slinked out of her dress and kicked it away, sending her teacup poodles clittering. She watched until I raised my camera; then, satisfied, she undid her stockings from their garters and rolled the stockings down her legs.

"Are you getting this? I don't hear your camera clicking." Her garter belt came next, and then, shimmying to silent tom-toms, she released her bra with a pop. "Shoot, woman! Shoot!" Her gaze locked on my lens, she hooked her pinky on her panties and pulled. She struck a lewd pose, staggered, then restruck it. "Would you shoot, damn it?"

Once she'd heard me advancing the film, she was all pussycat smiles, holding her breasts or showing me her rear. She paused to squint at me. "Why'd you stop? Did you stop when you were shooting Marilyn?"

Recording someone hurting herself like this was as dark as any of the dark places my camera had taken me. I realized, sometimes the unseen should stay unseen.

Joan's daughter Christina entered the dressing room. The poodles skittered over to her, yipping. Her face went as pale as her shiny ivory pageboy. "Mother!"

Joan teetered, then wobbled herself upright. "What?"

Christina hissed, “Put some clothes on.”

“This is art. My body is art. Eve Arnold is Marilyn Monroe’s photographer. Say hi, Eve.”

Marilyn Monroe’s photographer? No one had ever called me that. Did I like it?

“I’m sorry,” I said briskly, “but I’m all out of film.” It was the flimsiest of excuses, and weakest. Who runs out of film on a shoot, after only one roll? A sober person wouldn’t have fallen for it.

Joan squinted me into focus. “I expect prints in the morning. Good ones.” She sniffed. “Tasteful. Or,” she slurred, “you’ll never work in Hollywood again.” She slumped onto one of Tina Leser’s white leather couches and was out.

AT JOAN’S REQUEST, I’D FOUND—WELL, INGE HAD FOUND—tickets for that night’s performance of *The Diary of Anne Frank*, the hottest show in town. Somehow, Joan had roused herself, had me get her a town car, and then flounced into the theater to watch the play, with me trailing behind her with an armful of flowers for the leading lady. When the curtain fell at the play’s end, I sat next to Joan, the bouquet heavy on my lap. Less than twenty years earlier, many of Arnold’s family had been herded into cattle cars and murdered in camps during the Nazi occupation, which was the background of the play. Any members of my own family who’d fled the pogroms for Poland and Germany had perished then, too. How quickly their terror and suffering of just a decade earlier had become a part of the past, the pain of remembering them diluted by everyday life—nature’s way of allowing a survivor to go on. But when the players came out for a bow and most of the audience jumped to their feet, some viewers sat, planted where agony had found them. I marveled at how the trauma of loss and the guilt of survival never really go away. They only lie waiting to get you.

When I stood to clap, Joan shouted in my ear, "Christina would like to go backstage now."

I knew the star, Lee and Paula Strasberg's daughter, Susan, from the times I'd gone to the Actors Studio with you. She was a nice kid, so I cringed when, at Joan's insistence, we barged into her dressing room. She still had on the stage makeup and wig designed to make her look even younger than her eighteen years.

"Congratulations," I told her. "You were terrific. No wonder the play won a Pulitzer."

Joan pushed the flowers that I had bought into Susan's arms and kissed her on the lips. "I starred in a picture that was based on a Pulitzer winner, so we have the prize in common."

"Yes, Miss Crawford." Susan maintained her poise as only someone who'd grown up among actors could. "Very nice to meet you."

"This is my Christina." Joan edged her daughter forward. "You are to become fast friends."

Christina's eyes implored Susan to forgive her mother.

A disturbance arose in the hall. Joan blew out a sigh. "Oh dear, my fans must have found me." She swept around, smiling broadly.

You halted in the doorway, causing a pileup of the reporters and photographers behind you. You hiked up your filmy wrap with white-gloved hands as you beamed. "Miss Crawford? Eve?"

I don't know who was more surprised. "You're in town!"

"For Arthur's hearing." You imitated creeping in with your fingers. "We had to sneak in. We thought we could get away with seeing Susan's play, but—"

Arthur, just behind you, ushered us in and slammed the door on the clamor outside.

"What are you doing here?" Joan said. "And why are you shutting out my fans?"

You grabbed Susan's hands. "You were wonderful, Susie. You're my hero!" You saw Joan raise her chin. "Oh, Miss Crawford! You've always been my hero, ever since I was a little girl."

Joan sniffed, then turned to Arthur. "When are you going to write a picture for me, darling? I can bring you an Oscar. I've done it before."

He curled a corner of his mouth.

"Say!" you exclaimed. "Would you like to join us for dinner, Miss Crawford? Wouldn't that be fun?" you asked Arthur.

At your insistence, we left for Sardi's as a group, with Susan's promise that she would follow. Reporters ambushed us at the back door of the theater. I covered my eyes against the barrage of flashes. It was open season.

"—Mr. Miller, what do you say about the subpoena?"

"—Are you going to show up at court?"

"—You going to spill the beans on your commie friends?"

"—Are *you* a commie, Mr. Miller?"

"—I hear J. Edgar Hoover has a file a mile high on you. That true?"

"*I* am not a Communist," Joan announced to them.

The reporters paused, their hunt interrupted. They were keen for Arthur's blood—had been since the FBI recently subpoenaed him to testify about his Communist connections from some twenty years earlier. J. Edgar Hoover had taken up McCarthy's mantle. Too much power was to be had in riding the Red Scare to let it fade with the disgraced senator. Arthur was the latest prey.

You slipped under the arm of your Lincoln. "Arthur loves America," you told the reporters, "as much as I do."

"Is he going to report to court?" a reporter demanded. "Or is he going to go to jail?"

"He'll report," you said, "but he's been a little busy." You beamed up into Arthur's eyes. "We're going to get married."

Only Arthur's quick, slanted glance suggested that this was news to him.

The press pool surged forward.

"—You're getting married?"

"—You set a date?"

You reached on tiptoes to kiss his cheek. A Fourth of July finale of flashbulbs blinded us. I wondered if Arthur appreciated how you'd just gained the sympathy of the press for him.

To me, Joan snapped, "Let's go."

STILL BLEARY THE NEXT MORNING, AFTER A LONG NIGHT OF ENtertaining a fuming Joan at Sardi's while you were constantly interrupted by a stream of fans and she wasn't, I poked the contact sheet in its developing tray. The images were as bad as I feared. Even though I'd kept my camera trained above the shoulders whenever possible, there wasn't a single frame in which the woman didn't look plastered and desperate.

I destroyed the contact sheet but kept the negatives, then trudged upstairs, where Arnold was working on school papers at the kitchen table.

"My shots of Joan Crawford were pure smut." I dropped down across from him.

He sat back, frowning at the interruption. "What?"

I explained how she had stripped when sauced, demanding that I shoot as she struck pornographic poses. "I don't know what I'm going to do."

"Do you kid?" he said, his German accent heavier with his annoyance. "You are going to take them to that Hefner fellow at *Playboy* and see what he will give you for them—that is what you are going to do."

"You can't be serious."

"I am." He got up to look in the refrigerator.

Maybe he didn't understand me. "She was out of her mind. It was heartbreaking to see her—to see anyone—like that." I shuddered at the thought of her face twisted in the blurry sneer she imagined was sexy.

"Does she want you to publish them?"

"Yes. She's all over me to give them to *LHJ.* She's convinced herself that we had a groundbreaking shoot."

"Then do it." He rooted around in the fridge.

"I wouldn't do that to her. If those shots got out it would kill her career. It'd be just plain cruel."

"I thought you didn't like her."

"I don't, particularly, but that's beside the point. I'm not here to titillate."

"What is that they say here?" he said, moving the lettuce and the milk around. "'Holier than thou'?"

Did he really just say that? "You know what I meant—just that I'm not a sensationalist. No one at Magnum is."

He laughed. "Capa is famous for a photo of a guy getting shot."

I stared at him in disbelief. "There's a huge difference between exploitation and exposition."

He retrieved a package of deli meat, then hipped the door shut. "Do what you want to do. I don't care."

For a long, strained moment, our gazes locked, and then he turned away and started unwrapping the package. The wall he put around himself was as real as the smell of the corned beef.

Dread trickled into my gut. I went over and laid my head on his back.

"What is this?" he said as I put my arms around him.

"I miss you." Did I? Was that true? All I knew was that I was scared.

He kept making his sandwich. “Whose fault is that?”

I was trying to make peace here. “I do. I miss you.”

He ducked out of my arms, haphazardly put away the meat and bread, and then strolled to the family room, where he turned on the television and dropped into his chair.

Sorrow flooded my heart until it seemed to slide down from the weight of it, causing an ache that hurt me to my teeth. I knew we’d grown distant, even estranged, but I had not known that he no longer liked me.

DULL FROM MY NEW UNDERSTANDING, I ESCORTED JOAN AND poor Christina around town for the rest of the week, putting off Joan when she asked for the prints of our first session, and trying to pull things back together when I was home. With each passing day, those shots grew more wonderful in her mind. She imagined them to be some of her best, images of a magnificent, mature, sensual woman feeling her power. When I showed her contact sheets from other occasions but still wouldn’t produce the first roll, she accused me of wanting her to fail.

“Now, look here,” she said at our last meal—a quick treat at Maxfield’s before she and Christina left for the airport. “I don’t care what your deal is with *Ladies’ Home Journal.* I’ll make them pay you more. They’ll listen to me.”

The crowd at Maxfield’s was giving us little attention. Christina stared at the single scoop of ice cream her mother had ordered for her, and Joan made tiny divots in her own lone scoop. “You must understand, I came from nothing. When I was Christina’s age—”

Christina lifted cold eyes.

“—I got my first bit parts in silent pictures. With hard work, after making the most of any scrap they’d give me, I made myself a standout. You know flappers? I invented the concept. I was *the* flapper." She sighed. "And then talkies came. Few of the silent stars could make the transition. Norma Talmadge quacking like a Jersey girl in her role as a French countess—why, they laughed her off the screen! But I made the leap. I taught myself acting and elocution and bettered my lot. Do you think I was born sounding like this? I grew up in Texas!"

She ate a smidge of ice cream. "I took all the B roles that MGM lobbed my way, and I made them shine. I looked for a certain kind of character—the girl who came from nothing but, with grit and verve, made it big. I knew it would resound with women, because isn't that what all we women must do, fight our way up from nothing in our individual ways? Well, it did resound. And I did all right—three smashes a year!" Her triumphant smile faded. "But then, when I was in my thirties, younger actresses started getting the plum parts, and me, almost overnight, they called 'box office poison.' The studio thought I should be grateful for any shit role they flung at me. But I wasn't grateful." She licked the tip of her spoon. "I stopped taking parts."

An older woman came to our table and asked for an autograph. Joan provided one with a flourish, then went back to me.

"For two years, I turned down scripts—to hell with my contract! Your little Marilyn wasn't the first to stand up to Hollywood. I waited until a role came my way that I knew would speak to women, and I found it in Mildred Pierce. Now, here was a woman in middle life who tried to have it all—motherhood, work, love—and went down fighting for it. Oh, she made mistakes, but what woman in America didn't understand what Mildred Pierce was up against? I played her with everything I had." A waitress dropped a tray. Joan waited for the noise to subside, then leaned forward, her eyes bright beneath blue-powdered lids. "I not only won big against Hollywood, but I won the Oscar. Such sweet revenge. *I won the Oscar.* Can your Marilyn say that?"

She pushed her bowl away. "And now, *when I have reached my prime,* I must reinvent myself again. How many times must women reinvent themselves?" She felt her cheekbones as if to see if they were still there. "You see, Eve, those images that you took in our first creative session are what I need right now. I need to show who the New Joan is. Bold. Confident. In charge." She reached across the table and took my hand. "Won't you please do for me what you did for Marilyn?"

Christina wouldn't meet my eyes.

I drew an envelope from my purse and slid it across the table. "Here they are."

With a gasp of delight, Joan opened it, then held the negatives up to the Tiffany-shaded light above our booth.

She blanched under her makeup.

"That's all the negatives. I've kept nothing. They're yours."

She stashed the envelope in her handbag, then exhaled. She gave me a brittle smile. "You're getting a reputation within the acting community. Did you know? Everyone wants you to photograph them. I thought it was because you're Marilyn's photographer, but I can see that's not why." She snapped her bag closed. "It's because you can keep a secret."

# 25

ARNOLD WAS TO PICK ME UP IN PORT JEFFERSON AFTER I LEFT Miss Crawford in the city. I dreaded seeing him. Our marriage was like the tree that was still putting out leaves but was black at its core; I still straightened up the house and helped Francis with his homework, and Arnold still took out the trash and paid the nanny, but our relationship was hollow. I felt ashamed to be disliked, and not a little angry. Maybe I didn't like him—didn't *love* him—either. The thought made me sick.

Steeling myself, I stepped outside the train station. He wasn't there.

Had it already come to that?

A crowd had gathered in front of the display of TVs in the window of the appliance store across the street. By the solemn looks on their faces, I wondered if the Soviet Union had invaded another country or Eisenhower had died. My paranoia at the boiling point, I went over to the display. You and Arthur were on all the televisions.

Under a tree in the countryside somewhere, facing a pack of

reporters, you were wavering between smiling weakly into the cameras and tucking your head into Arthur's shoulder like a bat that had been pulled out into the light—or, more factually, like a feral child scraped from her hiding place. It was clear that something bad was going on, and you had no idea what to do with yourself before the cameras.

Arthur's heavy Brooklyn accent was audible through the open door of the appliance store. "A terrible accident just happened as the result of mobs coming by here. I knew it was going to happen—I suspected it was going to happen—because it's a road made for horse carts. Cars smash up because people don't know the roads around here. I wanted the press to assemble all at once in the hope that this could be avoided."

The man next to me, smelling of onions, exclaimed, "Look at her! She doesn't have the guts to look the cameras in the eye. A reporter's dead because of her."

A woman harrumphed. "She tries to make us think she's this new, serious person. Well, I'm not fooled. She's immoral."

"She's not worth getting killed over—I can tell you that," said the woman's husband.

"Chasing them because they were running off to get married," my oniony neighbor scoffed. "What a waste. Who cares about Marilyn Monroe anyway?"

I thought of the villagers in *Frankenstein*, disturbed by the strange creature on the loose, arguing about what to do. They wanted to hate you, yet here they were, transfixed.

"But you're watching her, aren't you?"

They turned to me in surprise.

A car came up, honking. Francis hung out the passenger window. "Mom! Over here!"

Arnold grinned as Francis scrambled over the seat and I got in, and then Arnold leaned over to plant a kiss on my lips.

Had I stepped into a time warp?

Francis tapped me on the shoulder. "Look what I got."

I turned around. He held up a cardboard box with a color picture of a battleship on it. "Nice."

"Dad's going to build it with me."

"We are celebrating." Arnold's voice was bright with happiness. "Parker Brothers is making Gold Rush."

My worry for you, Arnold's sudden affection—it was all too much. "They are?"

"I just got off the phone with my boss. Sorry I was late—I made Francis dress up. We're going out for dinner."

"They're making your game?"

"Yes. Isn't it grand?"

After champagne and filet mignon, there was celebrating in our backyard with "The Stars and Stripes Forever," sung to the waving of Zippos in lieu of sparklers. We acted like a family, though even as I sang along with my husband's bellow and my son's reedy warbling, a bruise hurt deep in my heart.

I'd come downstairs after tucking a happy and tired Francis into bed, and was getting some water at the kitchen sink, when Arnold came in behind me and wrapped me in his arms. He laid his chin on my head. "Things are going to get better."

The pit in my stomach burned. Did he think one game deal, one happy night, could bridge the gap between us? I was insulted that he thought it could be that simple.

He turned me around and kissed me.

"Arnold. We should talk."

"Talk?" He laughed. "Who wants to talk?"

He kept kissing me, murmuring in German, and it felt good, too good to stop him. Desire, and not a little hope, were stirring as he led me upstairs.

Later, as we lay next to kicked-away sheets, he rubbed two fingers idly on my back. "I've missed you."

Could it be this easy to pick up the pieces? I was willing to believe it was. I rolled against his side. His chest was warm beneath my cheek as I listened to the thump of his heart. "I've missed you, too."

# 26

## 1957

I HAD CANCER. WHY ELSE WOULD THE DOCTOR ASK ME TO come back to his office?

I took my hand from Arnold's sweaty one and smoothed my skirt. It was a nice dress, a Tina Leser sample with palm trees all over it. I'd picked it up last year, when I was with Joan Crawford. I figured I needed something cheerful to look at now, when I got the bad news.

I'd quit smoking several years earlier, but had I quit soon enough? Tobacco companies claimed there was no link between smoking and cancer. They took out ads with doctors puffing away while earnestly recommending their brands, but honestly, didn't we all know better? How could singeing your lungs with smoke possibly be good for you?

Maybe I was being punished for helping a life insurance company twist the truth by portraying a loving father driving a child who was allegedly (but not actually) his son, or for taking gorgeous shots of a countryside allegedly (but not actually) improved somehow by a plastics manufacturer. Maybe I was being punished for using my photographer's eye to make money and not for telling important truths. Henri would be ashamed of me. Capa would be ashamed of me. I was ashamed of myself. And now I was dying.

Dr. Wehrenberg strutted in with a clipboard, put out his cigarette in the freestanding ashtray, and shook Arnold's hand. "Hello, Arnold. How are you feeling, Eve?" He patted my knee and smiled. He was awfully cavalier for someone who was about to deliver a death sentence.

Warily, I said, "Good."

The doctor's smile broadened. "Well, you two, the *rabbit* didn't feel good."

Arnold and I squinted.

"The rabbit died. Eve is pregnant."

I broke the silence twanging from the mint green walls. "That can't be. I'm forty-five. I gave up on having a second baby a long time ago."

Arnold was still squinting. "A rabbit died?"

Dr. Wehrenberg propped himself against the counter. "Oh, you know the expression—though, actually, all the rabbits, or guinea pigs, or mice, or whichever, die, whether the patient is pregnant or not. The lab dissects them after injecting them with the patient's urine. If their ovaries are affected . . ."

I stopped listening. How could this have happened? Soon after our armistice, Arnold and I had fallen back into leading largely separate lives, sleeping together only once every other month, or less often, and usually after we'd both had something to drink. The last time we'd had sex was the day after Valentine's Day—he'd been in the city on the actual day—four months ago.

"How far along am I?"

The doctor, still explaining the mechanics of the rabbit test, blinked, but was agile enough to switch gears to ask the date of my last period and then figure from that.

"Four months."

He wrote on my chart, then lowered it. "Let's address Eve's age. I accept it as a challenge to bring mother and baby to term safely," he told Arnold.

A challenge?

"Come back in four weeks. We'll have to keep a close watch on your vitals. Meanwhile"—he put his hand out to Arnold—"good work, sir."

IT WAS AS A STUNNED PREGNANT LADY THAT I WENT TO YOUR premiere of *The Prince and the Showgirl* the next evening, and then to the after-party at the Waldorf. Shrieks of laughter rang out over the packed Grand Ballroom of the hotel, where an orchestra was bending into a string version of Elvis Presley's "Hound Dog." Men in natty suits and women in satin gowns crowded around you and Laurence Olivier, and to a lesser extent, around your spouses. Though I hadn't seen you since you'd gone to England to film, soon after the car crash that had killed the reporter, I was quickly giving up hope of talking to you that night. More well-wishers were orbiting you, awaiting their turn, while others chugged Manhattans and champagne and roared as if it were New Year's Eve in June, as if the film they'd just seen had not stunk.

Oh, Norma Jeane, I'm sorry. Even in my dazed state I could see that it reeked. You and Olivier seemed to be in two different films. He played it like a farce, hamming it up as the goofily greedy would-be prince . . . and the world's most famous Shakespearean actor did not do goofiness well. You played it as an altogether different kind of comedy, an intellectual one infused with a Method actor's realism and insight, a cross between *A Streetcar Named Desire* and *The Seven Year Itch.* Maybe the New Marilyn was more interested in being Mrs. Arthur Miller these days, but your acting chops had soared in your last film, *Bus Stop*, and in this one you were even better. Your engaging, lovable Elsie made Olivier look as stiff as the epaulets on his uniform. The whole film through, my brain tried and failed to peg the mishmash it was seeing. In a nutshell, *The Prince and the Showgirl* was unwatchable.

The orchestra struck up Presley's "Don't Be Cruel." A writer who'd taught with Arnold at the New School slapped him on the back and they launched into a conversation. I told Arnold I was going to get some fresh air.

He caught my hand. "Do we need to leave?"

Upon the news of my miraculous pregnancy, each of us became newly tender with the other. He was sweet, funny, and thoughtful, like the starving young man I'd fallen in love with. Oh, his cold shoulder had not been forgotten. Nor was his begrudging my success until he had some of his own, nor his resentment of my travel and my dedication to my work. But I had to let all that go. It was for the best. How often does a marriage—a family—get a second chance?

I knew how much he relished these showbiz events. "Stay. I'm fine. I'll be back in a minute."

I padded down thickly carpeted halls to the lobby, which was empty at this hour, save for the clerks behind the mahogany fortress of the reception desk. I dropped onto the upholstery of the bench encircling the famous gold tower clock, pried my shoes from my heels, and leaned back.

I must have drifted off, because the next thing I felt was pressure on the cushion next to me. I smelled Chanel No. 5.

"Miss Documentary Photographer, I presume."

I sat up to a grinning you. "Miss Most Advertised! What are you doing out here? You're missing your party."

"Giving Larry a rest from me." You twitched up a sculpted brow. "And vice versa."

I drew in a breath. "Loved your show. It was great."

"Eve. It's me. You can tell me the truth."

"I mean it. *You* were great."

You rolled your eyes. "Oh jeez, I wonder what Bosley Crowther's going to say now."

"He liked *Bus Stop*."

"You saw his review of it?"

"Yes."

You rested your head against the upholstery and recited to the ceiling. "'Hold on to your chairs, everybody, and get set for a rattling surprise. Marilyn Monroe has finally proved herself an actress in *Bus Stop*. She and the picture are swell! This piece of professional information may seem both implausible and absurd to those who have gauged the lady's talents by her performances in such films as *Niagara*, *Gentlemen Prefer Blondes*, and even *The Seven Year Itch*, wherein her magnetism was put forth by other qualities than her histrionic skill.'"

"I can't believe you can remember all that."

"I'm an actress, remember? I gotta know lines." You burst out laughing, and kept it up, straight from the belly. "Could he have been any more backhanded?"

"He's a putz. But you got your positive review from him."

You closed your eyes and lifted your soft, strained singing voice. "*'Af-ter you get what you want, you don't want it.'*" You'd sung that song in *There's No Business Like Show Business*. Strange how often your life mirrored the songs and roles you were famous for.

You sat up. "You know what really ticks me off? Crowther goes on in the review to give Josh Logan all the credit for my acting. He said it was Logan's directing that brought me out. According to him, without Logan I'd still be a bubblehead bumbling along on my 'other qualities.'"

"Okay, that was shitty."

"Live and learn." You grabbed a topknot of hair, as you did when frustrated or annoyed, crushing your hairstyle. "Every time Larry demanded that I do something a certain way in *Showgirl*, I thought of Crowther giving Josh all the credit for what I did in *Bus Stop*. Larry was hell-bent on making the picture his star vehicle, with me as the gasoline, but I saw it differently. It was my picture. So I did it my way." Your sigh was long and loud. "Maybe that was a bad idea. Oh well."

You sure were taking this in stride. A setback of this nature normally would have sent you into a spiral of doubt.

"Maybe I'll give up acting."

After devoting your every corpuscle to it since you were a child? "What? No!"

"I have something more important to do now." You grasped my wrist. "Eve, I'm going to have a baby."

I could feel the smile taking over my face. "Norma Jeane!"

"I know. It's crazy. Me, a mom!" You rolled back and kicked the flounced fishtail of your gown. "Can you imagine?"

"Yes. More than you think."

You laughed, but didn't take the hint. Your smile fell. "Problem is, I have no idea how to be a mother. I had no relationship with mine. She was too mentally ill to take care of me. Maybe I'll be crazy like she was, like my grandma was. I come from a long line of schizophrenics—uncles, aunts. Maybe I'm schizophrenic—" You blinked false eyelashes at me. "Am I?"

"No! Stop already! You'll be great. I know you will. And you'll have some company to help you." I grinned. "I'm expecting, too."

You shrieked. The desk manager craned his neck in alarm.

You wrapped your arms around me and snuggled me into your cloud of perfume. "Evie, oh, Evie. We're going to have babies!"

My whole body felt like it was beaming. Into your rumpled platinum waves, I murmured, "Can you imagine?"

# 27

## 1958

THE CREPE RUBBER SOLES OF MY KEDS (YES, YOU'D CONVERTED me) soaked up the rumble of the ferry's engine. I peered out from the railing. *Hello, foamy gray Pacific! Got any whales down there?* I pictured gargantuan cucumber babies nudging at their benevolent barnacled mothers, and just like that, the bleakness fell, again.

Even eight months after the miscarriage, and the following hysterectomy to clean out both baby and failed uterus, it didn't take much to set me back. Pinballing across forty-eight states on an ad campaign for Simplicity Pattern these past few months had only stoked the ache that had festered in me since I'd lain on that steel table in the hospital and gazed at the basin that contained my heart.

*It was just a fetus,* they said. *You're forty-five years old,* they said. *Surely you're better without it at this age.*

"It" was a girl, and I'd wanted her with all my being. Oh, I'd needed a couple days to wrap my head around being a new mother. Who wouldn't, after they'd given up eight years earlier? But once I did grasp that I was having a baby, I couldn't wait to inhale the sweet scent of her newborn scalp. I couldn't wait to look deep into her eyes, the way a mother does only with her infant, and have her gaze back, deep into my soul, the way an infant does only with her mother. I was getting a second chance at being the kind of mother I should have been to Francis. To honor him, I'd teach her all I'd learned about this strange and wonderful world, things I didn't know when he was young and I was young, too. When I'd started bleeding, I made a bargain with God that if he saved my baby, I would give up photography. Now, as I peered into the sudsy sea, I wondered if I could have gone through with it. Maybe God knew this.

The motor cut. Backwash sloshed against the hull of the slowing boat as we drifted toward land. Over the loudspeaker, the captain told us to return to our cars. I rolled down the window of the stuffy rented Chevy. Exhaust from all the revving machines rolled in, overpowering the stink of fish and the creosote of the piers, and fumigating the dress samples hanging in the back of the car. My assignment for Simplicity Pattern was to photograph a woman in each of the forty-eight states, each woman modeling a dress that she, ostensibly, had sewn, for a campaign called *Sewing Across America*—a job that seemed like a good idea when Inge proposed it, during my first month of bed rest, but not like such a great one after I'd been gone from Arnold and Francis for two weeks. At least the women I'd rounded up through my contacts across the country had been delightful, no matter that few could sew a button. They didn't need to. Simplicity had sent me on the road from New York with a carful of dresses professionally sewn by their seamstresses.

I drove the Biscayne down the ferry ramp and onto a road strewn with white sand. Above the palm trees, the whimsical turrets and towers of the Hotel del Coronado rose like a Victorian millionaire's fever dream. I'd done my California shoot for Simplicity in San Diego, as fond as I was of the place since visiting Dr. Seuss, and I had come over to Coronado after reading that you were filming a movie there. You and I hadn't spoken since the premiere of *The Prince and the Showgirl.* I'd called several times, and after I'd heard your news, I sent a letter, but Arthur kept you tightly under wraps. That was probably what you needed. Word had spread across America that you'd lost your baby, too.

After lugging my equipment into my room at the Del, I went to the beach, where I joined the crowd obediently standing behind a single rope, the ocean breeze rippling the women's sundresses and the men's open terry cloth jackets—it was a balmy day in September. On the other side of a grove of cameras and booms from which microphones and lights hung like metallic coconuts, you were charging up through the sand, chasing a beach ball thrown from a circle of frolicking young women in 1920s bathing suits. A saddle shoe–clad foot darted out from a hooded wicker beach chair. You went sprawling, and then up you popped, dusting your knees off as you spoke to the man on the wicker throne—Tony Curtis, I realized when he lowered his newspaper. I wondered if you liked him any better now than you did when he tried to own you at the advertising banquet. You were making this film to fulfill an old contract with Fox—would you have hired him if it had been one of your productions?

Billy Wilder yelled through his megaphone, "Cut!"

You trudged through the sand with Paula Strasberg, a Bedouin sheik in her black robes, toward a row of trailers and tents. Whitey Snyder met you at the door of a small Airstream, where you hid until everyone was called back.

Once again, you positioned yourself with the actors on the beach. Extras readied to play in the surf.

"Quiet on the set!" Wilder ordered.

Behind the rope, the spectators straightened.

"Roll cameras!"

"Rolling!" the cameramen shouted.

"Slate."

The clapper board clacked.

The women's beach ball game resumed. The ball sailed; you ran; you fell, then jumped up.

"Cut!"

"Poor Marilyn. That sand must hurt her knees," said a woman in cat-eye sunglasses next to me.

"I like how she bounces when she hits," commented her husband.

"I wonder how you'd bounce when you hit," I muttered.

I stared back when they looked at me in surprise.

This went on all afternoon. I lost track of the number of takes. At last, you ran, splatted, said your lines, and Wilder called, "That's a wrap!" Finally.

Afterward, I tracked you down at the Mar Vista cottage. The door opened to Paula Strasberg, as stern-faced as a prison guard. "Marilyn's resting."

"When can I come back?"

From the background, you called, "Am I dreaming? Miss Documentary Photographer, is that you?"

"Not a dream," I called back.

"Paula, let her in!"

I stepped into the darkened room made darker by the blanket thrown over the chiffon curtains at the window. You came out of the bathroom holding a glass of water. You looked bloated and ill. I stuffed back my alarm and held out my arms. "Come here, you."

We hugged, long and hard. "I had to see you," I murmured.

"Yeah?" you said when I let you go.

Tears began to stream down your face, streaking your makeup.

"What's wrong?"

"Oh, that bastard Billy, making me fall so much!" You swiped at your tears. "What's this going to do to my baby?"

You saw my surprise.

"Yes, I'm pregnant again." You patted your belly. "Do you think I'm this fat for nothing?"

You glanced at my midsection. "Wait. I'm so selfish. I haven't asked you—Eve, how is your baby?"

I shook my head.

Your face drained with dismay. "You—?"

"Miscarried."

"Oh, Eve." You held me tight. "I'm sorry. I didn't know. I've been going so nuts. What happened?"

I told her.

"You know, I lost my baby around then, too. I thought I would go out of my mind." You sunk your teeth into your cushiony lip. "I hope it doesn't make you feel bad that I'm pregnant."

"Are you kidding? No!"

"It used to kill me to see mothers with their babies."

"Oh, it kills me—believe me—but I'm happy for you. I mean it."

You kissed my hand. "I know you do."

"You should lie down." My heart warm with love and concern for you, I led you through a room full of bamboo furniture to the couch. I saw a bowl of fruit. "I'll feed you grapes."

You smiled wanly. Bement seemed so long ago.

I sat, and then you lay your head on my lap. "I'm just so tired. I can never sleep"—you glanced at Paula, who'd receded into the shadows—"even though I'm stuffed with pills."

"Doctor's orders," Paula said.

"Sleep now." I touched your forehead, and tried not to react when your once-silky skin felt hard, as if you were turning to stone.

You sighed deeply as I stroked your brow. "I took this part

right after my miscarriage. I didn't think I would get pregnant again so fast. It was my second miscarriage—did you know?"

I shook my head. "I didn't."

"I had the first one in England. Two miscarriages! Is God trying to tell me something?" You looked up from my lap. "Does he think I'll make a kooky mother?"

"Shh. No. That's not true."

You whooshed out a sigh. "I can't be falling in the sand over and over and over like I did today. All yesterday, I had to run onto the beach from the water and jump around with Jack Lemmon. Tomorrow I'm supposed to dash up the steps to the hotel, Lord knows how many times, and later I'm to run from the hotel down to the pier, down dozens of steps. Up, down, up, down. I can feel my heart pounding. It can't be good for the baby. What if I shake her loose?"

"You're not shaking her loose. But why don't you get a stand-in?"

"I can't let Billy know. Fox won't insure me. I'll get kicked off the picture just for being pregnant." You laughed bitterly. "Tony Curtis never has to worry about that."

"Shh. Shh."

You laid your hand on your belly. "Arthur's losing his enthusiasm to have a baby. He already has two kids. He says he doesn't need any more."

I had to change the subject. "What's this movie about?"

You paused to acknowledge that you knew you were being diverted. "I play a dumb blonde. Can you imagine?"

I pursed my lips.

"It's a comedy," Paula said from the shadows.

You rolled your head against my thighs. "I'm back to playing funny dummies. So much for the New Marilyn!"

"Infuse her with dignity," Paula intoned.

"I do!" To me you said, "But how much nuance can I give a ukulele-playing fluffhead?"

"Ukulele-playing fluffheads have feelings, too."

"Thank you!" Paula exclaimed from her corner.

You snorted. "I wouldn't have taken the part, but we have bills. Fighting the House Un-American Activities Committee cost a fortune. But Arthur's trying—don't get me wrong. He's writing a screenplay—with me as a lead."

"That's terrific!" Arthur's standing as America's greatest playwright had tumbled since *Death of a Salesman*, nearly a decade earlier, and though *The Crucible* had found some success, with each subsequent play he seemed further from regaining his mantle. His latest, *A View from the Bridge,* had received lukewarm reviews and closed after a few months.

Did you sense a note of my doubt? Because you frowned and added, "He was just awarded a gold medal by the National Institute of Arts and Letters."

"I read about it in the paper. Congrats to him. Grape?"

You shook your head. "Reporters kept wanting to take my picture. Arthur had to stand to the side at his own ceremony. He's got a lot of pride, you know? What's that going to do to a man like that?"

"He's proud of you, I'm sure."

"Is he? Of me?"

"Of course he is."

You inhaled deeply. "What'd Yeats say about only God being able to 'love you for yourself alone and not your yellow hair'?" You exhaled, then shut your eyes. The tough and dirty feral child was receding into herself. I'd never seen you give up. I was scared for you.

"What is Arthur's new script about?"

With closed eyes, you whispered, "Wild horses."

Your chest rose and fell quietly.

Paula's black robe separated from the shadows as she emerged to pull me away. At the door, she whispered, "If she can keep this baby, she'll be okay."

We stared at each other. And if you didn't keep it?

"Thanks for coming by." She closed the door.

I PHONED ARNOLD WHEN I WENT BACK TO MY ROOM.

"When do you come home?" he asked.

"How are you? How is Francis?"

"He is eating a TV dinner. Where are you?"

Dread overwhelmed me. Everything seemed on the verge of breaking.

"Eve?"

I croaked, "California."

"California! Christ, will you ever come home?"

The lump in my throat grew saltier.

"These long-distance charges will be murder." He didn't bother to hide his irritation. "Call Inge Bondi. She says she might have a story for you."

"What is it?"

"I don't know. But if it is out of state, do not take it. I am tired of running this show by myself."

If by "by myself" he meant with the help of Elaine or my mother taking the train over from Philly if Elaine needed a day off, yes, he was running the household single-handedly, as I did when I was home. Oh, why was I letting him irritate me now? We'd dug into our separate foxholes soon after we lost the baby. This was us now.

Heaviness gathered in my chest as I called Inge collect. *Please let her be in the office at this hour.*

"Magnum Photos," she answered; then she accepted charges.

"Arnold said you'd called."

"Well, are you sick of advertising yet?" Her kind Viennese voice was a balm to my heart.

"I was sick of it before I started."

"*Gut.* I might have the cure."

# 28

I POKED THE PRINT IN ITS SMELLY BATH, THE RED SAFELIGHT swaying as Arnold stomped overhead. I heard the bang of a pan on the stove, and the faint thunk of frozen hamburger meat hitting metal, and then the spongy shuffle of feet in Red Ball Jets, and Arnold's muffled voice: "Don't go down there. Your mother is busy."

My soul flew up through physical barriers to my son, even as I forced my attention back to my tray, where Thurgood Marshall's thick-lidded eyes were swimming into view. A smile wreathed the civil rights lawyer's fleshy face. His victory at the Supreme Court was written all over it. Individual states could not make their own timetables for compliance with *Brown v. Board of Education.* Every public school in the US had to make plans to integrate immediately. No more tricks or delays.

Overhead, Francis was asking his father when he could see me.

My heart broke a little as I moved on to the next tray. After this deadline, I'd make it up to him.

I glanced at a photo drying on the line, of Mr. Marshall laughing with his fellow NAACP lawyers, buttoned up in overcoats against the early-autumn wind. I had yet to visit him in his home for my feature for *Look*, or to meet his wife and kids—and his parents, too, if they were alive. I'd had no time to do my usual preparation since Inge had given me the story when I was out in California. And another angle was nagging at me.

When I was shooting the Marshall story on the Supreme Court steps, a local reporter had mentioned that, just across the river, in Arlington, some parents at his kids' junior high school were going to have an "integrated dinner" next week. His wife and some other Arlington parents, Black and white, had planned it, banking on the Supreme Court striking down Virginia's policy of "massive resistance," the term the state legislature used for closing every public school in the state rather than integrating them. No school at all, that legislature had ruled, was better than a mixed school.

These Arlington parents had bet that nonsense would not stand, the reporter said, and thought their kids, who'd been kept apart their whole lives, needed to learn how to be together. As I waited on the print in its tray, I remembered thinking how much I would love to be a fly on the wall at that dinner.

The hair on my arms stood up, the way it did when I smelled a good story. Why not go be that fly?

The sensible angel on my shoulder kicked into gear:

—Because absence had not made my husband's heart grow fonder. He'd been shunning me since I'd gotten home from doing the Thurgood Marshall story. I didn't know how much more tension Arnold, or I, could take.

—Because I was missing my son's childhood.

—Because what if I threw away any hope of healing my broken family and I couldn't get good shots?

*Stop!*

My tongs shaking, I transferred the print to the next bath, tore off my rubber apron, and ran upstairs.

Arnold and Francis were in the kitchen. *Just rip off the Band-Aid.* "I have to go away again."

Arnold turned from the ground meat sizzling on the stove. "Are you serious?"

*"Mo-om!"* Francis, now ten and as tall as me—not so hard a feat—kept slinging his Slinky from hand to hand. "You just got back!"

"I know." I spoke above the *zing-ching, zing-ching* of the Slinky. "I hate being away from you, but I have to go to Virginia. There's an important human rights story there that has to be told." I rubbed my face. "Hey! I have an idea! Why don't you go with me? Both of you. We can make a family trip of it—go to Washington, see the sights."

"Are you mad?" Arnold exclaimed. "He has school. I have work. The world does not revolve around you, Eve."

"Oh, ho ho ho, of *that* I'm acutely aware."

"Just—forget it."

"I can't! People need to see this story. Some things are more important than me—than us."

"I want to go!" Francis exclaimed.

"No." Arnold put out a hand like a traffic cop. "You are forbidden. If your mother does this, she must go on her own. She must decide what's more important to her, us or her snapshots. I'm the only man I know who has to cook dinner—"

"Once in a blue moon, when Elaine hasn't cooked or you've run out of the soup Mother left in the freezer or I just can't get to it."

He finished bitterly. "And I have three jobs." His voice was harsh. "You choose, Eve."

Capa didn't have to choose. He belonged to the world. But how could I belong to the world when I couldn't even leave my kitchen? "This is bigger than us. It's for humankind."

"Don't be grandiose, Eve. Choose."

"I shouldn't have to choose."

"Yet you do. Make a decision."

"I can't choose. I need all of it—you, Francis, my work."

Arnold stared at me, then laughed grimly. "Then you've already chosen."

My guts were still roiling with fury after I'd finished developing my prints and was packing my overnight bag. Couldn't Arnold see that I could no more stop documenting the unseen than I could swim the Strait of Gibraltar? Only one thing would kill me more surely than doing more trite and misleading advertising photography: doing no photography at all.

I grabbed my cold cream, toothbrush, and toothpaste from the bathroom. I'd make it right with them. I'd get such important shots that they'd see why I *had* to work, why it would be a crime for me to stop. I dropped my things into a zippered pouch and paused. Was I being grandiose? What if my ability to tell the story was all in my head? What if the pictures were good but no one had any use for them, like those of that bully McCarthy? I'd be further damaging my family for nothing. I could see my mother shaking her head. *Pauper, where are you crawling?*

I latched my suitcase and padded to the stairs in my Keds—all the better to run in.

I had to see this story out.

# 29

THE TARRY SMELL OF THE DEFUNCT FIREPLACE FOUGHT WITH the smoke of chain-lit cigarettes. On the mantel, a pine branch had been stuck in one of Capa's champagne bottles and smothered with tinsel. Beneath the "Christmas tree," the two Eliot(t)s, Elisofon and Erwitt, were arguing over who had made the best photos of Parisian women. An underpaid young woman was attacking the keys of the old Royal in the corner. Inge, on the telephone, was wringing out the terms for a still shoot for an Alfred Hitchcock film. It was just another day in early December at Magnum.

While I waited for Inge to get off the phone, I shuffled through the tear sheets of my integration-dinner story for *Look*, the sour school-cafeteria smells of mopped floors and spoiled milk unfurling through my memory. I could still feel how nervous those junior high kids, the girls in particular, had been at the start of the shoot. They'd all grown up within a mile or two of one another, they'd all had to deal with the physical changes of growing from girls to women, they'd all had to figure out where they stood as females in this world, and yet each group stole glances at the other over their plates of spaghetti as if the other were an alien species. Their parents were hardly more comfortable, exchanging polite comments as they shuffled stiffly in the background.

My hope when I was shooting the first roll had been to show how deftly kids managed to bridge the gap that generations of their elders had created between them. But when I saw, in reality, how hard it was for these older kids to change something that had been ingrained in them, the blues that I'd had since my hysterectomy welled up. A two-alarm headache began to rise.

I'd gone to the restroom to take some aspirin when two girls, one Black, one white, came out of their stalls. They washed their hands, got into their purses, and then bent, in unison, toward the mirror with their lipstick, moving their tubes in the same direction. They looked at each other and, lipsticks still to their mouths, cracked up. I swung up my camera, found my view, focused: *Oop!*

They switched their eyes to me.

"Don't mind me. I'm just a mom who's here to photograph the dinner."

They raised their brows at each other, now in cahoots against the weirdo taking their picture in the school bathroom. *This lady's crazy.*

*Oop!*

As I took the girls' shot, I realized I didn't need a gimmick, a "thing," like Halsman's shots of his subjects jumping. I didn't need clever setups or coaxing. Truth was, it was all up to the people I was photographing. I just had to be up close when they were ready—though shooting through the remove of a mirror might be something to remember. I thought of you in the Chicago airport, where, looking in the mirror, you first let me see Norma Jeane fully. I sighed loudly.

The girls glanced at me and then back at each other. *Nutso!* They giggled, new friends.

Now Inge ended her phone call. "So, where were we?"

"You said you had an assignment for me." I felt a twinge of apprehension. *Look* had been enthusiastic about these photos. More editors were remarking that they could count on me to take the pulse of our times . . . from a woman's point of view. With the attention my work had been getting, I should be picking through stories like chocolates in a Whitman's sampler, but still I was being sought only for stories fit for a lady photographer.

Inge reached over to the percolator. "Some?"

I shook my head.

She poured herself a cup. "Someone asked me for you."

"Yes?"

"The Mutual Life Insurance Company of New York."

An advertisement. My heart dropped. "Oh no."

She rested her nose on her knuckle, then rolled her gaze up to me. "They want a baby in it."

The Eliot(t)s stopped competing and looked at me. Was it that obvious that I'd gone through a bit of a rough patch since my miscarriage?

The teddy bear Eliott, Erwitt, broke the silence. "Did you hear that Marilyn Monroe lost another baby? Friend at *Time* told me."

*"Dummkopf!"* Inge cried. "Why do you bother Eve with this?"

"I hadn't heard," I said evenly. "When?"

"Just happened. She flew here from LA to save it."

"Where is she?"

"Here. At the Polyclinic Hospital—you know, in the Theater District. Every Tom, Dick, and Harry is trying to get a photo of her."

"When she's in the hospital?" I exclaimed.

He shrugged. "Marilyn shots sell. Especially when she's in trouble."

I got up. "Tell the insurance company to forget it," I told Inge.

I pushed through the agency door and into the roar of the city.

At the park, I strode by hot dog vendors' steaming carts and visitors with Kodaks strapped around their necks as they consulted maps; I heard the clopping and creaking of my father's horse and wagon—no, not Tata, just a carriage for tourists. From the zoo floated the distant barks of sea lions. I pictured them in their glass-and-concrete pool, a blur behind the foggy glass, circling, circling. They'd never know the ocean, never hunt for their own fish, or mate, or birth, or do anything but endlessly repeat their mindless circuit.

I ran.

My high heels clashed against the pavement. *Damn it*—where were my Keds? I dodged shoppers loaded with packages on Fifth Avenue, Salvation Army soldiers ringing their bells outside of stores, businessmen and secretaries in Midtown, playgoers lined up for matinees on Broadway. Out of breath at the Uris Theatre, footsore, frustrated, I snatched off my shoes and sprinted the last couple blocks in my stockings.

Gasping for air outside the tall bronze doors of the hospital, I reshod my feet and hobbled up the stairs. At the desk, I started to ask for you, then stopped. "I'd like to visit Zelda Zonk, please."

The receptionist's eyes narrowed behind steel-rimmed glasses.

The door behind me opened. May Reis blew in, carrying a suitcase in either hand.

"She says she wants to visit Zelda Zonk," the receptionist told her.

"Right. She's Zelda's sister." May held out a suitcase for me to take. "Help me take this up."

You were alone in the room, lying on the bed with your eyes wide-open, your face stricken. Without a stitch of makeup, you looked like the child who'd been dropped at the orphanage without warning. I went to you and scooped you into my arms.

I don't know how long you cried, your body quaking against mine as you gulped and gasped. When at last you were quiet, we pulled apart. Your clothes had been hung in the open closet. May was gone.

"I guess God thought I would be too kooky of a mother after all."

"Norma Jeane, that's just not true."

"The doctor said this is it. I can't have any more babies."

Your cheeks were slightly sticky when I brushed away your tears. There were no good words. I knew this from when well-meaning people tried to comfort me when I'd lost my baby.

"Arthur says, fine—he didn't want one anyway."

"He's trying to make you feel better," I said, stroking your matted hair.

"Well, he's doing a lousy job of it."

My gaze fell on a telegram partially covered by a book of Emily Dickinson's poems. I read the words WILL NOT APPEAR ANYMORE. WE ARE PREPARING BYLINE PIECES BY TONY CURTIS, JACK LEMMON AND BILLY WILDER. A STRONG UPBEAT APPROACH WILL BE BREAKING AROUND THE COUNTRY.

You saw what I was looking at. "I suppose you read the latest issue of *Time*, painting me as a freak. Tony told them that kissing me was like kissing Hitler. Nice, huh? And then there was Billy, saying he'd never work with me again. I was too late, too unprofessional, too nuts. They made me look like I was trying to be a brat, and a crazy brat at that. Well, I *was* crazy. The whole time we were shooting that goddamn picture, I was out of my mind with fear for the baby. You try kissing a man who you don't much like when your brain is on fire with worry. I think I did a pretty good job of it. You try getting to the set on time when the goofballs you have to take to get some sleep finally kick in at five, and the bennies you're given at six just can't cut through them. You try smiling and pleasing and kissing and being Marilyn Monroe when the thing you want most is dying inside you."

"I think you're brave."

"Ha. I'm not so brave." You wiped your face. The white polish was chipping from your nails. "I guess I'm stuck with being Marilyn now. How am I ever going to make a comeback?"

"You don't have to 'come back.' You're already there. You're already at the top."

Tears refilled your eyes. But it was true. Even when people rebuked you, the public couldn't get enough of you—maybe they wanted you even more. How the public loved seeing a great woman stumble.

An orderly pushed a squeaky cart down the hall. Out on the street, an ambulance wailed.

You sighed, then looked out the window, toward the Theater District. "Some place. What I have to do to get close to Broadway!"

I laughed. "Cut it out."

We listened to some nurses talking outside the room. "My headshrinker says people can't get better until they confront what's bugging them. I must have a lot wrong with me, because, four years into analysis, I'm still not past first grade." You rubbed your nose with the back of your hand. "How do I look?"

"Gorgeous." It was true. Even when gutted, charisma lit your small, flat face. You had the same otherworldly glow that set you apart in the crowd when you'd taken Art to Olivier at the Waldorf. That which was divine in you would not let the mortal rest.

"Help me up."

"Should you get out of bed?"

"It's not like I'll lose the baby."

I helped you onto your feet, then, at your orders, into your black trench coat and shoes. A scarf over your head, and you were Zelda Zonk.

"Is this a good idea? Where are we going?"

You snorted. "Therapy."

Hoping for May Reis to return, for a nosy nurse to butt in, for *somebody* to take you back to bed—where the hell was Arthur?—I held on to your arm. You padded toward the elevator.

"Floor, please?" the elevator operator asked when the door opened.

"Where is the nursery?" you asked. "The one with newborns."

Two floors down, the elevator car thudded to a stop. I followed you along the hall to a glassed-in room. There, behind the windows, a nurse was bathing a wiry infant who had screamed himself the color of borscht. Two other just-borns slept in their plastic bassinets, snug as pupae in their striped cotton swaddling. Through eyes matted with gooey drops, another one gazed at an overhead light, as inscrutable as a cat. *Baby Girl Sutherland*, the paper tag on her bassinet read.

What did she see? Having just exchanged a warm, wet world with its familiar, watery murmuring for this harsh, dry, blaring one, how did she feel? She'd just been cleaved from her mother, bathed, wrapped, and bedded, but did anyone here see her as something other than a task at hand? Above us, fluorescent lights buzzed. You reached over and wiped the tears from my cheek. "First, you cry."

We leaned our heads together, yours atop mine.

As we sniffed and swallowed, our grief flowing freely as from a lanced wound, an idea sent out quivering tendrils.

# 30

## 1959

"BURGEONING." THAT'S THE WORD FOR THE SORT OF SPRING day when the elms along the park sprout leaves that are tiny silver-green versions of themselves. Mothers pushed baby buggies overflowing with crocheted blankets, and toddlers strained at their mommies' hands. I was burgeoning with my own sort of baby, now cradled within the briefcase that I held up to let two little girls dart past me and into the zoo. Would Morris, Inge—anyone—like it?

When I got to the office, Morris was out. Inge sat back at her desk, rubbing her knuckles with Jergens while the newest underpaid young woman banged on her rickety typewriter. Inge nodded at the prints she had just reviewed. "You tried this before, with your sister." She dashed her brows. "How is your niece?"

"Wowing her teachers in kindergarten, thank you." I scooted my chair closer. "This is different. That shoot was of childbirth from an adult's point of view. This one is from the newborn's perspective. I call the story 'A Baby's First Five Minutes of Life.' I've written the copy."

She glanced at me.

"Yes, I am getting the cart before the horse. But I believe in this story. It's honest and eye-opening but shouldn't be objectionable." I laughed grimly. "Later, I'll record the forceps, the mothers going berserk under general anesthesia, the drugged-up babies. I'm not foolish enough to think that hospitals, let alone magazines, will let me open that can of worms now."

"*Das* is true." Inge held a print with the sides of her hands, so as not to get lotion on it.

I got up to go around her desk and peer over her shoulder. This story had to be told. People *had* to be curious about what infants go through, what all of us born in hospitals went through, to enter this world. Newborns were the littlest unseen.

"I tried not to show anything that could be construed as offensive, and there's nothing too scary for American readers to handle. The baby, now, must have been shocked. Can you imagine?"

"Imagine." The word begs the mind to burgeon. No wonder you claimed it.

Inge looked over her shoulder and saw me smiling. "*Ja*, these photos are special, this one in particular."

It had taken four months for the obstetricians to get used to having a little Jewish lady with a camera loitering in their delivery room and for nurses to trust that I'd get out of their way when they rushed babies to the resuscitation bed or needed to give emergency oxygen. I'd found a young mother from Long Island, Ruth Woods, who was interested in seeing what her child experienced at birth, and then the literal shoot of a lifetime—the baby's as well as mine—commenced.

The shoot flowed like magic. The mother determinedly labored for five and a half hours, and then the doctor announced that the baby was crowning. The scalp, as bunched and folded as a brain, pushed against the mother's taut flesh rim; her long groan broke the hush as the doctor guided the baby's head out. Another deep breath and another push, and then out popped the shoulders, like a cork from a sacred bottle, and then out slid the body. The sterile air rang with the doctor's pronouncement: "It's a boy!"

I sought this fresh human through my viewfinder, loving him, protecting him in my heart and in my mind, as he was slapped by the doctor and his umbilical cord was cut and clamped. I cradled him through my lens as he was passed to the nurse to suction, footprint, and suspend from his feet to measure him. He cried very little, mostly staring gravely at the nurse as she wiped him with gauze dipped in baby lotion and applied stinging drops to his trusting eyes. Before he was wrapped, he was held out to his mother in his rosy nakedness. From her table, she extended one finger, which he then clenched, clinging to his lifeline. My camera, with me behind it, swallowing tears, caught it all.

Inge examined the print in her hands, of the mother and baby first connecting. "I'm reminded of Michelangelo's painting in the Sistine Chapel, when God and Adam touch."

"*The Creation of Adam.*"

"Yes." She laughed. "And it is just that, isn't it, the creation of a person? Very clever, Eve." She looked up at me over her shoulder. "I think we do have something here."

TWO NIGHTS LATER, INGE STILL HADN'T PLACED MY "FIRST FIVE Minutes" story. Waiting with the throng in Times Square for you to arrive for the premiere of *Some Like It Hot*, I mentally scolded myself for thinking the story would ever find a home. I must have been nuts to believe that editors would think Americans were ready to let go of their delivery storks. Who wanted to see what babies went through at birth when they could laugh at Lucy and Ricky bumbling their way to the hospital and then sigh with relief when the Ricardos received their baby, nicely packaged and perfect?

Next to me, Arnold got knocked forward. "Hey!" The wild-eyed teenager who'd pushed him didn't acknowledge him, just kept worming his way through the crowd. "People," Arnold muttered to himself. He'd been extra irritable since, after several fits and starts, Parker Brothers had decided not to make Gold Rush after all. He was pursuing designing covers for record albums now instead.

One of the odd effects of our growing estrangement was that the closer Arnold and I were in actual, physical proximity, the more alone I felt. I could take the cooling of our marriage when I was on a shoot in, say, Boston, but to be together in the kitchen? Excruciating. Standing with him now, though we were shoulder to shoulder in a writhing mosaic of humans, I ached with loneliness. I hoped you were doing better with Arthur. Maybe that's why you hadn't called me back in the past few months—you had each other. That didn't mean I couldn't miss you.

You were still pulling in the crowds. Though many magazine writers had turned against you, grumbling that you were too spoiled, too troubled, too sexy, or too pretentious—*the nerve of Marilyn Monroe, thinking that she could be a serious actress!*—this crowd didn't care. When your limo finally got through and Arthur helped you out, the multitude surged forward in a great, shouting wave. Pushing and scrapping, everyone wanted a piece of you, to hell with your safety, with your need to breathe and keep your skin upon your body. Policemen wielded batons, but still people lunged at you. Arthur, trying to shield you, was cast aside like an angry stick.

I caught glimpses of your face through the melee. Your mouth hung ajar in a fixed smile that wasn't a smile, and your eyes were at half-mast. You looked as if you were wearing a Marilyn Monroe mask. I imagined the feral girl just behind it, flinching as the mob clawed for a scrap of her.

Your performance in the film was astonishing. *Some Like It Hot* was a comedy, and in it you were a joke, yet you made your character, Sugar "Kane" Kowalczyk, real and adorable. I can think of no other comedienne who could make her audience laugh with such affection. You looked like you were having a ball, though from my visit to the set, I knew differently.

No moviegoer would know how deathly ill you'd been, what a worried, sleep-deprived, strung-out ball of misery. How—*how*—had you dragged yourself to the set and then shone like this when the cameras rolled? Your fellow actors, who thought you were a spoiled brat for being tardy and calling in sick, had no idea that they were witnessing a miracle of fortitude. Here was a woman who'd already had two miscarriages and was acting her heart out in physically challenging roles in order to pay her husband's legal bills, when all she desperately wanted was to bring a baby to term. Servicemen get Purple Hearts for being wounded in action. You got a write-up about being a selfish bitch.

After the premiere, Arnold and I took a cab to the after-party at the Strasbergs' apartment, where Lee and Paula played your triumphant parents, hugging and coddling their A-plus daughter and showing her off to the Actors Studio crowd they'd invited. When you were changing clothes, Paula bragged about how you often spent the night there. Did Arthur stay, too? She showed you around to the other guests, you hanging your head and stammering under their praise. I saw Shelley Winters roll her eyes, but you weren't faking your shyness or your modesty. You knew that the junior high girls would take the dirty orphan girl down any chance they got.

On the couch, Susan Strasberg picked at a piece of strawberry cake. I sat next to her and raised my voice over loud, tipsy conversations and Ella Fitzgerald scatting on the record player. "Aren't you on tour with *Caesar and Cleopatra*?"

"I have the night off. My parents wanted me here." Though she was a Tony-nominated actress, the smile she put on failed to hide her jealousy. Her parents' favoritism for you wasn't doing you any favors with her.

As soon as you saw me, you broke from admiring the belly of the very pregnant Joanne Woodward with her and her husband Paul Newman, and came over. You kissed Susan on top of the head, then flopped onto the couch, legs in a knock-kneed splay like they'd been the day you collapsed upon that chair in Bement. But this time you weren't laughing. You had to be exhausted. I realized with a chill how tired—how sick—you must have been even as early as Bement, and how valiantly you railed against it. You'd tried to tell me, but I didn't understand how much you suffered with your endometriosis. I burned with my ignorance.

"Congratulations," I said. "You were magnificent."

"Oh," you groaned, "I was fat!"

"You were pregnant, friend."

Susan flashed her eyes at me, warning me away from forbidden ground.

But you just said, "I was. Four months gone." You struggled to sit upright. "Eve, I haven't told you—I found a doctor who says I can have a baby."

"You did?"

"Dr. Oscar Steinberg—have you heard of him? He says there's a surgery for what I have. I'm getting it as soon as I'm strong enough—he thinks in June."

Susan got up and left us.

"That's—that's fantastic," I said. How did you summon the courage to try again after so much loss? You'd been burned in pregnancy three times; how could you go around for a fourth?

You saw my face. "Don't worry. I can do this."

Arthur strolled over with a pipe between his teeth. He held a glass out to you. "Don't worry about what?"

You turned your face up to him. "About my surgery."

He nodded a curt hello to me, then prodded you with the glass. "It's water. Drink it." He took out his pipe. "You're not having surgery, honey."

"I am."

"You're not. Our film starts shooting in July. You can't have open abdominal surgery in June. And then what if you get pregnant?"

You laughed. "That's the point."

He smiled patiently, then explained, as if to a child, "We'd have to postpone the picture indefinitely, and we can't do that. I have already hired the best director, the best cinematographer, and the best actors there are. I've signed on Clark Gable, for Christ's sake, and Montgomery Clift and Eli Wallach. We can't do anything to slow things down. This is going to be the picture of the century."

I looked away. Modesty was not the man's strong suit. He'd been trumpeting to magazines everywhere about how his screenplay for *The Misfits* was the best ever written. No other movie would be as important. Compared with it, he implied, all other movies were trash—this before a single frame was shot.

Evidently he wasn't superstitious.

You put your glass down. "Do it without me."

"The movie? I can't!"

Any guests who weren't already listening paused. From the stereo console, Ella Fitzgerald's voice coursed up the scale and hung there.

"I wrote the part for you. The film's my love letter to my wife." He snatched up the glass and put it back in your hand. "It's your job now to stay healthy."

You put the glass against your cheek. Your chest heaved as if you were going to cry. Then, with a cackle, you burst into laughter, and kept it up until water spilled from the glass and down the front of your blouse.

Arnold, who'd been talking with one of Susan's young friends, strolled up. "What is so funny?"

"Not a damn thing." Arthur stalked away.

"Really," Arnold asked me, "what is the joke?"

You sniffed, still hiccuping a little from your outburst. Dabbing your wet shirtfront with a napkin, you said, "Eve's Husband, would you mind finding me another napkin?"

Arnold stared at where you were wiping. "Sure."

When he was across the room, asking Paula Strasberg for a napkin, you shook your head. "Arthur's movie will get made with me in it—don't worry—and when you see it, you tell me who it's a love letter to."

Arnold trotted back, touched the napkin to the wet spot, and then, remembering himself, turned purple. He handed you the napkin, then ran off for another one.

THE NEXT EVENING, INGE CALLED TO SAY THAT *LIFE* WOULD BE publishing my "First Five Minutes" story. Not only that, but they wanted to make it their cover story. I don't know how long I sat with the phone receiver to my chest after Inge hung up. The documentary that I had conceived of and carried out purely on spec was going to be the lead story in the world's most important magazine.

Arnold came into the kitchen. "Who called?" He saw my dazed expression. "What is it?"

"*Life* wants my baby story." I shook my head. "They actually want my baby story . . . for their cover."

He drew in a long breath, then stepped over and carefully folded me into his arms.

I absorbed his familiar smell, the remembered weight of his arms, the fit of his body against mine. He said into the top of my head, "Congratulations."

I nodded my head against his chest.

Too soon, he lowered his arms. He bent his head to look into my eyes. Quietly, he said, "I shall never see you now."

His sorrow panicked me. "Yes, you will! Of course you will."

He winced. "This is what I always feared. I know it is small of me, but I feared it."

"No! Arnold! You'll sell a game idea, or another book. Your dream will come true, too. You'll be the moneybags of the family—wait and see."

He stared at me. "What do you think I am talking about? All I was trying to say was that I can't bear being alone."

Francis burst into the kitchen, but upon seeing me, my little emotion reader stopped. "Mom? What's wrong?"

Arnold smiled coolly. "Congratulate your mother, Frank." He clapped my arm. "One of us is a success."

# 31

FOUR MONTHS LATER, THE STEAM BATH KNOWN AS AUGUST ARrived in Manhattan. Elbows rested on the drivers' windows of taxis. Sidewalks heaved with sweating men with their suit jackets drooping over their arms, and women with their dresses sticking to their backs. I was rowing through the humidity toward the *Life* office in the Time-Life Building—*Wait for me, delicious, frosty airconditioning!*—when the traffic light at the corner of Fifth and Forty-Eighth went out. The intersection instantly jammed.

I picked my way around blazing chrome bumpers and shouting cabbies with the other melting walkers. My tall, cool skyscraper waited just ahead. Finally, I ducked under the bas-relief of goldenhaired goddesses enjoying bunches of grapes—you and me?—and heaved through the door and into the lobby.

It was strangely dim. People were collecting in knots in the elevator bays. The power was out in here, too.

"When do they figure out that the elevators aren't coming?" said a man behind me.

I turned around. Gordon Parks's scarred face creased into a grin.

"Guess we got lucky today, Flip. Four minutes earlier and we'd be those poor wretches stuck between floors."

"Chicken! How are you?" I smelled the starch of his collar when we embraced. Did his wife iron his shirts? I imagined her fussing over him, and him being grateful to her, and felt the brokenness of my own marriage.

We determined that we were both going up to the editorial office on the eleventh floor and that we were not going to throw our lot in with the growing number of unadaptable souls waiting outside the elevators for the power to resume. We took the stairs.

"So," he asked me, our steps ringing in the stairwell, "when are you going to be on the staff of *Life*?" The doors at each floor had been propped open, so a feeble light diluted the darkness. I could hear climbers on the flights above and below us, but we had this stretch to ourselves.

"Is that what I'm working toward? Getting on *Life*?"

"Isn't everybody?"

"Not me. I like my independence."

He nodded, as if I were the one who decided my standing at *Life*. The magazine still had its token woman photographer in Margaret Bourke-White, although she now had Parkinson's disease and could no longer hold a camera. Nina Leen was listed on the masthead, too, but we all knew that she was only a contract photographer, like I was. I wondered who she was related to.

We kept trudging upward, side by side. "Well, congrats, Flip. I heard your 'Baby's First Five Minutes' story kicked some serious ass. They're saving it for November, the better for readers to admire the cover on their coffee tables when their families get together for Thanksgiving."

"I was wondering when they were going to run it. I guess it's good that they're waiting."

"Yes, it's good! You're the rising young star."

I laughed. *Young.* I was forty-seven.

"I still can't believe I'm getting a cover."

"I bet you can."

I looked at him.

"You wouldn't have kept going if you hadn't believed. Hey—a little arrogance isn't a bad thing for an artist. Someone's got to keep believing when nobody else does."

He caught my smile. In that dim stairwell, our shoes scraping against concrete, understanding hummed like a plucked cord between us.

*I see you and you see me. What do we do with this?*

I went with words that were easier to navigate. "I saw your feature on *A Raisin in the Sun* in last week's issue."

He paused to acknowledge what hadn't been said. He knew.

"Good play, good play."

"I went to it." With my husband. Why didn't I say so? "Your photos of Sidney Poitier did him justice."

"Thanks. This is going to sound like bragging, but you know what I'm proud of?"

"What?"

"My cover photo in May."

I smiled. Must be nice to have to specify which of his covers.

Every photojournalist studied the cover of *Life* when it came out, to see which of us was king for the week. I knew the cover he meant. I pictured the toothy wife of the ex-governor of New Hampshire, up to her thighs in rubber waders, her head thrown back in laughter as she and her flinty Yankee husband fly-fished.

"Former Governor and Mrs. Sherman Adams." He shook his head. "Possibly the whitest couple in America. I followed them around for a week, doing the whitest things rich, white Eastern WASPs could do. Forgive my boasting, but if this poor Black boy from Fort Scott, Kansas, can get into their heads, he can get into anyone's."

I didn't laugh. I knew he was serious. "Good work."

"Thanks. I thought I was a real champ. Who could beat me at empathy? Then this grown lady comes around and gets inside the head of a newborn."

Now I did laugh.

A huffing man tramped around a bend in the stairwell and down our flight. We spoke little after that. We didn't need to say much. We knew we were fellow travelers.

NINETY MINUTES LATER, WITH MY HEART STILL THRUMMING with affection for Gordon and with two new assignments from *Life* in hand, I was sitting on your cushy couch. The power was still out all over Manhattan, and the trains were down, so I couldn't get home. When I'd called, you said to come over and stay as long as I liked. Now, surrounded by photos of Carl Sandburg and Albert Einstein, and Arthur and his parents, and by your books—not just on Lincoln, but on philosophy, history, art, and, especially, poetry—I sipped a celebratory whiskey highball and forced my giddy brain to focus. You were in trouble.

"The operation didn't work," you said. "The surgeon opened me up, saw a bunch of endometriotic tissue and scarring on my Fallopian tubes, scooped out the damage, left in the tubes, and sewed me up. He'd better have left in my tubes! I'd pinned a note to my hospital gown ordering him to leave them." You took a gulp of your cocktail—your third drink since I'd arrived. "He said it was a salvage situation. That's what he called my operation, a salvage situation. Isn't that just me, a salvage situation?"

I'd seen, on the TV news, the mob swarming you as you left the hospital earlier that month. You were filmed as if you were arriving at a movie premiere, not leaving the hospital after a last-ditch, apparently unsuccessful surgery to have a baby. You smiled for the cameras from your wheelchair as the mob grabbed for pieces of you. They barely made room for Arthur to load you into the car. You kept your Fabulous Marilyn mask on as if you weren't in pain from major abdominal surgery, as if you hadn't just been dealt the worst of emotional blows. I remembered thinking, *Good Lord, they would kill you and then be shocked afterward that they had done it.*

"How do you feel?"

You swished your drink. "Crazy." You sighed. "If I could get just one full hour of sleep, maybe I wouldn't feel so nuts."

"I'm sorry, Norma Jeane."

"Don't be sorry. I found another doctor. I'm still going to have a baby, with or without Arthur." You caught my surprised look and half smiled. "A virgin birth, you know?"

This did not sound good. "Where is Arthur?"

"At our country house, working on the script."

"*The Misfits*?"

"Always on *The Misfits*. It's going to be the death of us."

"I thought it was done."

"Oh, it'll never be done. He's got to prove that he's more than Mr. Marilyn Monroe"—you laughed—"with his funny valentine."

I didn't know what you meant then.

"*The Misfits* is on ice—for now, anyway." You swirled the liquid in your glass, then drank it. "Clark Gable took another project while I was waiting for surgery. When he gets done, we'll start. Meanwhile, I'm doing another film, with this French guy, Yves Montand. I've got to keep working on *something*. Remodeling our country house doesn't pay for itself."

---

**MY MORTGAGE DIDN'T PAY FOR ITSELF, EITHER. BUT I TOOK AN**-other Joan Crawford story, out in California, for *Life* mainly in direct response to Gordon's remarks about getting into the head of someone completely foreign to one. The story was proving to be an interesting challenge. How *did* a poor Jewish girl from Philly get into the mind of Hollywood's reigning drama queen? Not just to document her, but to truly look at the world through her eyes.

"Would Marilyn have a part like this?" Joan asked me as her limousine arrived at the Twentieth Century-Fox lot where she was filming *The Best of Everything*. We got out, her tiny poodles yipping as I retrieved my cameras. Her chauffeur followed us, carrying her black alligator-skin gem case filled with matched sets of earrings, necklaces, and bracelets—not fake diamonds, rubies, and emeralds, she made clear, but the real deal, because they made her "feel more authentic." He also toted a tall thermos marked *Pepsi-Cola*, a vessel for her 140-proof vodka.

"My role in this picture is pivotal." She allowed me to walk next to her while her makeup artist, hairdresser, wardrobe mistress, secretary, and stand-in fell in line behind her goods-carrying chauffeur like the twelve little girls in *Madeline*. "Everyone respects and fears my character, although at heart she is kind and thoughtful—much like me. My character must *act* tough so that the young girls in the office don't think they can take her job without hard work. I chose the role so that I could model leadership for women." She lifted a languid hand in greeting to the workers positioning cameras and lights on the set as we cruised through. "I don't think Miss Monroe models anything but sleaziness in her roles."

I was puzzled by how often she put you down. When she had

a highly emotional scene, she would take her place twenty feet from the action, dash in high heels through the tangle of lights, hit her mark, and then—*Roll 'em!*—emote, genuinely breathlessly, for the camera. After delivering the scene, she'd pant to me, "Could Marilyn have done that?"

At her home, after I arrived each morning, she would descend her staircase like Cleopatra from her dais, only to stop halfway down. There, she'd genuflect at the niche in which her Oscar for *Mildred Pierce* was enshrined. "Does Marilyn have one of these?" she'd ask.

She would then bid me to sit on her ornate sofa, sheathed in clear plastic like the rest of her furniture, and we would make plans for the day. "I doubt if Marilyn has such a lovely home," she'd say, looking around.

Your name came up while I was shooting her frequent beauty-treatment sessions. Her lips—the rest of her face had been slathered in unguents and then mummified in bandages, leaving only her mouth and nostrils free—would say, "Would Marilyn go through such agony to be beautiful for her fans?" Once the wrappings were removed and her makeup was applied, she had me come close to shoot her curler crunching her eyelashes or her lip line being extended with a lip pencil. "Would Marilyn dare to show what she does to present her face to the world?"

One night we watched Walter Cronkite on her console TV, her twelve-year-old twin girls perched like beribboned sphinxes at her feet. When the program aired a live segment on Khrushchev's visit to Hollywood, I mentioned that my assignment for *Life* just before her had been photographing Khrushchev's wife in New York. "Madam Khrushchev was quite—"

"Shh!" Joan demanded. Her gaze was pinned to the screen, where a reporter had cornered you at a ceremonial dinner for the Soviet leader. Your eyes were open and your mouth tight. No Old

Marilyn lowering of the lids or twitching of the lips was in evidence here. The reporter asked, "What did you think of what Mr. Khrushchev had to say?"

You started to pucker like Old Marilyn, then stopped yourself. "Interesting," you said.

The reporter smiled. "How did you expect him to be?"

I could see you fight to control your face. You leaned toward the microphone. "Interesting."

The reporter shuffled, then asked, "How did you think the evening would go?" He tipped the microphone toward you.

You smiled impishly. "Interesting."

"What a dumb broad!" Joan cried. "Isn't she a dummy, girls?"

Two big bows bobbed obediently. "Yes, Mommy."

My heart broke for you. You aren't dumb. I'd seen you hold your own with Arthur's literary friends, swapping lines of poetry with Carl Sandburg and clever illustrated notes with Norm Rosten. Oh, you could make it look like you were playing your one-word response to the reporter as a joke, but that wasn't what was really going on. You hated exposing your unedited self on live television. You feared that Norma Jeane would fail.

My sorrow for you flashed into disgust for Joan. She and her furniture clad in plastic as if in condoms, her daily *Sunset Boulevard* descent down her staircase, her stern treatment of her children, repulsed me.

The last morning, I was prepping my camera for a final shoot while mentally tallying how much I would earn for the sacrifice of the two weeks with Francis and any remaining shred of goodwill from Arnold, when I looked up and saw Joan under a life-sized painting of herself when young. She was holding her hair up to strike the same pose as in her portrait.

She sighed, her air of Hollywood royalty gone. "I'll give you all the material you need. How can you make me sellable?"

I was fed up with her by then. "You don't need my help in that department."

"Please. I need to know. How can I be more sellable? I've taken the low road, and I've taken the high road, but I'm losing ground no matter what I do." She laughed, haughtily at first, and then her lacquered mouth fell. "Help me."

In that moment I saw that the great Joan Crawford was still ambitious, still striving, despite all she'd achieved. No matter how many accolades and trophies she racked up, she'd always be the girl from small-town Texas, unloved and gauche, and being the queen of Hollywood could never fix that. She'd always be looking over her shoulder for another gauche, unloved girl to come along and snatch away her crown, because she knew the awesome power of the ambitious, gauche girl with everything to gain and nothing to lose, and, knowing that power, she feared it in others. She knew that a dirty girl claiming her own was the most powerful force in nature.

"You have real clout," she said, honeying her voice. "Look what you've done for Marilyn."

"I didn't do anything for her. Whatever Marilyn has, she's gotten for herself."

An edge crept into her tone. "Well, then, she's certainly done a lot for you."

Had you? Hadn't I gotten whatever I had by myself?

She looked up at her portrait, her gaze lingering lovingly on her haughty and gorgeous former self. Now in her fifties, she was the same woman as in the portrait above her, but her glamorous shell had worn thin over time; I could glimpse the anxious girl crouched within it. And oh, that girl within her, that astonishing, eager girl! What a fighter, what a dreamer, what a girl who wouldn't say no; what a striver, what a thinker, what a doer who exhausted herself and yet *still* wouldn't say no. That girl wasn't your enemy or mine, Norma Jeane. She was all of us.

I raised my camera.

Later, at Magnum, when Inge was going over the contact sheets for the shoots, she paused on that image. She tipped her head to gaze at me over her glasses.

"I have never seen Joan Crawford look so"—she laughed—"likable. What did you give the old girl?"

I sighed. "A break."

# 32

## 1960

**A LOT CAN HAPPEN IN TWO HOURS. ONE TWO-HOUR TOUR OF** magazine editorial offices in July netted me (1) a request by *Life* to cover a Broadway play that was going to be aired on television, the first ever in color; (2) a feature on the wives of the presidential candidates for *Harper's Bazaar*; and (3) an assignment on the "school for sit-ins" in Petersburg, Virginia, for *Look*. Yes—surprise, surprise—they were all supposed to be from a woman's point of view, but they were good stories. Damn it, why shouldn't stories from the female ghetto be the *best* stories?

Therefore, a Monday on which I would have been packing sandwiches for the beach for Francis, had I been the kind of mother he yearned for and I sometimes wished I could be, found me driving through the web of toll roads from New York to Virginia for the sit-in story. My contact in Petersburg, Myra, had told me on the phone when I was preparing for the story that her community had called a strike at the local Woolworth's because it refused to serve Blacks at its lunch counters. The "Can't Eat, Don't Buy" campaign was a nonviolent means of hurting the dime-store chain at the cash register. *Don't put money in the pockets of those who revile you* was the idea.

To get their point across, Myra told me, volunteers "sat in" at the lunch counter and marched with placards in front of the store, where they were often met with vigilante harassment and sometimes violence. For that, the protesters needed training—hence my story for *Look*.

"Calmly sitting on a lunchroom stool or walking along with a sign while abuse and suffering rains down on you doesn't come naturally to a person," she told me when I got to Petersburg. She was accompanying me to the local AME church's basement, a painted cinder-block space that smelled of scorched coffee.

I rested my hand on the leather of the camera case around my neck, my familiar companion. "I imagine not."

She turned to me, her shiny curls piled atop her head. The overhead fluorescent lights reflected off her black-framed glasses. "No one can imagine such hatred coming from strangers until it comes for you. It feels unnatural, yet hate is the most natural thing in the world." She gave me a pointed look. "But so is love."

She introduced me to one of the college kids in the group, Priscilla, whose soft, serious face made her look younger than her twenty-two years. A lot of the volunteers were young moms and dads who were fighting for their children. Others, like Myra, were grandparents who were as concerned for their grown children as for their grandbabies. Priscilla was the newest recruit, and would therefore be the subject of my documentary.

I gauged the lighting as Priscilla seated herself at a wooden table, straightened her cardigan over her white blouse, and opened her Bible. I was close enough to see which book she turned to—John. She was reading a passage about loving thy neighbor when a sleek young woman in glossy spit curls walked up, examined her own nails, then lunged in and gave Priscilla's hair a yank. We both jumped. The man with her dragged on his cigarette, then leaned to within three inches of Priscilla's face and blew. Together, he and the woman took turns shoving her from behind, then shoved her in unison while calling her the worst racial slurs. "What you want anyway?" they sneered. "Haven't we done enough for you?"

The attacks went on for two hours, the length her stint on the picket line would be. For one hundred twenty minutes, I was close enough to Priscilla to get jostled, blinded by smoke, and showered with spittle as her abusers shouted into her ears.

I was shaking when their torture was over. "Is it really that bad?"

"Worse," said one of her tormentors, Florence, as the man helped Priscilla from her seat. "You can feel the hate of your attacker. There is no worse feeling in the world."

I accepted the tissue Florence took from the pocket of her dress. "And still you stay there," I said.

Florence put her arm around Priscilla. "And still you stay there."

"The bravest person," I said, "is the most terrified person, who goes on and gets it done."

She frowned at me as she rubbed her numb friend's shoulder.

She was right. Those were Gordon's words. What'd I know about bravery?

I had my cameras ready when Priscilla took up her sign and joined the picket line the next day. Policemen with dogs formed a barricade on the street, for whose protection, the hecklers' or the marchers', I wasn't sure. The air jangled with menace from the men and women who'd gathered behind them. I braced myself for violence.

For two hours, Priscilla carried her sign. For two hours, I waited for the taunts to erupt into something worse. Finally, her time on the line was up. I found that my neck and shoulders ached from clenching as she and I walked through the streets, back to the church.

Down in the safety of the basement, her colleagues took turns rocking her in their arms, and then she was given a lemonade before she slumped onto a folding chair.

"How'd you get through it?" I asked, sitting next to her. Myra brought me a lemonade, too.

"I recited poetry and chemical formulas."

"Chemical formulas!"

The anxiety on her young face dissolved. "I'm a chemistry major at Virginia State."

No one had physically attacked her or the other marchers this time. Myra heard that the police had decided to tamp down the heckling, and the worst of the vigilantes never showed up. Word had gotten out that someone from *Look* would be there. There are some unseen who want to stay that way.

Soon afterward, I was invited to follow Priscilla and her friends to their college, where they sang "We Shall Overcome" and other protest songs, accompanied by a white guitarist who'd come down from New York. I shot a few frames there, then loaded my car and made a melancholy two-hour drive up to DC. How did those protesters keep their chins up with so many obstacles before them? I hoped my pictures would help them in some way. Maybe I was dreaming. Maybe all of us at Magnum were kidding ourselves about photos mattering. There was no less evil in the world now than when Magnum was started, after the war. Yet I'd chosen photography over family. *Pauper, where are you crawling?*

LATER THAT AFTERNOON, MY CAR BUMPED OVER THE TONY cobblestone streets of Georgetown, where the subject of my article about the wives of the candidates lived. I knocked on the door of a town house that oozed money and prestige from its red Colonial-era bricks. Mrs. John F. Kennedy answered.

"Hello," she said, composed, in a pink Givenchy suit with a schoolgirl's rounded white collar. "You must be Mrs. Arnold." Her voice was as soft and sweet as a child's, her small nose and wide-spaced eyes equally girlish. She seemed much younger than the thirty-one years—your age, minus three—that my research stated she was. So soon after I'd photographed the picket line and people who just wanted to be able to eat at a dime-store lunch counter, my mood did not incline me to sympathize with this monied waif.

She ushered me among linen-covered club chairs and French china as we discussed where it would be best to set up the shoot. The back of the house had the best natural light at this time of day, she said.

I must have looked surprised that she knew lighting was a factor.

"I was the 'Inquiring Camera Girl' for the *Washington Times-Herald*," she said, in that funny little voice. "I suppose that didn't make it into the press kit on me."

"Then I guess you know that I'm looking for 'color.' What do you want to be doing in the photo? What setting would best reveal"—I spread my hands—"your personality?"

"Is it my personality you want, or that of the wife of Jack Kennedy?"

Our eyes met. There was more to this woman-child than I had given her credit for.

"Actually, yours."

"Then you'd hand me the camera and I'd be doing the photographing."

I laughed.

She remained serious. "What do you suggest I be doing as the potential first lady?"

I cleared my throat. *I see.* She preferred to keep it all business. Fine. Not everyone was the lighthearted sort. "Why don't we photograph you with your daughter?"

"Why does everyone always want her in the picture?" She held her belly. I realized then that her designer suit was hiding a waist expanded by pregnancy. "I want girls to know they are more than just mothers."

She was full of surprises. "Agreed. I'm just trying to get you on the cover, Mrs. Kennedy. *Harper's* plans to highlight all the candidates' wives in the same issue, and you're the youngest and prettiest, and the only one with a young child. I've been working with magazines for a decade, and one thing I know is that a young, pretty woman with a beautiful baby sells copies, whatever you and I might think of that." I caught her glance. "It also gets votes."

Her black brows shot up from their crooks. I thought of you. You had brows like that.

The doorbell rang. She went to answer it herself and returned with the hairdresser Kenneth Battelle, loaded down with two aqua-colored train cases. His sweet face lit up, which sweetened it all the more. "Eve!"

We kissed hello.

"You know each other?" Mrs. Kennedy looked at my plain, graying bun.

"For a couple years now," he said, "since I started doing Marilyn's hair." I noted Mrs. Kennedy's frown. "How are you?" he asked me.

"Busy. Good," I said. "And you?"

"Same. Busy is good. I've been seeing a lot of our friend Marilyn when she isn't jetting off to Hollywood. Where would you like me to set up?" he asked Mrs. Kennedy.

"My bedroom," she said, her baby voice sharp.

"Would you like Eve to join us? I know Eve specializes in these behind-the-scenes shots."

"No."

We both looked at her.

"No," she repeated.

Curbed, I sat on the couch, and wondered what I'd done wrong.

To pass the time, I got my camera out and framed shots from where I sat. A portrait of Mrs. Kennedy appeared in the viewfinder. I played with my focus, easing in on the wide-set eyes, the small nose with the bump on the end, the pretty lips. I realized with a jolt: You had a forehead like that. You had a nose like that, a mouth like that, even a voice like that when you were playing the original Marilyn. She was a dark version of you.

She came down the steps, her flipped bob swooped to the left—your hair, but the color of black coffee. Her little girl, Caroline, was on her hip, the child's feet, in patent leather shoes and lacy socks, dangling.

Mrs. Kennedy took us to the rear of the house and opened the door to a library, where her husband and another man were consulting some paperwork. She jabbed her thumb at the door, for them to leave.

Her husband got up. "You're the boss," he said with the good-natured nonchalance of a man who holds the reins in a relationship.

He started to leave, then quickly came back with his hand out to me. "I'm Jack Kennedy."

"She knows Marilyn Monroe," Mrs. Kennedy said, watching him.

"You do?" He smiled easily. "My, uh, wife thinks I'm an expert on Miss Monroe now that I've met her once. I had the honor, uh, of sitting next to her at dinner at my brother-in-law's house in Malibu—I was out there for the convention." He didn't mention that he'd won the nomination for president at that convention. "She's, uh, a nice young woman."

Mrs. Kennedy swallowed.

At our shoot, she was the opposite of you. While you took off and led me on a photographic safari, in the rare times that Mrs. Kennedy allowed herself to look into the camera, the woman behind her eyes ran away from me. She spoke little, throwing her attention into her toddler daughter as they arranged a vase of tulips and then read a book together. Was she always like this, or was my friendship with you her beef? I would encounter the same resistance in Grace Kelly, then the princess of Monaco, when I filmed her a few years later. I'd taken it personally until I learned that the princess had recently found out that her husband was straying. It wasn't me she was angry at, but her husband.

After two hours, I packed up and went to my hotel in downtown DC. Tomorrow, I would photograph Mrs. Richard Nixon in the morning and Mrs. Lyndon Johnson, the wife of Kennedy's running mate, in the afternoon. And then, the following morning, I could finally go home.

WHEN I WALKED INTO THE KITCHEN TWO DAYS LATER, FRANCIS—who, at eleven, preferred that I call him Frank—was dropping root beer Fizzies tablets into a glass of water. The screen door banged as I dropped my camera bags on the counter. I wheeled over and hugged him until he squirmed.

"Where's Dad?" I asked.

"At the grocery. He left a long time ago."

"He just left you here? Alone?"

"He always does." His glance was part accusation and part something else before he shrugged. "I'm used to it."

My heart got heavy. "Is that your lunch?" I nodded at the log of Velveeta with its peeled-back aluminum foil wrapper.

"I'm okay!"

It was nearly dusk when Arnold returned. From the bedroom window, I watched him walk from the garage. He did have a bag of groceries.

He stopped unloading when I came down to the kitchen, and then he continued.

"Hello, Arnold."

He put a bottle of ketchup in the cupboard. "Hi."

He wouldn't even look at me. I hadn't seen him in days. My hurt came out in a demand. "Where have you been?"

"You, who have been here exactly one full day over the past three weeks, are asking me where *I* have been?"

I glanced toward the living room, where Francis was watching an anvil crushing a cartoon roadrunner on TV. I lowered my voice. "You left Frank alone all day. Where's Elaine?"

"She had to leave." He scowled. "Frank is okay. He can fend for himself. He has had to—hasn't he?—while you do whatever the hell you please."

"It's called work."

Was there something so criminal about a woman doing what she pleased? Was it so wrong for me to love pursuing something I was good at, something that was of value to the world? But arguing this would not help me, not when I also wanted my husband. We'd had a good marriage, years ago.

"You'll be happy to hear that my next job will be in New York," I said. "I'm going to follow Mary Martin in her role as Peter Pan, and document the show being taken from the stage to color TV. What I don't get is why Broadway would agree to cannibalize itself by broadcasting it. Who's going to go to a play when they can see it at home on their TV?"

"They have to be home to do that," he said flatly.

"You know what I'm saying. I think we're seeing the end of—"

"Honestly, Eve, I don't care."

The telephone rang. He answered, then held the receiver out. "It's your buddy. Marilyn."

He was making me pay for following my vocation, and it was working. My guts were in a catfight when I took the phone.

You were phoning from Nevada, where you'd just begun filming *The Misfits.* You said Magnum photographers were taking turns following the shoot for its duration. Did I know?

Yes, I did. My dear Henri and Inge Morath, the newest Magnum photographer—and the "other Inge" at the agency, besides Inge Bondi—had been assigned the first two weeks of filming and were already on set. Another pair of photographers would take their place for the next couple of weeks, followed by other biweekly duos until filming was complete. I'd been offered a chance to go but had turned it down. I didn't have it in me to wrangle with Arnold for something as culturally inconsequential as a movie shoot. If I was going to nail my marriage into its coffin, I wasn't going to do it over Arthur's vanity project.

Now you were begging me to come before the next pair from Magnum was supposed to arrive. "Please, Eve, please. I'll give you all the best shots. You know how brilliant we are together."

"Oh, we're brilliant, but it's not about that."

"Please, Eve. Arthur—" I heard the suction sound of you cupping the receiver. You lowered your voice so someone there wouldn't hear. "He's cruel. He thinks I'm disappointing—I embarrass him in front of his friends. I'm ruining his career—his own words! I saw them in his journal in England, and now he no longer bothers to deny them. His contempt for me"—you swallowed—"it's all over the script."

"Oh, Norma Jeane."

"I'm not kidding, Eve. I need a friendly female face. It's been hell."

"Isn't Inge Morath there? Didn't Paula Strasberg go with you?"

"I need a *friend.* Someone who doesn't want something from me. Someone who actually . . . who actually likes me."

I opened the door for a housefly that was bouncing against the screen. It zoomed back into the room, away from its offered freedom.

Your sigh gushed over the phone line. "Oh, what am I saying? You must want to be with your little boy. Of course you want to be with him! I shouldn't take you away from him, or from Mr. Eve. I know you've been having rough times."

"Yeah," I murmured.

You were quiet. "I'm sorry, Eve. I should be more of a friend to you, huh? I'm such a jerk! Never mind. You shouldn't come. I mean it—please don't come. You take care of yourself. I'll be okay."

I stared at the fly, now crawling up the screen. You, a feral girl who knew only how to survive; you, who never knew how to think beyond yourself, because you were all you ever had; you, abandoned young, were concerned for me. That didn't come naturally to you. You had to work hard at seeing how to take care of others. And I wasn't getting much care at home. Tears needled my eyes.

I gulped them back. Crumbling at the thought of someone caring for me . . . *Don't be such a needy child!* But aren't we all just needy children at our core, scared and lonely and confused?

"What was that about?" Arnold asked when I hung up ten minutes later.

I drew in a breath. "She wants me to join the Magnum crew in Nevada, where they're shooting *The Misfits.* It's just for fourteen days," I added quickly.

"You told her no, right?"

I shook my head.

He stared at me.

"It's just for fourteen days, and I don't leave for a week. Until then, and after then, I will only take work in town. There are some advertising jobs I can take—"

"We don't have a marriage."

Acid trickled through my gut. The conversation I didn't want to have . . .

He leaned in to make sure Francis was still watching TV. "I do not know what you call this . . . this arrangement, but it is not a marriage. I am sick of it."

"You're sick of it? You work your damnedest to make me suffer."

"I have never laid a touch on you."

"A finger," I said. "You never laid a *finger* on me. And I guess, technically, that is true." He really didn't get it. "I'm exhausted, Arnold."

"You're exhausted, are you? What about me? What about me, having to hold everything together, cooking, cleaning, doing things no other man would do?"

"Yet still you can pursue whatever you want in the city, no explanations necessary."

Something flinched in his eyes.

I scrambled to understand what I was seeing.

"Mom? Dad?" Francis called. "You coming? Your show's going to be on."

Arnold and I slunk in to sit as a family in front of the television. We watched, my mind reeling with the implications of what had and hadn't been said, until Francis got up after *Father Knows Best.*

When he'd collected hugs and gone up to bed, Arnold and I sat in the dark, the TV flickering in front of us. Alfred Hitchcock teetered onto the screen. From above the stacked life buoys of his chins came his lugubrious "Good evening."

I looked over at the man with whom I'd shared my life for nineteen years. How I had loved that craggy profile, that man, still handsome in early middle age. How he had once loved me. Oh, to love and be loved like that again.

Since when did I not fight for what was mine? "It's just for two weeks," I said. "And then I will stay here, with both of you."

He looked at me, then laughed silently. I watched him stalk up the stairs.

A lot can happen in two hours. Two hours was all it took for it to become clear that I had to do something drastic to save my marriage.

# 33

A DISTURBANCE IN THE FRONT OF THE AIRPLANE: MY EYES SHOT open from a doze. Even in a plane picking up passengers in San Francisco, on a flight bound for Reno, I knew what that particular mix of excited cries and wolf whistles meant.

Your huge straw hat hadn't fooled anyone. Passengers who'd been on board offered napkins or pads of paper for you to autograph. People just getting on board held their tickets out for your signature before they squeezed down the aisle. Some guy who'd been drinking since Chicago wanted you to sign his forehead. Though you signed and smiled for the people clustering around you in the aisle, there was something about you, something precarious and frail, that made me hurl myself from my seat to run to you, only to get knocked back down into my chair by a man in a Hawaiian shirt.

Up at your row, Arthur shoved his skinny frame between you and your fans. "Leave her alone, why don't you? Have some decency."

May Reis fluttered around the edges of the gawkers, begging

to get by. When a stewardess finally herded your fans to their places, May dipped in and tucked blankets around you as if you were an invalid. Your eyes drifted shut and your lips, pale and dry, parted. You had to be drugged, if you were sleeping.

I sat back, leaving you to your rare rest. But why were you in San Francisco? You were supposed to be in Reno, on location, where I was to join you on the *Misfits* set.

The cabin still abuzz, though all were buckled in, the plane took off and the stewardesses worked their way down the aisle.

"Coffee?" asked Patty, who'd been serving me since New York. Her ash-blond hair, with its short flips and swoopy bangs, was styled like yours and Mrs. Kennedy's. The 'do that Kenneth called the "club cut" had migrated from your heads to that of every young woman in America, save for mine. I clung to my long, prematurely gray locks like a girl Samson. I could sit on my braid, if I ever let it down. The ends of my hair were still the brown of my youth.

Patty shook her coffeepot, waiting for an answer. "Sure. Please." Why not? I was wide-awake now. I'd slept little in the days before I left. Anxiety from Arnold's silent treatment, meant to control me, controlled nothing, only robbed me of sleep. I understood now why keeping prisoners awake was a form of torture. How *did* you endure your sleepless nights?

Patty leaned down to whisper, "Marilyn Monroe is on this plane."

"Is she?"

Coffee twirled from the spout of the pot and into my porcelain cup. "I heard she tried to kill herself with sleeping pills. Her husband caught her just in time and took her to the hospital in San Francisco."

My heart skipped. I was unaware that you'd been hospitalized.

"I don't know why she's the despondent one." She held up the cream. I nodded. "She cheated on *him*," she said as white clouds billowed in my coffee. "She was the one who had the affair with that French guy—what's his name, Yves something? You know, the guy who starred with her in her last movie."

I thought of how hard you'd toiled to become famous. Now you were so famous that stewardesses knew details of your affair, details you'd only recently shared with me, during a drunken call from the filming location. You'd been defensive, but you needn't have worried. I hadn't judged you. I knew the unloved child in you was lashing out at Arthur's disdain for you—the equivalent of abandonment to you.

When the plane landed in Reno, around midnight, I made my way to you through the crowd of other passengers being herded off. "Well, hello, Miss Most Advertised."

Your eyes lost some of their vacantness. "Miss Documentary Photographer," you whispered. "You came."

Arthur pulled at your arm. "Come on, Marilyn. Your fans are waiting. Let's get through this."

Fans were waiting at midnight?

After everyone else filed off, I followed behind you, with Arthur and May, as you stepped onto the airplane stairway and into floodlights. A brass band burst into "I Wanna Be Loved by You." A crowd of hundreds, even at this hour, even in this little town, roared. Reporters' flashbulbs popped as, smiling rigidly, you descended the steps on your way toward the terminal entrance, where a banner proclaimed, *Welcome Back, Marilyn!* All this hoopla for a woman recovering from a possible suicide attempt. Who had called this mob here at this hour, for this occasion? Oh, Norma Jeane, surely it wasn't you.

Still on Eastern time, I got up early the next morning and took a walk around Reno. The morning light, though hazy with desert dust, was not kind to the sleeping town. Without their blinking neon frames, the colored signs of the casino fronts looked on dully, as if to say, *It's not* my *job to hide the ugly buildings beneath me. It's not* my *job to warn people of the disappointment waiting inside.*

At the end of the block, the Mapes Casino and Hotel lorded over the shallow Truckee River. The cast, crew, and everyone else associated with *The Misfits* was staying there. I'd read that it was the tallest building in Nevada when it was built, just after the war. Its height and its elegant Art Deco façade set it apart from the tacky carnival of avarice over which it loomed. *I'm important,* it seemed to say. *Important things happen within.*

And they did. Presidents, movie stars, and European royalty had laid their heads there. At its bar, in 1957, the good senator McCarthy had gotten smashed with two reporters and admitted that he didn't have any actual names on his list of 205 Communists that had started the Red Scare and destroyed so many lives. Turned pariah almost overnight after he himself was put under investigation, he died of alcoholism less than three years later. Who would have dreamed of his swift demise when I photographed him?

Despite the stain of McCarthy, the Mapes held itself as if it were too important to be part of the Divorce Capital of America, too big to be a place just to stew in for the six weeks that it took to legally end a marriage. Only in Nevada were divorces granted if one simply put in the prescribed time, unlike in every other state in the union, where aggrieved spouses had to sue and countersue on the grounds of adultery, abandonment, cruelty, mental illness, or something else ugly. Let it never come to that with Arnold and me! Your Arthur had been one of the thousands who'd gone to Reno to get a "painless" divorce, which freed him to marry you, and now you were here—fresh from your very public affair and, if Patty the stewardess was to be believed, a suicide attempt—in town to play a part that Arthur had written for you. And here I was as well, to photograph you as your character went through a Reno divorce, even as I clung to the wreckage of my own marriage. How had our lives become such a Russian nesting doll of ironies?

The weather was already hot when I went inside and found Henri observing his fellow diners over his cup in the coffee shop of the Mapes. Tears sprang into my eyes as we kissed cheeks and then embraced. I kept my cheek to the linen lapel of his suit. The sound of his heart made the tears come harder.

He tucked his chin to look down at me. "*Chérie!* What is it?"

I pulled back, swiping at my eyes. "Nothing. Lack of sleep."

Not convinced, he aimed his high forehead, with its receding hairline, at me.

I sighed. "Pressure from home."

A waitress came with coffee. He waited until she'd finished pouring. "What is it that Capa said? 'The camera is a jealous partner. . . .'"

"Other couples make it. You're married. You've been married for over twenty years."

He winced. "Ratna and I, we no longer—" He sighed, then pushed his wire-rimmed glasses up until his kind eyes were centered within them. "It has been years since we have lived together. We share the title only."

"I'm sorry."

He took my hands, balled on the laminate table, and shook my closed fists. "I am seeing your stories everywhere now, *chérie.* One on the candidates' wives, in *Harper's,* one on your school for sit-ins in *Look.* But no matter the magazine, I always recognize your work, even before I read the credits."

"You do?"

"Your work is unmistakable. There is a quiet truth in your images that is yours alone."

Those words, from him—I could hardly bear how happy he made me. "I'm just trying to do what you taught me—to wait and look until the truth is revealed, and then *oop!* The decisive moment."

He inclined his head. "Then you do me honor. But there is something else to your work, something not I or anyone else could teach you. Your subjects trust you. You let them give you what they want. They want to give themselves to you. That is your special talent."

My eyes welled up again. I took my hands back to wipe my eyes. "I'm sorry. I'm just really weepy right now."

He sighed and shook his head. "I am sorry that I must go. I would have enjoyed working on this assignment with you."

I wouldn't have believed that from any other photographer. We are a competitive bunch.

He drew air over his teeth. "Your poor friend."

"Marilyn? I came in on the plane bringing her back from San Francisco."

His grimace acknowledged that what Patty the stewardess had told me was true. "I cannot understand her wish to destroy herself, yet of course I can. There's a certain myth of what we in France call *la femme éternelle. La femme éternelle* is a woman who is alert and vivid, with an intelligence in her personality and in her glance. It shines, then fades, then shines again, like the sun playing among clouds. This is our Marilyn." He paused to make sure I was following. "*Oui*, she has her beauty. It is like an apparition—we hunger to see it because we cannot believe what we are seeing. But it is this intelligence about which I speak. That is *la femme éternelle*."

The waitress came and took my order for breakfast. Then Henri resumed.

"I had the pleasure of sitting next to her at dinner last week. I saw this intelligence come fluidly, all the time, the amusing remarks, precise, pungent, direct, delivered without a shred of arrogance. There is almost a quality of naivety."

I smiled. You would have said it was because you were feral.

"But, as I said, *la femme éternelle* is a myth. For a flesh-and-blood woman to have it"—he shook his head—"it cannot be easy for her. She is like a unicorn among horses—she has no place." He aligned his spoon with his coffee cup. "The best we can do for her as photographers is to tell the truth about her—although she hides it from even herself, no?"

He sighed. "Listen to me, imposing my Gallic superstitions upon your friend. But I must say that I saw her great discipline as an actress. It is very clear that she is American."

"Really? How is that?"

His smile was gentle. "Only an American would not know that."

I laughed. "You just did my Ukrainian mother proud. Her greatest wish was that her children be American. Well, and to marry up. And to be professionals. And have lots of smart and attractive children."

"Ah, your mother is very much an American."

"And Marilyn?"

"Because she thinks there is always more, when she should be glad."

"I will tell her that."

He propped his head on his hand and studied me. *"Chérie?"*

"Yes?"

"I just realized—are you not *la femme éternelle*, too?"

I burst out laughing. "Yeah. Me and Marilyn. Two *femmes éternelles.*"

"I do not kid. You have the quicksilver intelligence." He smiled. "But, *chérie,* with you there is no naivety."

"That's right. Only ice-cold realism here."

"I would not say that. But as we do for Marilyn, perhaps the best we can do for you is to tell you the truth."

I posed it jokingly, though I was scared to hear the answer: "And that is . . . ?"

"That you do not realize your power."

Our waitress came to the table to tell us that Henri's driver was waiting to take him to the airport. He paid our bill and, with many kisses to my cheeks and the top of my head, left.

I ATE MY EGGS, THEN WANDERED TO THE LOBBY, WHERE THE crew had been lounging, waiting for you to come down so that filming could begin.

"EVE?" Whitey Snyder stepped out from the gift shop with a small paper bag.

We hugged. I stood back to behold him in his snap-button shirt and big oval belt buckle. "Aren't you the Western dude?"

His grin softened his sharp features. "When in REno . . ." He took a plastic figurine of a cowboy from his bag. When he pushed a button under its base, the little cowboy collapsed like a dropped marionette.

"This is ME out on location when it gets to be one hundred ten degrees in the shade." He released the button. The cowboy popped upright. "And this is me after a margarita. It's for my kids." He dropped it back into the bag. "I was glad to hear that you were going to be on this shift for Magnum."

"Here I am. How has the filming been?"

He made a face. Before he could speak, a youth sauntered up with a pencil and a pad of paper. "Who's got bets?"

"EVE, this is Jim Goode. He's writing a book about the filming. Jim, Eve Arnold, from Magnum Photos." I heard the flatness in Whitey's voice. He didn't like this young man.

"Photographer, eh? A picture's worth a thousand words, right? Well, I'm here to photograph with words. Frank hired me—Frank Taylor, the producer," he clarified for me, an obvious know-nothing. "He says an important film like this deserves a book. I say that I'm a firm believer that the reader wants a complete story of any situation, and that's what I'm going to give them."

Whitey started to pull me away.

"Right now, I'm taking bets on when Marilyn will come down this morning—*if* she comes down. Since you're new here, I'm going to give you a little tip. She hasn't graced the lobby before eleven since we located here, though start time is nine. And since she is just back from"—young Mr. Goode cleared his throat—"sick bay, today I'm going to say noon."

A crew member dressed in full Western wear slouched over. "Give me five bucks on ten o'clock, kid. After her shenanigans with the pills, she'll want to turn over a new leaf, so I say only an hour late—ten." Another fellow, in denim and embossed boots, stepped over to place his bet. Looking around, I realized all the crew members were outfitted like matinee cowboys.

Whitey led me off as Jim wrote down the bets. "Whitey?" he called after us.

"I'm not betting," he called over his shoulder. "SNAKES," he said to me. "Norma Jeane's lateness has poisoned the crew against her. Can you do your Jane Russell act and get her to the set on time?"

"What about Arthur?"

"That turd? He just makes it worse."

The elevator pinged. You strolled out, looking more radiant, in your simple white dress, than seemed possible for a person who'd recently tried to take her own life. Behind you glowered Arthur, who immediately snuffed his cigarette in the sand of one of the tall ashtrays outside the elevator, then stalked into the gift shop.

You sashayed out among the men draped on chairs or smoking in groups. "Good morning, boys!" I noticed that you used your breathiest Old Marilyn voice. "What are you waiting for? Load up!"

Interesting—you'd put on your Old Marilyn armor. And it

worked. Lighting men, soundmen, cameramen, assistants, and assistants' assistants hopped to their feet. A skinny guy cheered. "I picked nine!"

You saw me. With a cry, you clipped over on your high heels. You tackled me, engulfing me in your cloud of No. 5. "I'll make it up to you for coming. I promise."

"I'm glad I came. Stop it!"

"Okay." You touched your throat. "Then tell me the truth. Do I . . . do I look awful?"

You were as beautiful as I'd ever seen you, though there was a new fragility to you, a translucence like that of an iris bloom beaten by a storm. It worried me.

"You don't know how to look awful."

"Oh yes, I do." A faint blue wash rose to the surface of the sheer flesh beneath your eyes. "I'm thirty-four years old. I danced for six months on the other picture, then came straight to this one. I've had no rest. I'm exhausted. Where do I go from here?"

You were serious. You really didn't know.

Whitey grasped your arm. "You're going to go out to my CAR—that's where you are going—and get to the set on time, like the professional you are."

Arthur strolled out of the gift shop, tamping a pack of cigarettes on the back of his hand. He frowned when he saw you. "What are you doing?"

"Norma Jeane's riding with me," Whitey said.

Arthur snapped, "She can't. Marilyn, I need you to practice the lines I just rewrote for your scene. You can read them to me in the car." He took you from Whitey and tried to lead you off, but you pulled from his grasp. Holding the white flames of your hair high, you took the lead to your car.

# 34

*WELCOME TO DAYTON*, READ THE SIGN OUTSIDE THE TOWN where Whitey parked his car. My fellow passengers—your stand-in, your hairdresser, and your body makeup woman—got out of the back.

"Convincing set," I said to Whitey, joining everyone at the trunk to fetch our equipment.

"Oh, this is no set," said Evelyn Moriarty, your double. She was your carbon copy, but with everything slightly coarsened—skin, hair, bones—how you would look if you were like the rest of us. "This is an actual town. That's a real cowboy bar." She indicated the saloon into which the crew was lugging equipment. "Even the extras are genuine cowboys."

I became aware of the "townsfolk" loitering outside the saloon. Among them, I recognized an actor famous for playing drunks. Arnold and I had seen him on *The Ed Sullivan Show*, back when we used to watch television and then go upstairs to bed together.

Your Cadillac rolled up. Arthur left it outside the saloon for a crew member to dispose of, and then he joined the line of your people following you to one of the trailers parked along Main Street. Whitey ran off to catch them.

I was left to acclimate myself to the set. I'd shot the stills for Joan Crawford's movie, so I thought I knew what to expect. Despite Joan's demands and her efforts to control everyone, the crew had been relaxed and efficient, comrades in creating the big illusion. They joked, pranked, and worked hard. This set felt different. The crew members were sharp with one another, as if sick and hungover, which they likely were.

John Huston, haggard in his tan safari suit, shambled among them like a pirate king, his eyes submerged within their bags. It seemed like decades since I'd seen him at the party at which you and I'd met, though it had been only eight years. He hadn't aged well. The talk this morning was that he'd lost fifteen thousand dollars at the craps table at the Mapes last night. Whose brilliant idea was it to base a movie production at a casino?

Onto this voyage of the damned, you stepped from your trailer like a goddess of fertility in a tight white dress printed with ripe cherries. Arthur stalked ahead to beat you to Huston, and the two men immediately huddled, leaving you to stand alone in the hot, bright sun.

Whitey, clutching his makeup case to his chest like a shield, asked, "How do you like Norma Jeane's dress?"

"Cherries—maybe a little heavy-handed on the symbolism."

"I know! Guess who picked it out."

"Not her?"

"Never. SHE's got class. Arthur did, like he picked out almost everything about this production, from the crew to the location." He laughed. "The only thing Norma JEANE picked was ME."

*And me,* I thought. "Where's Huston in all this?"

"He lets Miller call the shots. I'm not sure why—because one of Miller's plays won a Pulitzer?" Whitey snorted. "But that was eleven years ago. What's he won since?"

Over at the bar, Huston held the door open. Arthur and you went in.

"SHOWtime," Whitey said. We followed.

Crewmen, extras, and equipment jammed the establishment. Montgomery Clift, his head swathed in white gauze bandages for his role, and Clark Gable, leaning on his elbow with his patented smirk, drank at the bar. When they saw you, they pushed themselves up and strolled over. Eli Wallach then appeared, and the four of you picked your way past the lighting and sound booms to a dance floor next to a jukebox, where you stroked Clift's arm as the others talked.

Huston and Miller climbed into their adjacent folding chairs. "Places," Huston growled.

The scene was a barroom celebration after a rodeo. The actor who played a drunk readied himself to snatch up his "grandchild," who was the little son of the producer. Extras stood at the bar and sat at tables. Clark Gable, who was playing your main love interest, and Eli Wallach took their own table and turned toward the dance floor, where you and Montgomery Clift, your characters just friends, practiced dancing in a loose embrace. I found a spot near the action but out of the lines of the actors' vision, out of the movie camera's range, and where I would cast no shadows into the scene. There's no place where a photographer needs to be more unseen than on a movie set.

Huston waved his arms as if to the beat of "Skip to My Lou," which would be dubbed in during postproduction. "Roll film."

Everyone froze in a barroom tableau.

"Action."

The actor who played a drunk hoisted the boy up by the seat

of his pants and airplaned him through the saloon. Clift, his cowboy hat perched on top of his turban of bandages, took you by the waist and began to lead you in a Texas shuffle, to the beat of Huston's imaginary music. Gable and Wallach glowered at you over their drinks.

I centered you and Clift in my viewfinder. You were playing a lost divorcée who'd just befriended the reckless young rodeo rider, but your tenderness toward Clift went beyond acting. When you returned to him after a twirl, you squeezed his shoulder with affection. Arthur leaned toward Huston. The director yelled, "Cut."

You looked surprised. You pulled from Clift and waited for an explanation.

"That's not the way Perce would dance," your husband said, his Brooklyn accent ringing with annoyance. "This isn't an Arthur Murray ballroom class."

"How should I do it?" Clift asked. "You said like a square dance."

"Well, do it like a *kid* doing a square dance. Remember, you're just some dumb young buck." By the disdain on his face, it was obvious that he didn't mean just Clift's character.

"Perce is not just some dumb young buck!" you exclaimed. "He's a twenty-year-old who's got no place in the world. His father died and his mother has rejected him. He's looking for approval from someone, somehow, and Roslyn cares for him. It's your screenplay. Read it."

Arthur's stare was cold enough to frost a mug. He remained standing while the scene was reset.

Huston called, "Action." To the wave of his arms, the drunk grandfather again ramrodded his grandson through the bar. You and Clift danced again, but this time you were hardly able to keep from laughing as you two galumphed around.

"Cut!" Arthur yelled. He turned to Huston. "Sorry."

"Cut," Huston said wearily.

Arthur strode out to the dance floor and stood over you and Clift. "You think this is a joke? We're two weeks behind schedule and a hundred thousand over budget. Want to know how to do it? Here's how." He grabbed your waist and your hand, then pushed you around the floor. You lowered your head, not in submission but as if ashamed for him.

Furious, I snapped the shot.

THE NEXT DAY WAS WORSE. THE ACTION CALLED FOR YOU AND Clift to leave the bar during the dance because "Perce" was feeling the effects of a kick to the head by a bull at the rodeo and he had to get some fresh air outside. The afternoon was a scorcher, 111 degrees in the shade of the white canvas tarp stretched over the set. Booms dripping with can lights and microphones were aimed at you and Clift, sitting on ripped car seats in what was supposed to be a dump outside the saloon. Weeks before filming was to begin, Reno kids had been given a penny for each beer can they collected. Now a heap worth hundreds of dollars in pennies, along with other refuse, buzzed with flies, the stink so strong that it was almost visible. You were to sit with Perce on junked car seats at the foot of this fetid mountain while you delivered what was to be more than five minutes of continuously filmed dialogue. A stretch of speech that long would be a record in this world of make-believe, in which each scene was cobbled together from dozens of cuts.

I could tell you were nervous. You paced around the set, flapping your hands like you were shaking them dry as you whispered lines from a crib sheet. Arthur had rewritten your lines on the way to the location and then rewritten them again after you and Clift ran them on the set. Now you had to memorize fresh changes made to the most important scene you'd ever played in your life, in this film produced by *your* company, formed to show your acting prowess. No pressure.

Save for the buzzing of the flies, the set was silent. Everyone seemed to be holding their breath. No one, not even a seasoned actor, had ever pulled off five minutes of dialogue perfection without a break, and now here was this blond bimbo, this mere comedienne, a lightweight known for blowing her lines, going for the record. In the lobby that morning, Jim Goode had taken bets on whether you'd blow it. Now the crew was quiet. Were they for or against you?

Huston came over to you. "Ready?" His pity was obvious in his ruined eyes. He didn't believe you could do it.

You looked at Clift. "Brother, are you ready?"

"Yeah, Sis, if you are."

Huston receded to his chair.

You dropped your crib sheet and took your place with Clift on the ripped car seats.

"Roll cameras."

You became Roslyn, the divorcée trapped in a body so beautiful that no one could see the lonely woman within it, and Clift became your friend, young Perce, who was just as lost and lonely and undervalued. For five minutes, you forged with your colleague a real emotional bond that transcended the overwrought words Arthur had written for you. You literally glowed with compassion. The crew, everyone, watched in stunned silence.

*Oop.*

"Cut!" Arthur shouted.

Huston shook his head as if coming up for air. "What?"

"Marilyn," Arthur said, "that wasn't your line."

"Yes, it was."

"Well, that's not how you were to play it."

"Roslyn would have said it that way."

Arthur looked amazed. "You're telling me what my character would say?"

You glared up from the base of the buzzing garage heap. "You're telling me what *my* character would say?"

"Stick to the dialogue as written," Huston said wearily from his chair.

"I did, though he keeps rewriting it. Why don't you stop trying to sabotage me?" you asked Arthur.

"Are you kidding? My whole reputation rides on this film. If you weren't so goddamn selfish, you'd see that there's no way I would want to sabotage something so important to me." He indicated the crew, the other actors. "Everyone here is depending on me, so I ask, kindly, for you to *get it fucking right.*"

You crooked your mouth in a wry smile. You had just a wee little stake in the film, too. "All right, Arthur. We'll get this right for you."

"Thank you." He crossed his arms. "Where's the guy with the bug spray? Flies are crawling all over her."

An assistant came over with a can of spray.

"Get her face."

You closed your eyes, your face clenched in determination as he blasted you.

My heart broke for you. And still I shot. When you opened your eyes, you looked for me.

*Yes, Norma Jeane, I'm getting it all.*

The actors and crew reset the scene as the sun and heat baked through the white tarpaulin. Take after take in the brutal heat, you and Clift acted out your lines with real emotion, and perfectly, as far as I could tell, but not according to Arthur. Finally, on the sixth take, even he hushed. You and Clift were tender and real, not just as actors, but as two humans reaching for connection. Whatever it was that bonded you, it was so pure that I found that I was crying.

"It's a wrap," Huston called.

The crew cheered.

Clift pulled you to your feet. Everyone rushed forward to congratulate you—save for Arthur, who sat with his cowboy boots hooked on a rung of his chair.

You stopped Clift's dresser after she congratulated him. "You notice that Monty's jeans are a little saggy? Have you ever tried wetting them before he puts them on? Brother," you said to Clift, "if you let them dry on you, they'll stay tight and you'll stay sexy. Trick of the trade."

You two kissed lightly, then went your separate ways.

"Eve, Whitey," you said gaily, "may I take your chariot back with you to the hotel?" You left Arthur to glower from the smelly set.

Whitey's other passengers found rides, and the three of us piled in, you in the passenger seat, me in the back, with my camera thumping on my chest. Only after Whitey pulled the car onto the road did he exclaim, "Marilyn, are you TRYing to piss off Arthur?"

You laughed. "No."

"He does seem jealous of Monty," I said from the back, checking how many exposures were left on my roll of film. One.

"All he sees is a man trying to take away his possession. I'd say 'most prized,' but I'm not that. That would be his Pulitzer medal. Me—he thinks I'm beneath him. I found that out early in our marriage." You turned around to me with a crunch of upholstery. "Such a wise and sensitive man Arthur Miller is, the truth teller of our times, our American seer! He's so busy crying out for humankind that he can't see the simple fact that Brother likes men. He can't imagine that Brother and I are something more important than lovers—we're friends."

You turned back around. I could see your reflection in the side-view mirror, your hand to your mouth as you stared out over the sage-tufted desert. Those faint purple smudges deepened under your eyes.

I raised my camera, focused on the mirror. Your reflection rolled your gaze to me.

Whitey said, "Is Yves Montand queer?"

"No." You looked at me in the mirror. On your face grew the grin of a thirteen-year-old dirty girl fighting her belittlers with the only power at hand. "Arthur's right to be mad about him."

I got the shot.

It's one of my favorites.

YOU TOOK A SEPARATE ROOM AT THE MAPES WHEN WE RE-turned. "Stay with me," you asked.

I pulled back in surprise. "In your room?"

"No. I'm looking forward to the breathing space. No, I meant in Reno, until the filming is done. Having you here—it gives me courage."

"I can't."

"You can't?"

I really couldn't. "You don't need me."

Your eyes were full of begging, but you just sighed. "I understand. I'm not being a good friend to you to ask you to stay. You've got Francis and Arnold to think about." Your flat little face crumpled into a smile. "I'm still trying to get the hang of this friendship thing. Forgive me."

# 35

AFTER YOUR ACTING BREAKTHROUGH WITH CLIFT, AND YOUR public breakup with Arthur, you had some pressure taken off, yet you were even more anxious, more jittery, more insecure. Maybe the action in the film itself was getting to you. All the characters were careening to their existential cliffs. Or maybe you were unstable because Arthur changed your lines so frequently and so drastically that you were in a constant state of panic to learn them. But it wasn't just you. The entire production company had gone *meshuganeh.*

Suddenly, everyone had their hands on you and you had your hands on them between takes. I took snaps of you cuddling on the laps of everyone from Huston to the clapper loader, and then snaps of the men cuddling on *your* lap. Soon you were getting rubdowns between takes, and not just from your ever-present masseur, the gentle giant Ralph Roberts, but from Clift, the producer, the soundman, your hairdresser . . . Everyone seemed to have a hand in kneading your neck and back. On one roll of film I caught Clift, his bandages unspooling from his head like a ball of yarn, massaging big Ralph Roberts, who was himself massaging you. It was grooming time in the monkey house.

Then a bunch of you decided to form a human pyramid, with you at the apex. The pyramid shakily in place, Clift crowed, "It's better than taking wages!"

The pyramid wobbled from laughter. How many times did the script call for the male characters in the movie to spout this motto, their characters' excuse to do whatever cruel and appalling thing it took to keep them from working for "the man"?

You adjusted your hands and knees on the backs of your colleagues. "Come on, Eve. Get up here. You're little—you can be the cherry on top!"

"No, thank you." I took photos until the lot of you collapsed in a heap, with you in its handsy core.

It was in this bizarre state that we'd gone out on location in the desert. The thermometer had boiled up to 116 degrees, with no trees, shrubs, or even clumps of sage there to mitigate the heat. Hot wind swept across the cracked surface of what had once been a lake, driving stinging dust deep into everyone's eyes, nose, and mouth. Your hair could not stand up to such a pounding; you wore a wig even though your hair was just in pigtails.

We were between takes of the scene in which your Roslyn forced Gable's character, Gay, to admit that the horses he was trapping were to be slaughtered to make food for "the dog and the cat," not sold as children's pets, as he'd led Roslyn to believe. This was just after Roslyn had learned, in the previous scene, that only a few wild mustangs remained. Eli Wallach's character had spied only fifteen of them when he'd scouted the canyons in his rickety biplane. The men, therefore, would be driving the animals to extinction to net themselves just a few hundred bucks, making it hard for them to claim that it was "better than taking wages."

Gable sat in his chair, calmly letting his makeup man powder his face for his close-up. He certainly had a lot of close-ups in this movie that Arthur had so publicly proclaimed was his love letter to you. Clearly, Gable was the star of this show about men wrestling with the manly art of being free, a subject that seemed to weigh heavily on Arthur. As he'd written your part, you were just the pretty catalyst for the hero to examine his life. Some valentine.

I'd gone over to the air-conditioned trailer to get some more film when a station wagon appeared, spraying a rooster tail of dust. Gable's wife, Kay, got out, then called me over to her.

Kay, a former actress, might have given up the craft when she'd married Gable, but in her jodhpurs and starched white shirt, her blond waves piled behind a black headband, she was still camera ready. "Look at this!"

I followed her to the back of the car, where she swung the rear gate open. An old spindle-sided cradle squatted in the bed of the station wagon. "Isn't it great? I found it in an antique store in Reno."

"Does this mean what I think it does?"

She lifted her black sunglasses and grinned.

I embraced her, happy for her, for Gable. Like a tongue to a wiggly tooth, I checked for baby envy. Negligible. I thought about Gable, and his lost child with Loretta Young. Here was his chance, when he was nearly sixty, to be a good father.

"Don't tell Clark," Kay said. "I want to surprise him."

"I won't."

And I wouldn't. I wouldn't tell anyone. Especially not you. I didn't know how you would take it.

Kay and I went to the filming location. You were sitting in Huston's lap as you two discussed your character's motivation. Wallach came over and rubbed your back, and Clift leaned in for an embrace. Arthur, long legs sprawled from his chair next to Huston's, watched you all with the shuttered eyes of a man ready to blow.

"It sure is getting awfully steamy for a desert around here," Kay said.

Arthur snorted. "You think?"

Huston called for everyone to take their mark. When you hopped off his lap, Arthur reached over and grabbed your leg.

The crew, the cast—everyone—froze.

I raised my camera to my eye, focused. He hung on as he gave you instructions, kindly, concerned, a thoughtful dictator—an interested McCarthy. You recoiled.

If cameras could kill . . . I pulled my trigger.

But then, as firmly as a chef lifting a lid from a pan, you removed his hand. Arthur gaped in astonishment.

"That felt better," you said, "than taking wages."

There was a slight shift in the pressure among us all. A titter burst loose—from Clift?

"All right, all right," Huston growled. "Places."

Everyone went back into motion, and then: "Lights, camera, action."

You, Monty, Gable, and Wallach performed the scene in a single brilliant take.

You rode back to the Mapes with Monty. I found a ride with Whitey, who gossiped with Bunny, the body makeup woman, the scorching wind blasting through the open windows of the Chevy as we trundled across the desert. Mountains rose, jagged, in the distance. Closer to Reno, cattle grazed in shank-high, dun-colored grass, their square bodies black against the blue sky. They lifted their heads from contentedly readying themselves for slaughter and watched our car scuttle past.

"You're quiet," Whitey said. We passed a sign advertising the Mustang Ranch—not a ranch at all, but a brothel. It occurred to me to photograph the women there. I'd photographed prostitutes in Cuba, but not in America. What was it like to have to be intimate with strangers for money?

I laughed. That was a good photographer's job, too.

Whitey, hopeful, ready to share a chuckle, glanced at me.

I shook my head. For nearly two weeks, I'd watched you carry this show for men and about men, but not one of your colleagues, save for Whitey and Monty, could see that. Save for those two, no one could see that you were bailing out your genius husband, saving his pretentious movie by giving it a real heart. You—just a comedienne, a babe, a blonde, a girl whose greatest potential was to be dominated—were carrying it alone.

Whitey readjusted his hands on the steering wheel. "Are you okay?"

"I will be."

In my room at the hotel, I went right for the phone. Better to get it over with. I got a phone connection to New York.

Arnold picked up after four rings. It was ten o'clock on a Friday night back home. He'd be watching *The Twilight Zone.*

His voice cooled when he heard it was me calling.

*Do it.* "Arnold, I have to stay out here another three weeks, possibly four."

A cold silence fell. *"Plop, plop, fizz, fizz, oh, what a relief it is"*—the Alka-Seltzer song floated, tinny, from the distant TV.

Arnold said, "You have to stay, or you need to stay?"

"Both."

Neither of us spoke. I could hear the faint, eerie *Twilight Zone* music returning to his television.

"I guess you really don't care about me or Frank," he said.

"I do, very much so. Why does it have to be mutually exclusive? Why can't I work and care? It's that way for you."

"I don't write the rules, Eve."

"Then who does write them? Why not you? Why not me?"

A television scream sounded in the background. Arnold sniffed with anger. "Your work had better be worth it to you."

The line went dead.

YOU WERE UPSET ABOUT THE HORSES. SEVERAL WEEKS HAD passed; we were at the dry lake bed again, to film the climax of the show. You were hanging over the side of the metal corral the animal handlers had put up for the wild horses in the scene. I was right over your shoulder, your persistent shadow. Already, one of my cameras had been felled by the dust. If there were a place more inhospitable to life on Earth, I couldn't imagine it.

You leaned against the top rail, pressing the paper bib that your dresser had put on you to protect your white blouse and jean jacket against the galvanized steel. "Hey!" you shouted at a handler roping a foal for the scene. "Does that hurt him?"

He squinted at you as if you were crazy.

You went over to the representative from the ASPCA, who was watching from her open car.

"Is that foal going to be okay?"

The ASPCA woman, her eyes piercing blue in her leathery face, didn't budge her gaze from the young horse. "Under my watch," she growled, "he had better be."

Your white bib rose on a sigh. You'd been disturbed about the horses for weeks, since hearing that a wild mare had been killed during a plane chase. A biplane had flushed a herd from the hills. The horses were streaking flat out across the lake bed when a mare just under the plane unexpectedly lifted her head and broke her neck. It angered you that Arthur, in his quest for authenticity, insisted on using live horses in the action. No movie was so important that animals should be harmed for it, you argued, let alone a breed struggling to exist. Could he be more arrogant?

You wandered away from the horses, the wind tugging at the pigtails of your wig. "Something's wrong," you said as I followed. "Can't you feel it? It's not just that everyone's been so hopped-up. It's like there's this *curse* over this movie, and someone has to die to break it. Something has to be appeased for the harm we're doing."

I kept my hands on my cameras in their leather cases, as if that could protect them from the prying dust. "It's just a big scene—that's all. You're nervous. Everyone is."

"I can feel it." You shaded your eyes to peer toward the distant mountain range rising from vast white plain. "The animal in me feels it." You looked at me. "You know what I mean?"

I knew what you meant. The atmosphere seethed with your frenzy to touch and be touched, and with the sense of off-footedness caused by Arthur's constant changes to the dialogue, compounded by the suffering of the horses, Arthur's hostility toward you, and the relentless dust, heat, and sun. Something had to break, but spooky talk wasn't helping you. "I think we're just nervous. This is an important scene."

"You're right." You glanced at me. To protect me from worry, you were willing to pretend I was being honest.

Your dresser came over and took off your bib. "Five minutes, Marilyn."

You nodded, then pulled your crib sheet from your jacket pocket. "Well, if I'm ever going to get Arthur his Oscar, I had better know my lines."

You drifted away from me, reading the new dialogue Arthur had just given you. Soon you were whispering your lines, flapping your hands, then balling them at your mouth in concentration. Arthur, as heavy-handed with symbolism as ever, had you in pigtails again, a blatant tip-off that your character was just a girl-woman in a man's world. But I was seeing something else.

I released one of my cameras from its case and got you in my viewfinder. I noticed the harsh beauty of the range of mountains behind you; I switched cameras. Through my 35mm lens you were but a small girl in a jean jacket on a vast, bleak plain. Dwarfed and alone on the hostile expanse, you bunched into yourself like Rocky Marciano in a crouch and, with fists to your mouth, incanted the lines. What did Gordon say about bravery?

You glanced at me.

Yes, I saw you, friend.

Reassured, you went back to saving Arthur's picture, because he'd once saved you.

*Oop.*

Huston gathered everyone back to the set, where animal handlers were standing guard over a wild horse lying in the dust, its back and front hooves trussed together. In an earlier scene, the mustang had been roped, weighted with tires, and run to exhaustion so that Gable's character, Gay, could tie it down. Who knew how long it had been hog-tied like this? Fear for it burned in my gut.

Huston raised his megaphone. "Roll camera. Action!"

With the protesting ASPCA woman restrained by a guard off camera, the foal was brought over and released. It trotted up to the fallen mare and nudged her with his nose, Gable and Wallach's characters looking on with satisfaction. They discussed how much money they would make on that pair and three other horses. Your Roslyn watched until she could no longer bear it. She ran from them, then turned to face them. "Butchers! Killers! Murderers!" You coiled down into yourself, into a tortured squat, your screams terrible and real. "You're liars! All of you! Liars! You're only happy when you can see something die."

You screamed and kept screaming, screams that should have come when reporters asked you to bend over while you were trying to tell them about a serious role, when studio bosses locked you in their offices, when the girls in the lunchroom laughed at you—screams you couldn't scream, for fear that you'd lose the public's attention, your contract would be dropped, you'd get carted off to juvenile hall. When you were spent, you dropped to your knees.

The camera was still rolling when Huston got up, stalked out, and swept you into his arms. "My star. My darling star."

"Cut!" Arthur snapped, then stood. "She's overacting." He loped off to his car.

For a moment, everyone else was motionless. They knew that it wasn't playacting they'd just seen.

You pulled away from Huston. "If I could have played it my way, I wouldn't have screamed when pushed to the limit. Arthur thinks women get things done by screaming. He's wrong. We don't have that luxury."

I advanced my film. I'd gotten it all.

A COUPLE WEEKS LATER, EVERYONE WENT TO THE LOUNGE AT the Mapes to celebrate the end of the filming on location—even you, who never went, and Gable and Kay, who, like gods upon Olympus, usually kept apart from the flailing mortals below. I was there, in the smoky din, with my camera to my eye, circulating among the jolly cast and crew, part of the gang yet not. Once an outsider, always an outsider.

Over steaks and cocktails at dinner, Kay rose, setting silverware jingling against plates. She wanted to make an announcement. The already-tipsy troupe gathered around the table stopped laughing and scoring jabs against one another to listen.

Gable was going to be a daddy.

I looked for you, but you were already up and rushing toward Kay. You kissed her cheek, then drew something from your white patent leather purse: a baby rattle fluttering with pink and blue ribbons. You presented it to Gable. He stood stiffly—he'd been dragged clear across the lake bed by a truck in a scene that afternoon, having insisted upon doing all his own stunts. The man you'd once dreamed was your own father, the good papa who brought coloring books to the orphanage before claiming you and whisking you away, now cradled you in a hug. You'd done a love scene with him in the film; he was fully dressed, but you were naked under your sheet. I realized with a jolt—was that when things had gone so crazy?

"Nice touch," I told you in the casino later. You'd just been stopped for your autograph by a large man in a shiny blue suit. Burly casino security men had kept your fans at bay through dinner but must have been told to let this one through. I wondered how much he'd had to lose at the casino for that privilege.

"By giving my autograph?"

"No, the baby rattle for Gable. I didn't know that you knew."

"Kay told me weeks ago and told me not to tell a soul. You knew?"

"Yes. For a while."

Her brow cocked from its joint. "And you didn't tell me? Were you trying to protect my feelings? How am I to protect myself if I don't know things?" you exclaimed. You were truly angry.

"When will you understand that you can lean on me?" I was just as angry now. "It offends me that you won't accept my help. Friends protect one another."

"Protect you from what, honey?" Huston lumbered up and put his arm around you.

"From you."

He laughed. "Too late."

I watched through the viewfinder as he led you to a gambling table. He handed you a pair of dice.

"How do I do this?" you said.

His laughter stayed deep within his chest. "You women overthink things. Don't think about it," he said, as if we have that privilege. "Just roll."

# 36

YOU SAID YOU WANTED TO BE A BOTTICELLI VENUS, THE ONE on a clamshell.

You thought it was hilarious that you were a modern sex goddess—you, Norma Jeane Baker. Or was it Mortensen, the surname of one of your mother's husbands, which she put on some of your records? Mortensen was certainly not the name of your blood father, who wouldn't even meet you, the bum. No wonder you'd taken a whole new name; you had no idea what to call yourself. But when I asked you how you wanted to look in our studio shoot, you assumed the confidence of a blue blood. You said you thought you should go full Venus. I got the joke.

You know how I avoid studio shoots, how much I hate artifice and manipulation. But studio stills were required for the publicity for *The Misfits,* and you begged for me to do them, so for you I broke my rules. I rented a studio, hung it with a specially ordered blue-paper backdrop printed with fluffy white clouds, carted in a café chair, a mattress, and silk sheets, laid in two magnums of

Dom Pérignon and a liter of caviar, and gathered all your favorite Sinatra records. Nothing was too good for an immortal.

"Willow Weep for Me" was playing when you arrived—only an hour late, a virtual compliment—with May Reis, Bunny the body makeup woman, your publicist, your studio hairdresser, your wardrobe woman, and Whitey trailing you like Joan Crawford's well-trained retinue following her onto her movie set. Unlike Joan, you had no makeup on and your hair was tousled like a boy's. You looked to be about twelve. Yet even without your Marilyn trappings, and though you were exhausted from two months of giving performances beyond yourself and from cutting Arthur loose, the light still burned from within your human shell. I couldn't stop looking at you. No one could. Who can take their eyes from a unicorn among horses?

"For me?" You gazed at the blue-sky paper backdrop illuminated by cantilevered lanterns. "This looks like heaven."

"Botticelli's idea of it, at least. Sorry I couldn't find a big clamshell. Will white silk sheets strewn at your feet do?"

You laughed from the belly, in that way I loved.

"Do you remember, after we just met, you thought you'd stage a riot at the beach for my benefit? Did I ever tell you, when you stepped onto the Achitoffs' cliff, you looked just like a Botticelli Venus . . . in army boots? All these years, I've been meaning to tell you, the boots were brilliant."

I was disconcerted to see . . . were those tears glittering in your eyes?

Whitey must have seen them, too, because he exclaimed, clapping, "Okay, everybody! SHOWtime!"

He, Bunny, and the hairdresser went to work on you, like so many Michelangelos chipping away at their bra-clad *David.* First Whitey applied a film of Vaseline followed by Pan-Cake makeup, the unglamorous secret to your dewy look. After Whitey crafted your eyes and lips, the hairdresser sculpted your waves, and then the wardrobe woman fitted you into a three-hundred-dollar bikini—the poor girl in you couldn't get over the price of it. Finally, Bunny fluffed her shadow and light onto your collarbones, breasts, and belly, and, after three hours, one magnum, and a half liter of beluga indulged in by all, you emerged from their hands. Heavenly trumpets should have blown. We just clapped.

"This is really nice," you said as I positioned you under the lights, with Sinatra crooning from the record player. Whitey stayed close by with his powder puff, but the others respectfully faded behind the white paper screen I'd put up.

"Good. I want you to be comfortable." I arranged the sheet under your feet in my best approximation of a cloud. When I straightened, you were fanning your eyes with your pearly fingertips.

"What is it?"

"You're so good to me."

"No!" I exclaimed. "You're so good to me!"

Whitey stepped up and dabbed your eyes. "What I mean is," you said when he'd receded, "every other photographer—all the men—they all want something from me. They give me treats like this, but there's always a price."

I heard Whitey gulp. He retreated behind the white paper, leaving us alone.

"I'm not just paying them back for the goodies and because they're nice to me. I'm not that dumb. And it's not really because I'm grateful that they're trying to make me look good in my photos, though I guess that is part of it." You toed the satin piled at your feet. "The guy and I always develop a sort of closeness through the lens. And things get hot in the moment, you know? It feels good to give them what they want. But even when I really like the guy and I know that he really likes me, it hurts. It physically hurts."

You looked to see if I understood. I didn't, yet.

"Endometriosis doesn't just cause me to lose my babies. It makes having sex painful. Torture, really. It's like getting stabbed over and over there." You rolled your eyes. "I'm supposed to be so sexy, and here, having sex kills me. Isn't that a laugh? I can't even enjoy this body."

"Oh, Norma Jeane. I'm so sorry."

You looked away, suddenly shy. "That's why doing a photo session I know is never going to hurt, that it's just going to be pure pleasure, pure fun, pure . . . *creativity*—well, it's a dream for me." You took a breath, then met my eyes. "Eve, we actually get to *play*!"

And oh, friend, play we did. Something got into us after that. Soon we were laughing like kids as you camped it up on your half-shell sheet. You must have known the Botticelli painting well, because you struck the pose of Venus exactly, tipping your head and crossing your legs demurely, cracking me up until I could hardly hold my camera.

You then struck every stock pose of sex symbols through the ages, turning your rear to me à la Betty Grable, then touching your décolleté in surprise like a naughty flapper, then resting your cheek on your hands like a Victorian sweetheart. After stops in the Renaissance and Cleopatra's Egypt, your siren's journey back in time ended with you grabbing a loaf of French bread for the caviar and squatting like the rough-hewn fertility idol in Bement. I howled.

Oh, my friend, my friend, I didn't have to tell you to "give me" anything. You flung your inventiveness at me, and I just had to know how to catch it. We didn't think about what couldn't or shouldn't be done; we just did it, two women sparking off each other's creativity. Oy, we laughed, giddy with the wonder of it all. We felt brilliant.

Too soon, we finished six rolls of film. When I'd reloaded and was ready to shoot again, I put my camera to my eye, eager to see what you would show me next. And this time, you just lowered your chin, looked straight into my camera, and released the relaxed, unglamorous smile of a friend.

I felt a burning behind my sternum. You were giving me pure you.

I positioned my eye behind the lens. *I'm here, Norma Jeane.*

I pressed the shutter button.

WE DECIDED YOU'D BETTER CHANGE INTO THE SLIP YOU'D worn at the start of the movie. It cost seven hundred dollars—holy moly! Once sheathed in this pricey piece of silk, you sat backward in the French café chair, in homage to Marlene Dietrich.

"When are you ever going to do an appreciation of me?"

I clicked the shutter. "Isn't that what I'm doing?"

You sat forward, hugging your knee. "No, you're taking stills to promote my picture. You're not doing this to show me."

I was hurt. "The hell I'm not. Then what am I doing?"

"I mean, can't you do photos for an article that is just about me? One that has nothing to do with my movies, just a shoot, friend to friend?"

I lowered my camera. "I've been wanting to do an appreciation for a long time, but you got wrapped up in Arthur, and I got wrapped up in—"

"Being famous," you said staunchly.

I laughed. "I am far from famous." I thought of Gordon telling me what the editors at *Life* had said. "But I could be rising. Maybe forty-nine will be my lucky year. Anyhow, I'd like to do it."

"Then let's do!"

"All right. Let's do."

We grinned at each other.

"When?" I said.

"Soon. Call May."

"Where do you want to do it? Not in a studio."

"Somewhere good. We'll have to figure something out."

"Right."

"Right!"

But working at peak creativeness had tired us, and we still had to re-create the scene in the movie in which you woke wearing only a sheet and Gable had come in to kiss you.

"Well," you said, "let's get this over with, and then we can get back to having some fun."

You took off your clothes—I turned my back—and then you sat on the bed, covered with the satin sheet.

"Arthur knew that I thought of Gable as my father." You pulled the sheet to your chin, like a child scared of ghosts. "I told him that—I told him everything about me—and yet he wrote a scene in which I had to kiss Gable in bed, with Clark fully dressed and me naked save for a sheet. What kind of husband does that? He knew it would break my heart."

"I wondered how you felt about that scene."

"Terrible. That's how."

You settled down to give me a shot, but your energy was flagging.

I lowered my camera. "Here's what I think, Norma Jeane. Arthur was trying to break you. He's afraid of you. He knows how much power you have. It was clear to everyone on that set how much power you have. It was your energy that kept things going. The love scene designed to crush you? All the changing of your lines, all the hurting of animals just to wound your soul? They were meant to break your power, but they couldn't." I thought of something you once said. "Arthur knows it's your world and he's just living in it, and that makes him cruel."

You lay back with your arms over the sheet. Even in full makeup and with your hair done, you had the innocence of a child ready for a bedtime story. "Maybe you're right."

"I know I'm right."

Whitey pulled back the white paper screen. Behind him, May, Bunny, your publicist, and the rest looked in nervously. "How we doing in here?"

"Come in," you said.

You gazed up at all of us gathered over you. I shook off a chill. It was as if you were on your deathbed.

"Oh, Whitey, remember our first photo session?" You reached up to him; he clasped your hand. "There was just you and me, but we had hope then."

He kissed your palm. "We did, didn't we?"

"Hey!" I said, "we have hope now."

"Yeah," you whispered. You took your hand from him, then let it fall as you closed your eyes. A sigh parted your lips.

Later, people would think the photo was of you looking sexy, as if the image were a come-on to take your body, or a shot of postcoital bliss. They would project onto that image whatever they needed from it, as they did with you yourself. But I knew the truth. It was just an image of you, exhausted beyond human limits.

# 37

## 1961

I WAS AT THE KITCHEN TABLE, PUTTING MY PINKY THROUGH THE cigarette-burn holes in the back of my tan cardigan, when you phoned.

"Can you come take pictures?"

For our "appreciation" session? I wondered. Now? It was July, and I was months into a feature on Malcolm X for *Life* magazine. The story was taking a toll on my time, stamina, and clothing, to which the burned sweater testified. Arnold and I were also in the middle of selling our house and readying to move to England.

After I'd come home from the shoot with you in the studio, in one last-ditch effort to stitch up the shreds of our marriage, Arnold and I decided that Francis should go to the school that had once sheltered Arnold from the Holocaust, and that we would follow him. The idea was to stay close to Francis, though it became clear that Arnold was sure I'd taken up with Malcolm X soon after I'd started documenting him, and he wanted to distance me from Malcolm. How little he knew me. I'd never do that to Malcolm's wife and daughters. I'd never do that to Arnold; I would have pursued Gordon years ago if that were my way.

Though now Gordon was getting a divorce.

Well, if it was a meshuga time for me, it was worse for you.

*The Misfits* had flopped when it came out in February. At an advance screening I'd gone to in New York, the audience had actually *laughed* during your screaming scene, the scene in which you'd so honestly opened a vein and spilled. I wanted to cry.

Truth was, the public mood was setting against you. It had turned on you when Gable had died, just a week after filming, just days after you'd given him the baby rattle. Everyone, even his wife, blamed you for his heart attack. They said you'd brought it on by keeping him waiting for you in the hot desert sun. No matter that the man had done his own stunts knowing he had a heart condition. Among other stunts, he'd insisted on tumbling over the hood of a car and being dragged across the desert by a horse. His own macho refusal to see his limitations had killed him, not you, but it was so much easier to blame the dirty girl. How it destroyed you to be held responsible for the death of the man who you once wished were your father and had recently become your treasured friend.

As if that hadn't crushed you enough, Arthur had taken up with the other Inge from my agency, Inge Morath, whom he'd met on the set of the film. He'd moved on and was making sure you damn well knew it. I'd heard rumors about you seeing certain famous married men, major public figures whose jobs depended on their staying married. Why would you do that to yourself? No wonder you had ended up in a mental hospital last winter, completing your trifecta of crises. It was a miracle you'd survived.

But when you asked me to come shoot photos, I just said, "When?"

"Tomorrow?"

"Tomorrow!"

"I'm sorry. I should have thought—I know you're crazy busy. I've been in the hospital, and time kind of stops in there, you know?"

My heart dropped. *Not hospitalized again.* I knew—all of America knew—of your hospitalization in February, when you'd committed yourself to the Payne Whitney Psychiatric Clinic. Your psychiatrist had convinced you that it was the right thing to do. What she hadn't told you was that Payne Whitney was a full-blown mental institution, from which you had little chance of leaving, the quack.

I don't know how you survived. You'd been straitjacketed and put in isolation, just like your mother and your grandparents had been—your biggest fear come true. Knee-deep in my own *mishigas,* I tried to see you, but no visitors were allowed. It took Joe DiMaggio's damn near tearing the place down to get you out. He took you to heal in the less radical Columbia Presbyterian Hospital, where you stayed for almost a month. When you got out, TV coverage showed you with bodyguards walking you to your car as you waved to the crush of fans as if you were just leaving another gala. Oh, my dear. You didn't have to keep smiling. You owed the jackals nothing.

You were always good at reading my silences, even over the phone. "No, Eve, I wasn't in the nuthouse. Not this time. I was in for my endometriosis. It had messed with my gallbladder and I had to have it taken out."

"Oh no! How do you feel?"

"I've been in for thirteen days—good enough to go home now."

I tried to keep the alarm from my voice. "You're in the hospital still?"

"I get out tomorrow."

"Oh, Norma Jeane."

"I'd like you to come to my apartment, if you could, and then go with me to Kenneth's."

"The hairdresser?"

"Yes, our dear Kenneth."

I couldn't understand. "You want me to go with you to the hairdresser?"

"Yes. Right after I get out. I want photographs to prove to the world that Marilyn is okay, and I need a friend to shoot it." You inhaled, then sighed. "And you're my only real friend, you know?"

THE REPORTERS LEANING AGAINST THE PARKED CARS AND stunted sycamores along the sidewalk pushed upright when the cab dropped me at your apartment.

"Who's that?" someone asked.

"One of us," another said. "She's got cameras."

I turned to glare at whoever would lump me with this pack of vultures. "Why don't you leave Marilyn alone?"

"Easy for you to say." A stocky, tanned fellow nodded at the cameras around my neck. "I know you. You're Marilyn's personal photographer. Well, all we want is what you want—photos for cash."

"Really? That's all she is to you? Cash?"

"Easy, lady," said the fireplug with the Florida tan. "We're just doing what she wants. Don't you get it?" He lifted a Rheingold from an ice-filled coal scuttle under one of the sycamores. "Who do you think sent us these beers? What do you think she's using you for?"

Marilyn's burly doorman, Fred, strolled out and tipped his cap back, exposing his curly sideburns. "What's going on here? These guys giving you trouble, Mrs. Arnold?"

"I can handle them." I meant it. In my job, I'd had to hold my own against pimps, agitators, and mobs. Little Evie from Philly had become a force.

He failed to see it. "You jackasses leave her alone." He threw his arm around me and walked me to the door. Once we were inside, he ushered me between the off-duty policemen guarding the lobby and up the elevator to your third-floor apartment. "There you go, little lady."

All right, if it gave him a sense of value. Isn't that what we all want—more than sex, more than comfort, maybe even more than love—to be valued? "Thank you, Fred."

You let me in. "Miss Documentary Photographer."

"Miss Most Advertised." I almost gasped. You didn't even look like yourself. Your light was gone. You looked . . . mortal.

You read my eyes and sighed. "You know how it is in hospitals. I couldn't sleep a wink."

"Oh, Norma Jeane."

"I'm okay. Tell me what you've been up to."

"Maybe we shouldn't go to your appointment."

"No! I know what I'm doing."

I sighed. "Well, then, we'd better not be late."

"Ha! Kenneth wouldn't know what to do if I came on time. So, tell me, how's your little boy?"

I told you about his going to school in England, and that I was moving there to be with him.

"You're moving to England!"

"Honestly, Norma Jeane, it's not so tough. This country is so mired in racial problems, I don't know how we're ever going to get past it. All this ugliness I've seen makes me think less of humans, and I don't want to think like that."

"Have you been documenting all this?"

I told you about the hate, the human folly that I'd recorded these past few months, covering Malcolm X at the Black Muslim rallies. I'd had run-ins with American Nazis, who, as hearty supporters of the Black Muslim aim to have their own society separate from whites, showed up dressed in their tan shirts and leather cross-body straps like a band of high school Hitlers. I'd been up front at a rally, photographing Malcolm, when their lumpish leader snarled, "Go home, Jew, or we'll make you into a lampshade."

Oy vey, what idiots. "As long as I'm not a bar of soap," I'd snapped, and kept on shooting.

They weren't the only ones who hadn't wanted me there. No one did except Malcolm, who understood the importance of getting into *Life*, and therefore let me follow him through the crowd. I was so intent on my shooting that I hadn't known the danger I was in until I got home and found the burn holes all over the back of my sweater. His followers had put their cigarettes out on me.

I told you I understood their rage. I'd covered too many marches, gone into too many migrant camps, heard too much casual bigotry, not to empathize. But if I'd not had my lens between myself and them, putting me at a remove, I don't know how I could have withstood their hate. I'm strong, but I'm human.

"It makes me respect Gordon Parks even more, for tolerating hostility to get his shots at the same shoots I'd covered with ease," I said. *Oh, Chicken.* How was I ever going to let him go?

"Can I see the photos?"

"I don't have any with me. But they'll be in *Life*."

"I'll tell you who's charismatic—our president, Mr. Kennedy. I like him very much. I could talk to him all day." You tucked your bare feet, with those stubby toes, under you on the sofa. "But, you know, it's his brother Bobby I adore. He cares so much about people, about civil rights, about doing the right thing. He has so many plans—" Enthusiasm lit your wan face. "He's a good man. You'd like him."

We stared at each other. Then the rumors were true. You

wanted me to understand that you were sleeping with the president and his brother. I wanted you to understand that I wished I could pursue a relationship with Gordon.

"Do you think it's wise?" I said.

"Seeing them? It's my honor." You wrapped your arms around yourself.

A friend tells a friend the hard stuff. "Each piece of yourself that you give away leaves less for you. You've got to leave something for yourself."

"Who says I'm not getting something back?"

"Are you? These guys are never leaving their wives. Do you think he's giving up the presidency for you?"

"Do you think Gordon would risk being blacklisted for you if you ever became a couple?"

Friends tell each other the hard stuff.

We stared at each other.

"How did you know?" I asked.

"He told me, at the shoot in LA, how much he 'dug you,' but he didn't have to tell me. I saw it in your eyes. So when I heard rumors—"

"Rumors?"

"—that you and Gordon . . ."

My stomach lurched. Before I moved to England, we hadn't slept together, or even kissed. We'd just met for dinner or in the park, and talked and talked and talked, the way two soulmates do. Though his marriage had broken up, mine hadn't, not completely, and I wouldn't do that to Arnold—though that didn't make me an angel. There are worse ways of betraying someone than with your body.

You saw my face. "Welcome to the feral side." You put on Jane Russell's tough-girl voice. "Come on, kid. We'd better go to Kenneth's." You took me by the arm.

---

I WAS TAKING CANDIDS AFTER WE'D GOTTEN TO KENNETH'S and had drunk champagne and exchanged gossip. Your head was tipped back on the shampoo bowl, and Kenneth's slender fingers were kneading suds through your wet, platinum mass. You were telling him about your stay in the mental institution.

"When I demanded that they let me go, they asked me why I wanted to leave. I thought, *Are you kidding?* You'd have to be mental to want to stay in that cell! I mean, that's what it was, a cell, with cinder-block walls and no furniture except for a crummy bed and desk and chair."

"Oh, my poor Baby Marilyn!" Kenneth exclaimed. I got a shot of him as he sudsed, dapper in his suit and pink candy-striped tie.

"I sat on the bed, sweating out over what I should do, when I thought: *What would I do if I were given this situation for an acting improvisation?*"

"An acting improvisation!" Kenneth exclaimed.

"Like what we did at the Actors Studio." You swiveled your Crayola blues up to him. "All life is but one great big improvisation."

"Oh, Baby Marilyn, you are right about that."

"I remembered a scene in *Don't Bother to Knock*."

"Oh, I know that movie!" He sprayed water against his wrist, testing the temperature the way I used to test the water in Francis's bathinette. Somehow, he avoided wetting his shirt cuff and diamond bracelet.

Your face, protected from the spray by his hand, brightened. "I picked up a lightweight chair and slammed it against the glass of my door, which was hard for me to do, because I'd never broken a thing in my life! I had to whack it a lot to break off even a small piece of glass, but when I'd gotten one, I concealed it in my hand

and then waited on the bed. When the attendants came, I told them, 'If you're going to treat me like a nut, then I'm going to act like a nut.'"

"Oh, my baby girl!"

"I admit, the next thing I did was corny." Your pink smock heaved in a chuckle. "I did it in the movie, except with a razor blade. I said, 'If you don't let me out, I'll harm myself'—which was the furthest thing from my mind, you know, since I'm an actress and would never intentionally mark or mar myself." You laughed as shampoo bubbles swirled down the drain. "I'm just that vain."

"You'd better never hurt yourself!"

"Oh, you know I wouldn't. I may drink too much and take too many pills—I lose track of how many sometimes, you know?—but I'm not going anywhere." You looked up at me. "Am I, Eve?"

I took the shot. "Nope."

"Well, you'd better not," Kenneth said, his soft face furious. "You're my favorite client."

"I am?" You glowed. "Not Mrs. Kennedy?"

"Oh, I love her," he said, pushing water through your hair, "but she's not you."

"Well, they call you 'Mrs. Kennedy's Kenneth' in the magazines. Eve"—anchored to the bowl, you reached for me—"you won't call him that in the captions when these photos run in *Life*, will you?"

I tilted my camera to check how many exposures I had left. "I'll call him 'Miss Monroe's Kenneth.' How's that?"

Kenneth blinked mournfully. "Can't you just list me as 'Kenneth Battelle'?"

You were agreeing that was the best idea when, flanked by two sturdy men in black suits, the real Mrs. Kennedy came in. For her to appear at that moment was so implausible, it seemed like something out of a Hollywood farce, life imitating art.

"Oh," Mrs. Kennedy breathed, her voice more babyish than you'd ever made yours, "I thought you could squeeze me in."

Kenneth turned the water off and went over to kiss her. "For you, Baby Jackie, anything, if you don't mind waiting a little bit. I have your favorite, Dom Pérignon 1955."

Your neck still against the sink, you raised your glass.

Mrs. Kennedy froze. I don't think she'd seen you until that moment.

She stared at you, and you back at her, images in the same mirror.

"Never mind."

Mrs. Kennedy left, having never acknowledged me. She didn't need me and my still-life camera. She'd invented the White House television special, a surprisingly efficient way to spread her fame.

Kenneth, his kind face red, came back from escorting her out. He started rubbing your hair with a fluffy white towel. "Well, that was uncomfortable! She's normally very nice."

You started laughing, so much that Kenneth pulled back. "What?"

"She was afraid of me. I'm the scary dirty girl."

He brought his fist to his lips, his big pearl pinky ring brushing his nose. "Oh, Baby Marilyn."

"Don't worry, I'll be okay. But I am going to need some more of this champagne."

WHEN OUR TAXI PULLED UP OUTSIDE YOUR APARTMENT, PHOtographers swarmed over and knocked on your window, rolled up to protect Kenneth's creation though it must have been close to ninety outside. The driver turned around and rested his hairy arm on the top of the seat. "Say, Marilyn. Want me to beat them up?"

You gasped. "No!"

"Then let me walk you in. Those guys are animals."

"Oh, they're not so bad."

He refused your money when you went to pay. "It's an honor to have you in my car." He extended a fare receipt from a hand just as furry as his arm. "But if you wanted to sign this . . ."

I opened the door, activating the hive of reporters. The driver was holding the door for us, the autographed scrap of paper clutched to his chest, when you paused.

"Would you like a picture of us? This is Eve Arnold. She's a famous photographer. She'll take it, won't you, Eve?"

I think the man stopped breathing.

"Where do you want us, Eve?"

I readied the camera around my neck as they positioned themselves next to the car. Though sweat coursed down his face, his gap-toothed smile was beatific. And so, I saw in my viewfinder, was yours. I realized with a jolt: it wasn't so much power that you found in making others happy, but relief.

"Please come up," you asked me when I was done. "For just a little while."

You looked weary under the exaggerated swoops of your club cut. You'd just gotten out of the hospital after a half-a-month stay, for Pete's sake. "I should go."

"Please, Eve. Let's take a couple of photos together."

"I think I got some good ones at Kenneth's. Bet I can get them into *Life*. We'll show everyone—Marilyn Monroe is a tiger."

"Eve, please stay. We can improvise like old times! Or I can give you the scoop on Jack Kennedy. He is not the great lover a person would think he was, although for a woman with endometriosis, *wham bam* is sort of a blessing. Compared to Frank Sinatra—"

"Stop! I'll come in if that's what you want."

Your voice went small. "I do."

The cabbie helped me carry in my equipment while Fred, the doorman, cleared our way through the shouting photographers. Once inside, you went to your bedroom to change. I realized after all these years why you got into a robe the second that you could—tight clothes hurt your abdomen, sore with endometriosis. Funny how we can't see something right in front of our eyes.

One of my folded-up light reflectors toppled over. Rising from the sofa to get it, I knocked into the coffee table and sent a stack of letters sliding to the floor. Picking up the letters, I saw the telegram from André de Dienes, one of your early photographers, the first of the long line of horse's asses to pose you in a bathing suit on the beach. An old friend, according to you. It was dated February 11, the day Joe DiMaggio broke you out of the mental institution.

STOP FEELING SORRY FOR YOURSELF. GET OUT OF THE HOSPITAL. LET'S GO DRIVING AND HIKING THROUGH THE REDWOODS, INCOGNITO, AND TAKE BEAUTIFUL PICTURES LIKE NOBODY COULD EVER TAKE. IT WILL CURE YOU OF ALL YOUR ILLS.

I was sick. Pitying yourself wasn't what had landed you in the hospital. Sheer exhaustion, from dreaming, from creating, from fighting, from giving beyond what any mortal had to give of themselves, from being a goddamn unicorn, was what had gotten you there. Yet, this man, who was supposed to be your friend, could only see a diva, a crybaby, a potential screw. You were beyond his experience, beyond most everyone's experience, really. Who could imagine who you were when there was no one else like you?

You came out and we got on the phone and ordered spaghetti from Gino's down the street. One of the waiters ran the gauntlet of reporters to bring it to us. We were slurping it up and watching *The Dick Van Dyke Show* when you said, "She's the new thing now."

On the screen, a young woman in a tighter, cuter club cut was sobbing adorably because her plans had gone awry.

A spaghetti strand slapped sauce onto my nose. "Mary Tyler Moore?" I said, wiping it.

"She's funny. She's cute. She's what people want now."

The young actress, now smiling through her tears at her TV husband, had your big wide-spaced eyes and an expressive mouth, though her club cut was a medium brown shade between your blond and Jackie Kennedy's chocolate.

"I feel so old," you said.

"Thirty-five looks pretty good from where I'm sitting. Try forty-nine."

You weren't listening. "I have to make Marilyn more compelling. Different. I can't let people forget her."

"Are you kidding? Do you see all those madmen out your window? Nobody's forgotten you."

You bit at your nail, and then, tasting polish, stopped. "They love me and they don't even know me. They can hate me just as easily."

"Hell with them."

Your eyes grew solemn under the angel wings of your hair. "Oh, no, Eve. They're the only thing keeping me alive."

Being July, darkness had already fallen when I left at close to ten. Traffic, heavy for that time of night, especially on a side street, slowed as it neared your apartment, allowing for gawkers. The photographers were still on the sidewalk. Oh, your public had not forgotten you. Yet, as I stepped around the men with cameras, I knew your fears were real. Your control was weakening, after Gable's death, your second sensationalized divorce, and your mental institutionalization, and once the lions you were feeding smelled it, they would pounce. Or, maybe worse for an unloved child, they would turn on their great clawed paws and slink away.

"She's not coming out, guys," I told them.

One of them snapped my photo, blinding me with his flash.

"What'd you do that for?"

He ejected his bulb, then fitted in another. "Gotta turn in something."

I laughed in disbelief. "What's your angle?"

He took another shot, then shrugged. "Marilyn's photographer."

"Get out of here," I growled.

I went home and developed the film. The images were good, but we could do better. Somehow, we would have to do that shoot, do your appreciation.

# 38

## 1962

"THERE YOU ARE," YOU SAID. ICE CUBES CLICKED AGAINST GLASS on the other end of the phone line. Though it was morning, I feared that it wasn't iced tea you were drinking. I'd heard that you had, well, trouble at the Golden Globe Awards in March. Elliott Erwitt told me that you slurred your speech and smiled so widely that you looked like a caricature of yourself. Remembering how charming and funny you'd been when he photographed you for *The Seven Year Itch*, how adorably you'd worn your mantle of fame, he was upset to see you like that.

"How'd you find me?" I hadn't been in the city for two hours, having just flown into New York from London, where I was still acclimating from an overseas move made all the more crushing by England's coldest winter in over a hundred years. Pipes froze, daily living patterns broke down, we could never get warm. Arnold hadn't lasted six months, though there was more to his decampment than the cold. Still, as nuts as it had been for me since I'd last seen you, I felt guilty for not reaching out since I'd moved. I should have at least told you I was coming. From the bits I'd heard on the grapevine and seen in magazines, you were on shaky ground, too.

"I'm going to be in New York for all of three minutes."

"Make that five days," you said. "You're back to photograph Malcolm X again—the Black Muslims are having a mass wedding. I talked to Inge—the *nice* Inge—at Magnum. She said Gordon Parks is shooting it, too. Will you get to see him?"

I never could bullshit you. But it was hard to talk about. Arnold had left a sweetheart in the States, one he'd had for years. Surprise, surprise, it was to her he'd rushed back. This was why, when Malcolm cabled to ask me to shoot the wedding, I'd agreed, then contacted Gordon to let him know I would be in town, as one professional to another. Or so I'd told myself.

I just said, "God, I hope."

"Well, here's to love." Ice cubes clashed in a glass. I heard you sip and then swallow. "Tomorrow night I'm going to be singing for Jack at his birthday party at Madison Square Garden. Top of the bill! Can you imagine?"

I knew just the Jack you meant. "Norma Jeane, I can always imagine."

You chuckled. "Eve, I want you to come. I want you to be my escort."

"Your escort?"

I just sighed—that's how overwhelmed I was. Not to mention that I was still half-deaf from the transatlantic plane ride and my ankles were swollen like salamis. And, honestly? I didn't much like Mr. Wham Bam Kennedy. I hated how he treated his tough little wife. I hated how he toyed with you. It was a relationship in which you were destined to get hurt when he shed you like a napkin at a hot dog stand.

"I can't, Norma Jeane. I've got a ton of work to do."

You took a drink. You were waiting for me to come around.

"You wouldn't want me. I'd be rotten company." Just say it: "Arnold wants a divorce."

You sucked in your breath. "Ohhh, Eve. I'm sorry. Were you ready for that?"

"He came back to the States to get married."

You inhaled again. "Shit. To who?"

"I really can hardly talk about it. It hurts."

"Then you'd better not." You inhaled deeply, then let it out with a whoosh. "I guess I could get Arthur's father to accompany me. He still loves me, even if Arthur doesn't, and his wife just died and he needs some cheering up."

I realized how much a Madison Square Garden gig for the president would mean for you. "I don't know—maybe I should come."

"No, that's okay. You don't feel good. You should rest." In the background, May told you that your masseur, Mr. Roberts, had come for your massage.

"I don't know what to do," I said.

"Rest, I tell you." You took a breath. "I love you."

You hung up.

THE NEXT DAY, I MADE TONS OF CALLS, CULMINATING WITH A conversation with Malcolm X himself. Not only was he enthusiastic about me covering the mass wedding, but he said he'd like me to do a shoot of him personally. Do an appreciation, so to speak. I nearly skipped to the *Life* office to tell them of my coup.

Waiting for the elevator, I fantasized about where I could do a groundbreaking shoot with Malcolm. Should I photograph at his headquarters? At home with his family? Playing the drums? He was a good drummer. I then realized that I'd have no say in it—Malcolm X was not a person open to collaboration. He called all the shots. I was simply an instrument to get out his message. He wasn't like you. We were equals on each side of the lens.

A man behind me said, "I know a quicker way to get upstairs."

When I turned around, Gordon put his arms out for me to walk into them. "Flip!"

"Chicken?"

We hugged. His warmth went through me like a shot of Chivas.

We grinned at each other. "How was England?" he asked.

"Cold. And I'm not talking about the weather."

"What's up? Cold for photographers?"

I wasn't going to ruin our time talking about Arnold. "No, chilly for Yanks. A lot of people seem to kind of wince around me, like they're bracing themselves for the American foolishness that's sure to come out of my mouth. People from waiters in a tearoom to the woman showing me a flat keep me at arm's length, mildly bemused if not vaguely hostile. It's weird."

"I guess you've never been a Black person at a board meeting before."

I grimaced. "No, but I've been a woman at one."

He laughed silently. "At least you have that working for you when you're getting assignments."

"Working for me? Being a woman? You mean working against me."

"That true? Being one of the rare women in our field?" He shook his head. "If I were you, I would work that lode. Half the population sees things through eyes like yours. You don't realize your power."

The footsteps of businesspeople rang from the granite floors of the lobby. "My friend Henri once told me something like that."

"Because it's true?"

"All right," I joked, "if you say."

He told me he had an appointment and asked me if I was still planning to shoot the mass wedding with Malcolm X. I told him yes, and about my coup of Malcolm's request to do his portrait—which was not as much of a coup when I learned that Malcolm had asked Gordon to take his portrait, too. We laughed, then said it would be fun to get together afterward to see if our portraits turned out to be the same, as they always did.

He patted my arm. "Except mine will be better. Sorry, Flip."

"No, I'm sorry, Chicken—remember my power you were talking about? I'm just going to have to smoke you with it. Sorry."

"That so. See why I stay so mad?"

He kissed my cheek, then hurried off to his appointment.

Even after I'd dropped some proofs off at *Life*, my heart was still humming from seeing him. I went on to the Magnum office, walking, it being a fine day in May, Manhattan-style, with office building windows cranked to the sun and women—why was it always women?—tending to plants or gazing outside like indoor cats. Magnum had moved to a new building over by Bryant Park, to a soulless modern office full of partitions, with Capa's champagne magnums nowhere in sight. I found Inge Bondi ("the nice Inge," according to you) in one of the partitions.

She jumped up and ran around her desk, trailing her scent of Jergens. "*Meine Freundin!* My favorite seer of the unseen! How are you?"

I gushed to her about good things and bad, how being in England was hard, but that I wouldn't leave Francis on another continent to move home. "At least the *Sunday Times* is interested in my work."

"*Ja*, the photo of the vicar mowing the lawn in his gown was amusing." She opened a file cabinet and started digging. "I have the tear sheet around here somewhere."

"That's okay." I sagged against her desk. "I'm still figuring out how my curiosity about the world and the *Sunday Times*'s focus on all things English can jibe."

She lifted her hands. "That is easy! Just do for women what you did for babies. Show us what it is like for us, English, American, Chinese, all of us. Don't try to think what men would like to see. Think what women would like, and then show us . . . *us.* It's your special power, *meine Liebe.*"

"You're the second person to tell me this today."

Her phone rang. She waved it off. "Let it go to my recording machine. So, are you going to the president's party to see your friend tonight?"

I shook my head.

"No? She did not reach you? She called here looking for you. I gave her your hotel. She sounded very sad."

I sighed. "She got hold of me."

"She told me to tell Inge Morath congratulations."

"About her wedding to Arthur?"

"No. Did you not hear? Inge's pregnant. The baby is due this fall."

I felt slapped. My darling friend, how must you feel? A flash of offense that you hadn't told me was replaced by the understanding of why you couldn't speak of it. You were shielding me from the burden of your pain: Arthur's new wife was getting what you'd so desperately wanted and could not have. You'd been willing to give up everything for a baby. And tonight, I realized, you would be singing for something else you could not have.

Fear iced through my body. Because I knew you. I knew the feral child would jump for the stars, not knowing what should not, what could not, be done. You would woo that undeserving man in public tonight. And you would be vilified for it.

I looked at my watch: four forty-five. "May I use your phone?"

"*Ja.* Sure."

No one answered at your apartment.

"I've got to go." I kissed Inge hurriedly and ran for the elevator.

The taxi driver looked shocked when I threw myself onto his back seat. "Four forty-four Fifty-Seventh Street. Fast!"

"Marilyn Monroe's apartment?"

"How'd you know?"

A gap-toothed grin spread over his bristly face. "We all know Marilyn's address. Tourists."

"I'm not a tourist."

"You her friend?"

"Yes. Yes, I am. And she needs me. Can you hurry?"

He answered by throwing his cab in gear and gunning in front of a delivery truck, then weaved through traffic under a hail of honks. How he didn't ram a car or get rammed, I didn't know. I closed my eyes, hearing the astonishment in your voice when you said that you, Norma Jeane, would be singing for the president. Top of the bill! What had it taken for you to claw your way to this moment? Everything you did—act, sing, perform before millions of judging peers—went against every instinct in your animal bones to hide. And now that you'd gotten to the top, you needed to go even higher. But you didn't, Norma Jeane. You were already enough.

"Fred," I panted to your doorman when we got there, "Marilyn here?"

"No. She left"—he looked at his watch—"ten minutes ago."

The one time you would be punctual!

My driver was still at the curb, taking a call from his dispatcher.

"Can you take me somewhere else?"

He told his dispatcher to never mind. "Where we going?"

"Madison Square Garden."

He whistled. "President's having a party there. Gonna be a madhouse."

I looked in my purse. I hadn't exchanged money yet and only had a five left. I held it up. "I'll give you all I've got if you can step on it."

"Save it. I ain't taking no more money from a friend of Marilyn."

I didn't have time to argue. "Then to the Garden—like someone's life depended on it!"

The car darted from the curb, throwing me back.

He did everything short of drive down the sidewalks to get around gridlocked cars, until even he had to come to a stop, four blocks from the Garden. I gave him the five against his protests and hopped out, where I slipped out of my heels—I knew how to do this—and ran.

I pushed through the crowd of onlookers lining the sidewalks. I must have looked crazy—they let me through. At the door, the guard was not impressed with my appearance nor my winded explanation. "Lady, this event isn't for you."

A cop said, "Hey, I know her."

I thumped my throat. "Yes! Thank you! I am Marilyn's friend."

He pushed back his leather-billed cap. "Are you? I thought you were the photographer, Eve Arnold."

"I'm that, too!"

He waved me in. "Follow me."

Whitey was standing before you, applying your makeup. You gasped and pulled away from his brush. "Miss Documentary Photographer! What are you doing here?"

"Miss Most Advertised, I presume."

You hugged me against your white terry robe, then pulled back. "Oh, no, Mr. Miller thinks he's going to accompany me. And"—you scanned my shirtdress and my laddered hose—"you're not dressed." You peered over your shoulder. "Maybe they have something around here."

"It's okay. I don't need to accompany you." I asked Whitey if he could give us a minute.

"I just wanted to tell you—"

You were glowing with hopefulness. I hadn't seen you this happy since before you married Arthur.

You raised those arched brows. "Tell me what?"

I drew a breath. "That it's a woman's world, only the guys"—I spread my hands—"the guys just don't know it."

You gave me a funny look, and then you chuckled until your robe shook. "Oh, Eve, I told you that."

"No. Norma Jeane. What I'm saying is, you have everything you need. You don't *have* to have the president. You're already the greatest there is—without him. Without any man."

"And you are telling me this now . . . why?"

"He's married."

"Who?"

"The president."

You laughed. "I know. I don't want him."

A woman, Olga—"Hello!"—stood by with a nude-colored dress covered with tiny mirrors, ready to sew you in it. You'd look naked in that thing. I saw visions of the *Ciné Revue* lady and your hairbrush.

"Please, please, don't do something to embarrass yourself."

Your hair was so stiff with spray, the massive tidal wave swooping from the side stayed rigid when you shook your head. "If it were anyone else, I'd be insulted. But from you, because you care in your demented way, I'm complimented."

I clasped my hands as in prayer. "Please."

"Oh, Eve, don't you get it? I'm not doing this for the president. I'm doing this for us. Tonight is a victory for all the dirty girls."

---

HUMANS ARE NOTHING IF NOT ADAPTABLE. WE CAN GET USED to almost anything. Take being in a crowd of fifteen thousand people listening to Jack Benny whining up onstage in Madison Square Garden. Some of these fifteen thousand creatures will be clearing their cigarette-shredded throats, others whispering from behind white gloves, still others shuffling their wing tips or dragging their high heels against the carpet or blowing their noses, chewing gum, slipping on lipstick, stealing kisses, yawning. Humans can acclimate to sensory chaos in moments, taking it in stride as if they were packed together with tens of thousands of pungent, snuffling strangers every day. Not most other animals. Certainly not the two tiny poufy dogs imprisoned by their owner in the seat next to me. The little guys, much like Joan Crawford's tiny poodles except these were dyed pink, cowered within the belled sleeves of their mistress's raspberry swing coat. I sympathized. I was so nervous for you, I wished I had a good sleeve to hide in, too.

Now I glanced at my squirrel-sized seatmates, their bright eyes peering from the shelter of their keeper's Dior. "Wish her luck tonight."

Onstage, Jack Benny had given way to Peter Lawford, suave from his Brylcreemed hair to his gleaming shoes, the master of ceremonies and, not coincidentally, President Kennedy's brother-in-law. Lawford had been pretending to introduce you all night, only to move on to the next guest because supposedly you were late, playing on the running joke of your infamous dumb-girl tardiness. If only they knew what a feat of willpower it was for this shy, unschooled girl to arrive anywhere at any time.

Now Lawford said your name, then gasped as if shocked when you appeared from the curtain like the sun coming from behind a cloud. Your gown, spangled with thousands of tiny mirrors, blazed in the spotlight. The crowd's deafening roar sent the dogs deeply into their Dior.

You inched out in that dress incompatible with walking and breathing. Your tiny winking mirrors dared—no, demanded—the crowd to look into them. They'd see who made an outcast child named Norma Jeane share her otherworldly light in her fierce bid for respect.

Lawford crowed, "Here she is, the late, great Marilyn Monroe!"

You minced to him with the tiny steps of a geisha, your hair, your makeup, your body, absurd exaggerations of the ideal woman—a mock fertility goddess, and you knew it. You leaned into the microphone. Without the aid of a piano, your wispiest Marilyn voice floated above the sea of humanity.

They thought you were singing for the president. That's not true. You were singing for you.

# 39

BACK IN ENGLAND THAT SUMMER, AFTER MADISON SQUARE Garden, it was as sweltering as that first winter had been cold. Fortified with dress shields under my dewy arms and my new mission to reveal women to themselves in all our variety and splendor, I was all over that hot sceptered isle. I shot four young secretaries ingeniously making ends meet in their one-bedroom Cambridge flat, a joyfully rowdy lesbian wedding in Devon, Vanessa Redgrave in her dressing room in London, wearing little but a nun's black veil. (There, Gordon, I photographed a white woman's backside.) I even covered Queen Elizabeth, cheery under her umbrella, opening a factory in Manchester. Inspired by you and encouraged by Gordon, I was feeling my special power—letting heretofore unseen women speak for themselves through my lens. I couldn't wait to photograph just you, for an appreciation, as you'd asked. How brilliant we'd be! With my Black Muslim wedding shoot and the media storm that followed your appearance at the Garden, we'd had no time to get together when

I was there in June. But we would, we would, soon, we said. And until I got back, I knew you'd be okay. You were tough.

But time melts more quickly than the ice in a Tom Collins in the sun. Two months zinged by without a thought about shooting your appreciation. Everyone was in such a hurry.

I found myself that August with my movie camera trained on Grace Kelly, Her Serene Highness, Princess of Monaco, looking serene, indeed, in leopard skin from her pillbox hat to her pointed high heels (although the poor leopard wasn't so tranquil anymore). With the prince, stuffed within a uniform shingled with medals, she strolled across the balustrade of their palace, klieg lights glaring, my camera whirring. The film was to make history for Grace Kelly and Monaco like Jackie Kennedy's televised White House tour had done for her and her husband's presidency. I was making personal history, too. It was my first television shoot.

TV, the scourge. But if you can't beat 'em . . .

I pivoted my camera to the former Grace Kelly as she stopped to wave to her subjects below. She was as sanguine as her title suggested, the very look of cool royal contentment.

Oy vey, she was a bore.

Maybe I was just irritated that day. I had awakened with a feeling of dread that I hadn't been able to shake. The whole shoot felt wrong, and it wasn't just because I was using a new medium. Her Serene Highness boring my tail off didn't help, but I needed to cut Grace some slack. Not everyone can be as brilliant as you.

In a break in the filming, I went to the bowels of the palace to the servants' quarters, where some of the crew had brought in a blue metal Pepsi-Cola cooler filled with drinks. For the weeks that we'd been on this production, the princess hadn't provided us with snacks nor even a single cup of tea. It seemed the Principality of Monaco was broke.

A pair of roadies were drinking bottles of ale and playing a

BBC program on one of those tiny new plastic transistor radios when a song came on, featuring some nasally boys on guitars, drums, and a harmonica.

"Turn it up!" a roadie exclaimed. "It's the Beatles."

"Who?" said the other, a tall lad with the crowded teeth of the British.

"The Beatles! Turn it up."

The singers were begging, *"Please, please me,"* when the music stopped. Dead air thrummed over the radio.

The silence wailed like a siren, throwing the animal in me into a panic. I held my mouth, choked back a pack mate's howl. Because I knew, even before the announcer spoke, across time and space and experience, I knew.

Oh, my Norma Jeane.

# 1982

THE BABY BLUE CADILLAC CONVERTIBLE SAILED THROUGH THE sizzling ocean of tasseled corn. I undid my hair and let it fly like I was a girl, not the seventy-year-old I could not believe I actually was. Finally, nearly two years after deciding at my first exhibition in Brooklyn to do so, I was on the road to document America.

Over behind the wheel, my driver asked, "Mind if I turn on the radio?"

I did, but the girl, a twenty-one-year-old harpist from Milwaukee, had been nice enough to offer to ferry me across the Midwest in her papa's car for the week. "Go ahead."

She peered over the top of the square sunglasses that covered half of her small face and rolled the dial, releasing blurts of music and speech. I grabbed at my whipping hair—should have worn a bandana like her—and tried to relax. I was looking forward to photographing small-town America. Already I'd documented women taking pregnancy exercise classes, organizing parades, and running the family stud horse farm, much more enjoyable subjects than the men in the Ku Klux Klan whom I'd just shot swanning around in their robes in Texas. Not that I ruffle easily.

In Russia, I'd fled a KGB goon after I'd snapped photos of dissidents being tortured in bathtubs in a Soviet mental hospital. In Dubai, I'd dined on sheep brains roasted with raisins, rice, and spices and served in its own head, after a toast that I later learned meant "Western women are so stupid that even a sheep's brain might help them." I'd been pummeled with fists and screams when I shot a street market in a village near Beijing. "A fine photographer?" a seller shouted when my interpreter tried to intervene. "How could she be a fine photographer! She doesn't even have a studio!"

I did get ruffled, though—make that I damn near crumbled—when I photographed mothers and babies dying of malnutrition in South Africa. Their hopeless eyes still haunt me.

And there I was in all that corn, hair flying, still kicking. I'd had solo exhibitions across America, starting at that one in Brooklyn Museum when I was sixty-eight. (So much for the rising young star, Gordon.) I'd won enough awards to put in a niche and genuflect to, had I been Joan Crawford, and photographed more arts people than Busby Berkeley had dancers: Liz Taylor, Richard Burton, Mia Farrow, Anne Bancroft, Audrey Hepburn, Vanessa Redgrave, Michael Caine, Andy Warhol—you get the idea. It had taken only four decades, but I was a respected photojournalist now, a "truth teller," a "one-woman cultural exchange," as said in the *New York Times*, or, in John Huston's words, "an adornment to this earth." The man was always as over-the-top as his eyes were baggy.

I guess I'd had a life, and the pauper wasn't done crawling yet. My mother had tried to spare me from hard times by discouraging me, but all she had done was to make me stronger. I put my arm over my eyes to protect them from the violence of my hair thrashing in the wind. Wait—had that been Mother's plan all along? The things one figures out late in life!

I kept up my arm against the wind as I let waves of yearning for my mother wash over me. It had been my big idea to pull over to put down the top once we'd cleared Madison. Something about being in a convertible in fields of corn had made me do it. As the green rows had spun by, I'd seen you perched on the seat back of the Eldorado, sunglasses on, gloved hand waving, your dress white against the red of the car and the emerald of the corn, on our way to Bement and all those fake Lincolns. Now, surrounded by the unending corn, your face replaced my mother's in my mind. It was still glowing there, as it had done so often since I'd allowed myself to get out your photos and reexamine them after my exhibition in Brooklyn, when two words leaped from the radio: Marilyn Monroe.

My driver dialed on.

"Wait! Go back!" I felt a frisson of fear. Had I conjured the words? At seventy, one is always on the lookout for signs of dementia.

She tuned in to a station. A female speaker's words floated out over the cornscape. ". . . such a pity Marilyn had died."

"There. Thanks," I told my driver.

"She would have been such a great feminist," the speaker was saying. "She knew so much about being a sex object and being exploited. How powerful it would have been to hear her testimony. If only she could have lived long enough to rise up and refuse to wear the cloak of sexiness her oppressors so cruelly made her wear. What an inspiration she would have been."

"And on that note," said another speaker, "we end our celebration of the twentieth anniversary of Marilyn's death with a song that so poignantly captures her struggle: 'Candle in the Wind,' by Elton John."

I pushed up my sunglasses. With my packed schedule, I'd forgotten what day it was. Every August fourth since '62, your death was rehashed, your supposed flaws exhumed, your lovers who caused your demise hinted at. Why didn't people try celebrating your life for once?

I was so perturbed that it was hard to settle down and listen to the lyrics. No sooner than I did, out floated *"Hollywood created a superstar / And pain was the price you paid."*

Hollywood created? No! That wasn't how it was at all. "Turn it off!"

My driver started at my tone, then snapped off the radio. "I know. That song always makes me cry. Poor Marilyn."

"You don't have to feel sorry for her." I gripped my hair in a topknot—your move of exasperation—exposing my face to the full force of the wind. I did not understand the value of convertibles at all.

"But what they did to her!"

"Who's 'they'?"

"Hollywood, like in the song. They made her and then they broke her."

"No. That's not right. Marilyn wasn't a victim."

"But she was, wasn't she?" She dipped her sunglass-heavy face. "Respectfully. I don't mean to argue." She glanced at me, then added in a mournful voice, "I'm sorry for your loss, Mrs. Arnold."

"Eve. Just Eve."

"You were friends, right?"

The day after you'd left us, I fled for home. When I arrived at Heathrow, every newsstand in the airport featured magazine covers with glamorous shots of you or endearing ones or others that weren't as complimentary. It seemed that every photographer who'd ever taken your shot had joined the gold rush. But it was the photo of you in the morgue, with just your toes showing, that stopped my heart. Had they no decency?

The minute I got back to my flat, I called Magnum and put an embargo on every photo of you I'd taken that wasn't already in circulation. I swore I would not make a single dime off your images, unlike those ghouls. Yet, for all my silence on the subject, after these twenty years, somehow all my conversations with the public circled back to you. It was uncanny.

"You were her photographer on the set of her last big movie. *The Misfits*, right? I saw the pictures in *Life*."

How was that possible? This girl would have been a baby in '61 when those pictures came out.

"I researched." She smiled shyly. "I'm obsessed with Marilyn Monroe. When my father's friend from Magnum said you knew her, I begged him to let me be your driver."

I buttoned my lip. Oy. Not again. After all I've given up and all I've achieved, still it was my friendship with you that people were most interested in.

I heard a hearty chuckle. *Imagine!*

I peered out over the corn. Tassels stirred languidly in the wind.

"Look, they have Marilyn all wrong. She wasn't a victim."

My driver gave a dainty cough. "Again, respectfully—they did drive her to suicide."

"That's not what happened." I wasn't hashing it out with this girl, but here's the truth. In your unrequited quest to find sleep, you'd awakened after taking pills and, too groggy to know how many you'd already taken, swallowed more. You'd told Kenneth you could never harm your beautiful body and you'd meant it. You were not a liar.

"But . . . didn't they? You can see that she was in trouble. Look at these pictures." My driver pulled a flat paper bag from under her seat, swerving. Tires crunched on the stony edge of the berm. "Was it the Kennedys?"

"Careful!"

Car corrected and eyes on the road, she blindly dumped the bag on the seat between us. A Payday, packs of Beemans gum, and a *Life* magazine slid out, the most recent edition. "I got this before I left home."

You were on the cover. I recognized the shot. Bert Stern's. One you'd tried to block.

"Don't tell me there are more photos like that inside."

"Lots," she said. "A whole article."

I flipped to the photos as she drove. Photo after photo showed you at your sickest. They were no better than the one at the morgue. What drugs, what drink, had Stern given you to make you like this? You'd not wanted him to print these. You'd not only X'd them out; you'd poked holes in the negatives with a bobby pin so he could never use them. And still he did, their damaged state making you look even crazier.

"This isn't right."

"Says in the article that he has a book coming out with these pictures and more."

"A book! She hated these!"

"She told you that?"

"She would have."

"So you were friends." That goofy smile I used to see on people around you came over her face. "What was she like?"

"Not like this," I muttered.

"Then how was she?"

I stared at a photo of you, haggard or drunken or both, wearing only a sheer orange scarf while tearing at a strand of pearls with your teeth. Should I let this picture, that song, those rumors, stand when I had photos that proved otherwise?

I knew how this would work. I'd become known as Marilyn Monroe's photographer. My decades of other work would recede into the background, my name as the woman who saw the unseen would fade, my other subjects would fade away, too. Because that's how it is with Marilyn Monroe. She overshadows everyone around her. Even you, Norma Jeane. Especially you.

Yet, how was anyone to know differently if I didn't set them straight? Who else was there that could? What was I so afraid of?

The bravest person is the most terrified person . . .

Oh, but I was never the bravest one.

# 1992

I HUDDLED WITHIN THE BLACK CASHMERE SWEATER-COAT GIVEN to me by Khrushchev's wife. I'd made the mistake of admiring the bulky garment while taking her picture in 1966, thinking to myself how lustrous and pretty the wool looked hanging on the goats I'd seen in actual Kashmir, when she shrugged it from her ample shoulders and laid it, still warm and smelling of bread and her strong perfume, on mine. She'd insisted that I keep it, the coat in exchange for a favorable report from my tour of the Soviet Union, I suppose. I'd found the coat recently and had taken to wearing it.

That morning on the North Shore of Long Island, I was thanking the goats for their soft wool. The watery edge of the Atlantic, all heaving surf and pebbles rolling in the tide, was chilly at dawn, even on August fourth. My eighty-year-old bones, which had once tolerated sleeping on a mud floor of a yurt in Mongolia and on a blanket over a wooden platform in Sichuan, were tetchier by the year. Lugging camera equipment across six continents for forty-some years had finally caught up with me.

"Eve?" said the producer, Jennifer. She was a pleasant young woman, sweet-faced, modest, probably from the American Midwest, judging by her chipperness. She had that same milk-and-roses look of the English producer who'd filmed during my first program for the BBC, the subject of which was the same as this one.

"Eve, are you ready with your lines?" Jennifer asked.

"Yes." I stroked the wool of the collar with my jowls. Age gives even skinny little people extra chins.

"Good. Let's start again." Jennifer indicated that I should commence trudging through the sand. In front of me, the cameraman plodded backward under the weight of his television equipment. TV guys had it so much worse than I did with my Nikons, once upon a time.

Justice, right? Since TV had wiped out the magazines. Who'd have ever thought?

I began my intonations. "'I've found many things on this beach—'"

I stopped. The words had winged right out of my mind, replaced with the memory of my mother, her knife slicing into a cooked beet, her hands as red as if she'd just murdered a guy. *This one, she could have been a doctor! Anyone can take a picture. Pauper, where are you crawling?*

Dear Mother, you knew just how to make me crawl even faster. But what was it that I was crawling to, really?

I glanced at Jennifer, smiling in encouragement. I'd done my little spiel about you so much I couldn't keep my mind on it. I guess I was bored—the script was so trite. It was meant to encapsulate us. Us! Can you imagine?

I heard another voice in my head, that of a tough girl, chuckling until her laugh reached her belly.

My heart swelled; it actually hurt in my chest.

Behind her clipboard, Jennifer grimaced. "Are you okay?"

"Sure."

"Want to start over?"

"Please."

I screwed deeper into my goat fur, caught the cameraman's eye to roll 'em. "'I've found many things on this beach. Shells, logs, beached fish. But the most incredible thing I found was Marilyn Monroe, walking along one day with Norman Rosten, the poet.'"

Jennifer beamed, motioning for me to continue.

"'Norm said, "Do you remember Marilyn?"'"

Oy vey, that was a dumb question then, and time hadn't made it any smarter. Forget you? I think of you every time I shoot! Try as I might to find them, no one has ever seized the lead and run with it like you did. No one has been as inventive, as clever, as smart, as fun, as . . . frightening. Yes, frightening. Seeing the unseen is not for sissies. It wasn't always easy to take, but you turned yourself inside out for me.

Why?

Jennifer was watching.

I straightened up. "'I told Norm that I remembered her, though she was a starlet then. I'd met her at a cocktail party given for John Huston.'"

You chose me. You had hundreds, probably thousands, of men photograph you, all the best ones in the business, true artists. You name them, they sought you out. Yet you wanted me. You saved your best work for me. You looked different in my shots than in anyone else's.

Under her brown fringe, Jennifer's young blue gaze went from her clipboard to my face. Ah, right. Back to The Story.

"'She saw some pictures I'd done of Marlene Dietrich and wanted me to do some of her.'"

I stopped.

"And?" Jennifer tipped her head forward in expectancy. She was all but ready to mouth the words with me. She probably could have. I had told my "Meeting Marilyn" story so many times that she knew what was coming next. Everyone knew The Story. Since our book had come out in '87, five years after I'd begun it, I was made to talk about us at every exhibition, press conference, and party. All my work, all my sleeping in yurts, eating of sheep brains, and witnessing atrocities and kindnesses had come down to one thing: I was Marilyn Monroe's favorite photographer.

My goat coat was suddenly too hot.

"Ms. Arnold, are you okay?"

"Let me tell you how it was. Marilyn and I were two young women starting out in this quite male world, so we just played together, had the most fun we could. She made me feel as if I were brilliant, and I suppose I made her feel the same. We fed off one another until I couldn't tell where I began and she left off." I wanted to say more but the truth was smacking me with the force of the waves on the pebbly shingle: Being your photographer was the best thing that ever happened to me. You brought out my best, and then your star power brought people to my work, people who would have never seen all my other subjects had it not been for you. You gave them, me, a voice. You once said, "Can you imagine what I could do for you?" Oh, Norma Jeane, did I do enough for you?

"Ms. Arnold?" Jennifer said gingerly, as one would to a balky child. You chuckled. Or was it just the sea, raking the stones at the water's edge? "Would you like to tell us why your photos of Marilyn look like no one else's? It has been said that in a display of Marilyn Monroe pictures, a viewer can always pick yours out."

Tears rose behind my eyes. You know what was so scary? What I had run from when we were together, then all those years after you'd left me? You saw me. Eve Arnold, the great seer of the unseen, thought she could get away with not being seen herself, but you saw me. And through my pictures of you, you turned around and revealed me to the world. You made me seen. My pictures of you are as much of me as they are of you. My heart is right there, should anyone care to see.

"It's the mark of your special genius," Jennifer was saying. "Your trademark Eve Arnold empathy is perfectly evidenced in your Marilyn photos. How do you get your subjects—how did you get Marilyn—to open up to you like that?"

Oh, I didn't get you to open up. You willingly turned yourself inside out for me. More than anyone I'd ever photographed, you turned yourself inside out for me. And do you know why? Because I turned myself inside out for you. It wasn't my camera that loved you. It was me.

Jennifer consulted her clipboard. I was proving a difficult subject. "Ms. Arnold, let's take a break."

I waved my hand. "I'm okay."

She drew in a breath. "Then let's try something else." She handed me a volume. "Could you please hold up your book?"

I passed my hand, knotty with years of use, over the cover. The photo I'd chosen for it was of you, buttoned up in your jean jacket, the Nevada desert wind whipping your hair in your eyes as, chin up in defiance, a dirty, brave girl to the end, you blew me a kiss. It was right there for all to see, a most private photo of you. Of me.

Tears burned behind my eyes. From the very beginning, I was the camera. And you, Norma Jeane, were you. But, most importantly, we, together, were us.

"Can we see the title?" Jennifer asked.

Swallowing, I lifted the book. Who could ever imagine how brilliant we could be?

She nodded to the TV man to make sure the film was rolling. "Very nice. Read the title for us, please."

I cleared my throat and read, *"Marilyn Monroe: An Appreciation."*

# ACKNOWLEDGMENTS

I first saw Marilyn Monroe on my living room television, in *The Seven Year Itch*, when I was eight. To this impressionable little girl, she seemed to be a glorious butterfly flitting from everyone's net just in the nick of time. I didn't see sexy; I saw brave. Yet everyone in the 1960s, even eight-year-old girls, knew that she died at her own hand. It crushed me. When I grew up and became a writer, I longed to write a novel about her, just to try to understand her. I would have done so early in my career but couldn't find a fresh angle for telling her story. And then along came Eve.

I had been wishing, once again, that I could write about Marilyn, when I thought to do an internet search on the women who'd photographed her. My hunt led me straight to Eve Arnold . . . because there was only Eve Arnold. Almost inconceivably, out of the hundreds of photographers for whom Marilyn sat, only one was a woman.

Eve's photos of Marilyn looked different from everyone else's, easily identifiable when lined up with other photographers' shots. Yes, Eve (please forgive me; I can think of her and Marilyn only on a first-name basis after spending so much time with them) was a photojournalist who shot film using whatever lighting was available, unlike most of Marilyn's other photographers, who worked in a studio or in controlled outdoor settings. But that didn't explain everything. Turning the pages of Eve's 1987 coffee table book, *Marilyn Monroe: An Appreciation*, I not only found a side of

Marilyn that had eluded everyone else but discovered Eve's deeply empathetic photography and writing. Before I'd finished, I knew I'd spend the next few years of my life with these women.

While Eve's personal take on Marilyn in *An Appreciation* (recently rereleased in a sumptuous reprint) became the springboard for my novel, her other books, in particular *In Retrospect, Flashback! The 50s* and *In America*, directly contributed to the development of my story. I am grateful to Eve's grandson Michael Arnold for generously answering my questions, and especially for maintaining her flame through a gorgeous website, www.evearnold.com. Many of the photos of Marilyn that I refer to in my book can be found there (and even more in Eve's *Marilyn Monroe*). I dare you to come away from a visit to Eve's website unawed by her talent for quietly distilling a moment into truth. She famously said that she let her subjects give her what they wanted to give her, and you can see that they gave her—and, by extension, us—so much.

Beyond Eve's own books, the biography *Eve Arnold: Magnum Legacy* by Janine di Giovanni offered an authoritative examination of her life and work. Through it, I discovered a discrepancy between Eve's dating of her first meeting with Marilyn in *Marilyn Monroe: An Appreciation* and that documented in her photo archives. I decided not only to stick with Eve's timeline of her relationship with Marilyn but to plot around it. My story, then, would take off from the story I imagined that Eve wanted to tell about herself and Marilyn. Their friendship would be the crux of my novel.

Every novelist should be so lucky as to have a timeline documenting one of her subjects' daily life. I found such in *Marilyn Monroe Day by Day* by Carl Rollyson. This chronicle became part of the framework from which I wove my fiction. From the wealth of nonfiction books about Marilyn and Eve, those written by people who would become my characters, such as Norman Rosten,

Ralph Roberts, Milton Greene, and Sam Shaw, were particularly useful. I should note here that all the characters based on real people in my book should be understood to be my interpretations of them. They are meant to be read as characters in a novel, not the subjects of a biographer. My book is this storyteller's creation, written to explore what the lives of Marilyn Monroe and Eve Arnold might say to us about what it means to be human.

But even fiction requires a ton of research. I had a host of help:

Thanks to Adrienne Sharpe-Weseman and Mary Ellen Budney at the Yale University Library, I was able to root through Eve's papers at the Beinecke Rare Book and Manuscript Library.

Thanks to Matt Murphy, global director of archives and production, Magnum Photos, New York, I was able to track down the agency offices that so often figured into the book.

Thanks to my daughters, Lauren Lynch, Megan Cayes, and Alison Cullen, I had good company with whom to trudge around New York City in search of places Marilyn and Eve lived or worked. Megan, who made three such trips with me, even caught a photo of me with my long wrap flying up around me, caught by a freak wind on a sultry summer evening, when I was standing on the subway grate made famous in *The Seven Year Itch.* I'll admit that was spooky.

Thanks to psychologist Jacqueline Walker, I was given insight into possible motives for Marilyn's and Eve's behavior. Psychoanalyst and dear friend Carol Levy is due my huge thanks for delving into their behavior with me as well.

I am grateful to photographer Emily Thomas for helping me understand the technical side of photography. And I am lucky to have a sister like Arlene Eifrid to watch Marilyn's movies with.

I'm thankful to all the friends who cheered me on from the start, including Jani Taylor, Karen Torghele, Jan Johnstone, Colleen Oakley, Alison Law, Tori Whitaker, Mary Kay Andrews, and the Drinks on the Driveway Gang. And to all of you wonderful new friends I've made at book clubs, and to my dear old pals in our long-term neighborhood book club: Thank you for welcoming me into your homes and hearts. You give me courage.

And to my husband, Michael, I owe my biggest thanks. This whole operation hinges on you.

And for the publishing side of this book's journey:

I wish to thank my beloved agent, Margaret Sutherland Brown, for the gift of her extreme patience, wisdom, and time devoted to advising me on a barrage of early drafts, and for her huge support in every way.

I'm also wildly grateful to the great Amanda Bergeron at Berkley for her editorial letters, emails, texts, and phone and in-person conversations that further clarified my thinking in the many additional drafts, and for her tremendous energy freely given to make this book a reality.

A fond thanks goes to Randi Kramer for lending her sharp editorial eye, and for her thoughts on her careful readings. Another thanks goes out to Zach Vigna for his masterful copyediting, and to designer Vikki Chu and artist Guy Parkhomenko for making the book so beautiful.

The fact is, I'm lucky, and so very grateful, for the huge support of the entire team at Berkley: Craig Burke, Jeanne-Marie Hudson, Claire Zion, Christine Ball, Theresa Tran, Kate Whitman, Dan Walsh, and Katheryn Gao. It is by their hard work, and from the support of booksellers—in particular the doughty independents—that this book has reached your hands. As Norma Jeane herself would say, *Imagine!*